BURNIN
DAYLIGHT
JACK LONDON

Publication date: 1910

JACK LONDON 1876-1916

" Man is made with *such large discourse,*
looking before and after. "

PART I

PART II

PART I

CHAPTER 1

It was a quiet night in the Shovel. At the bar, which ranged along one side of the large chinked-log room, leaned half a dozen men, two of whom were discussing the relative merits of spruce-tea and lime-juice as remedies for scurvy. They argued with an air of depression and with intervals of morose silence. The other men scarcely heeded them. In a row, against the opposite wall, were the gambling games. The crap-table was deserted. One lone man was playing at the faro-table. The roulette-ball was not even spinning, and the gamekeeper stood by the roaring, red-hot stove, talking with the young, dark-eyed woman, comely of face and figure, who was known from Juneau to Fort Yukon as the Virgin. Three men sat in at stud-poker, but they played with small chips and without enthusiasm, while there were no onlookers. On the floor of the dancing-room, which opened out at the rear, three couples were waltzing drearily to the strains of a violin and a piano.

Circle City was not deserted, nor was money tight. The miners were in from Moseyed Creek and the other diggings to the west, the summer washing had been good, and the men's pouches were heavy with dust and nuggets. The Klondike had not yet been discovered, nor had the miners of the Yukon learned the possibilities of deep digging and wood-firing. No work was done in the winter, and they made a practice of hibernating in the large camps like Circle City during the long Arctic night. Time was heavy on their hands, their pouches were well filled, and the only social diversion to be found was in the saloons. Yet the Shovel was practically deserted, and the Virgin, standing by the stove, yawned with uncovered mouth and said to Charley Bates: --

"If something don't happen soon, I'm gin' to bed. What's the matter with the camp, anyway? Everybody dead?"

Bates did not even trouble to reply, but went on moodily rolling a cigarette. Dan MacDonald, pioneer saloonman and gambler on the upper Yukon, owner and proprietor of the Tivoli and all its games, wandered forlornly across the great vacant space of floor and joined the two at the stove.

"Anybody dead?" the Virgin asked him.

"Looks like it," was the answer.

"Then it must be the whole camp," she said with an air of finality and with another yawn.

MacDonald grinned and nodded, and opened his mouth to speak, when the front door swung wide and a man appeared in the light. A rush of frost, turned to vapor by the heat of the room, swirled about him to his knees and poured on across the floor, growing thinner and thinner, and perishing a dozen feet from the stove. Taking the wisp broom from its nail inside the door, the newcomer brushed the snow from his moccasins and high German socks. He would have appeared a large man had not a huge French-Canadian stepped up to him from the bar and gripped his hand.

"Hello, Daylight!" was his greeting. "By Gar, you good for sore eyes!"

"Hello, Louis, when did you-all blow in?" returned the newcomer. "Come up and have a drink and tell us all about Bone Creek. Why, dog-gone you-all, shake again. Where's that pardner of yours? I'm looking for him."

Another huge man detached himself from the bar to shake hands. Olaf Henderson and French Louis, partners together on Bone Creek, were the two largest men in the country, and though they were but half a head taller than the newcomer, between them he was dwarfed completely.

"Hello, Olaf, you're my meat, savvee that," said the one called Daylight. "To-morrow's my birthday, and I'm going to put you-all on your back--savvee? And you, too, Louis. I can put you-all on your back on my birthday--savvee? Come up and drink, Olaf, and I'll tell you-all about it."

The arrival of the newcomer seemed to send a flood of warmth through the place. "It's Burning Daylight," the Virgin cried, the first to recognize him as he came into the light. Charley Bates' tight features relaxed at the sight, and MacDonald went over and joined the three at the bar. With the advent of Burning Daylight the whole place became suddenly brighter and cheerier. The barkeepers were active. Voices were raised. Somebody laughed. And when the fiddler, peering into the front room, remarked to the pianist, "It's Burning Daylight," the waltz-time perceptibly quickened, and the dancers, catching the contagion, began to whirl about as if they really enjoyed it. It was known to them of old time that nothing languished when Burning Daylight was around.

He turned from the bar and saw the woman by the stove and the eager look of welcome she extended him.

"Hello, Virgin, old girl," he called. "Hello, Charley. What's the matter with you-all? Why wear faces like that when coffins cost only three ounces? Come up, you-all, and drink. Come up, you unburied dead, and name your poison. Come up, everybody. This is my night, and I'm going to ride it. To-morrow I'm thirty, and then I'll be an old man. It's the last fling of youth. Are you-all with me? Surge along, then. Surge along."

"Hold on there, Davis," he called to the faro-dealer, who had shoved his chair back from the table. "I'm going you one flutter to see whether you-all drink with me or we-all drink with you."

Pulling a heavy sack of gold-dust from his coat pocket, he dropped it on the *high card*.

"Fifty," he said.

The faro-dealer slipped two cards. The high card won. He scribbled the amount on a pad, and the weigher at the bar balanced fifty dollars' worth of dust in the gold-scales and poured it into Burning Daylight's sack. The waltz in the back room being finished, the three couples, followed by the fiddler and the pianist and heading for the bar, caught Daylight's eye.

"Surge along, you-all" he cried. "Surge along and name it. This is my night, and it ain't a night that comes frequent. Surge up, you Siwashes and Salmon-eaters. It's my night, I tell you-all--"

"A blame mangy night," Charley Bates interpolated.

"You're right, my son," Burning Daylight went on gaily. "A mangy night, but it's MY night, you see. I'm the mangy old he-wolf. Listen to me howl."

And howl he did, like a lone gray timber wolf, till the Virgin thrust her pretty fingers in her ears and shivered. A minute later she was whirled away in his arms to the dancing-floor, where, along with the other three women and their partners, a rollicking Virginia reel was soon in progress. Men and women danced in moccasins, and the place was soon a-roar, Burning Daylight the centre of it and the animating spark, with quip and jest and rough merriment rousing them out of the slough of despond in which he had found them.

The atmosphere of the place changed with his coming. He seemed to fill it with his tremendous vitality. Men who entered from the street felt it immediately, and in response to their queries the barkeepers nodded at the back room, and said comprehensively, "Burning Daylight's on the tear." And the men who entered remained, and kept the barkeepers busy. The gamblers took heart of life, and soon the tables were filled, the click of chips and whir of the roulette-ball rising monotonously and imperiously above the hoarse rumble of men's voices and their oaths and heavy laughs.

Few men knew Elam Harnish by any other name than Burning Daylight, the name which had been given him in the early days in the land because of his habit of routing his comrades out of their blankets with the complaint that daylight was burning. Of the pioneers in that far Arctic wilderness, where all men were pioneers, he was reckoned among the oldest. Men like Al Mayo and Jack McQuestion antedated him; but they had entered the land by crossing the Rockies from the Hudson Bay country to the east. He, however, had been the pioneer over the Chilcoot and Chilcat passes. In the spring of 1883, twelve years before, a stripling of eighteen, he had crossed over the Chilcoot with five comrades. In the fall he had crossed back with one. Four had perished by mischance in the bleak, uncharted vastness. And for twelve years Elam Harnish had continued to grope for gold among the shadows of the Circle.

And no man had groped so obstinately nor so enduringly. He had grown up with the land. He knew no other land. Civilization was a dream of some previous life. Camps like Forty Mile and Circle City were to him metropolises. And not alone had he grown up with the land, for, raw as it was, he had helped to make it. He had made history and geography, and those that followed wrote of his traverses and charted the trails his feet had broken.

Heroes are seldom given to hero-worship, but among those of that young land, young as he was, he was accounted an elder hero. In point of time he was before them. In point of deed he was beyond them. In point of endurance it was acknowledged that he could kill the hardiest of them. Furthermore, he was accounted a nervy man, a square man, and a white man.

In all lands where life is a hazard lightly played with and lightly flung aside, men turn, almost automatically, to gambling for diversion and relaxation. In the Yukon men gambled their lives for gold, and those that won gold from the ground gambled for it with one another. Nor was Elam Harnish an exception. He was a man's man primarily, and the instinct in him to play the game of life was strong. Environment had determined what form that game should take. He was born on an Iowa farm, and his father had emigrated to eastern Oregon, in which mining country Elam's boyhood was lived. He had known nothing but hard knocks for big stakes. Pluck and endurance counted in the game, but the great god Chance dealt the cards. Honest work for sure but meagre returns did not count. A man played big. He risked everything for everything, and anything less than everything meant that he was a loser. So for twelve Yukon years, Elam Harnish had been a loser. True, on Moosehide Creek the past summer he had taken out twenty thousand dollars, and what was left in the ground was twenty thousand more. But, as he himself proclaimed, that was no more than getting his ante back. He had ante'd his life for a dozen years, and forty thousand was a small pot for such a stake--the price of a drink and a dance at the Tivoli, of a winter's flutter at Circle City, and a grubstake for the year to come.

The men of the Yukon reversed the old maxim till it read: *hard come, easy go*. At the end of the reel, Elam Harnish called the house up to drink again. Drinks were a dollar apiece, gold rated at sixteen dollars an ounce; there were thirty in the house that accepted his invitation, and between every dance the house was Elam's guest. This was his night, and nobody was to be allowed to pay for anything. Not that Elam Harnish was a drinking man. Whiskey meant little to him. He was too vital and robust, too untroubled in mind and body, to incline to the slavery of alcohol. He spent months at a time on trail and river when he drank nothing stronger than coffee, while he had gone a year at a time without even coffee. But he was gregarious, and since the sole social expression of the Yukon was the saloon, he expressed himself that way. When he was a lad in the mining camps of the West, men had always done that. To him it was the proper way for a man to express himself socially. He knew no other way.

He was a striking figure of a man, despite his garb being similar to that of all the men in the Tivoli. Soft-tanned moccasins of moose-hide, beaded in Indian designs, covered his feet. His trousers were ordinary overalls, his coat was made from a blanket. Long-gauntleted leather mittens, lined with wool, hung by his side. They were connected in the Yukon fashion, by a leather thong passed around the neck and across the shoulders. On his head was a fur cap, the ear-flaps raised and the tying-cords dangling. His face, lean and slightly long, with the suggestion of hollows under the cheek-bones, seemed almost Indian. The burnt skin and keen dark eyes contributed to this effect, though the bronze of the skin and the eyes themselves were essentially those of a white man. He looked older than thirty, and yet, smooth-shaven and without wrinkles, he was almost boyish. This impression of age was based on no tangible evidence. It came from the abstracter facts of the man, from what he had endured and survived, which was far beyond that of ordinary men. He had lived life naked and tensely, and something of all this smouldered in his eyes, vibrated in his voice, and seemed forever a-whisper on his lips.

The lips themselves were thin, and prone to close tightly over the even, white teeth. But their harshness was retrieved by the upward curl at the corners of his mouth. This curl gave to him sweetness, as the minute puckers at the corners of the eyes gave him laughter. These necessary graces saved him from a nature that was essentially savage and that otherwise would have been cruel and bitter. The nose was lean, full-nostrilled, and delicate, and of a size to fit the face; while the high forehead, as if to atone for its narrowness, was splendidly domed and symmetrical. In line with the Indian effect was his hair, very straight and very black, with a gloss to it that only health could give.

"Burning Daylight's burning candlelight," laughed Dan MacDonald, as an outburst of exclamations and merriment came from the dancers.

"An' he is der boy to do it, eh, Louis?" said Olaf Henderson.

"Yes, by Gar! you bet on dat," said French Louis. "Dat boy is all gold--"

"And when God Almighty washes Daylight's soul out on the last big slucin' day," MacDonald interrupted, "why, God Almighty'll have to shovel gravel along with him into the sluice-boxes."

"Dot iss goot," Olaf Henderson muttered, regarding the gambler with profound admiration.

"Ver' good," affirmed French Louis. "I t'ink we take a drink on dat one time, eh?"

CHAPTER 2

It was two in the morning when the dancers, bent on getting something to eat, adjourned the dancing for half an hour. And it was at this moment that Jack Kearns suggested poker. Jack Kearns was a big, bluff-featured man, who, along with Bettles, had made the disastrous attempt to found a post on the head-reaches of the Koyokuk, far inside the Arctic Circle. After that, Kearns had fallen back on his posts at Forty Mile and Sixty Mile and changed the direction of his ventures by sending out to the States for a small sawmill and a river steamer. The former was even then being sledded across Chilcoot Pass by Indians and dogs, and would come down the Yukon in the early summer after the ice-run. Later in the summer, when Bering Sea and the mouth of the Yukon cleared of ice, the steamer, put together at St. Michaels, was to be expected up the river loaded to the guards with supplies.

Jack Kearns suggested poker. French Louis, Dan MacDonald, and Hal Campbell (who had make a strike on Moosehide), all three of whom were not dancing because there were not girls enough to go around, inclined to the suggestion. They were looking for a fifth man when Burning Daylight emerged from the rear room, the Virgin on his arm, the train of dancers in his wake. In response to the hail of the poker-players, he came over to their table in the corner.

"Want you to sit in," said Campbell. "How's your luck?"

"I sure got it to-night," Burning Daylight answered with enthusiasm, and at the same time felt the Virgin press his arm warningly. She wanted him for the dancing. "I sure got my luck with me, but I'd sooner dance. I ain't hankerin' to take the money away from you-all."

Nobody urged. They took his refusal as final, and the Virgin was pressing his arm to turn him away in pursuit of the supper-seekers, when he experienced a change of heart. It was not that he did not want to dance, nor that he wanted to hurt her; but that insistent pressure on his arm put his free man-nature in revolt. The thought in his mind was that he did not want any woman running him. Himself a favorite with women, nevertheless they did not bulk big with him. They were toys, playthings, part of the relaxation from the bigger game of life. He met women along with the whiskey and gambling, and from observation he had found that it was far easier to break away from the drink and the cards than from a woman once the man was properly entangled.

He was a slave to himself, which was natural in one with a healthy ego, but he rebelled in ways either murderous or panicky at being a slave to anybody else. Love's sweet servitude was a thing of which he had no comprehension. Men he had seen in love impressed him as lunatics, and lunacy was a thing he had never considered worth analyzing. But comradeship with men was different from love with women. There was no servitude in comradeship. It was a business proposition, a square deal between men who did not pursue each other, but who shared the risks of trail and river and mountain in the pursuit of life and treasure. Men and women pursued each other, and one must needs bend the other to his will or hers. Comradeship was different. There was no slavery about it; and though he, a strong man beyond strength's seeming, gave far more than he received, he gave not something due but in royal largess, his gifts of toil or heroic effort falling generously from his hands. To pack for days over the gale-swept passes or across the mosquito-ridden marshes, and to pack double the weight his comrade packed, did not involve unfairness or compulsion. Each did his best. That was the business essence of it. Some

8

men were stronger than others--true; but so long as each man did his best it was fair exchange, the business spirit was observed, and the square deal obtained.

But with women--no. Women gave little and wanted all. Women had apron-strings and were prone to tie them about any man who looked twice in their direction. There was the Virgin, yawning her head off when he came in and mightily pleased that he asked her to dance. One dance was all very well, but because he danced twice and thrice with her and several times more, she squeezed his arm when they asked him to sit in at poker. It was the obnoxious apron-string, the first of the many compulsions she would exert upon him if he gave in. Not that she was not a nice bit of a woman, healthy and strapping and good to look upon, also a very excellent dancer, but that she was a woman with all a woman's desire to rope him with her apron-strings and tie him hand and foot for the branding. Better poker. Besides, he liked poker as well as he did dancing.

He resisted the pull on his arm by the mere negative mass of him, and said: --

"I sort of feel a hankering to give you-all a flutter."

Again came the pull on his arm. She was trying to pass the apron-string around him. For the fraction of an instant he was a savage, dominated by the wave of fear and murder that rose up in him. For that infinitesimal space of time he was to all purposes a frightened tiger filled with rage and terror at the apprehension of the trap. Had he been no more than a savage, he would have leapt wildly from the place or else sprung upon her and destroyed her. But in that same instant there stirred in him the generations of discipline by which man had become an inadequate social animal. Tact and sympathy strove with him, and he smiled with his eyes into the Virgin's eyes as he said: --

"You-all go and get some grub. I ain't hungry. And we'll dance some more by and by. The night's young yet. Go to it, old girl."

He released his arm and thrust her playfully on the shoulder, at the same time turning to the poker-players.

"Take off the limit and I'll go you-all."

"Limit's the roof," said Jack Kearns.

"Take off the roof."

The players glanced at one another, and Kearns announced, "The roof's off."

Elam Harnish dropped into the waiting chair, started to pull out his gold-sack, and changed his mind. The Virgin pouted a moment, then followed in the wake of the other dancers.

"I'll bring you a sandwich, Daylight," she called back over her shoulder.

He nodded. She was smiling her forgiveness. He had escaped the apron-string, and without hurting her feelings too severely.

"Let's play markers," he suggested. "Chips do everlastingly clutter up the table....If it's agreeable to you-all?"

"I'm willing," answered Hal Campbell. "Let mine run at five hundred."

"Mine, too," answered Harnish, while the others stated the values they put on their own markers, French Louis, the most modest, issuing his at a hundred dollars each.

In Alaska, at that time, there were no rascals and no tin-horn gamblers. Games were conducted honestly, and men trusted one another. A man's word was as good as his gold in the blower. A marker was a flat, oblong composition chip worth, perhaps, a cent. But when a man betted a marker in a game and said it was worth five hundred dollars, it was accepted as worth five hundred dollars. Whoever won it knew that the man who issued it would redeem it with five hundred dollars' worth of dust weighed out on the scales. The markers being of different colors, there was no difficulty in identifying the owners. Also, in that early Yukon day, no one dreamed of playing table-stakes. A man was good in a game for all that he possessed, no matter where his possessions were or what was their nature.

Harnish cut and got the deal. At this good augury, and while shuffling the deck, he called to the barkeepers to set up the drinks for the house. As he dealt the first card to Dan MacDonald, on his left, he called out: --

"Get down to the ground, you-all, Malemutes, huskies, and Siwash purps! Get down and dig in! Tighten up them traces! Put your weight into the harness and bust the breast-bands! Whoop-la! Yow! We're off and bound for Helen Breakfast! And I tell you-all clear and plain there's goin' to be stiff grades and fast goin' to-night before we win to that same lady. And somebody's goin' to bump...hard."

Once started, it was a quiet game, with little or no conversation, though all about the players the place was a-roar. Elam Harnish had ignited the spark. More and more miners dropped in to the Tivoli and remained. When Burning Daylight went on the tear, no man cared to miss it. The dancing-floor was full. Owing to the shortage of women, many of the men tied bandanna handkerchiefs around their arms in token of femininity and danced with other men. All the games were crowded, and the voices of the men talking at the long bar and grouped about the stove were accompanied by the steady click of chips and the sharp whir, rising and falling, of the roulette-ball. All the materials of a proper Yukon night were at hand and mixing.

The luck at the table varied monotonously, no big hands being out. As a result, high play went on with small hands though no play lasted long. A filled straight belonging to French Louis gave him a pot of five thousand against two sets of threes held by Campbell and Kearns. One pot of eight hundred dollars was won by a pair of trays on a showdown. And once Harnish called Kearns for two thousand dollars on a cold steal. When Kearns laid down his hand it showed a bobtail flush, while Harnish's hand proved that he had had the nerve to call on a pair of tens.

But at three in the morning the big combination of hands arrived. It was the moment of moments that men wait weeks for in a poker game. The news of it tingled over the Tivoli. The onlookers became quiet. The men farther away ceased talking and moved over to the table. The players deserted the other games, and the dancing-floor was forsaken, so that all stood at last, fivescore and more, in a compact and silent group, around the poker-table. The high betting had begun before the draw, and still the high betting went on, with the draw not in sight. Kearns had dealt, and French Louis had opened the pot with one marker--in his case one hundred dollars. Campbell had merely "seen" it, but Elam Harnish, corning next, had tossed in five hundred dollars, with the remark to MacDonald that he was letting him in easy.

MacDonald, glancing again at his hand, put in a thousand in markers. Kearns, debating a long time over his hand, finally "saw." It then cost French Louis nine hundred to remain in the game, which he contributed after a similar debate. It cost Campbell likewise nine hundred to remain and draw cards, but to the surprise of all he saw the nine hundred and raised another thousand.

"You-all are on the grade at last," Harnish remarked, as he saw the fifteen hundred and raised a thousand in turn. "Helen Breakfast's sure on top this divide, and you-all had best look out for bustin' harness."

"Me for that same lady," accompanied MacDonald's markers for two thousand and for an additional thousand-dollar raise.

It was at this stage that the players sat up and knew beyond peradventure that big hands were out. Though their features showed nothing, each man was beginning unconsciously to tense. Each man strove to appear his natural self, and each natural self was different. Hal Campbell affected his customary cautiousness. French Louis betrayed interest. MacDonald retained his whole-souled benevolence, though it seemed to take on a slightly exaggerated tone. Kearns was coolly dispassionate and noncommittal, while Elam Harnish appeared as quizzical and jocular as ever. Eleven thousand dollars were already in the pot, and the markers were heaped in a confused pile in the centre of the table.

"I ain't go no more markers," Kearns remarked plaintively. "We'd best begin I.O.U.'s."

"Glad you're going to stay," was MacDonald's cordial response.

"I ain't stayed yet. I've got a thousand in already. How's it stand now?"

"It'll cost you three thousand for a look in, but nobody will stop you from raising."

"Raise--hell. You must think I got a pat like yourself." Kearns looked at his hand. "But I'll tell you what I'll do, Mac. I've got a hunch, and I'll just see that three thousand."

He wrote the sum on a slip of paper, signed his name, and consigned it to the centre of the table.

French Louis became the focus of all eyes. He fingered his cards nervously for a space. Then, with a "By Gar! Ah got not one leetle beet hunch," he regretfully tossed his hand into the discards.

The next moment the hundred and odd pairs of eyes shifted to Campbell.

"I won't hump you, Jack," he said, contenting himself with calling the requisite two thousand.

The eyes shifted to Harnish, who scribbled on a piece of paper and shoved it forward.

"I'll just let you-all know this ain't no Sunday-school society of philanthropy," he said. "I see you, Jack, and I raise you a thousand. Here's where you-all get action on your pat, Mac."

"Action's what I fatten on, and I lift another thousand," was MacDonald's rejoinder. "Still got that hunch, Jack?"

"I still got the hunch." Kearns fingered his cards a long time. "And I'll play it, but you've got to know how I stand. There's my steamer, the *Bella*--worth twenty thousand if she's worth an ounce. There's Sixty Mile with five thousand in stock on the shelves. And you know I got a sawmill coming in. It's at Linderman now, and the scow is building. Am I good?"

"Dig in; you're sure good," was Daylight's answer. "And while we're about it, I may mention casual that I got twenty thousand in Mac's safe, there, and there's twenty thousand more in the ground on Moosehide. You know the ground, Campbell. Is they that-all in the dirt?"

"There sure is, Daylight."

"How much does it cost now?" Kearns asked.

"Two thousand to see."

"We'll sure hump you if you-all come in," Daylight warned him.

"It's an almighty good hunch," Kearns said, adding his slip for two thousand to the growing heap. "I can feel her crawlin' up and down my back."

"I ain't got a hunch, but I got a tolerable likeable hand," Campbell announced, as he slid in his slip; "but it's not a raising hand."

"Mine is," Daylight paused and wrote. "I see that thousand and raise her the same old thousand."

The Virgin, standing behind him, then did what a man's best friend was not privileged to do. Reaching over Daylight's shoulder, she picked up his hand and read it, at the same time shielding the faces of the five cards close to his chest. What she saw were three queens and a pair of eights, but nobody guessed what she saw. Every player's eyes were on her face as she scanned the cards, but no sign did she give. Her features might have been carved from ice, for her expression was precisely the same before, during, and after. Not a muscle quivered; nor was there the slightest dilation of a nostril, nor the slightest increase of light in the eyes. She laid the hand face down again on the table, and slowly the lingering eyes withdrew from her, having learned nothing.

MacDonald smiled benevolently. "I see you, Daylight, and I hump this time for two thousand. How's that hunch, Jack?"

"Still a-crawling, Mac. You got me now, but that hunch is a rip-snorter persuadin' sort of a critter, and it's my plain duty to ride it. I call for three thousand. And I got another hunch: Daylight's going to call, too."

"He sure is," Daylight agreed, after Campbell had thrown up his hand. "He knows when he's up against it, and he plays accordin'. I see that two thousand, and then I'll see the draw."

In a dead silence, save for the low voices of the three players, the draw was made. Thirty-four thousand dollars were already in the pot, and the play possibly not half over. To the Virgin's amazement, Daylight held up his three queens, discarding his eights and calling for two cards. And this time not even she dared look at what he had drawn. She knew her limit of control. Nor did he look. The two new cards lay face down on the table where they had been dealt to him.

"Cards?" Kearns asked of MacDonald.

"Got enough," was the reply.

"You can draw if you want to, you know," Kearns warned him.

"Nope; this'll do me."

Kearns himself drew two cards, but did not look at them.

Still Harnish let his cards lie.

"I never bet in the teeth of a pat hand," he said slowly, looking at the saloon-keeper. "You-all start her rolling, Mac."

MacDonald counted his cards carefully, to make doubles sure it was not a foul hand, wrote a sum on a paper slip, and slid it into the pot, with the simple utterance:-

"Five thousand."

Kearns, with every eye upon him, looked at his two-card draw, counted the other three to dispel any doubt of holding more than five cards, and wrote on a betting slip.

"I see you, Mac," he said, "and I raise her a little thousand just so as not to keep Daylight out."

The concentrated gaze shifted to Daylight. He likewise examined his draw and counted his five cards.

"I see that six thousand, and I raise her five thousand...just to try and keep you out, Jack."

"And I raise you five thousand just to lend a hand at keeping Jack out," MacDonald said, in turn.

His voice was slightly husky and strained, and a nervous twitch in the corner of his mouth followed speech.

12

Kearns was pale, and those who looked on noted that his hand trembled as he wrote his slip. But his voice was unchanged.

"I lift her along for five thousand," he said.

Daylight was now the centre. The kerosene lamps above flung high lights from the rash of sweat on his forehead. The bronze of his cheeks was darkened by the accession of blood. His black eyes glittered, and his nostrils were distended and eager. They were large nostrils, tokening his descent from savage ancestors who had survived by virtue of deep lungs and generous air-passages.

Yet, unlike MacDonald, his voice was firm and customary, and, unlike Kearns, his hand did not tremble when he wrote.

"I call, for ten thousand," he said. "Not that I'm afraid of you-all, Mac. It's that hunch of Jack's."

"I hump his hunch for five thousand just the same," said MacDonald. "I had the best hand before the draw, and I still guess I got it."

"Mebbe this is a case where a hunch after the draw is better'n the hunch before," Kearns remarked; "wherefore duty says, 'Lift her, Jack, lift her,' and so I lift her another five thousand."

Daylight leaned back in his chair and gazed up at the kerosene lamps while he computed aloud.

"I was in nine thousand before the draw, and I saw and raised eleven thousand--that makes thirty. I'm only good for ten more." He leaned forward and looked at Kearns. "So I call that ten thousand."

"You can raise if you want," Kearns answered. "Your dogs are good for five thousand in this game."

"Nary dawg. You-all can win my dust and dirt, but nary one of my dawgs. I just call."

MacDonald considered for a long time. No one moved or whispered. Not a muscle was relaxed on the part of the onlookers. Not the weight of a body shifted from one leg to the other. It was a sacred silence. Only could be heard the roaring draft of the huge stove, and from without, muffled by the log-walls, the howling of dogs. It was not every night that high stakes were played on the Yukon, and for that matter, this was the highest in the history of the country. The saloon-keeper finally spoke.

"If anybody else wins, they'll have to take a mortgage on the Tivoli."

The two other players nodded.

"So I call, too."

MacDonald added his slip for five thousand.

Not one of them claimed the pot, and not one of them called the size of his hand. Simultaneously and in silence they faced their cards on the table, while a general tiptoeing and craning of necks took place among the onlookers. Daylight showed four queens and an ace; MacDonald four jacks and an ace; and Kearns four kings and a trey. Kearns reached forward with an encircling movement of his arm and drew the pot in to him, his arm shaking as he did so.

Daylight picked the ace from his hand and tossed it over alongside MacDonald's ace, saying: --

"That's what cheered me along, Mac. I knowed it was only kings that could beat me, and he had them.

"What did you-all have?" he asked, all interest, turning to Campbell.

"Straight flush of four, open at both ends--a good drawing hand."

"You bet! You could a' made a straight, a straight flush, or a flush out of it."

"That's what I thought," Campbell said sadly. "It cost me six thousand before I quit."

"I wisht you-all'd drawn," Daylight laughed. "Then I wouldn't a' caught that fourth queen. Now I've got to take Billy Rawlins' mail contract and *mush* for Dyea. What's the size of the killing, Jack?"

Kearns attempted to count the pot, but was too excited. Daylight drew it across to him, with firm fingers separating and stacking the markers and I.O.U.'s and with clear brain adding the sum.

"One hundred and twenty-seven thousand," he announced. "You-all can sell out now, Jack, and head for home."

The winner smiled and nodded, but seemed incapable of speech.

"I'd shout the drinks," MacDonald said, "only the house don't belong to me any more."

"Yes, it does," Kearns replied, first wetting his lips with his tongue. "Your note's good for any length of time. But the drinks are on me."

"Name your snake-juice, you-all--the winner pays!" Daylight called out loudly to all about him, at the same time rising from his chair and catching the Virgin by the arm. "Come on for a reel, you-all dancers. The night's young yet, and it's Helen Breakfast and the mail contract for me in the morning. Here, you-all Rawlins, you--I hereby do take over that same contract, and I start for salt water at nine A.M.--savvee? Come on, you-all! Where's that fiddler?"

CHAPTER 3

It was Daylight's night. He was the centre and the head of the revel, unquenchably joyous, a contagion of fun. He multiplied himself, and in so doing multiplied the excitement. No prank he suggested was too wild for his followers, and all followed save those that developed into singing imbeciles and fell warbling by the wayside. Yet never did trouble intrude. It was known on the Yukon that when Burning Daylight made a night of it, wrath and evil were forbidden. On his nights men dared not quarrel. In the younger days such things had happened, and then men had known what real wrath was, and been man-handled as only Burning Daylight could man-handle. On his nights men must laugh and be happy or go home.

Daylight was inexhaustible. In between dances he paid over to Kearns the twenty thousand in dust and transferred to him his Moosehide claim. Likewise he arranged the taking over of Billy Rawlins' mail contract, and made his preparations for the start. He despatched a messenger to rout out Kama, his dog-driver--a Tananaw Indian, far-wandered from his tribal home in the service of the invading whites. Kama entered the Tivoli, tall, lean, muscular, and fur-clad, the pick of his barbaric race and barbaric still, unshaken and unabashed by the revellers that rioted about him while Daylight gave his orders.

"Um," said Kama, tabling his instructions on his fingers. "Get um letters from Rawlins. Load um on sled. Grub for Selkirk--you think um plenty dog-grub stop Selkirk?"

"Plenty dog-grub, Kama."

"Um, bring sled this place nine um clock. Bring um snowshoes. No bring um tent. Mebbe bring um fly? um little fly?"

"No fly," Daylight answered decisively.

"Um much cold."

"We travel light--savvee? We carry plenty letters out, plenty letters back. You are strong man. Plenty cold, plenty travel, all right."

"Sure all right," Kama muttered, with resignation. "Much cold, no care a damn. Um ready nine um clock."

He turned on his moccasined heel and walked out, imperturbable, sphinx-like, neither giving nor receiving greetings nor looking to right or left. The Virgin led Daylight away into a corner.

"Look here, Daylight," she said, in a low voice, "you're busted."

"Higher'n a kite."

"I've eight thousand in Mac's safe--" she began.

But Daylight interrupted. The apron-string loomed near and he shied like an unbroken colt.

"It don't matter," he said. "Busted I came into the world, busted I go out, and I've been busted most of the time since I arrived. Come on; let's waltz."

"But listen," she urged. "My money's doing nothing. I could lend it to you--a grub-stake," she added hurriedly, at sight of the alarm in his face.

"Nobody grub-stakes me," was the answer. "I stake myself, and when I make a killing it's sure all mine. No thank you, old girl. Much obliged. I'll get my stake by running the mail out and in."

"Daylight," she murmured, in tender protest.

But with a sudden well-assumed ebullition of spirits he drew her toward the dancing-floor, and as they swung around and around in a waltz she pondered on the iron heart of the man who held her in his arms and resisted all her wiles.

At six the next morning, scorching with whiskey, yet ever himself, he stood at the bar putting every man's hand down. The way of it was that two men faced each other across a corner, their right elbows resting on the bar, their right hands gripped together, while each strove to press the other's hand down. Man after man came against him, but no man put his hand down, even Olaf Henderson and French Louis failing despite their hugeness. When they contended it was a trick, a trained muscular knack, he challenged them to another test.

"Look here, you-all" he cried. "I'm going to do two things: first, weigh my sack; and second, bet it that after you-all have lifted clean from the floor all the sacks of flour you-all are able, I'll put on two more sacks and lift the whole caboodle clean."

"By Gar! Ah take dat!" French Louis rumbled above the cheers.

"Hold on!" Olaf Henderson cried. "I ban yust as good as you, Louis. I yump half that bet."

Put on the scales, Daylight's sack was found to balance an even four hundred dollars, and Louis and Olaf divided the bet between them. Fifty-pound sacks of flour were brought in from MacDonald's cache. Other men tested their strength first. They straddled on two chairs, the flour sacks beneath them on the floor and held together by rope-lashings. Many of the men were able, in this manner, to lift four or five hundred pounds, while some succeeded with as high as six hundred. Then the two giants took a hand, tying at seven hundred. French Louis then added another sack, and swung seven hundred and fifty clear. Olaf duplicated the performance, whereupon both failed to clear eight hundred. Again and again they strove, their foreheads beaded with sweat, their frames crackling with the effort. Both were able to shift the weight and to bump it, but clear the floor with it they could not.

"By Gar! Daylight, dis tam you mek one beeg meestake," French Louis said, straightening up and stepping down from the chairs. "Only one damn iron man can do dat. One hundred pun' more--my frien', not ten poun' more." The sacks were unlashed, but when two sacks were added, Kearns interfered. "Only one sack more."

"Two!" some one cried. "Two was the bet."

"They didn't lift that last sack," Kearns protested.

"They only lifted seven hundred and fifty."

But Daylight grandly brushed aside the confusion.

"What's the good of you-all botherin' around that way? What's one more sack? If I can't lift three more, I sure can't lift two. Put 'em in."

He stood upon the chairs, squatted, and bent his shoulders down till his hands closed on the rope. He shifted his feet slightly, tautened his muscles with a tentative pull, then relaxed again, questing for a perfect adjustment of all the levers of his body.

French Louis, looking on sceptically, cried out: --

"Pool lak hell, Daylight! Pool lak hell!"

Daylight's muscles tautened a second time, and this time in earnest, until steadily all the energy of his splendid body was applied, and quite imperceptibly, without jerk or strain, the bulky nine hundred pounds rose from the door and swung back and forth, pendulum like, between his legs.

Olaf Henderson sighed a vast audible sigh. The Virgin, who had tensed unconsciously till her muscles hurt her, relaxed. While French Louis murmured reverently: --

"M'sieu Daylight, *salut!* Ay am one beeg baby. You are one beeg man."

Daylight dropped his burden, leaped to the floor, and headed for the bar.

"Weigh in!" he cried, tossing his sack to the weigher, who transferred to it four hundred dollars from the sacks of the two losers.

16

"Surge up, everybody!" Daylight went on. "Name your snake-juice! The winner pays!"

"This is my night! " he was shouting, ten minutes later. "I'm the lone he-wolf, and I've seen thirty winters. This is my birthday, my one day in the year, and I can put any man on his back. Come on, you-all! I'm going to put you-all in the snow. Come on, you *chechaquos*[1] and sourdoughs[2], and get your baptism!"

The rout streamed out of doors, all save the barkeepers and the singing Bacchuses. Some fleeting thought of saving his own dignity entered MacDonald's head, for he approached Daylight with outstretched hand.

"What? You first?" Daylight laughed, clasping the other's hand as if in greeting.

"No, no," the other hurriedly disclaimed. "Just congratulations on your birthday. Of course you can put me in the snow. What chance have I against a man that lifts nine hundred pounds?"

MacDonald weighed one hundred and eighty pounds, and Daylight had him gripped solely by his hand; yet, by a sheer abrupt jerk, he took the saloon-keeper off his feet and flung him face downward in the snow. In quick succession, seizing the men nearest him, he threw half a dozen more. Resistance was useless. They flew helter-skelter out of his grips, landing in all manner of attitudes, grotesquely and harmlessly, in the soft snow. It soon became difficult, in the dim starlight, to distinguish between those thrown and those waiting their turn, and he began feeling their backs and shoulders, determining their status by whether or not he found them powdered with snow.

"Baptized yet?" became his stereotyped question, as he reached out his terrible hands.

Several score lay down in the snow in a long row, while many others knelt in mock humility, scooping snow upon their heads and claiming the rite accomplished. But a group of five stood upright, backwoodsmen and frontiersmen, they, eager to contest any man's birthday.

Graduates of the hardest of man-handling schools, veterans of multitudes of rough-and-tumble battles, men of blood and sweat and endurance, they nevertheless lacked one thing that Daylight possessed in high degree--namely, an almost perfect brain and muscular coordination. It was simple, in its way, and no virtue of his. He had been born with this endowment. His nerves carried messages more quickly than theirs; his mental processes, culminating in acts of will, were quicker than theirs; his muscles themselves, by some immediacy of chemistry, obeyed the messages of his will quicker than theirs. He was so made, his muscles were high-power explosives. The levers of his body snapped into play like the jaws of steel traps. And in addition to all this, his was that super-strength that is the dower of but one human in millions--a strength depending not on size but on degree, a supreme organic excellence residing in the stuff of the muscles themselves. Thus, so swiftly could he apply a stress, that, before an opponent could become aware and resist, the aim of the stress had been accomplished. In turn, so swiftly did he become aware of a stress applied to him, that he saved himself by resistance or by delivering a lightning counter-stress.

"It ain't no use you-all standing there," Daylight addressed the waiting group. "You-all might as well get right down and take your baptizing.

---

[1] Tenderfeet.

[2] Old-timers.

You-all might down me any other day in the year, but on my birthday I want you-all to know I'm the best man. Is that Pat Hanrahan's mug looking hungry and willing? Come on, Pat."

Pat Hanrahan, ex-bare-knuckle-prize fighter and roughhouse-expert, stepped forth. The two men came against each other in grips, and almost before he had exerted himself the Irishman found himself in the merciless vise of a half-Nelson that buried him head and shoulders in the snow. Joe Hines, ex-lumber-jack, came down with an impact equal to a fall from a two-story building--his overthrow accomplished by a cross-buttock, delivered, he claimed, before he was ready.

There was nothing exhausting in all this to Daylight. He did not heave and strain through long minutes. No time, practically, was occupied. His body exploded abruptly and terrifically in one instant, and on the next instant was relaxed. Thus, Doc Watson, the gray-bearded, iron bodied man without a past, a fighting terror himself, was overthrown in the fraction of a second preceding his own onslaught. As he was in the act of gathering himself for a spring, Daylight was upon him, and with such fearful suddenness as to crush him backward and down. Olaf Henderson, receiving his cue from this, attempted to take Daylight unaware, rushing upon him from one side as he stooped with extended hand to help Doc Watson up. Daylight dropped on his hands and knees, receiving in his side Olaf's knees. Olaf's momentum carried him clear over the obstruction in a long, flying fall. Before he could rise, Daylight had whirled him over on his back and was rubbing his face and ears with snow and shoving handfuls down his neck.

"Ay ban yust as good a man as you ban, Daylight," Olaf spluttered, as he pulled himself to his feet; "but by Yupiter, I ban navver see a grip like that."

French Louis was the last of the five, and he had seen enough to make him cautious. He circled and baffled for a full minute before coming to grips; and for another full minute they strained and reeled without either winning the advantage. And then, just as the contest was becoming interesting, Daylight effected one of his lightning shifts, changing all stresses and leverages and at the same time delivering one of his muscular explosions. French Louis resisted till his huge frame crackled, and then, slowly, was forced over and under and downward.

"The winner pays!" Daylight cried; as he sprang to his feet and led the way back into the Tivoli. "Surge along you-all! This way to the snake-room!"

They lined up against the long bar, in places two or three deep, stamping the frost from their moccasined feet, for outside the temperature was sixty below. Bettles, himself one of the gamest of the old-timers in deeds and daring ceased from his drunken lay of the "Sassafras Root," and titubated over to congratulate Daylight. But in the midst of it he felt impelled to make a speech, and raised his voice oratorically.

"I tell you fellers I'm plum proud to call Daylight my friend. We've hit the trail together afore now, and he's eighteen carat from his moccasins up, damn his mangy old hide, anyway. He was a shaver when he first hit this country. When you fellers was his age, you wa'n't dry behind the ears yet. He never was no kid. He was born a full-grown man. An' I tell you a man had to be a man in them days. This wa'n't no effete civilization like it's come to be now." Bettles paused long enough to put his arm in a proper bear-hug around Daylight's neck. "When you an' me *mushed*[1] into the Yukon in the good ole days, it didn't rain soup and they wa'n't no free-lunch joints. Our

---

[1] Drove dogs; travelled.

18

camp fires was lit where we killed our game, and most of the time we lived on salmon-tracks and rabbit-bellies--ain't I right?"

But at the roar of laughter that greeted his inversion, Bettles released the bear-hug and turned fiercely on them.

"Laugh, you mangy short-horns, laugh! But I tell you plain and simple, the best of you ain't knee-high fit to tie Daylight's moccasin strings.

Ain't I right, Campbell? Ain't I right, Mac? Daylight's one of the old guard, one of the real sour-doughs. And in them days they wa'n't ary a steamboat or ary a trading-post, and we cusses had to live offen salmon-bellies and rabbit-tracks."

He gazed triumphantly around, and in the applause that followed arose cries for a speech from Daylight. He signified his consent. A chair was brought, and he was helped to stand upon it. He was no more sober than the crowd above which he now towered--a wild crowd, uncouthly garmented, every foot moccasined or *muc-lucked*[1], with mittens dangling from necks and with furry ear-flaps raised so that they took on the seeming of the winged helmets of the Norsemen. Daylight's black eyes were flashing, and the flush of strong drink flooded darkly under the bronze of his cheeks. He was greeted with round on round of affectionate cheers, which brought a suspicious moisture to his eyes, albeit many of the voices were inarticulate and inebriate. And yet, men have so behaved since the world began, feasting, fighting, and carousing, whether in the dark cave-mouth or by the fire of the squatting-place, in the palaces of imperial Rome and the rock strongholds of robber barons, or in the sky-aspiring hotels of modern times and in the boozing-kens of sailor-town. Just so were these men, empire-builders in the Arctic Light, boastful and drunken and clamorous, winning surcease for a few wild moments from the grim reality of their heroic toil. Modern heroes they, and in nowise different from the heroes of old time.

"Well, fellows, I don't know what to say to you-all," Daylight began lamely, striving still to control his whirling brain. "I think I'll tell you-all a story. I had a pardner wunst, down in Juneau. He come from North Caroliney, and he used to tell this same story to me. It was down in the mountains in his country, and it was a wedding. There they was, the family and all the friends. The parson was just puttin' on the last touches, and he says, 'They as the Lord have joined let no man put asunder.'

"'Parson,' says the bridegroom, 'I rises to question your grammar in that there sentence. I want this weddin' done right.'

"When the smoke clears away, the bride she looks around and sees a dead parson, a dead bridegroom, a dead brother, two dead uncles, and five dead wedding-guests.

"So she heaves a mighty strong sigh and says, 'Them new-fangled, self-cocking revolvers sure has played hell with my prospects.'

"And so I say to you-all," Daylight added, as the roar of laughter died down, "that them four kings of Jack Kearns sure has played hell with my prospects. I'm busted higher'n a kite, and I'm hittin' the trail for Dyea--"

"Goin' out?" some one called.

A spasm of anger wrought on his face for a flashing instant, but in the next his good-humor was back again.

---

[1] *Muc-luc*: a water-tight, Eskimo boot, made from walrus-hide and trimmed with fur.

"I know you-all are only pokin' fun asking such a question," he said, with a smile. "Of course I ain't going out."

"Take the oath again, Daylight," the same voice cried.

"I sure will. I first come over Chilcoot in '83. I went out over the Pass in a fall blizzard, with a rag of a shirt and a cup of raw flour. I got my grub-stake in Juneau that winter, and in the spring I went over the Pass once more. And once more the famine drew me out. Next spring I went in again, and I swore then that I'd never come out till I made my stake. Well, I ain't made it, and here I am. And I ain't going out now. I get the mail and I come right back. I won't stop the night at Dyea. I'll hit up Chilcoot soon as I change the dogs and get the mail and grub. And so I swear once more, by the mill-tails of hell and the head of John the Baptist, I'll never hit for the Outside till I make my pile. And I tell you-all, here and now, it's got to be an almighty big pile."

"How much might you call a pile?" Bettles demanded from beneath, his arms clutched lovingly around Daylight's legs.

"Yes, how much? What do you call a pile?" others cried.

Daylight steadied himself for a moment and debated.

"Four or five millions," he said slowly, and held up his hand for silence as his statement was received with derisive yells. "I'll be real conservative, and put the bottom notch at a million. And for not an ounce less'n that will I go out of the country."

Again his statement was received with an outburst of derision. Not only had the total gold output of the Yukon up to date been below five millions, but no man had ever made a strike of a hundred thousand, much less of a million.

"You-all listen to me. You seen Jack Kearns get a hunch to-night. We had him sure beat before the draw. His ornery three kings was no good. But he just knew there was another king coming--that was his hunch--and he got it. And I tell you-all I got a hunch. There's a big strike coming on the Yukon, and it's just about due. I don't mean no ornery Moosehide, Birch-Creek kind of a strike. I mean a real rip-snorter hair-raiser. I tell you-all she's in the air and hell-bent for election. Nothing can stop her, and she'll come up river. There's where you-all track my moccasins in the near future if you-all want to find me--somewhere in the country around Stewart River, Indian River, and Klondike River. When I get back with the mail, I'll head that way so fast you-all won't see my trail for smoke. She's a-coming, fellows, gold from the grass roots down, a hundred dollars to the pan, and a stampede in from the Outside fifty thousand strong. You-all'll think all hell's busted loose when that strike is made."

He raised his glass to his lips.

"Here's kindness, and hoping you-all will be in on it."

He drank and stepped down from the chair, falling into another one of Bettles' bear-hugs.

"If I was you, Daylight, I wouldn't *mush* to-day," Joe Hines counselled, coming in from consulting the spirit thermometer outside the door. "We're in for a good cold snap. It's sixty-two below now, and still goin' down. Better wait till she breaks."

Daylight laughed, and the old sour-doughs around him laughed.

"Just like you short-horns," Bettles cried, "afeard of a little frost. And blamed little you know Daylight, if you think frost kin stop 'm."

"Freeze his lungs if he travels in it," was the reply.

"Freeze pap and lollypop! Look here, Hines, you only ben in this here country three years. You ain't seasoned yet. I've seen Daylight do fifty miles up on the Koyokuk on a day when the thermometer busted at seventy-two."

Hines shook his head dolefully.

"Them's the kind that does freeze their lungs," he lamented. "If Daylight pulls out before this snap breaks, he'll never get through--an' him travelin' without tent or fly."

"It's a thousand miles to Dyea," Bettles announced, climbing on the chair and supporting his swaying body by an arm passed around Daylight's neck. "It's a thousand miles, I'm sayin' an' most of the trail unbroke, but I bet any *chechaquo*--anything he wants--that Daylight makes Dyea in thirty days."

"That's an average of over thirty-three miles a day," Doc Watson warned, "and I've travelled some myself. A blizzard on Chilcoot would tie him up for a week."

"Yep," Bettles retorted, "an' Daylight'll do the second thousand back again on end in thirty days more, and I got five hundred dollars that says so, and damn the blizzards."

To emphasize his remarks, he pulled out a gold-sack the size of a bologna sausage and thumped it down on the bar. Doc Watson thumped his own sack alongside.

"Hold on!" Daylight cried. "Bettles's right, and I want in on this. I bet five hundred that sixty days from now I pull up at the Tivoli door with the Dyea mail."

A sceptical roar went up, and a dozen men pulled out their sacks.

Jack Kearns crowded in close and caught Daylight's attention.

"I take you, Daylight," he cried. "Two to one you don't--not in seventy-five days."

"No charity, Jack," was the reply. "The bettin's even, and the time is sixty days."

"Seventy-five days, and two to one you don't," Kearns insisted. "Fifty Mile'll be wide open and the rim-ice rotten."

"What you win from me is yours," Daylight went on. "And, by thunder, Jack, you can't give it back that way. I won't bet with you. You're trying to give me money. But I tell you-all one thing, Jack, I got another hunch. I'm goin' to win it back some one of these days. You-all just wait till the big strike up river. Then you and me'll take the roof off and sit in a game that'll be full man's size. Is it a go?"

They shook hands.

"Of course he'll make it," Kearns whispered in Bettles' ear. "And there's five hundred Daylight's back in sixty days," he added aloud.

Billy Rawlins closed with the wager, and Bettles hugged Kearns ecstatically.

"By Yupiter, I ban take that bet," Olaf Henderson said, dragging Daylight away from Bettles and Kearns.

"Winner pays!" Daylight shouted, closing the wager.

"And I'm sure going to win, and sixty days is a long time between drinks, so I pay now. Name your brand, you *hoochinoos!* Name your brand!"

Bettles, a glass of whiskey in hand, climbed back on his chair, and swaying back and forth, sang the one song he knew: --

> "O, it's Henry Ward Beecher
> And Sunday-school teachers
>   All sing of the sassafras-root;
> But you bet all the same,
> If it had its right name
>   It's the juice of the forbidden fruit."

The crowd roared out the chorus: --

> "But you bet all the same,
>   If it had its right name,
>   It's the juice of the forbidden fruit."

Somebody opened the outer door. A vague gray light filtered in.

"Burning daylight, burning daylight," some one called warningly.

Daylight paused for nothing, heading for the door and pulling down his ear-flaps. Kama stood outside by the sled, a long, narrow affair, sixteen inches wide and seven and a half feet in length, its slatted bottom raised six inches above the steel-shod runners. On it, lashed with thongs of moose-hide, were the light canvas bags that contained the mail, and the food and gear for dogs and men. In front of it, in a single line, lay curled five frost-rimed dogs. They were huskies[1], matched in size and color, all unusually large and all gray. From their cruel jaws to their bushy tails they were as like as peas in their likeness to timber-wolves. Wolves they were, domesticated, it was true, but wolves in appearance and in all their characteristics. On top the sled load, thrust under the lashings and ready for immediate use, were two pairs of snowshoes.

Bettles pointed to a robe of Arctic hare skins, the end of which showed in the mouth of a bag.

"That's his bed," he said. "Six pounds of rabbit skins. Warmest thing he ever slept under, but I'm damned if it could keep me warm, and I can go some myself. Daylight's a hell-fire furnace, that's what he is."

"I'd hate to be that Indian," Doc Watson remarked.

"He'll kill'm, he'll kill'm sure," Bettles chanted exultantly. "I know. I've ben with Daylight on trail. That man ain't never ben tired in his life. Don't know what it means. I seen him travel all day with wet socks at forty five below. There ain't another man living can do that."

While this talk went on, Daylight was saying good-by to those that clustered around him. The Virgin wanted to kiss him, and, fuddled slightly though he was with the whiskey, he saw his way out without compromising with the apron-string. He kissed the Virgin, but he kissed the other three women with equal partiality. He pulled on his long mittens, roused the dogs to their feet, and took his Place at the gee-pole[2].

"*Mush*, you beauties!" he cried.

The animals threw their weights against their breastbands on the instant, crouching low to the snow, and digging in their claws. They whined eagerly, and before the sled had gone half a dozen lengths both Daylight and Kama (in the rear) were running to keep up. And so, running, man and dogs dipped over the bank and down to the frozen bed of the Yukon, and in the gray light were gone.

---

[1] Husky: a wolf-dog of tremendous strength, endurance, viciousness, and sagacity.

[2] A gee-pole: stout pole projecting forward from one side of the front end of the sled, by which the sled is steered.

22

CHAPTER 4

On the river, where was a packed trail and where snowshoes were unnecessary, the dogs averaged six miles an hour. To keep up with them, the two men were compelled to run. Daylight and Kama relieved each other regularly at the gee-pole, for here was the hard work of steering the flying sled and of keeping in advance of it. The man relieved dropped behind the sled, occasionally leaping upon it and resting.

It was severe work, but of the sort that was exhilarating.

They were flying, getting over the ground, making the most of the packed trail. Later on they would come to the unbroken trail, where three miles an hour would constitute good going. Then there would be no riding and resting, and no running. Then the gee-pole would be the easier task, and a man would come back to it to rest after having completed his spell to the fore, breaking trail with the snowshoes for the dogs. Such work was far from exhilarating also, they must expect places where for miles at a time they must toil over chaotic ice-jams, where they would be fortunate if they made two miles an hour. And there would be the inevitable bad jams, short ones, it was true, but so bad that a mile an hour would require terrific effort.

Kama and Daylight did not talk. In the nature of the work they could not, nor in their own natures were they given to talking while they worked. At rare intervals, when necessary, they addressed each other in monosyllables, Kama, for the most part, contenting himself with grunts. Occasionally a dog whined or snarled, but in the main the team kept silent. Only could be heard the sharp, jarring grate of the steel runners over the hard surface and the creak of the straining sled.

As if through a wall, Daylight had passed from the hum and roar of the Tivoli into another world--a world of silence and immobility. Nothing stirred. The Yukon slept under a coat of ice three feet thick. No breath of wind blew. Nor did the sap move in the hearts of the spruce trees that forested the river banks on either hand. The trees, burdened with the last infinitesimal pennyweight of snow their branches could hold, stood in absolute petrification. The slightest tremor would have dislodged the snow, and no snow was dislodged. The sled was the one point of life and motion in the midst of the solemn quietude, and the harsh churn of its runners but emphasized the silence through which it moved.

It was a dead world, and furthermore, a gray world. The weather was sharp and clear; there was no moisture in the atmosphere, no fog nor haze; yet the sky was a gray pall. The reason for this was that, though there was no cloud in the sky to dim the brightness of day, there was no sun to give brightness. Far to the south the sun climbed steadily to meridian, but between it and the frozen Yukon intervened the bulge of the earth. The Yukon lay in a night shadow, and the day itself was in reality a long twilight-light. At a quarter before twelve, where a wide bend of the river gave a long vista south, the sun showed its upper rim above the sky-line. But it did not rise perpendicularly. Instead, it rose on a slant, so that by high noon it had barely lifted its lower rim clear of the horizon. It was a dim, wan sun. There was no heat to its rays, and a man could gaze squarely into the full orb of it without hurt to his eyes. No sooner had it reached meridian than it began its slant back beneath the horizon, and at quarter past twelve the earth threw its shadow again over the land.

The men and dogs raced on. Daylight and Kama were both savages so far as their stomachs were concerned. They could eat irregularly in time and quantity, gorging hugely on occasion, and on occasion going long

23

stretches without eating at all. As for the dogs, they ate but once a day, and then rarely did they receive more than a pound each of dried fish. They were ravenously hungry and at the same time splendidly in condition. Like the wolves, their forebears, their nutritive processes were rigidly economical and perfect. There was no waste. The last least particle of what they consumed was transformed into energy. And Kama and Daylight were like them. Descended themselves from the generations that had endured, they, too, endured. Theirs was the simple, elemental economy. A little food equipped them with prodigious energy. Nothing was lost. A man of soft civilization, sitting at a desk, would have grown lean and woe-begone on the fare that kept Kama and Daylight at the top-notch of physical efficiency. They knew, as the man at the desk never knows, what it is to be normally hungry all the time, so that they could eat any time. Their appetites were always with them and on edge, so that they bit voraciously into whatever offered and with an entire innocence of indigestion.

By three in the afternoon the long twilight faded into night. The stars came out, very near and sharp and bright, and by their light dogs and men still kept the trail. They were indefatigable. And this was no record run of a single day, but the first day of sixty such days. Though Daylight had passed a night without sleep, a night of dancing and carouse, it seemed to have left no effect. For this there were two explanations first, his remarkable vitality; and next, the fact that such nights were rare in his experience. Again enters the man at the desk, whose physical efficiency would be more hurt by a cup of coffee at bedtime than could Daylight's by a whole night long of strong drink and excitement.

Daylight travelled without a watch, *feeling* the passage of time and largely estimating it by subconscious processes. By what he considered must be six o'clock, he began looking for a camping-place. The trail, at a bend, plunged out across the river. Not having found a likely spot, they held on for the opposite bank a mile away. But midway they encountered an ice-jam which took an hour of heavy work to cross. At last Daylight glimpsed what he was looking for, a dead tree close by the bank. The sled was run in and up. Kama grunted with satisfaction, and the work of making camp was begun.

The division of labor was excellent. Each knew what he must do. With one ax Daylight chopped down the dead pine. Kama, with a snowshoe and the other ax, cleared away the two feet of snow above the Yukon ice and chopped a supply of ice for cooking purposes. A piece of dry birch bark started the fire, and Daylight went ahead with the cooking while the Indian unloaded the sled and fed the dogs their ration of dried fish. The food sacks he slung high in the trees beyond leaping-reach of the huskies. Next, he chopped down a young spruce tree and trimmed off the boughs. Close to the fire he trampled down the soft snow and covered the packed space with the boughs. On this flooring he tossed his own and Daylight's gear-bags, containing dry socks and underwear and their sleeping-robes. Kama, however, had two robes of rabbit skin to Daylight's one.

They worked on steadily, without speaking, losing no time. Each did whatever was needed, without thought of leaving to the other the least task that presented itself to hand. Thus, Kama saw when more ice was needed and went and got it, while a snowshoe, pushed over by the lunge of a dog, was stuck on end again by Daylight. While coffee was boiling, bacon frying, and flapjacks were being mixed, Daylight found time to put on a big pot of beans. Kama came back, sat down on the edge of the spruce boughs, and in the interval of waiting, mended harness.

"I t'ink dat Skookum and Booga make um plenty fight maybe," Kama remarked, as they sat down to eat.

"Keep an eye on them," was Daylight's answer.

And this was their sole conversation throughout the meal. Once, with a muttered imprecation, Kama leaped away, a stick of firewood in hand, and clubbed apart a tangle of fighting dogs. Daylight, between mouthfuls, fed chunks of ice into the tin pot, where it thawed into water. The meal finished, Kama replenished the fire, cut more wood for the morning, and returned to the spruce bough bed and his harness-mending. Daylight cut up generous chunks of bacon and dropped them in the pot of bubbling beans. The moccasins of both men were wet, and this in spite of the intense cold; so when there was no further need for them to leave the oasis of spruce boughs, they took off their moccasins and hung them on short sticks to dry before the fire, turning them about from time to time. When the beans were finally cooked, Daylight ran part of them into a bag of flour-sacking a foot and a half long and three inches in diameter. This he then laid on the snow to freeze. The remainder of the beans were left in the pot for breakfast.

It was past nine o'clock, and they were ready for bed. The squabbling and bickering among the dogs had long since died down, and the weary animals were curled in the snow, each with his feet and nose bunched together and covered by his wolf's brush of a tail. Kama spread his sleeping-furs and lighted his pipe. Daylight rolled a brown-paper cigarette, and the second conversation of the evening took place.

"I think we come near sixty miles," said Daylight.

"Um, I t'ink so," said Kama.

They rolled into their robes, all-standing, each with a woolen Mackinaw jacket on in place of the *parkas*[1] they had worn all day. Swiftly, almost on the instant they closed their eyes, they were asleep. The stars leaped and danced in the frosty air, and overhead the colored bars of the aurora borealis were shooting like great searchlights.

In the darkness Daylight awoke and roused Kama. Though the aurora still flamed, another day had begun. Warmed-over flapjacks, warmed-over beans, fried bacon, and coffee composed the breakfast. The dogs got nothing, though they watched with wistful mien from a distance, sitting up in the snow, their tails curled around their paws. Occasionally they lifted one fore paw or the other, with a restless movement, as if the frost tingled in their feet. It was bitter cold, at least sixty-five below zero, and when Kama harnessed the dogs with naked hands he was compelled several times to go over to the fire and warm the numbing finger-tips. Together the two men loaded and lashed the sled. They warmed their hands for the last time, pulled on their mittens, and mushed the dogs over the bank and down to the river-trail. According to Daylight's estimate, it was around seven o'clock; but the stars danced just as brilliantly, and faint, luminous streaks of greenish aurora still pulsed overhead.

Two hours later it became suddenly dark--so dark that they kept to the trail largely by instinct; and Daylight knew that his time-estimate had been right. It was the darkness before dawn, never anywhere more conspicuous than on the Alaskan winter-trail. Slowly the gray light came stealing through the gloom, imperceptibly at first, so that it was almost with surprise that they noticed the vague loom of the trail underfoot. Next, they were able to see the wheel-dog, and then the whole string of running dogs and snow-stretches on either side. Then the near bank loomed for a

---

[1] Parka: a light, hooded, smock-like garment made of cotton drill.

moment and was gone, loomed a second time and remained. In a few minutes the far bank, a mile away, unobtrusively came into view, and ahead and behind, the whole frozen river could be seen, with off to the left a wide-extending range of sharp-cut, snow-covered mountains. And that was all. No sun arose. The gray light remained gray.

Once, during the day, a lynx leaped lightly across the trail, under the very nose of the lead-dog, and vanished in the white woods. The dogs' wild impulses roused. They raised the hunting-cry of the pack, surged against their collars, and swerved aside in pursuit. Daylight, yelling "Whoa!" struggled with the gee-pole and managed to overturn the sled into the soft snow. The dogs gave up, the sled was righted, and five minutes later they were flying along the hard-packed trail again. The lynx was the only sign of life they had seen in two days, and it, leaping velvet-footed and vanishing, had been more like an apparition.

At twelve o'clock, when the sun peeped over the earth-bulge, they stopped and built a small fire on the ice. Daylight, with the ax, chopped chunks off the frozen sausage of beans. These, thawed and warmed in the frying-pan, constituted their meal. They had no coffee. He did not believe in the burning of daylight for such a luxury. The dogs stopped wrangling with one another, and looked on wistfully. Only at night did they get their pound of fish. In the meantime they worked.

The cold snap continued. Only men of iron kept the trail at such low temperatures, and Kama and Daylight were picked men of their races. But Kama knew the other was the better man, and thus, at the start, he was himself foredoomed to defeat. Not that he slackened his effort or willingness by the slightest conscious degree, but that he was beaten by the burden he carried in his mind. His attitude toward Daylight was worshipful. Stoical, taciturn, proud of his physical prowess, he found all these qualities incarnated in his white companion. Here was one that excelled in the things worth excelling in, a man-god ready to hand, and Kama could not but worship--withal he gave no signs of it. No wonder the race of white men conquered, was his thought, when it bred men like this man. What chance had the Indian against such a dogged, enduring breed? Even the Indians did not travel at such low temperatures, and theirs was the wisdom of thousands of generations; yet here was this Daylight, from the soft Southland, harder than they, laughing at their fears, and swinging along the trail ten and twelve hours a day. And this Daylight thought that he could keep up a day's pace of thirty-three miles for sixty days! Wait till a fresh fall of snow came down, or they struck the unbroken trail or the rotten rim-ice that fringed open water.

In the meantime Kama kept the pace, never grumbling, never shirking. Sixty-five degrees below zero is very cold. Since water freezes at thirty-two above, sixty-five below meant ninety-seven degrees below freezing-point. Some idea of the significance of this may be gained by conceiving of an equal difference of temperature in the opposite direction. One hundred and twenty-nine on the thermometer constitutes a very hot day, yet such a temperature is but ninety-seven degrees above freezing. Double this difference, and possibly some slight conception may be gained of the cold through which Kama and Daylight travelled between dark and dark and through the dark.

Kama froze the skin on his cheek-bones, despite frequent rubbings, and the flesh turned black and sore. Also he slightly froze the edges of his lung-tissues--a dangerous thing, and the basic reason why a man should not unduly exert himself in the open at sixty-five below. But Kama never complained, and Daylight was a furnace of heat, sleeping as warmly under his six pounds of rabbit skins as the other did under twelve pounds.

On the second night, fifty more miles to the good, they camped in the vicinity of the boundary between Alaska and the Northwest Territory. The rest of the journey, save the last short stretch to Dyea, would be travelled on Canadian territory. With the hard trail, and in the absence of fresh snow, Daylight planned to make the camp of Forty Mile on the fourth night. He told Kama as much, but on the third day the temperature began to rise, and they knew snow was not far off; for on the Yukon it must get warm in order to snow. Also, on this day, they encountered ten miles of chaotic ice-jams, where, a thousand times, they lifted the loaded sled over the huge cakes by the strength of their arms and lowered it down again. Here the dogs were well-nigh useless, and both they and the men were tried excessively by the roughness of the way. An hour's extra running that night caught up only part of the lost time.

In the morning they awoke to find ten inches of snow on their robes. The dogs were buried under it and were loath to leave their comfortable nests. This new snow meant hard going. The sled runners would not slide over it so well, while one of the men must go in advance of the dogs and pack it down with snowshoes so that they should not wallow. Quite different was it from the ordinary snow known to those of the Southland. It was hard, and fine, and dry. It was more like sugar. Kick it, and it flew with a hissing noise like sand. There was no cohesion among the particles, and it could not be moulded into snow- balls. It was not composed of flakes, but of crystals--tiny, geometrical frost-crystals. In truth, it was not snow, but frost.

The weather was warm, as well, barely twenty below zero, and the two men, with raised ear-flaps and dangling mittens, sweated as they toiled. They failed to make Forty Mile that night, and when they passed that camp next day Daylight paused only long enough to get the mail and additional grub. On the afternoon of the following day they camped at the mouth of the Klondike River. Not a soul had they encountered since Forty Mile, and they had made their own trail. As yet, that winter, no one had travelled the river south of Forty Mile, and, for that matter, the whole winter through they might be the only ones to travel it. In that day the Yukon was a lonely land. Between the Klondike River and Salt Water at Dyea intervened six hundred miles of snow-covered wilderness, and in all that distance there were but two places where Daylight might look forward to meeting men. Both were isolated trading-posts, Sixty Mile and Fort Selkirk. In the summer-time Indians might be met with at the mouths of the Stewart and White rivers, at the Big and Little Salmons, and on Lake Le Barge; but in the winter, as he well knew, they would be on the trail of the moose-herds, following them back into the mountains.

That night, camped at the mouth of the Klondike, Daylight did not turn in when the evening's work was done. Had a white man been present, Daylight would have remarked that he felt his "hunch" working. As it was, he tied on his snowshoes, left the dogs curled in the snow and Kama breathing heavily under his rabbit skins, and climbed up to the big flat above the high earth-bank. But the spruce trees were too thick for an outlook, and he threaded his way across the flat and up the first steep slopes of the mountain at the back. Here, flowing in from the east at right angles, he could see the Klondike, and, bending grandly from the south, the Yukon. To the left, and downstream, toward Moosehide Mountain, the huge splash of white, from which it took its name, showing clearly in the starlight. Lieutenant Schwatka had given it its name, but he, Daylight, had first seen it long before that intrepid explorer had crossed the Chilcoot and rafted down the Yukon.

But the mountain received only passing notice. Daylight's interest was centered in the big flat itself, with deep water all along its edge for steamboat landings.

"A sure enough likely town site," he muttered. "Room for a camp of forty thousand men. All that's needed is the gold-strike." He meditated for a space. "Ten dollars to the pan'll do it, and it'd be the all-firedest stampede Alaska ever seen. And if it don't come here, it'll come somewhere hereabouts. It's a sure good idea to keep an eye out for town sites all the way up."

He stood a while longer, gazing out over the lonely flat and visioning with constructive imagination the scene if the stampede did come. In fancy, he placed the sawmills, the big trading stores, the saloons, and dance-halls, and the long streets of miners' cabins. And along those streets he saw thousands of men passing up and down, while before the stores were the heavy freighting-sleds, with long strings of dogs attached. Also he saw the heavy freighters pulling down the main street and heading up the frozen Klondike toward the imagined somewhere where the diggings must be located.

He laughed and shook the vision from his eyes, descended to the level, and crossed the flat to camp. Five minutes after he had rolled up in his robe, he opened his eyes and sat up, amazed that he was not already asleep. He glanced at the Indian sleeping beside him, at the embers of the dying fire, at the five dogs beyond, with their wolf's brushes curled over their noses, and at the four snowshoes standing upright in the snow.

"It's sure hell the way that hunch works on me" he murmured. His mind reverted to the poker game. "Four kings!" He grinned reminiscently. "That WAS a hunch!"

He lay down again, pulled the edge of the robe around his neck and over his ear-flaps, closed his eyes, and this time fell asleep.

CHAPTER 5

At Sixty Mile they restocked provisions, added a few pounds of letters to their load, and held steadily on. From Forty Mile they had had unbroken trail, and they could look forward only to unbroken trail clear to Dyea. Daylight stood it magnificently, but the killing pace was beginning to tell on Kama. His pride kept his mouth shut, but the result of the chilling of his lungs in the cold snap could not be concealed. Microscopically small had been the edges of the lung-tissue touched by the frost, but they now began to slough off, giving rise to a dry, hacking cough. Any unusually severe exertion precipitated spells of coughing, during which he was almost like a man in a fit. The blood congested in his eyes till they bulged, while the tears ran down his cheeks. A whiff of the smoke from frying bacon would start him off for a half-hour's paroxysm, and he kept carefully to windward when Daylight was cooking.

They plodded days upon days and without end over the soft, unpacked snow. It was hard, monotonous work, with none of the joy and blood-stir that went with flying over hard surface. Now one man to the fore in the snowshoes, and now the other, it was a case of stubborn, unmitigated plod. A yard of powdery snow had to be pressed down, and the wide-webbed shoe, under a man's weight, sank a full dozen inches into the soft surface. Snowshoe work, under such conditions, called for the use of muscles other than those used in ordinary walking. From step to step the rising foot could not come up and forward on a slant. It had to be raised perpendicularly. When the snowshoe was pressed into the snow, its nose was confronted by a vertical wall of snow twelve inches high. If the foot, in rising, slanted forward the slightest bit, the nose of the shoe penetrated the obstructing wall and tipped downward till the heel of the shoe struck the man's leg behind. Thus up, straight up, twelve inches, each foot must be raised every time and all the time, ere the forward swing from the knee could begin.

On this partially packed surface followed the dogs, the man at the gee-pole, and the sled. At the best, toiling as only picked men could toil, they made no more than three miles an hour. This meant longer hours of travel, and Daylight, for good measure and for a margin against accidents, hit the trail for twelve hours a day. Since three hours were consumed by making camp at night and cooking beans, by getting breakfast in the morning and breaking camp, and by thawing beans at the midday halt, nine hours were left for sleep and recuperation, and neither men nor dogs wasted many minutes of those nine hours.

At Selkirk, the trading post near Pelly River, Daylight suggested that Kama lay over, rejoining him on the back trip from Dyea. A strayed Indian from Lake Le Barge was willing to take his place; but Kama was obdurate. He grunted with a slight intonation of resentment, and that was all. The dogs, however, Daylight changed, leaving his own exhausted team to rest up against his return, while he went on with six fresh dogs.

They travelled till ten o'clock the night they reached Selkirk, and at six next morning they plunged ahead into the next stretch of wilderness of nearly five hundred miles that lay between Selkirk and Dyea. A second cold snap came on, but cold or warm it was all the same, an unbroken trail. When the thermometer went down to fifty below, it was even harder to travel, for at that low temperature the hard frost-crystals were more like sand-grains in the resistance they offered to the sled runners. The dogs had to pull harder than over the same snow at twenty or thirty below zero. Daylight increased the day's travel to thirteen hours. He jealously guarded the margin he had gained, for he knew there were difficult stretches to come.

It was not yet quite midwinter, and the turbulent Fifty Mile River vindicated his judgment. In many places it ran wide open, with precarious rim-ice fringing it on either side. In numerous places, where the water dashed against the steep-sided bluffs, rim-ice was unable to form. They turned and twisted, now crossing the river, now coming back again, sometimes making half a dozen attempts before they found a way over a particularly bad stretch. It was slow work. The ice-bridges had to be tested, and either Daylight or Kama went in advance, snowshoes on their feet, and long poles carried crosswise in their hands. Thus, if they broke through, they could cling to the pole that bridged the hole made by their bodies. Several such accidents were the share of each. At fifty below zero, a man wet to the waist cannot travel without freezing; so each ducking meant delay. As soon as rescued, the wet man ran up and down to keep up his circulation, while his dry companion built a fire. Thus protected, a change of garments could be made and the wet ones dried against the next misadventure.

To make matters worse, this dangerous river travel could not be done in the dark, and their working day was reduced to the six hours of twilight. Every moment was precious, and they strove never to lose one. Thus, before the first hint of the coming of gray day, camp was broken, sled loaded, dogs harnessed, and the two men crouched waiting over the fire. Nor did they make the midday halt to eat. As it was, they were running far behind their schedule, each day eating into the margin they had run up. There were days when they made fifteen miles, and days when they made a dozen. And there was one bad stretch where in two days they covered nine miles, being compelled to turn their backs three times on the river and to portage sled and outfit over the mountains.

At last they cleared the dread Fifty Mile River and came out on Lake Le Barge. Here was no open water nor jammed ice. For thirty miles or more the snow lay level as a table; withal it lay three feet deep and was soft as flour. Three miles an hour was the best they could make, but Daylight celebrated the passing of the Fifty Mile by traveling late. At eleven in the morning they emerged at the foot of the lake. At three in the afternoon, as the Arctic night closed down, he caught his first sight of the head of the lake, and with the first stars took his bearings. At eight in the evening they left the lake behind and entered the mouth of the Lewes River. Here a halt of half an hour was made, while chunks of frozen boiled beans were thawed and the dogs were given an extra ration of fish. Then they pulled on up the river till one in the morning, when they made their regular camp.

They had hit the trail sixteen hours on end that day, the dogs had come in too tired to fight among themselves or even snarl, and Kama had perceptibly limped the last several miles; yet Daylight was on trail next morning at six o'clock. By eleven he was at the foot of White Horse, and that night saw him camped beyond the Box Canon, the last bad river-stretch behind him, the string of lakes before him.

There was no let up in his pace. Twelve hours a day, six in the twilight, and six in the dark, they toiled on the trail. Three hours were consumed in cooking, repairing harnesses, and making and breaking camp, and the remaining nine hours dogs and men slept as if dead. The iron strength of Kama broke. Day by day the terrific toil sapped him. Day by day he consumed more of his reserves of strength. He became slower of movement, the resiliency went out of his muscles, and his limp became permanent. Yet he labored stoically on, never shirking, never grunting a hint of complaint.

Daylight was thin-faced and tired. He looked tired; yet somehow, with that marvelous mechanism of a body that was his, he drove on, ever on, remorselessly on. Never was he more a god in Kama's mind than in the last days of the south-bound traverse, as the failing Indian watched him, ever to the fore, pressing onward with urgency of endurance such as Kama had never seen nor dreamed could thrive in human form.

The time came when Kama was unable to go in the lead and break trail, and it was a proof that he was far gone when he permitted Daylight to toil all day at the heavy snowshoe work. Lake by lake they crossed the string of lakes from Marsh to Linderman, and began the ascent of Chilcoot. By all rights, Daylight should have camped below the last pitch of the pass at the dim end of day; but he kept on and over and down to Sheep Camp, while behind him raged a snow-storm that would have delayed him twenty-four hours.

This last excessive strain broke Kama completely. In the morning he could not travel. At five, when called, he sat up after a struggle, groaned, and sank back again. Daylight did the camp work of both, harnessed the dogs, and, when ready for the start, rolled the helpless Indian in all three sleeping robes and lashed him on top of the sled. The going was good; they were on the last lap; and he raced the dogs down through Dyea Canon and along the hard-packed trail that led to Dyea Post. And running still, Kama groaning on top the load, and Daylight leaping at the gee-pole to avoid going under the runners of the flying sled, they arrived at Dyea by the sea.

True to his promise, Daylight did not stop. An hour's time saw the sled loaded with the ingoing mail and grub, fresh dogs harnessed, and a fresh Indian engaged. Kama never spoke from the time of his arrival till the moment Daylight, ready to depart, stood beside him to say good-by. They shook hands.

"You kill um dat damn Indian," Kama said. "Sawee, Daylight? You kill um."

"He'll sure last as far as Pelly," Daylight grinned.

Kama shook his head doubtfully, and rolled over on his side, turning his back in token of farewell.

Daylight won across Chilcoot that same day, dropping down five hundred feet in the darkness and the flurrying snow to Crater Lake, where he camped. It was a 'cold' camp, far above the timber-line, and he had not burdened his sled with firewood. That night three feet of snow covered them, and in the black morning, when they dug themselves out, the Indian tried to desert. He had had enough of traveling with what he considered a madman. But Daylight persuaded him in grim ways to stay by the outfit, and they pulled on across Deep Lake and Long Lake and dropped down to the level-going of Lake Linderman.

It was the same killing pace going in as coming out, and the Indian did not stand it as well as Kama. He, too, never complained. Nor did he try again to desert. He toiled on and did his best, while he renewed his resolve to steer clear of Daylight in the future. The days slipped into days, nights and twilight's alternating, cold snaps gave way to snow-falls, and cold snaps came on again, and all the while, through the long hours, the miles piled up behind them.

But on the Fifty Mile accident befell them. Crossing an ice-bridge, the dogs broke through and were swept under the down-stream ice. The traces that connected the team with the wheel-dog parted, and the team was never seen again. Only the one wheel-dog remained, and Daylight harnessed the Indian and himself to the sled. But a man cannot take the place of a dog at such work, and the two men were attempting to do the work of five dogs. At the end of the first hour, Daylight lightened up. Dog-food, extra gear, and the spare ax were thrown away. Under the extraordinary exertion the dog snapped a tendon the following day, and was hopelessly disabled. Daylight shot it, and abandoned the sled. On his back he took one hundred and sixty pounds of mail and grub, and on the Indian's put one hundred and twenty-five pounds. The stripping of gear was remorseless. The Indian was appalled when he saw every pound of worthless mail matter retained, while beans, cups, pails, plates, and extra clothing were thrown by the board. One robe each was kept, one ax, one tin pail, and a scant supply of bacon and flour. Bacon could be eaten raw on a pinch, and flour, stirred in hot water, could keep men going. Even the rifle and the score of rounds of ammunition were left behind.

And in this fashion they covered the two hundred miles to Selkirk. Daylight travelled late and early, the hours formerly used by camp-making and dog-tending being now devoted to the trail. At night they crouched over a small fire, wrapped in their robes, drinking flour broth and thawing bacon on the ends of sticks; and in the morning darkness, without a word, they arose, slipped on their packs, adjusted head-straps, and hit the trail. The last miles into Selkirk, Daylight drove the Indian before him, a hollow-cheeked, gaunt-eyed wraith of a man who else would have lain down and slept or abandoned his burden of mail.

At Selkirk, the old team of dogs, fresh and in condition, were harnessed, and the same day saw Daylight plodding on, alternating places at the gee-pole, as a matter of course, with the Le Barge Indian who had volunteered on the way out. Daylight was two days behind his schedule, and falling snow and unpacked trail kept him two days behind all the way to Forty Mile. And here the weather favored. It was time for a big cold snap, and he gambled on it, cutting down the weight of grub for dogs and men. The men of Forty Mile shook their heads ominously, and demanded to know what he would do if the snow still fell.

"That cold snap's sure got to come," he laughed, and mushed out on the trail.

A number of sleds had passed back and forth already that winter between Forty Mile and Circle City, and the trail was well packed. And the cold snap came and remained, and Circle City was only two hundred miles away. The Le Barge Indian was a young man, unlearned yet in his own limitations, and filled with pride. He took Daylight's pace with joy, and even dreamed, at first, that he would play the white man out. The first hundred miles he looked for signs of weakening, and marveled that he saw them not. Throughout the second hundred miles he observed signs in himself, and gritted his teeth and kept up. And ever Daylight flew on and on, running at the gee-pole or resting his spell on top the flying sled. The last day, clearer and colder than ever, gave perfect going, and they covered seventy miles. It was ten at night when they pulled up the earth-bank and flew along the main street of Circle City; and the young Indian, though it was his spell to ride, leaped off and ran behind the sled. It was honorable braggadocio, and despite the fact that he had found his limitations and was pressing desperately against them, he ran gamely on.

CHAPTER 6

A crowd filled the Tivoli--the old crowd that had seen Daylight depart two months before; for this was the night of the sixtieth day, and opinion was divided as ever as to whether or not he would compass the achievement. At ten o'clock bets were still being made, though the odds rose, bet by bet, against his success. Down in her heart the Virgin believed he had failed, yet she made a bet of twenty ounces with Charley Bates, against forty ounces, that Daylight would arrive before midnight.

She it was who heard the first yelps of the dogs.

"Listen!" she cried. "It's Daylight!"

There was a general stampede for the door; but where the double storm-doors were thrown wide open, the crowd fell back. They heard the eager whining of dogs, the snap of a dog-whip, and the voice of Daylight crying encouragement as the weary animals capped all they had done by dragging the sled in over the wooden floor. They came in with a rush, and with them rushed in the frost, a visible vapor of smoking white, through which their heads and backs showed, as they strained in the harness, till they had all the seeming of swimming in a river. Behind them, at the gee-pole, came Daylight, hidden to the knees by the swirling frost through which he appeared to wade.

He was the same old Daylight, withal lean and tired-looking, and his black eyes were sparkling and flashing brighter than ever. His *parka* of cotton drill hooded him like a monk, and fell in straight lines to his knees. Grimed and scorched by camp-smoke and fire, the garment in itself told the story of his trip. A two-months' beard covered his face; and the beard, in turn, was matted with the ice of his breathing through the long seventy-mile run.

His entry was spectacular, melodramatic; and he knew it. It was his life, and he was living it at the top of his bent. Among his fellows he was a great man, an Arctic hero. He was proud of the fact, and it was a high moment for him, fresh from two thousand miles of trail, to come surging into that bar-room, dogs, sled, mail, Indian, paraphernalia, and all. He had performed one more exploit that would make the Yukon ring with his name--he, Burning Daylight, the king of travelers and dog-mushers.

He experienced a thrill of surprise as the roar of welcome went up and as every familiar detail of the Tivoli greeted his vision--the long bar and the array of bottles, the gambling games, the big stove, the weigher at the gold-scales, the musicians, the men and women, the Virgin, Celia, and Nellie, Dan MacDonald, Bettles, Billy Rawlins, Olaf Henderson, Doc Watson,--all of them. It was just as he had left it, and in all seeming it might well be the very day he had left. The sixty days of incessant travel through the white wilderness suddenly telescoped, and had no existence in time. They were a moment, an incident. He had plunged out and into them through the wall of silence, and back through the wall of silence he had plunged, apparently the next instant, and into the roar and turmoil of the Tivoli.

A glance down at the sled with its canvas mail-bags was necessary to reassure him of the reality of those sixty days and the two thousand miles over the ice. As in a dream, he shook the hands that were thrust out to him. He felt a vast exaltation. Life was magnificent. He loved it all. A great sense of humanness and comradeship swept over him. These were all his, his own kind. It was immense, tremendous. He felt melting in the heart of him, and he would have liked to shake hands with them all at once, to gather them to his breast in one mighty embrace.

He drew a deep breath and cried: "The winner pays, and I'm the winner, ain't I? Surge up, you-all Malemutes and Siwashes, and name your poison! There's your Dyea mail, straight from Salt Water, and no hornswogglin about it! Cast the lashings adrift, you-all, and wade into it!"

A dozen pairs of hands were at the sled-lashings, when the young Le Barge Indian, bending at the same task, suddenly and limply straightened up. In his eyes was a great surprise. He stared about him wildly, for the thing he was undergoing was new to him. He was profoundly struck by an unguessed limitation. He shook as with a palsy, and he gave at the knees, slowly sinking down to fall suddenly across the sled and to know the smashing blow of darkness across his consciousness.

"Exhaustion," said Daylight. "Take him off and put him to bed, some of you-all. He's sure a good Indian."

"Daylight's right," was Doc Watson's verdict, a moment later. "The man's plumb tuckered out."

The mail was taken charge of, the dogs driven away to quarters and fed, and Bettles struck up the paean of the sassafras root as they lined up against the long bar to drink and talk and collect their debts.

A few minutes later, Daylight was whirling around the dance-floor, waltzing with the Virgin. He had replaced his *parka* with his fur cap and blanket-cloth coat, kicked off his frozen moccasins, and was dancing in his stocking feet. After wetting himself to the knees late that afternoon, he had run on without changing his foot-gear, and to the knees his long German socks were matted with ice. In the warmth of the room it began to thaw and to break apart in clinging chunks. These chunks rattled together as his legs flew around, and every little while they fell clattering to the floor and were slipped upon by the other dancers. But everybody forgave Daylight. He, who was one of the few that made the Law in that far land, who set the ethical pace, and by conduct gave the standard of right and wrong, was nevertheless above the Law. He was one of those rare and favored mortals who can do no wrong. What he did had to be right, whether others were permitted or not to do the same things. Of course, such mortals are so favored by virtue of the fact that they almost always do the right and do it in finer and higher ways than other men. So Daylight, an elder hero in that young land and at the same time younger than most of them, moved as a creature apart, as a man above men, as a man who was greatly man and all man. And small wonder it was that the Virgin yielded herself to his arms, as they danced dance after dance, and was sick at heart at the knowledge that he found nothing in her more than a good friend and an excellent dancer. Small consolation it was to know that he had never loved any woman. She was sick with love of him, and he danced with her as he would dance with any woman, as he would dance with a man who was a good dancer and upon whose arm was tied a handkerchief to conventionalize him into a woman.

One such man Daylight danced with that night. Among frontiersmen it has always been a test of endurance for one man to whirl another down; and when Ben Davis, the faro-dealer, a gaudy bandanna on his arm, got Daylight in a Virginia reel, the fun began. The reel broke up and all fell back to watch. Around and around the two men whirled, always in the one direction. Word was passed on into the big bar-room, and bar and gambling tables were deserted. Everybody wanted to see, and they packed and jammed the dance-room. The musicians played on and on, and on and on the two men whirled. Davis was skilled at the trick, and on the Yukon he had put many a strong man on his back. But after a few minutes it was clear that he, and not Daylight, was going.

For a while longer they spun around, and then Daylight suddenly stood still, released his partner, and stepped back, reeling himself, and fluttering his hands aimlessly, as if to support himself against the air. But Davis, a giddy smile of consternation on his face, gave sideways, turned in an attempt to recover balance, and pitched headlong to the floor. Still reeling and staggering and clutching at the air with his hands, Daylight caught the nearest girl and started on in a waltz. Again he had done the big thing. Weary from two thousand miles over the ice and a run that day of seventy miles, he had whirled a fresh man down, and that man Ben Davis.

Daylight loved the high places, and though few high places there were in his narrow experience, he had made a point of sitting in the highest he had ever glimpsed. The great world had never heard his name, but it was known far and wide in the vast silent North, by whites and Indians and Eskimos, from Bering Sea to the Passes, from the head reaches of remotest rivers to the tundra shore of Point Barrow. Desire for mastery was strong in him, and it was all one whether wrestling with the elements themselves, with men, or with luck in a gambling game. It was all a game, life and its affairs. And he was a gambler to the core. Risk and chance were meat and drink. True, it was not altogether blind, for he applied wit and skill and strength; but behind it all was the everlasting Luck, the thing that at times turned on its votaries and crushed the wise while it blessed the fools--Luck, the thing all men sought and dreamed to conquer. And so he. Deep in his life-processes Life itself sang the siren song of its own majesty, ever a-whisper and urgent, counseling him that he could achieve more than other men, win out where they failed, ride to success where they perished. It was the urge of Life healthy and strong, unaware of frailty and decay, drunken with sublime complacence, ego-mad, enchanted by its own mighty optimism.

And ever in vaguest whisperings and clearest trumpet-calls came the message that sometime, somewhere, somehow, he would run Luck down, make himself the master of Luck, and tie it and brand it as his own. When he played poker, the whisper was of four aces and royal flushes. When he prospected, it was of gold in the grass-roots, gold on bed-rock, and gold all the way down. At the sharpest hazards of trail and river and famine, the message was that other men might die, but that he would pull through triumphant. It was the old, old lie of Life fooling itself, believing itself--immortal and indestructible, bound to achieve over other lives and win to its heart's desire.

And so, reversing at times, Daylight waltzed off his dizziness and led the way to the bar. But a united protest went up. His theory that the winner paid was no longer to be tolerated. It was contrary to custom and common sense, and while it emphasized good-fellowship, nevertheless, in the name of good-fellowship it must cease. The drinks were rightfully on Ben Davis, and Ben Davis must buy them. Furthermore, all drinks and general treats that Daylight was guilty of ought to be paid by the house, for Daylight brought much custom to it whenever he made a night. Bettles was the spokesman, and his argument, tersely and offensively vernacular, was unanimously applauded.

Daylight grinned, stepped aside to the roulette-table, and bought a stack of yellow chips. At the end of ten minutes he weighed in at the scales, and two thousand dollars in gold-dust was poured into his own and an extra sack. Luck, a mere flutter of luck, but it was his. Elation was added to elation. He was living, and the night was his. He turned upon his well-wishing critics.

"Now the winner sure does pay," he said.

35

And they surrendered. There was no withstanding Daylight when he vaulted on the back of life, and rode it bitted and spurred.

At one in the morning he saw Elijah Davis herding Henry Finn and Joe Hines, the lumber-jack, toward the door. Daylight interfered.

"Where are you-all going?" he demanded, attempting to draw them to the bar.

"Bed," Elijah Davis answered.

He was a lean tobacco-chewing New Englander, the one daring spirit in his family that had heard and answered the call of the West shouting through the Mount Desert back odd-lots.

"Got to," Joe Hines added apologetically. "We're mushing out in the mornin'."

Daylight still detained them.

"Where to? What's the excitement?"

"No excitement," Elijah explained. "We're just a-goin' to play your hunch, an' tackle the Upper Country. Don't you want to come along?"

"I sure do," Daylight affirmed.

But the question had been put in fun, and Elijah ignored the acceptance.

"We're tacklin' the Stewart," he went on. "Al Mayo told me he seen some likely lookin' bars first time he come down the Stewart, and we're goin' to sample 'em while the river's froze. You listen, Daylight, an' mark my words, the time's comin' when winter diggin's'll be all the go. There'll be men in them days that'll laugh at our summer stratchin' an' ground-wallerin'."

At that time, winter mining was undreamed of on the Yukon. From the moss and grass the land was frozen to bed-rock, and frozen gravel, hard as granite, defied pick and shovel. In the summer the men stripped the earth down as fast as the sun thawed it. Then was the time they did their mining. During the winter they freighted their provisions, went moose-hunting, got all ready for the summer's work, and then loafed the bleak, dark months through in the big central camps such as Circle City and Forty Mile.

"Winter diggin's sure comin'," Daylight agreed. "Wait till that big strike is made up river. Then you-all'll see a new kind of mining. What's to prevent wood-burning and sinking shafts and drifting along bed-rock? Won't need to timber. That frozen muck and gravel'll stand till hell is froze and its mill-tails is turned to ice-cream. Why, they'll be working pay-streaks a hundred feet deep in them days that's comin'. I'm sure going along with you-all, Elijah."

Elijah laughed, gathered his two partners up, and was making a second attempt to reach the door

"Hold on," Daylight called. "I sure mean it."

The three men turned back suddenly upon him, in their faces surprise, delight, and incredulity.

"G'wan, you're foolin'," said Finn, the other lumberjack, a quiet, steady, Wisconsin man.

"There's my dawgs and sled," Daylight answered. "That'll make two teams and halve the loads--though we-all'll have to travel easy for a spell, for them dawgs is sure tired."

The three men were overjoyed, but still a trifle incredulous.

"Now look here," Joe Hines blurted out, "none of your foolin, Daylight. We mean business. Will you come?"

Daylight extended his hand and shook.

"Then you'd best be gettin' to bed," Elijah advised. "We're mushin' out at six, and four hours' sleep is none so long."

"Mebbe we ought to lay over a day and let him rest up," Finn suggested.

Daylight's pride was touched.

"No you don't," he cried. "We all start at six. What time do you-all want to be called? Five? All right, I'll rouse you-all out."

"You oughter have some sleep," Elijah counselled gravely. "You can't go on forever."

Daylight was tired, profoundly tired. Even *his* iron body acknowledged weariness. Every muscle was clamoring for bed and rest, was appalled at continuance of exertion and at thought of the trail again. All this physical protest welled up into his brain in a wave of revolt. But deeper down, scornful and defiant, was Life itself, the essential fire of it, whispering that all Daylight's fellows were looking on, that now was the time to pile deed upon deed, to flaunt his strength in the face of strength. It was merely Life, whispering its ancient lies. And in league with it was whiskey, with all its consummate effrontery and vain-glory.

"Mebbe you-all think I ain't weaned yet?" Daylight demanded. "Why, I ain't had a drink, or a dance, or seen a soul in two months. You-all get to bed. I'll call you-all at five."

And for the rest of the night he danced on in his stocking feet, and at five in the morning, rapping thunderously on the door of his new partners' cabin, he could be heard singing the song that had given him his name:--

"Burning daylight, you-all Stewart River hunchers! Burning daylight! Burning daylight! Burning daylight!"

CHAPTER 7

This time the trail was easier. It was better packed, and they were not carrying mail against time. The day's run was shorter, and likewise the hours on trail. On his mail run Daylight had played out three Indians; but his present partners knew that they must not be played out when they arrived at the Stewart bars, so they set the slower pace. And under this milder toil, where his companions nevertheless grew weary, Daylight recuperated and rested up. At Forty Mile they laid over two days for the sake of the dogs, and at Sixty Mile Daylight's team was left with the trader. Unlike Daylight, after the terrible run from Selkirk to Circle City, they had been unable to recuperate on the back trail. So the four men pulled on from Sixty Mile with a fresh team of dogs on Daylight's sled.

The following night they camped in the cluster of islands at the mouth of the Stewart. Daylight talked town sites, and, though the others laughed at him, he staked the whole maze of high, wooded islands.

"Just supposing the big strike does come on the Stewart," he argued. "Mebbe you-all'll be in on it, and then again mebbe you-all won't. But I sure will. You-all'd better reconsider and go in with me on it."

But they were stubborn.

"You're as bad as Harper and Joe Ladue," said Joe Hines. "They're always at that game. You know that big flat jest below the Klondike and under Moosehide Mountain? Well, the recorder at Forty Mile was tellin' me they staked that not a month ago--The Harper & Ladue Town Site. Ha! Ha! Ha!"

Elijah and Finn joined him in his laughter; but Daylight was gravely in earnest.

"There she is!" he cried. "The hunch is working! It's in the air, I tell you-all! What'd they-all stake the big flat for if they-all didn't get the hunch? Wish I'd staked it."

The regret in his voice was provocative of a second burst of laughter.

"Laugh, you-all, laugh! That's what's the trouble with you-all. You-all think gold-hunting is the only way to make a stake. But let me tell you-all that when the big strike sure does come, you-all'll do a little surface-scratchin' and muck-raking, but danged little you-all'll have to show for it. You-all laugh at quicksilver in the riffles and think flour gold was manufactured by God Almighty for the express purpose of fooling suckers and *chechaquos*. Nothing but coarse gold for you-all, that's your way, not getting half of it out of the ground and losing into the tailings half of what you-all do get.

"But the men that land big will be them that stake the town sites, organize the tradin' companies, start the banks--"

Here the explosion of mirth drowned him out. Banks in Alaska! The idea of it was excruciating.

"Yep, and start the stock exchanges--"

Again they were convulsed. Joe Hines rolled over on his sleeping-robe, holding his sides.

"And after them will come the big mining sharks that buy whole creeks where you-all have been scratching like a lot of picayune hens, and they-all will go to hydraulicking in summer and steam-thawing in winter--"

Steam-thawing! That was the limit. Daylight was certainly exceeding himself in his consummate fun-making. Steam-thawing--when even wood-burning was an untried experiment, a dream in the air!

"Laugh, dang you, laugh! Why your eyes ain't open yet. You-all are a bunch of little mewing kittens. I tell you-all if that strike comes on Klondike,

Harper and Ladue will be millionaires. And if it comes on Stewart, you-all watch the Elam Harnish town site boom. In them days, when you-all come around makin' poor mouths..." He heaved a sigh of resignation. "Well, I suppose I'll have to give you-all a grub-stake or soup, or something or other."

Daylight had vision. His scope had been rigidly limited, yet whatever he saw, he saw big. His mind was orderly, his imagination practical, and he never dreamed idly. When he superimposed a feverish metropolis on a waste of timbered, snow-covered flat, he predicated first the gold-strike that made the city possible, and next he had an eye for steamboat landings, sawmill and warehouse locations, and all the needs of a far-northern mining city. But this, in turn, was the mere setting for something bigger, namely, the play of temperament. Opportunities swarmed in the streets and buildings and human and economic relations of the city of his dream. It was a larger table for gambling. The limit was the sky, with the Southland on one side and the aurora borealis on the other. The play would be big, bigger than any Yukoner had ever imagined, and he, Burning Daylight, would see that he got in on that play.

In the meantime there was naught to show for it but the hunch. But it was coming. As he would stake his last ounce on a good poker hand, so he staked his life and effort on the hunch that the future held in store a big strike on the Upper River. So he and his three companions, with dogs, and sleds, and snowshoes, toiled up the frozen breast of the Stewart, toiled on and on through the white wilderness where the unending stillness was never broken by the voices of men, the stroke of an ax, or the distant crack of a rifle. They alone moved through the vast and frozen quiet, little mites of earth-men, crawling their score of miles a day, melting the ice that they might have water to drink, camping in the snow at night, their wolf-dogs curled in frost-rimed, hairy bunches, their eight snowshoes stuck on end in the snow beside the sleds.

No signs of other men did they see, though once they passed a rude poling-boat, cached on a platform by the river bank. Whoever had cached it had never come back for it; and they wondered and mushed on. Another time they chanced upon the site of an Indian village, but the Indians had disappeared; undoubtedly they were on the higher reaches of the Stewart in pursuit of the moose-herds. Two hundred miles up from the Yukon, they came upon what Elijah decided were the bars mentioned by Al Mayo. A permanent camp was made, their outfit of food cached on a high platform to keep it from the dogs, and they started work on the bars, cutting their way down to gravel through the rim of ice.

It was a hard and simple life. Breakfast over, and they were at work by the first gray light; and when night descended, they did their cooking and camp-chores, smoked and yarned for a while, then rolled up in their sleeping-robes, and slept while the aurora borealis flamed overhead and the stars leaped and danced in the great cold. Their fare was monotonous: sour-dough bread, bacon, beans, and an occasional dish of rice cooked along with a handful of prunes. Fresh meat they failed to obtain. There was an unwonted absence of animal life. At rare intervals they chanced upon the trail of a snowshoe rabbit or an ermine; but in the main it seemed that all life had fled the land. It was a condition not unknown to them, for in all their experience, at one time or another, they had travelled one year through a region teeming with game, where, a year or two or three years later, no game at all would be found.

Gold they found on the bars, but not in paying quantities. Elijah, while on a hunt for moose fifty miles away, had panned the surface gravel of a large creek and found good colors. They harnessed their dogs, and with light outfits sledded to the place. Here, and possibly for the first time in the history of the Yukon, wood-burning, in sinking a shaft, was tried. It was Daylight's initiative. After clearing away the moss and grass, a fire of dry spruce was built. Six hours of burning thawed eight inches of muck. Their picks drove full depth into it, and, when they had shoveled out, another fire was started. They worked early and late, excited over the success of the experiment. Six feet of frozen muck brought them to gravel, likewise frozen. Here progress was slower. But they learned to handle their fires better, and were soon able to thaw five and six inches at a burning. Flour gold was in this gravel, and after two feet it gave away again to muck. At seventeen feet they struck a thin streak of gravel, and in it coarse gold, testpans running as high as six and eight dollars. Unfortunately, this streak of gravel was not more than an inch thick. Beneath it was more muck, tangled with the trunks of ancient trees and containing fossil bones of forgotten monsters. But gold they had found--coarse gold; and what more likely than that the big deposit would be found on bed-rock? Down to bed-rock they would go, if it were forty feet away. They divided into two shifts, working day and night, on two shafts, and the smoke of their burning rose continually.

It was at this time that they ran short of beans and that Elijah was despatched to the main camp to bring up more grub. Elijah was one of the hard-bitten old-time travelers himself. The round trip was a hundred miles, but he promised to be back on the third day, one day going light, two days returning heavy. Instead, he arrived on the night of the second day. They had just gone to bed when they heard him coming.

"What in hell's the matter now?" Henry Finn demanded, as the empty sled came into the circle of firelight and as he noted that Elijah's long, serious face was longer and even more serious.

Joe Hines threw wood on the fire, and the three men, wrapped in their robes, huddled up close to the warmth. Elijah's whiskered face was matted with ice, as were his eyebrows, so that, what of his fur garb, he looked like a New England caricature of Father Christmas.

"You recollect that big spruce that held up the corner of the cache next to the river?" Elijah began.

The disaster was quickly told. The big tree, with all the seeming of hardihood, promising to stand for centuries to come, had suffered from a hidden decay. In some way its rooted grip on the earth had weakened. The added burden of the cache and the winter snow had been too much for it; the balance it had so long maintained with the forces of its environment had been overthrown; it had toppled and crashed to the ground, wrecking the cache and, in turn, overthrowing the balance with environment that the four men and eleven dogs had been maintaining. Their supply of grub was gone. The wolverines had got into the wrecked cache, and what they had not eaten they had destroyed.

"They plumb e't all the bacon and prunes and sugar and dog-food," Elijah reported, "and gosh darn my buttons, if they didn't gnaw open the sacks and scatter the flour and beans and rice from Dan to Beersheba. I found empty sacks where they'd dragged them a quarter of a mile away."

Nobody spoke for a long minute. It was nothing less than a catastrophe, in the dead of an Arctic winter and in a game-abandoned land, to lose their grub. They were not panic-stricken, but they were busy looking the situation squarely in the face and considering. Joe Hines was the first to speak.

"We can pan the snow for the beans and rice... though there wa'n't more'n eight or ten pounds of rice left."

"And somebody will have to take a team and pull for Sixty Mile," Daylight said next.

"I'll go," said Finn.

They considered a while longer.

"But how are we going to feed the other team and three men till he gets back?" Hines demanded.

"Only one thing to it," was Elijah's contribution. "You'll have to take the other team, Joe, and pull up the Stewart till you find them Indians. Then you come back with a load of meat. You'll get here long before Henry can make it from Sixty Mile, and while you're gone there'll only be Daylight and me to feed, and we'll feed good and small."

"And in the morning we-all'll pull for the cache and pan snow to find what grub we've got." Daylight lay back, as he spoke, and rolled in his robe to sleep, then added: "Better turn in for an early start. Two of you can take the dogs down. Elijah and me'll skin out on both sides and see if we-all can scare up a moose on the way down."

CHAPTER 8

No time was lost. Hines and Finn, with the dogs, already on short rations, were two days in pulling down. At noon of the third day Elijah arrived, reporting no moose sign. That night Daylight came in with a similar report. As fast as they arrived, the men had started careful panning of the snow all around the cache. It was a large task, for they found stray beans fully a hundred yards from the cache. One more day all the men toiled. The result was pitiful, and the four showed their caliber in the division of the few pounds of food that had been recovered.

Little as it was, the lion's share was left with Daylight and Elijah. The men who pulled on with the dogs, one up the Stewart and one down, would come more quickly to grub. The two who remained would have to last out till the others returned. Furthermore, while the dogs, on several ounces each of beans a day, would travel slowly, nevertheless, the men who travelled with them, on a pinch, would have the dogs themselves to eat. But the men who remained, when the pinch came, would have no dogs. It was for this reason that Daylight and Elijah took the more desperate chance. They could not do less, nor did they care to do less. The days passed, and the winter began merging imperceptibly into the Northland spring that comes like a thunderbolt of suddenness. It was the spring of 1896 that was preparing. Each day the sun rose farther east of south, remained longer in the sky, and set farther to the west. March ended and April began, and Daylight and Elijah, lean and hungry, wondered what had become of their two comrades. Granting every delay, and throwing in generous margins for good measure, the time was long since passed when they should have returned. Without doubt they had met with disaster. The party had considered the possibility of disaster for one man, and that had been the principal reason for despatching the two in different directions. But that disaster should have come to both of them was the final blow.

In the meantime, hoping against hope, Daylight and Elijah eked out a meagre existence. The thaw had not yet begun, so they were able to gather the snow about the ruined cache and melt it in pots and pails and gold pans. Allowed to stand for a while, when poured off, a thin deposit of slime was found on the bottoms of the vessels. This was the flour, the infinitesimal trace of it scattered through thousands of cubic yards of snow. Also, in this slime occurred at intervals a water-soaked tea-leaf or coffee-ground, and there were in it fragments of earth and litter. But the farther they worked away from the site of the cache, the thinner became the trace of flour, the smaller the deposit of slime.

Elijah was the older man, and he weakened first, so that he came to lie up most of the time in his furs. An occasional tree- squirrel kept them alive. The hunting fell upon Daylight, and it was hard work. With but thirty rounds of ammunition, he dared not risk a miss; and, since his rifle was a 45-90, he was compelled to shoot the small creatures through the head. There were very few of them, and days went by without seeing one. When he did see one, he took infinite precautions. He would stalk it for hours. A score of times, with arms that shook from weakness, he would draw a sight on the animal and refrain from pulling the trigger. His inhibition was a thing of iron. He was the master. Not til absolute certitude was his did he shoot. No matter how sharp the pangs of hunger and desire for that palpitating morsel of chattering life, he refused to take the slightest risk of a miss. He, born gambler, was gambling in the bigger way. His life was the stake, his cards were the cartridges, and he played as only a big gambler could play, with infinite precaution, with infinite consideration. Each shot meant a squirrel, and though days elapsed between shots, it never changed his method of play.

Of the squirrels, nothing was lost. Even the skins were boiled to make broth, the bones pounded into fragments that could be chewed and swallowed. Daylight prospected through the snow, and found occasional patches of mossberries. At the best, mossberries were composed practically of seeds and water, with a tough rind of skin about them; but the berries he found were of the preceding year, dry and shrivelled, and the nourishment they contained verged on the minus quality. Scarcely better was the bark of young saplings, stewed for an hour and swallowed after prodigious chewing.

April drew toward its close, and spring smote the land. The days stretched out their length. Under the heat of the sun, the snow began to melt, while from down under the snow arose the trickling of tiny streams. For twenty-four hours the Chinook wind blew, and in that twenty-four hours the snow was diminished fully a foot in depth. In the late afternoons the melting snow froze again, so that its surface became ice capable of supporting a man's weight. Tiny white snow-birds appeared from the south, lingered a day, and resumed their journey into the north. Once, high in the air, looking for open water and ahead of the season, a wedged squadron of wild geese honked northwards. And down by the river bank a clump of dwarf willows burst into bud. These young buds, stewed, seemed to posess an encouraging nutrition. Elijah took heart of hope, though he was cast down again when Daylight failed to find another clump of willows.

The sap was rising in the trees, and daily the trickle of unseen streamlets became louder as the frozen land came back to life. But the river held in its bonds of frost. Winter had been long months in riveting them, and not in a day were they to be broken, not even by the thunderbolt of spring. May came, and stray last-year's mosquitoes, full-grown but harmless, crawled out of rock crevices and rotten logs. Crickets began to chirp, and more geese and ducks flew overhead. And still the river held. By May tenth, the ice of the Stewart, with a great rending and snapping, tore loose from the banks and rose three feet. But it did not go down-stream. The lower Yukon, up to where the Stewart flowed into it, must first break and move on. Until then the ice of the Stewart could only rise higher and higher on the increasing flood beneath. When the Yukon would break was problematical. Two thousand miles away it flowed into Bering Sea, and it was the ice conditions of Bering Sea that would determine when the Yukon could rid itself of the millions of tons of ice that cluttered its breast.

On the twelfth of May, carrying their sleeping-robes, a pail, an ax, and the precious rifle, the two men started down the river on the ice. Their plan was to gain to the cached poling-boat they had seen, so that at the first open water they could launch it and drift with the stream to Sixty Mile. In their weak condition, without food, the going was slow and difficult. Elijah developed a habit of falling down and being unable to rise. Daylight gave of his own strength to lift him to his feet, whereupon the older man would stagger automatically on until he stumbled and fell again.

On the day they should have reached the boat, Elijah collapsed utterly. When Daylight raised him, he fell again. Daylight essayed to walk with him, supporting him, but such was Daylight's own weakness that they fell together. Dragging Elijah to the bank, a rude camp was made, and Daylight started out in search of squirrels. It was at this time that he likewise developed the falling habit. In the evening he found his first squirrel, but darkness came on without his getting a certain shot. With primitive patience he waited till next day, and then, within the hour, the squirrel was his.

The major portion he fed to Elijah, reserving for himself the tougher parts and the bones. But such is the chemistry of life, that this small creature, this trifle of meat that moved, by being eaten, transmuted to the meat of the men the same power to move. No longer did the squirrel run up spruce trees, leap from branch to branch, or cling chattering to giddy perches. Instead, the same energy that had done these things flowed into the wasted muscles and reeling wills of the men, making them move--nay, moving them--till they tottered the several intervening miles to the cached boat, underneath which they fell together and lay motionless a long time.

Light as the task would have been for a strong man to lower the small boat to the ground, it took Daylight hours. And many hours more, day by day, he dragged himself around it, lying on his side to calk the gaping seams with moss. Yet, when this was done, the river still held. Its ice had risen many feet, but would not start down-stream. And one more task waited, the launching of the boat when the river ran water to receive it. Vainly Daylight staggered and stumbled and fell and crept through the snow that was wet with thaw, or across it when the night's frost still crusted it beyond the weight of a man, searching for one more squirrel, striving to achieve one more transmutation of furry leap and scolding chatter into the lifts and tugs of a man's body that would hoist the boat over the rim of shore-ice and slide it down into the stream.

Not till the twentieth of May did the river break. The down-stream movement began at five in the morning, and already were the days so long that Daylight sat up and watched the ice-run. Elijah was too far gone to be interested in the spectacle. Though vaguely conscious, he lay without movement while the ice tore by, great cakes of it caroming against the bank, uprooting trees, and gouging out earth by hundreds of tons. All about them the land shook and reeled from the shock of these tremendous collisions. At the end of an hour the run stopped. Somewhere below it was blocked by a jam. Then the river began to rise, lifting the ice on its breast till it was higher than the bank. From behind ever more water bore down, and ever more millions of tons of ice added their weight to the congestion. The pressures and stresses became terrific. Huge cakes of ice were squeezed out till they popped into the air like melon seeds squeezed from between the thumb and forefinger of a child, while all along the banks a wall of ice was forced up. When the jam broke, the noise of grinding and smashing redoubled. For another hour the run continued. The river fell rapidly. But the wall of ice on top the bank, and extending down into the falling water, remained.

The tail of the ice-run passed, and for the first time in six months Daylight saw open water. He knew that the ice had not yet passed out from the upper reaches of the Stewart, that it lay in packs and jams in those upper reaches, and that it might break loose and come down in a second run any time; but the need was too desperate for him to linger. Elijah was so far gone that he might pass at any moment. As for himself, he was not sure that enough strength remained in his wasted muscles to launch the boat. It was all a gamble. If he waited for the second ice-run, Elijah would surely die, and most probably himself. If he succeeded in launching the boat, if he kept ahead of the second ice-run, if he did not get caught by some of the runs from the upper Yukon; if luck favored in all these essential particulars, as well as in a score of minor ones, they would reach Sixty Mile and be saved, if--and again the if--he had strength enough to land the boat at Sixty Mile and not go by.

44

He set to work. The wall of ice was five feet above the ground on which the boat rested. First prospecting for the best launching-place, he found where a huge cake of ice shelved upward from the river that ran fifteen feet below to the top of the wall. This was a score of feet away, and at the end of an hour he had managed to get the boat that far. He was sick with nausea from his exertions, and at times it seemed that blindness smote him, for he could not see, his eyes vexed with spots and points of light that were as excruciating as diamond-dust, his heart pounding up in his throat and suffocating him. Elijah betrayed no interest, did not move nor open his eyes; and Daylight fought out his battle alone. At last, falling on his knees from the shock of exertion, he got the boat poised on a secure balance on top the wall. Crawling on hands and knees, he placed in the boat his rabbit-skin robe, the rifle, and the pail. He did not bother with the ax. It meant an additional crawl of twenty feet and back, and if the need for it should arise he well knew he would be past all need.

Elijah proved a bigger task than he had anticipated. A few inches at a time, resting in between, he dragged him over the ground and up a broken rubble of ice to the side of the boat. But into the boat he could not get him. Elijah's limp body was far more difficult to lift and handle than an equal weight of like dimensions but rigid. Daylight failed to hoist him, for the body collapsed at the middle like a part-empty sack of corn. Getting into the boat, Daylight tried vainly to drag his comrade in after him. The best he could do was to get Elijah's head and shoulders on top the gunwale. When he released his hold, to heave from farther down the body, Elijah promptly gave at the middle and came down on the ice.

In despair, Daylight changed his tactics. He struck the other in the face. "God Almighty, ain't you-all a man?" he cried. "There! damn you-all! there! "

At each curse he struck him on the cheeks, the nose, the mouth, striving, by the shock of the hurt, to bring back the sinking soul and far-wandering will of the man. The eyes fluttered open.

"Now listen!" he shouted hoarsely. "When I get your head to the gunwale, hang on! Hear me? Hang on! Bite into it with your teeth, but HANG ON! "

The eyes fluttered down, but Daylight knew the message had been received. Again he got the helpless man's head and shoulders on the gunwale.

"Hang on, damn you! Bite in" he shouted, as he shifted his grip lower down.

One weak hand slipped off the gunwale, the fingers of the other hand relaxed, but Elijah obeyed, and his teeth held on. When the lift came, his face ground forward, and the splintery wood tore and crushed the skin from nose, lips, and chin; and, face downward, he slipped on and down to the bottom of the boat till his limp middle collapsed across the gunwale and his legs hung down outside. But they were only his legs, and Daylight shoved them in; after him. Breathing heavily, he turned Elijah over on his back, and covered him with his robes.

The final task remained--the launching of the boat. This, of necessity, was the severest of all, for he had been compelled to load his comrade in aft of the balance. It meant a supreme effort at lifting. Daylight steeled himself and began. Something must have snapped, for, though he was unaware of it, the next he knew he was lying doubled on his stomach across the sharp stern of the boat. Evidently, and for the first time in his life, he had fainted. Furthermore, it seemed to him that he was finished, that he had not one more movement left in him, and that, strangest of all, he did not care. Visions came to him, clear-cut and real, and concepts sharp as steel

45

cutting-edges. He, who all his days had looked on naked Life, had never seen so much of Life's nakedness before. For the first time he experienced a doubt of his own glorious personality. For the moment Life faltered and forgot to lie. After all, he was a little earth-maggot, just like all the other earth-maggots, like the squirrel he had eaten, like the other men he had seen fail and die, like Joe Hines and Henry Finn, who had already failed and were surely dead, like Elijah lying there uncaring, with his skinned face, in the bottom of the boat. Daylight's position was such that from where he lay he could look up river to the bend, around which, sooner or later, the next ice-run would come. And as he looked he seemed to see back through the past to a time when neither white man nor Indian was in the land, and ever he saw the same Stewart River, winter upon winter, breasted with ice, and spring upon spring bursting that ice asunder and running free. And he saw also into an illimitable future, when the last generations of men were gone from off the face of Alaska, when he, too, would be gone, and he saw, ever remaining, that river, freezing and fresheting, and running on and on.

Life was a liar and a cheat. It fooled all creatures. It had fooled him, Burning Daylight, one of its chiefest and most joyous exponents. He was nothing--a mere bunch of flesh and nerves and sensitiveness that crawled in the muck for gold, that dreamed and aspired and gambled, and that passed and was gone. Only the dead things remained, the things that were not flesh and nerves and sensitiveness, the sand and muck and gravel, the stretching flats, the mountains, the river itself, freezing and breaking, year by year, down all the years. When all was said and done, it was a scurvy game. The dice were loaded. Those that died did not win, and all died. Who won? Not even Life, the stool-pigeon, the arch-capper for the game--Life, the ever flourishing graveyard, the everlasting funeral procession.

He drifted back to the immediate present for a moment and noted that the river still ran wide open, and that a moose-bird, perched on the bow of the boat, was surveying him impudently. Then he drifted dreamily back to his meditations.

There was no escaping the end of the game. He was doomed surely to be out of it all. And what of it? He pondered that question again and again.

Conventional religion had passed Daylight by. He had lived a sort of religion in his square dealing and right playing with other men, and he had not indulged in vain metaphysics about future life. Death ended all. He had always believed that, and been unafraid. And at this moment, the boat fifteen feet above the water and immovable, himself fainting with weakness and without a particle of strength left in him, he still believed that death ended all, and he was still unafraid. His views were too simply and solidly based to be overthrown by the first squirm, or the last, of death-fearing life.

He had seen men and animals die, and into the field of his vision, by scores, came such deaths. He saw them over again, just as he had seen them at the time, and they did not shake him. What of it? They were dead, and dead long since. They weren't bothering about it. They weren't lying on their bellies across a boat and waiting to die. Death was easy--easier than he had ever imagined; and, now that it was near, the thought of it made him glad.

A new vision came to him. He saw the feverish city of his dream--the gold metropolis of the North, perched above the Yukon on a high earth-bank and far-spreading across the flat. He saw the river steamers tied to the bank and lined against it three deep; he saw the sawmills working and the long dog-teams, with double sleds behind, freighting supplies to the diggings. And he saw, further, the gambling-houses, banks, stock-exchanges, and all the gear and chips and markers, the chances and opportunities, of a vastly bigger gambling game than any he had ever seen. It was sure hell, he thought, with the hunch a-working and that big strike coming, to be out of it all. Life thrilled and stirred at the thought and once more began uttering his ancient lies.

Daylight rolled over and off the boat, leaning against it as he sat on the ice. He wanted to be in on that strike. And why shouldn't he? Somewhere in all those wasted muscles of his was enough strength, if he could gather it all at once, to up-end the boat and launch it. Quite irrelevantly the idea suggested itself of buying a share in the Klondike town site from Harper and Joe Ladue. They would surely sell a third interest cheap. Then, if the strike came on the Stewart, he would be well in on it with the Elam Harnish town site; if on the Klondike, he would not be quite out of it.

In the meantime, he would gather strength. He stretched out on the ice full length, face downward, and for half an hour he lay and rested. Then he arose, shook the flashing blindness from his eyes, and took hold of the boat. He knew his condition accurately. If the first effort failed, the following efforts were doomed to fail. He must pull all his rallied strength into the one effort, and so thoroughly must he put all of it in that there would be none left for other attempts.

He lifted, and he lifted with the soul of him as well as with the body, consuming himself, body and spirit, in the effort. The boat rose. He thought he was going to faint, but he continued to lift. He felt the boat give, as it started on its downward slide. With the last shred of his strength he precipitated himself into it, landing in a sick heap on Elijah's legs. He was beyond attempting to rise, and as he lay he heard and felt the boat take the water. By watching the tree-tops he knew it was whirling. A smashing shock and flying fragments of ice told him that it had struck the bank. A dozen times it whirled and struck, and then it floated easily and free.

Daylight came to, and decided he had been asleep. The sun denoted that several hours had passed. It was early afternoon. He dragged himself into the stern and sat up. The boat was in the middle of the stream. The wooded banks, with their base-lines of flashing ice, were slipping by. Near him floated a huge, uprooted pine. A freak of the current brought the boat against it. Crawling forward, he fastened the painter to a root. The tree, deeper in the water, was travelling faster, and the painter tautened as the boat took the tow. Then, with a last giddy look around, wherein he saw the banks tilting and swaying and the sun swinging in pendulum-sweep across the sky, Daylight wrapped himself in his rabbit-skin robe, lay down in the bottom, and fell asleep.

When he awoke, it was dark night. He was lying on his back, and he could see the stars shining. A subdued murmur of swollen waters could be heard. A sharp jerk informed him that the boat, swerving slack into the painter, had been straightened out by the swifter-moving pine tree. A piece of stray drift-ice thumped against the boat and grated along its side. Well, the following jam hadn't caught him yet, was his thought, as he closed his eyes and slept again.

It was bright day when next he opened his eyes. The sun showed it to be midday. A glance around at the far-away banks, and he knew that he was on the mighty Yukon. Sixty Mile could not be far away. He was abominably weak. His movements were slow, fumbling, and inaccurate, accompanied by panting and head-swimming, as he dragged himself into a sitting-up position in the stern, his rifle beside him. He looked a long time at Elijah, but could not see whether he breathed or not, and he was too immeasurably far away to make an investigation.

47

He fell to dreaming and meditating again, dreams and thoughts being often broken by sketches of blankness, wherein he neither slept, nor was unconscious, nor was aware of anything. It seemed to him more like cogs slipping in his brain. And in this intermittent way he reviewed the situation. He was still alive, and most likely would be saved, but how came it that he was not lying dead across the boat on top the ice-rim? Then he recollected the great final effort he had made. But why had he made it? he asked himself. It had not been fear of death. He had not been afraid, that was sure. Then he remembered the hunch and the big strike he believed was coming, and he knew that the spur had been his desire to sit in for a hand at that big game. And again why? What if he made his million? He would die, just the same as those that never won more than grub-stakes. Then again why? But the blank stretches in his thinking process began to come more frequently, and he surrendered to the delightful lassitude that was creeping over him.

He roused with a start. Something had whispered in him that he must awake. Abruptly he saw Sixty Mile, not a hundred feet away. The current had brought him to the very door. But the same current was now sweeping him past and on into the down-river wilderness. No one was in sight. The place might have been deserted, save for the smoke he saw rising from the kitchen chimney. He tried to call, but found he had no voice left. An unearthly guttural hiss alternately rattled and wheezed in his throat. He fumbled for the rifle, got it to his shoulder, and pulled the trigger. The recoil of the discharge tore through his frame, racking it with a thousand agonies. The rifle had fallen across his knees, and an attempt to lift it to his shoulder failed. He knew he must be quick, and felt that he was fainting, so he pulled the trigger of the gun where it lay. This time it kicked off and overboard. But just before darkness rushed over him, he saw the kitchen door open, and a woman look out of the big log house that was dancing a monstrous jig among the trees.

CHAPTER 9

Ten days later, Harper and Joe Ladue arrived at Sixty Mile, and Daylight, still a trifle weak, but strong enough to obey the hunch that had come to him, traded a third interest in his Stewart town site for a third interest in theirs on the Klondike. They had faith in the Upper Country, and Harper left down-stream, with a raft-load of supplies, to start a small post at the mouth of the Klondike.

"Why don't you tackle Indian River, Daylight?" Harper advised, at parting. "There's whole slathers of creeks and draws draining in up there, and somewhere gold just crying to be found. That's my hunch. There's a big strike coming, and Indian River ain't going to be a million miles away."

"And the place is swarming with moose," Joe Ladue added. "Bob Henderson's up there somewhere, been there three years now, swearing something big is going to happen, living off'n straight moose and prospecting around like a crazy man."

Daylight decided to go Indian River a flutter, as he expressed it; but Elijah could not be persuaded into accompanying him. Elijah's soul had been seared by famine, and he was obsessed by fear of repeating the experience.

"I jest can't bear to separate from grub," he explained. "I know it's downright foolishness, but I jest can't help it. It's all I can do to tear myself away from the table when I know I'm full to bustin' and ain't got storage for another bite. I'm going back to Circle to camp by a cache until I get cured."

Daylight lingered a few days longer, gathering strength and arranging his meagre outfit. He planned to go in light, carrying a pack of seventy-five pounds and making his five dogs pack as well, Indian fashion, loading them with thirty pounds each. Depending on the report of Ladue, he intended to follow Bob Henderson's example and live practically on straight meat. When Jack Kearns' scow, laden with the sawmill from Lake Linderman, tied up at Sixty Mile, Daylight bundled his outfit and dogs on board, turned his town-site application over to Elijah to be filed, and the same day was landed at the mouth of Indian River.

Forty miles up the river, at what had been described to him as Quartz Creek, he came upon signs of Bob Henderson's work, and also at Australia Creek, thirty miles farther on. The weeks came and went, but Daylight never encountered the other man. However, he found moose plentiful, and he and his dogs prospered on the meat diet. He found "pay" that was no more than "wages" on a dozen surface bars, and from the generous spread of flour gold in the muck and gravel of a score of creeks, he was more confident than ever that coarse gold in quantity was waiting to be unearthed. Often he turned his eyes to the northward ridge of hills, and pondered if the gold came from them. In the end, he ascended Dominion Creek to its head, crossed the divide, and came down on the tributary to the Klondike that was later to be called Hunker Creek. While on the divide, had he kept the big dome on his right, he would have come down on the Gold Bottom, so named by Bob Henderson, whom he would have found at work on it, taking out the first pay-gold ever panned on the Klondike. Instead, Daylight continued down Hunker to the Klondike, and on to the summer fishing camp of the Indians on the Yukon.

Here for a day he camped with Carmack, a squaw-man, and his Indian brother-in-law, Skookum Jim, bought a boat, and, with his dogs on board, drifted down the Yukon to Forty Mile. August was drawing to a close, the days were growing shorter, and winter was coming on. Still with unbounded faith in his hunch that a strike was coming in the Upper

Country, his plan was to get together a party of four or five, and, if that was impossible, at least a partner, and to pole back up the river before the freeze-up to do winter prospecting. But the men of Forty Mile were without faith. The diggings to the westward were good enough for them.

Then it was that Carmack, his brother-in-law, Skookum Jim, and Cultus Charlie, another Indian, arrived in a canoe at Forty Mile, went straight to the gold commissioner, and recorded three claims and a discovery claim on Bonanza Creek. After that, in the Sourdough Saloon, that night, they exhibited coarse gold to the sceptical crowd. Men grinned and shook their heads. They had seen the motions of a gold strike gone through before. This was too patently a scheme of Harper's and Joe Ladue's, trying to entice prospecting in the vicinity of their town site and trading post. And who was Carmack? A squaw-man. And who ever heard of a squaw-man striking anything? And what was Bonanza Creek? Merely a moose pasture, entering the Klondike just above its mouth, and known to old-timers as Rabbit Creek. Now if Daylight or Bob Henderson had recorded claims and shown coarse gold, they'd known there was something in it. But Carmack, the squaw-man! And Skookum Jim! And Cultus Charlie! No, no; that was asking too much.

Daylight, too, was sceptical, and this despite his faith in the Upper Country. Had he not, only a few days before, seen Carmack loafing with his Indians and with never a thought of prospecting? But at eleven that night, sitting on the edge of his bunk and unlacing his moccasins, a thought came to him. He put on his coat and hat and went back to the Sourdough. Carmack was still there, flashing his coarse gold in the eyes of an unbelieving generation. Daylight ranged alongside of him and emptied Carmack's sack into a blower. This he studied for a long time. Then, from his own sack, into another blower, he emptied several ounces of Circle City and Forty Mile gold. Again, for a long time, he studied and compared. Finally, he pocketed his own gold, returned Carmack's, and held up his hand for silence.

"Boys, I want to tell you-all something," he said. "She's sure come--the up-river strike. And I tell you-all, clear and forcible, this is it. There ain't never been gold like that in a blower in this country before. It's new gold. It's got more silver in it. You-all can see it by the color. Carmack's sure made a strike. Who-all's got faith to come along with me?"

There were no volunteers. Instead, laughter and jeers went up.

"Mebbe you got a town site up there," some one suggested.

"I sure have," was the retort, "and a third interest in Harper and Ladue's. And I can see my corner lots selling out for more than your hen-scratching ever turned up on Birch Creek."

"That's all right, Daylight," one Curly Parson interposed soothingly. "You've got a reputation, and we know you're dead sure on the square. But you're as likely as any to be mistook on a flimflam game, such as these loafers is putting up. I ask you straight: When did Carmack do this here prospecting? You said yourself he was lying in camp, fishing salmon along with his Siwash relations, and that was only the other day."

"And Daylight told the truth," Carmack interrupted excitedly. "And I'm telling the truth, the gospel truth. I wasn't prospecting. Hadn't no idea of it. But when Daylight pulls out, the very same day, who drifts in, down river, on a raft-load of supplies, but Bob Henderson. He'd come out to Sixty Mile, planning to go back up Indian River and portage the grub across the divide between Quartz Creek and Gold Bottom--"

"Where in hell's Gold Bottom?" Curly Parsons demanded.

50

"Over beyond Bonanza that was Rabbit Creek," the squaw-man went on. "It's a draw of a big creek that runs into the Klondike. That's the way I went up, but I come back by crossing the divide, keeping along the crest several miles, and dropping down into Bonanza. 'Come along with me, Carmack, and get staked,' says Bob Henderson to me. 'I've hit it this time, on Gold Bottom. I've took out forty-five ounces already.' And I went along, Skookum Jim and Cultus Charlie, too. And we all staked on Gold Bottom. I come back by Bonanza on the chance of finding a moose. Along down Bonanza we stopped and cooked grub. I went to sleep, and what does Skookum Jim do but try his hand at prospecting. He'd been watching Henderson, you see. He goes right slap up to the foot of a birch tree, first pan, fills it with dirt, and washes out more'n a dollar coarse gold. Then he wakes me up, and I goes at it. I got two and a half the first lick. Then I named the creek 'Bonanza,' staked Discovery, and we come here and recorded."

He looked about him anxiously for signs of belief, but found himself in a circle of incredulous faces--all save Daylight, who had studied his countenance while he told his story.

"How much is Harper and Ladue givin' you for manufacturing a stampede?" some one asked.

"They don't know nothing about it," Carmack answered. "I tell you it's the God Almighty's truth. I washed out three ounces in an hour."

"And there's the gold," Daylight said. "I tell you-all boys they ain't never been gold like that in the blower before. Look at the color of it."

"A trifle darker," Curly Parson said. "Most likely Carmack's been carrying a couple of silver dollars along in the same sack. And what's more, if there's anything in it, why ain't Bob Henderson smoking along to record?"

"He's up on Gold Bottom," Carmack explained. "We made the strike coming back."

A burst of laughter was his reward.

"Who-all'll go pardners with me and pull out in a poling-boat to-morrow for this here Bonanza?" Daylight asked.

No one volunteered.

"Then who-all'll take a job from me, cash wages in advance, to pole up a thousand pounds of grub?"

Curly Parsons and another, Pat Monahan, accepted, and, with his customary speed, Daylight paid them their wages in advance and arranged the purchase of the supplies, though he emptied his sack in doing so. He was leaving the Sourdough, when he suddenly turned back to the bar from the door.

"Got another hunch?" was the query.

"I sure have," he answered. "Flour's sure going to be worth what a man will pay for it this winter up on the Klondike. Who'll lend me some money?"

On the instant a score of the men who had declined to accompany him on the wild-goose chase were crowding about him with proffered gold-sacks.

"How much flour do you want?" asked the Alaska Commercial Company's storekeeper.

"About two ton."

The proffered gold-sacks were not withdrawn, though their owners were guilty of an outrageous burst of merriment.

"What are you going to do with two tons?" the store-keeper demanded.

"Son," Daylight made reply, "you-all ain't been in this country long enough to know all its curves. I'm going to start a sauerkraut factory and combined dandruff remedy."

He borrowed money right and left, engaging and paying six other men to bring up the flour in half as many more poling-boats. Again his sack was empty, and he was heavily in debt.

Curly Parsons bowed his head on the bar with a gesture of despair.

"What gets me," he moaned, "is what you're going to do with it all."

"I'll tell you-all in simple A, B, C and one, two, three." Daylight held up one finger and began checking off. "Hunch number one: a big strike coming in Upper Country. Hunch number two: Carmack's made it. Hunch number three: ain't no hunch at all. It's a cinch. If one and two is right, then flour just has to go sky-high. If I'm riding hunches one and two, I just got to ride this cinch, which is number three. If I'm right, flour'll balance gold on the scales this winter. I tell you-all boys, when you-all got a hunch, play it for all it's worth. What's luck good for, if you-all ain't to ride it? And when you-all ride it, ride like hell. I've been years in this country, just waiting for the right hunch to come along. And here she is. Well, I'm going to play her, that's all. Good night, you-all; good night."

CHAPTER 10

Still men were without faith in the strike. When Daylight, with his heavy outfit of flour, arrived at the mouth of the Klondike, he found the big flat as desolate and tenantless as ever. Down close by the river, Chief Isaac and his Indians were camped beside the frames on which they were drying salmon. Several old-timers were also in camp there. Having finished their summer work on Ten Mile Creek, they had come down the Yukon, bound for Circle City. But at Sixty Mile they had learned of the strike, and stopped off to look over the ground. They had just returned to their boat when Daylight landed his flour, and their report was pessimistic.

"Damned moose-pasture," quoth one, Long Jim Harney, pausing to blow into his tin mug of tea. "Don't you have nothin' to do with it, Daylight. It's a blamed rotten sell. They're just going through the motions of a strike. Harper and Ladue's behind it, and Carmack's the stool-pigeon. Whoever heard of mining a moose-pasture half a mile between rim-rock and God alone knows how far to bed-rock!"

Daylight nodded sympathetically, and considered for a space.

"Did you-all pan any?" he asked finally.

"Pan hell!" was the indignant answer. "Think I was born yesterday! Only a chechaquo'd fool around that pasture long enough to fill a pan of dirt. You don't catch me at any such foolishness. One look was enough for me. We're pulling on in the morning for Circle City. I ain't never had faith in this Upper Country. Head-reaches of the Tanana is good enough for me from now on, and mark my words, when the big strike comes, she'll come down river. Johnny, here, staked a couple of miles below Discovery, but he don't know no better."

Johnny looked shamefaced.

"I just did it for fun," he explained. "I'd give my chance in the creek for a pound of Star plug."

"I'll go you," Daylight said promptly. "But don't you-all come squealing if I take twenty or thirty thousand out of it."

Johnny grinned cheerfully.

"Gimme the tobacco," he said.

"Wish I'd staked alongside," Long Jim murmured plaintively.

"It ain't too late," Daylight replied.

"But it's a twenty-mile walk there and back."

"I'll stake it for you to-morrow when I go up," Daylight offered. "Then you do the same as Johnny. Get the fees from Tim Logan. He's tending bar in the Sourdough, and he'll lend it to me. Then fill in your own name, transfer to me, and turn the papers over to Tim."

"Me, too," chimed in the third old-timer.

And for three pounds of Star plug chewing tobacco, Daylight bought outright three five-hundred-foot claims on Bonanza. He could still stake another claim in his own name, the others being merely transfers.

"Must say you're almighty brash with your chewin' tobacco," Long Jim grinned. "Got a factory somewheres?"

"Nope, but I got a hunch," was the retort, "and I tell you-all it's cheaper than dirt to ride her at the rate of three plugs for three claims."

But an hour later, at his own camp, Joe Ladue strode in, fresh from Bonanza Creek. At first, non-committal over Carmack's strike, then, later, dubious, he finally offered Daylight a hundred dollars for his share in the town site.

"Cash?" Daylight queried.

"Sure. There she is."

So saying, Ladue pulled out his gold-sack. Daylight hefted it absent-mindedly, and, still absent-mindedly, untied the strings and ran some of the gold-dust out on his palm. It showed darker than any dust he had ever seen, with the exception of Carmack's. He ran the gold back tied the mouth of the sack, and returned it to Ladue.

"I guess you-all need it more'n I do," was Daylight's comment.

"Nope; got plenty more," the other assured him.

"Where that come from?"

Daylight was all innocence as he asked the question, and Ladue received the question as stolidly as an Indian. Yet for a swift instant they looked into each other's eyes, and in that instant an intangible something seemed to flash out from all the body and spirit of Joe Ladue. And it seemed to Daylight that he had caught this flash, sensed a secret something in the knowledge and plans behind the other's eyes.

"You-all know the creek better'n me," Daylight went on. "And if my share in the town site's worth a hundred to you-all with what you-all know, it's worth a hundred to me whether I know it or not."

"I'll give you three hundred," Ladue offered desperately.

"Still the same reasoning. No matter what I don't know, it's worth to me whatever you-all are willing to pay for it."

Then it was that Joe Ladue shamelessly gave over. He led Daylight away from the camp and men and told him things in confidence.

"She's sure there," he said in conclusion. "I didn't sluice it, or cradle it. I panned it, all in that sack, yesterday, on the rim-rock. I tell you, you can shake it out of the grassroots. And what's on bed-rock down in the bottom of the creek they ain't no way of tellin'. But she's big, I tell you, big. Keep it quiet, and locate all you can. It's in spots, but I wouldn't be none surprised if some of them claims yielded as high as fifty thousand. The only trouble is that it's spotted."

* *

A month passed by, and Bonanza Creek remained quiet. A sprinkling of men had staked; but most of them, after staking, had gone on down to Forty Mile and Circle City. The few that possessed sufficient faith to remain were busy building log cabins against the coming of winter. Carmack and his Indian relatives were occupied in building a sluice box and getting a head of water. The work was slow, for they had to saw their lumber by hand from the standing forest. But farther down Bonanza were four men who had drifted in from up river, Dan McGilvary, Dave McKay, Dave Edwards, and Harry Waugh. They were a quiet party, neither asking nor giving confidences, and they herded by themselves. But Daylight, who had panned the spotted rim of Carmack's claim and shaken coarse gold from the grass-roots, and who had panned the rim at a hundred other places up and down the length of the creek and found nothing, was curious to know what lay on bed-rock. He had noted the four quiet men sinking a shaft close by the stream, and he had heard their whip-saw going as they made lumber for the sluice boxes. He did not wait for an invitation, but he was present the first day they sluiced. And at the end of five hours' shovelling for one man, he saw them take out thirteen ounces and a half of gold. It was coarse gold, running from pinheads to a twelve-dollar nugget, and it had come from off bed-rock. The first fall snow was flying that day, and the Arctic winter was closing down; but Daylight had no eyes for the bleak-gray sadness of the dying, short-lived summer. He saw his vision coming true, and on the big flat was upreared anew his golden city of the snows. Gold had been found on bed-rock. That was the big thing. Carmack's strike was assured. Daylight staked a claim in his own name adjoining the three he

54

had purchased with his plug tobacco. This gave him a block of property two thousand feet long and extending in width from rim-rock to rim-rock.

Returning that night to his camp at the mouth of Klondike, he found in it Kama, the Indian he had left at Dyea. Kama was travelling by canoe, bringing in the last mail of the year. In his possession was some two hundred dollars in gold-dust, which Daylight immediately borrowed. In return, he arranged to stake a claim for him, which he was to record when he passed through Forty Mile. When Kama departed next morning, he carried a number of letters for Daylight, addressed to all the old-timers down river, in which they were urged to come up immediately and stake. Also Kama carried letters of similar import, given him by the other men on Bonanza.

"It will sure be the gosh-dangdest stampede that ever was," Daylight chuckled, as he tried to vision the excited populations of Forty Mile and Circle City tumbling into poling-boats and racing the hundreds of miles up the Yukon; for he knew that his word would be unquestioningly accepted.

With the arrival of the first stampeders, Bonanza Creek woke up, and thereupon began a long-distance race between unveracity and truth, wherein, lie no matter how fast, men were continually overtaken and passed by truth. When men who doubted Carmack's report of two and a half to the pan, themselves panned two and a half, they lied and said that they were getting an ounce. And long ere the lie was fairly on its way, they were getting not one ounce but five ounces. This they claimed was ten ounces; but when they filled a pan of dirt to prove the lie, they washed out twelve ounces. And so it went. They continued valiantly to lie, but the truth continued to outrun them.

One day in December Daylight filled a pan from bed rock on his own claim and carried it into his cabin. Here a fire burned and enabled him to keep water unfrozen in a canvas tank. He squatted over the tank and began to wash. Earth and gravel seemed to fill the pan. As he imparted to it a circular movement, the lighter, coarser particles washed out over the edge. At times he combed the surface with his fingers, raking out handfuls of gravel. The contents of the pan diminished. As it drew near to the bottom, for the purpose of fleeting and tentative examination, he gave the pan a sudden sloshing movement, emptying it of water. And the whole bottom showed as if covered with butter. Thus the yellow gold flashed up as the muddy water was flirted away. It was gold--gold-dust, coarse gold, nuggets, large nuggets. He was all alone. He set the pan down for a moment and thought long thoughts. Then he finished the washing, and weighed the result in his scales. At the rate of sixteen dollars to the ounce, the pan had contained seven hundred and odd dollars. It was beyond anything that even he had dreamed. His fondest anticipation's had gone no farther than twenty or thirty thousand dollars to a claim; but here were claims worth half a million each at the least, even if they were spotted.

He did not go back to work in the shaft that day, nor the next, nor the next. Instead, capped and mittened, a light stampeding outfit, including his rabbit skin robe, strapped on his back, he was out and away on a many-days' tramp over creeks and divides, inspecting the whole neighboring territory. On each creek he was entitled to locate one claim, but he was chary in thus surrendering up his chances. On Hunker Creek only did he stake a claim. Bonanza Creek he found staked from mouth to source, while every little draw and pup and gulch that drained into it was like-wise staked. Little faith was had in these side-streams. They had been staked by the hundreds of men who had failed to get in on Bonanza. The most popular of these creeks was Adams. The one least fancied was

Eldorado, which flowed into Bonanza, just above Karmack's Discovery claim. Even Daylight disliked the looks of Eldorado; but, still riding his hunch, he bought a half share in one claim on it for half a sack of flour. A month later he paid eight hundred dollars for the adjoining claim. Three months later, enlarging this block of property, he paid forty thousand for a third claim; and, though it was concealed in the future, he was destined, not long after, to pay one hundred and fifty thousand for a fourth claim on the creek that had been the least liked of all the creeks.

In the meantime, and from the day he washed seven hundred dollars from a single pan and squatted over it and thought a long thought, he never again touched hand to pick and shovel. As he said to Joe Ladue the night of that wonderful washing: --

"Joe, I ain't never going to work hard again. Here's where I begin to use my brains. I'm going to farm gold. Gold will grow gold if you-all have the savvee and can get hold of some for seed. When I seen them seven hundred dollars in the bottom of the pan, I knew I had the seed at last."

"Where are you going to plant it?" Joe Ladue had asked.

And Daylight, with a wave of his hand, definitely indicated the whole landscape and the creeks that lay beyond the divides.

"There she is," he said, "and you-all just watch my smoke. There's millions here for the man who can see them. And I seen all them millions this afternoon when them seven hundred dollars peeped up at me from the bottom of the pan and chirruped, 'Well, if here ain't Burning Daylight come at last.'"

CHAPTER 11

The hero of the Yukon in the younger days before the Carmack strike, Burning Daylight now became the hero of the strike. The story of his hunch and how he rode it was told up and down the land. Certainly he had ridden it far and away beyond the boldest, for no five of the luckiest held the value in claims that he held. And, furthermore, he was still riding the hunch, and with no diminution of daring. The wise ones shook their heads and prophesied that he would lose every ounce he had won. He was speculating, they contended, as if the whole country was made of gold, and no man could win who played a placer strike in that fashion.

On the other hand, his holdings were reckoned as worth millions, and there were men so sanguine that they held the man a fool who coppered[1] any bet Daylight laid. Behind his magnificent free-handedness and careless disregard for money were hard, practical judgment, imagination and vision, and the daring of the big gambler. He foresaw what with his own eyes he had never seen, and he played to win much or lose all.

"There's too much gold here in Bonanza to be just a pocket," he argued. "It's sure come from a mother-lode somewhere, and other creeks will show up. You-all keep your eyes on Indian River. The creeks that drain that side the Klondike watershed are just as likely to have gold as the creeks that drain this side."

And he backed this opinion to the extent of grub-staking half a dozen parties of prospectors across the big divide into the Indian River region. Other men, themselves failing to stake on lucky creeks, he put to work on his Bonanza claims. And he paid them well--sixteen dollars a day for an eight-hour shift, and he ran three shifts. He had grub to start them on, and when, on the last water, the Bella arrived loaded with provisions, he traded a warehouse site to Jack Kearns for a supply of grub that lasted all his men through the winter of 1896. And that winter, when famine pinched, and flour sold for two dollars a pound, he kept three shifts of men at work on all four of the Bonanza claims. Other mine-owners paid fifteen dollars a day to their men; but he had been the first to put men to work, and from the first he paid them a full ounce a day. One result was that his were picked men, and they more than earned their higher pay.

One of his wildest plays took place in the early winter after the freeze-up. Hundreds of stampeders, after staking on other creeks than Bonanza, had gone on disgruntled down river to Forty Mile and Circle City. Daylight mortgaged one of his Bonanza dumps with the Alaska Commercial Company, and tucked a letter of credit into his pouch. Then he harnessed his dogs and went down on the ice at a pace that only he could travel. One Indian down, another Indian back, and four teams of dogs was his record. And at Forty Mile and Circle City he bought claims by the score. Many of these were to prove utterly worthless, but some few of them were to show up more astoundingly than any on Bonanza. He bought right and left, paying as low as fifty dollars and as high as five thousand. This highest one he bought in the Tivoli Saloon. It was an upper claim on Eldorado, and when he agreed to the price, Jacob Wilkins, an old-timer just returned from a look at the moose-pasture, got up and left the room, saying: --

"Daylight, I've known you seven year, and you've always seemed sensible till now. And now you're just letting them rob you right and left. That's what it is--robbery. Five thousand for a claim on that damned

---

[1] *To copper:* a term in faro, meaning to play a card to lose.

moose-pasture is bunco. I just can't stay in the room and see you buncoed that way."

"I tell you-all," Daylight answered, "Wilkins, Carmack's strike's so big that we-all can't see it all. It's a lottery. Every claim I buy is a ticket. And there's sure going to be some capital prizes."

Jacob Wilkins, standing in the open door, sniffed incredulously.

"Now supposing, Wilkins," Daylight went on, "supposing you-all knew it was going to rain soup. What'd you-all do? Buy spoons, of course. Well, I'm sure buying spoons. She's going to rain soup up there on the Klondike, and them that has forks won't be catching none of it."

But Wilkins here slammed the door behind him, and Daylight broke off to finish the purchase of the claim.

Back in Dawson, though he remained true to his word and never touched hand to pick and shovel, he worked as hard as ever in his life. He had a thousand irons in the fire, and they kept him busy. Representation work was expensive, and he was compelled to travel often over the various creeks in order to decide which claims should lapse and which should be retained. A quartz miner himself in his early youth, before coming to Alaska, he dreamed of finding the mother-lode. A placer camp he knew was ephemeral, while a quartz camp abided, and he kept a score of men in the quest for months. The mother-lode was never found, and, years afterward, he estimated that the search for it had cost him fifty thousand dollars.

But he was playing big. Heavy as were his expenses, he won more heavily. He took lays, bought half shares, shared with the men he grub-staked, and made personal locations. Day and night his dogs were ready, and he owned the fastest teams; so that when a stampede to a new discovery was on, it was Burning Daylight to the fore through the longest, coldest nights till he blazed his stakes next to Discovery. In one way or another (to say nothing of the many worthless creeks) he came into possession of properties on the good creeks, such as Sulphur, Dominion, Excelsis, Siwash, Cristo, Alhambra, and Doolittle. The thousands he poured out flowed back in tens of thousands. Forty Mile men told the story of his two tons of flour, and made calculations of what it had returned him that ranged from half a million to a million. One thing was known beyond all doubt, namely, that the half share in the first Eldorado claim, bought by him for a half sack of flour, was worth five hundred thousand. On the other hand, it was told that when Freda, the dancer, arrived from over the passes in a Peterborough canoe in the midst of a drive of mush-ice on the Yukon, and when she offered a thousand dollars for ten sacks and could find no sellers, he sent the flour to her as a present without ever seeing her. In the same way ten sacks were sent to the lone Catholic priest who was starting the first hospital.

His generosity was lavish. Others called it insane. At a time when, riding his hunch, he was getting half a million for half a sack of flour, it was nothing less than insanity to give twenty whole sacks to a dancing-girl and a priest. But it was his way. Money was only a marker. It was the game that counted with him. The possession of millions made little change in him, except that he played the game more passionately. Temperate as he had always been, save on rare occasions, now that he had the wherewithal for unlimited drinks and had daily access to them, he drank even less. The most radical change lay in that, except when on trail, he no longer did his own cooking. A broken-down miner lived in his log cabin with him and now cooked for him. But it was the same food: bacon, beans, flour, prunes, dried fruits, and rice. He still dressed as formerly: overalls, German socks, moccasins, flannel shirt, fur cap, and blanket coat. He did not take up with cigars, which cost, the cheapest, from half a dollar to a dollar each. The same Bull Durham and brown-paper cigarette, hand-rolled, contented him. It was true that he kept more dogs, and paid enormous prices for them. They were not a luxury, but a matter of business. He needed speed in his travelling and stampeding. And by the same token, he hired a cook. He was too busy to cook for himself, that was all. It was poor business, playing for millions, to spend time building fires and boiling water.

Dawson grew rapidly that winter of 1896. Money poured in on Daylight from the sale of town lots. He promptly invested it where it would gather more. In fact, he played the dangerous game of pyramiding, and no more perilous pyramiding than in a placer camp could be imagined. But he played with his eyes wide open.

"You-all just wait till the news of this strike reaches the Outside," he told his old-timer cronies in the Moosehorn Saloon. "The news won't get out till next spring. Then there's going to be three rushes. A summer rush of men coming in light; a fall rush of men with outfits; and a spring rush, the next year after that, of fifty thousand. You-all won't be able to see the landscape for *chechaquos*. Well, there's the summer and fall rush of 1897 to commence with. What are you-all going to do about it?"

"What are you going to do about it?" a friend demanded.

"Nothing," he answered. "I've sure already done it. I've got a dozen gangs strung out up the Yukon getting out logs. You-all'll see their rafts coming down after the river breaks. Cabins! They sure will be worth what a man can pay for them next fall. Lumber! It will sure go to top- notch. I've got two sawmills freighting in over the passes. They'll come down as soon as the lakes open up. And if you-all are thinking of needing lumber, I'll make you-all contracts right now -- three hundred dollars a thousand, undressed."

Corner lots in desirable locations sold that winter for from ten to thirty thousand dollars. Daylight sent word out over the trails and passes for the newcomers to bring down log-rafts, and, as a result, the summer of 1897 saw his sawmills working day and night, on three shifts, and still he had logs left over with which to build cabins. These cabins, land included, sold at from one to several thousand dollars. Two-story log buildings, in the business part of town, brought him from forty to fifty thousand dollars apiece. These fresh accretions of capital were immediately invested in other ventures. He turned gold over and over, until everything that he touched seemed to turn to gold.

But that first wild winter of Carmack's strike taught Daylight many things. Despite the prodigality of his nature, he had poise. He watched the lavish waste of the mushroom millionaires, and failed quite to understand it. According to his nature and outlook, it was all very well to toss an ante away in a night's frolic. That was what he had done the night of the poker-game in Circle City when he lost fifty thousand--all that he possessed. But he had looked on that fifty thousand as a mere ante. When it came to millions, it was different. Such a fortune was a stake, and was not to be sown on bar-room floors, literally sown, flung broadcast out of the moosehide sacks by drunken millionaires who had lost all sense of proportion. There was McMann, who ran up a single bar-room bill of thirty-eight thousand dollars; and Jimmie the Rough, who spent one hundred thousand a month for four months in riotous living, and then fell down drunk in the snow one March night and was frozen to death; and Swiftwater Bill, who, after spending three valuable claims in an extravagance of debauchery, borrowed three thousand dollars with which to leave the country, and who, out of this sum, because the lady-love that had jilted him liked eggs, cornered the one hundred and ten dozen eggs on the Dawson market, paying twenty-four dollars a dozen for them and promptly feeding them to the wolf-dogs.

Champagne sold at from forty to fifty dollars a quart, and canned oyster stew at fifteen dollars. Daylight indulged in no such luxuries. He did not mind treating a bar-room of men to whiskey at fifty cents a drink, but there was somewhere in his own extravagant nature a sense of fitness and arithmetic that revolted against paying fifteen dollars for the contents of an oyster can. On the other hand, he possibly spent more money in relieving hard-luck cases than did the wildest of the new millionaires on insane debauchery. Father Judge, of the hospital, could have told of far more important donations than that first ten sacks of flour. And old-timers who came to Daylight invariably went away relieved according to their need. But fifty dollars for a quart of fizzy champagne! That was appalling.

And yet he still, on occasion, made one of his old-time hell-roaring nights. But he did so for different reasons. First, it was expected of him because it had been his way in the old days. And second, he could afford it. But he no longer cared quite so much for that form of diversion. He had developed, in a new way, the taste for power. It had become a lust with him. By far the wealthiest miner in Alaska, he wanted to be still wealthier. It was a big game he was playing in, and he liked it better than any other game. In a way, the part he played was creative. He was doing something. And at no time, striking another chord of his nature, could he take the joy in a million-dollar Eldorado dump that was at all equivalent to the joy he took in watching his two sawmills working and the big down river log-rafts swinging into the bank in the big eddy just above Moosehide Mountain. Gold, even on the scales, was, after all, an abstraction. It represented things and the power to do. But the sawmills were the things themselves, concrete and tangible, and they were things that were a means to the doing of more things. They were dreams come true, hard and indubitable realizations of fairy gossamers.

With the summer rush from the Outside came special correspondents for the big newspapers and magazines, and one and all, using unlimited space, they wrote Daylight up; so that, so far as the world was concerned, Daylight loomed the largest figure in Alaska. Of course, after several months, the world became interested in the Spanish War, and forgot all about him; but in the Klondike itself Daylight still remained the most prominent figure. Passing along the streets of Dawson, all heads turned to follow him, and in the saloons *chechaquos* watched him awesomely, scarcely taking their eyes from him as long as he remained in their range of vision. Not alone was he the richest man in the country, but he was Burning Daylight, the pioneer, the man who, almost in the midst of antiquity of that young land, had crossed the Chilcoot and drifted down the Yukon to meet those elder giants, Al Mayo and Jack McQuestion. He was the Burning Daylight of scores of wild adventures, the man who carried word to the ice-bound whaling fleet across the tundra wilderness to the Arctic Sea, who raced the mail from Circle to Salt Water and back again in sixty days, who saved the whole Tanana tribe from perishing in the winter of '91--in short, the man who smote the chechaquos' imaginations more violently than any other dozen men rolled into one.

He had the fatal facility for self-advertisement. Things he did, no matter how adventitious or spontaneous, struck the popular imagination as remarkable. And the latest thing he had done was always on men's lips, whether it was being first in the heartbreaking stampede to Danish Creek, in killing the record baldface grizzly over on Sulphur Creek, or in winning the single-paddle canoe race on the Queen's Birthday, after being forced to participate at the last moment by the failure of the sourdough representative to appear. Thus, one night in the Moosehorn, he locked horns with Jack Kearns in the long-promised return game of poker. The sky and eight o'clock in the morning were made the limits, and at the close of the game Daylight's winnings were two hundred and thirty thousand dollars. To Jack Kearns, already a several-times millionaire, this loss was not vital. But the whole community was thrilled by the size of the stakes, and each one of the dozen correspondents in the field sent out a sensational article.

CHAPTER 12

Despite his many sources of revenue, Daylight's pyramiding kept him pinched for cash throughout the first winter. The pay-gravel, thawed on bed-rock and hoisted to the surface, immediately froze again. Thus his dumps, containing several millions of gold, were inaccessible. Not until the returning sun thawed the dumps and melted the water to wash them was he able to handle the gold they contained. And then he found himself with a surplus of gold, deposited in the two newly organized banks; and he was promptly besieged by men and groups of men to enlist his capital in their enterprises.

But he elected to play his own game, and he entered combinations only when they were generally defensive or offensive. Thus, though he had paid the highest wages, he joined the Mine-owners' Association, engineered the fight, and effectually curbed the growing insubordination of the wage-earners. Times had changed. The old days were gone forever. This was a new era, and Daylight, the wealthy mine-owner, was loyal to his class affiliations. It was true, the old-timers who worked for him, in order to be saved from the club of the organized owners, were made foremen over the gang of *chechaquos*; but this, with Daylight, was a matter of heart, not head. In his heart he could not forget the old days, while with his head he played the economic game according to the latest and most practical methods.

But outside of such group-combinations of exploiters, he refused to bind himself to any man's game. He was playing a great lone hand, and he needed all his money for his own backing. The newly founded stock-exchange interested him keenly. He had never before seen such an institution, but he was quick to see its virtues and to utilize it. Most of all, it was gambling, and on many an occasion not necessary for the advancement of his own schemes, he, as he called it, went the stock-exchange a flutter, out of sheer wantonness and fun.

"It sure beats faro," was his comment one day, when, after keeping the Dawson speculators in a fever for a week by alternate bulling and bearing, he showed his hand and cleaned up what would have been a fortune to any other man.

Other men, having made their strike, had headed south for the States, taking a furlough from the grim Arctic battle. But, asked when he was going Outside, Daylight always laughed and said when he had finished playing his hand. He also added that a man was a fool to quit a game just when a winning hand had been dealt him.

It was held by the thousands of hero-worshipping *chechaquos* that Daylight was a man absolutely without fear. But Bettles and Dan MacDonald and other sourdoughs shook their heads and laughed as they mentioned *women*. And they were right. He had always been afraid of them from the time, himself a lad of seventeen, when Queen Anne, of Juneau, made open and ridiculous love to him. For that matter, he never had known women. Born in a mining-camp where they were rare and mysterious, having no sisters, his mother dying while he was an infant, he had never been in contact with them. True, running away from Queen Anne, he had later encountered them on the Yukon and cultivated an acquaintance with them--the pioneer ones who crossed the passes on the trail of the men who had opened up the first diggings. But no lamb had ever walked with a wolf in greater fear and trembling than had he walked with them. It was a matter of masculine pride that he should walk with them, and he had done so in fair seeming; but women had remained to him a closed book, and he preferred a game of solo or seven-up any time.

And now, known as the King of the Klondike, carrying several other royal titles, such as Eldorado King, Bonanza King, the Lumber Baron, and the Prince of the Stampeders, not to omit the proudest appellation of all, namely, the Father of the Sourdoughs, he was more afraid of women than ever. As never before they held out their arms to him, and more women were flocking into the country day by day. It mattered not whether he sat at dinner in the gold commissioner's house, called for the drinks in a dancehall, or submitted to an interview from the woman representative of the New York *Sun*, one and all of them held out their arms.

There was one exception, and that was Freda, the girl that danced, and to whom he had given the flour. She was the only woman in whose company he felt at ease, for she alone never reached out her arms. And yet it was from her that he was destined to receive next to his severest fright. It came about in the fall of 1897. He was returning from one of his dashes, this time to inspect Henderson, a creek that entered the Yukon just below the Stewart. Winter had come on with a rush, and he fought his way down the Yukon seventy miles in a frail Peterborough canoe in the midst of a run of mush-ice. Hugging the rim-ice that had already solidly formed, he shot across the ice-spewing mouth of the Klondike just in time to see a lone man dancing excitedly on the rim and pointing into the water. Next, he saw the fur-clad body of a woman, face under, sinking in the midst of the driving mush-ice. A lane opening in the swirl of the current, it was a matter of seconds to drive the canoe to the spot, reach to the shoulder in the water, and draw the woman gingerly to the canoe's side. It was Freda. And all might yet have been well with him, had she not, later, when brought back to consciousness, blazed at him with angry blue eyes and demanded: "Why did you? Oh, why did you?"

This worried him. In the nights that followed, instead of sinking immediately to sleep as was his wont, he lay awake, visioning her face and that blue blaze of wrath, and conning her words over and over. They rang with sincerity. The reproach was genuine. She had meant just what she said. And still he pondered.

The next time he encountered her she had turned away from him angrily and contemptuously. And yet again, she came to him to beg his pardon, and she dropped a hint of a man somewhere, sometime,--she said not how,--who had left her with no desire to live. Her speech was frank, but incoherent, and all he gleaned from it was that the event, whatever it was, had happened years before. Also, he gleaned that she had loved the man.

That was the thing--love. It caused the trouble. It was more terrible than frost or famine. Women were all very well, in themselves good to look upon and likable; but along came this thing called love, and they were seared to the bone by it, made so irrational that one could never guess what they would do next. This Freda-woman was a splendid creature, full-bodied, beautiful, and nobody's fool; but love had come along and soured her on the world, driving her to the Klondike and to suicide so compellingly that she was made to hate the man that saved her life.

Well, he had escaped love so far, just as he had escaped smallpox; yet there it was, as contagious as smallpox, and a whole lot worse in running its course. It made men and women do such fearful and unreasonable things. It was like delirium tremens, only worse. And if he, Daylight, caught it, he might have it as badly as any of them. It was lunacy, stark lunacy, and contagious on top of it all. A half dozen young fellows were crazy over Freda. They all wanted to marry her. Yet she, in turn, was crazy over that some other fellow on the other side of the world, and would have nothing to do with them.

63

But it was left to the Virgin to give him his final fright. She was found one morning dead in her cabin. A shot through the head had done it, and she had left no message, no explanation. Then came the talk. Some wit, voicing public opinion, called it a case of too much Daylight. She had killed herself because of him. Everybody knew this, and said so. The correspondents wrote it up, and once more Burning Daylight, King of the Klondike, was sensationally featured in the Sunday supplements of the United States. The Virgin had straightened up, so the feature-stories ran, and correctly so. Never had she entered a Dawson City dance-hall. When she first arrived from Circle City, she had earned her living by washing clothes. Next, she had bought a sewing-machine and made men's drill *parkas*, fur caps, and moosehide mittens. Then she had gone as a clerk into the First Yukon Bank. All this, and more, was known and told, though one and all were agreed that Daylight, while the cause, had been the innocent cause of her untimely end.

And the worst of it was that Daylight knew it was true. Always would he remember that last night he had seen her. He had thought nothing of it at the time; but, looking back, he was haunted by every little thing that had happened. In the light of the tragic event, he could understand everything--her quietness, that calm certitude as if all vexing questions of living had been smoothed out and were gone, and that certain ethereal sweetness about all that she had said and done that had been almost maternal. He remembered the way she had looked at him, how she had laughed when he narrated Mickey Dolan's mistake in staking the fraction on Skookum Gulch. Her laughter had been lightly joyous, while at the same time it had lacked its old-time robustness. Not that she had been grave or subdued. On the contrary, she had been so patently content, so filled with peace. She had fooled him, fool that he was. He had even thought that night that her feeling for him had passed, and he had taken delight in the thought, and caught visions of the satisfying future friendship that would be theirs with this perturbing love out of the way.

And then, when he stood at the door, cap in hand, and said good night. It had struck him at the time as a funny and embarrassing thing, her bending over his hand and kissing it. He had felt like a fool, but he shivered now when he looked back on it and felt again the touch of her lips on his hand. She was saying good-by, an eternal good-by, and he had never guessed. At that very moment, and for all the moments of the evening, coolly and deliberately, as he well knew her way, she had been resolved to die. If he had only known it! Untouched by the contagious malady himself, nevertheless he would have married her if he had had the slightest inkling of what she contemplated. And yet he knew, furthermore, that hers was a certain stiff-kneed pride that would not have permitted her to accept marriage as an act of philanthropy. There had really been no saving her, after all. The love-disease had fastened upon her, and she had been doomed from the first to perish of it.

Her one possible chance had been that he, too, should have caught it. And he had failed to catch it. Most likely, if he had, it would have been from Freda or some other woman. There was Dartworthy, the college man who had staked the rich fraction on Bonanza above Discovery. Everybody knew that old Doolittle's daughter, Bertha, was madly in love with him. Yet, when he contracted the disease, of all women, it had been with the wife of Colonel Walthstone, the great Guggenhammer mining expert. Result, three lunacy cases: Dartworthy selling out his mine for one-tenth its value; the poor woman sacrificing her respectability and sheltered nook in society to flee with him in an open boat down the Yukon; and Colonel Walthstone, breathing murder and destruction, taking out after them in another open boat. The whole impending tragedy had moved on down the muddy Yukon, passing Forty Mile and Circle and losing itself in the wilderness beyond. But there it was, love, disorganizing men's and women's lives, driving toward destruction and death, turning topsy-turvy everything that was sensible and considerate, making bawds or suicides out of virtuous women, and scoundrels and murderers out of men who had always been clean and square.

For the first time in his life Daylight lost his nerve. He was badly and avowedly frightened. Women were terrible creatures, and the love-germ was especially plentiful in their neighborhood. And they were so reckless, so devoid of fear. *They* were not frightened by what had happened to the Virgin. They held out their arms to him more seductively than ever. Even without his fortune, reckoned as a mere man, just past thirty, magnificently strong and equally good-looking and good-natured, he was a prize for most normal women. But when to his natural excellences were added the romance that linked with his name and the enormous wealth that was his, practically every free woman he encountered measured him with an appraising and delighted eye, to say nothing of more than one woman who was not free. Other men might have been spoiled by this and led to lose their heads; but the only effect on him was to increase his fright. As a result he refused most invitations to houses where women might be met, and frequented bachelor boards and the Moosehorn Saloon, which had no dance-hall attached.

CHAPTER 13

Six thousand spent the winter of 1897 in Dawson, work on the creeks went on apace, while beyond the passes it was reported that one hundred thousand more were waiting for the spring. Late one brief afternoon, Daylight, on the benches between French Hill and Skookum Hill, caught a wider vision of things. Beneath him lay the richest part of Eldorado Creek, while up and down Bonanza he could see for miles. It was a scene of a vast devastation. The hills, to their tops, had been shorn of trees, and their naked sides showed signs of goring and perforating that even the mantle of snow could not hide. Beneath him, in every direction were the cabins of men. But not many men were visible. A blanket of smoke filled the valleys and turned the gray day to melancholy twilight. Smoke arose from a thousand holes in the snow, where, deep down on bed-rock, in the frozen muck and gravel, men crept and scratched and dug, and ever built more fires to break the grip of the frost. Here and there, where new shafts were starting, these fires flamed redly. Figures of men crawled out of the holes, or disappeared into them, or, on raised platforms of hand-hewn timber, windlassed the thawed gravel to the surface, where it immediately froze. The wreckage of the spring washing appeared everywhere--piles of sluice-boxes, sections of elevated flumes, huge water-wheels,--all the debris of an army of gold-mad men.

"It-all's plain gophering," Daylight muttered aloud.

He looked at the naked hills and realized the enormous wastage of wood that had taken place. From this bird's-eye view he realized the monstrous confusion of their excited workings. It was a gigantic inadequacy. Each worked for himself, and the result was chaos. In this richest of diggings it cost out by their feverish, unthinking methods another dollar was left hopelessly in the earth. Given another year, and most of the claims would be worked out, and the sum of the gold taken out would no more than equal what was left behind.

Organization was what was needed, he decided; and his quick imagination sketched Eldorado Creek, from mouth to source, and from mountain top to mountain top, in the hands of one capable management. Even steam-thawing, as yet untried, but bound to come, he saw would be a makeshift. What should be done was to hydraulic the valley sides and benches, and then, on the creek bottom, to use gold-dredges such as he had heard described as operating in California.

There was the very chance for another big killing. He had wondered just what was precisely the reason for the Guggenhammers and the big English concerns sending in their high-salaried experts. That was their scheme. That was why they had approached him for the sale of worked-out claims and tailings. They were content to let the small mine-owners gopher out what they could, for there would be millions in the leavings.

And, gazing down on the smoky inferno of crude effort, Daylight outlined the new game he would play, a game in which the Guggenhammers and the rest would have to reckon with him. Cut along with the delight in the new conception came a weariness. He was tired of the long Arctic years, and he was curious about the Outside--the great world of which he had heard other men talk and of which he was as ignorant as a child. There were games out there to play. It was a larger table, and there was no reason why he with his millions should not sit in and take a hand. So it was, that afternoon on Skookum Hill, that he resolved to play this last best Klondike hand and pull for the Outside.

It took time, however. He put trusted agents to work on the heels of great experts, and on the creeks where they began to buy he likewise bought. Wherever they tried to corner a worked-out creek, they found him standing in the way, owning blocks of claims or artfully scattered claims that put all their plans to naught.

"I play you-all wide open to win--am I right" he told them once, in a heated conference.

Followed wars, truces, compromises, victories, and defeats. By 1898, sixty thousand men were on the Klondike and all their fortunes and affairs rocked back and forth and were affected by the battles Daylight fought. And more and more the taste for the larger game urged in Daylight's mouth. Here he was already locked in grapples with the great Guggenhammers, and winning, fiercely winning. Possibly the severest struggle was waged on Ophir, the veriest of moose-pastures, whose low-grade dirt was valuable only because of its vastness. The ownership of a block of seven claims in the heart of it gave Daylight his grip and they could not come to terms. The Guggenhammer experts concluded that it was too big for him to handle, and when they gave him an ultimatum to that effect he accepted and bought them out.

The plan was his own, but he sent down to the States for competent engineers to carry it out. In the Rinkabilly watershed, eighty miles away, he built his reservoir, and for eighty miles the huge wooden conduit carried the water across country to Ophir. Estimated at three millions, the reservoir and conduit cost nearer four. Nor did he stop with this. Electric power plants were installed, and his workings were lighted as well as run by electricity. Other sourdoughs, who had struck it rich in excess of all their dreams, shook their heads gloomily, warned him that he would go broke, and declined to invest in so extravagant a venture. But Daylight smiled, and sold out the remainder of his town-site holdings. He sold at the right time, at the height of the placer boom. When he prophesied to his old cronies, in the Moosehorn Saloon, that within five years town lots in Dawson could not be given away, while the cabins would be chopped up for firewood, he was laughed at roundly, and assured that the mother-lode would be found ere that time. But he went ahead, when his need for lumber was finished, selling out his sawmills as well. Likewise, he began to get rid of his scattered holdings on the various creeks, and without thanks to any one he finished his conduit, built his dredges, imported his machinery, and made the gold of Ophir immediately accessible. And he, who five years before had crossed over the divide from Indian River and threaded the silent wilderness, his dogs packing Indian fashion, himself living Indian fashion on straight moose meat, now heard the hoarse whistles calling his hundreds of laborers to work, and watched them toil under the white glare of the arc-lamps.

But having done the thing, he was ready to depart. And when he let the word go out, the Guggenhammers vied with the English concerns and with a new French company in bidding for Ophir and all its plant. The Guggenhammers bid highest, and the price they paid netted Daylight a clean million. It was current rumor that he was worth anywhere from twenty to thirty millions. But he alone knew just how he stood, and that, with his last claim sold and the table swept clean of his winnings, he had ridden his hunch to the tune of just a trifle over eleven millions.

His departure was a thing that passed into the history of the Yukon along with his other deeds. All the Yukon was his guest, Dawson the seat of the festivity. On that one last night no man's dust save his own was good. Drinks were not to be purchased. Every saloon ran open, with extra relays of exhausted bartenders, and the drinks were given away. A man who refused this hospitality, and persisted in paying, found a dozen fights on his hands. The veriest *chechaquos* rose up to defend the name of Daylight from such insult. And through it all, on moccasined feet, moved Daylight, hell-roaring Burning Daylight, over-spilling with good nature and *camaraderie*, howling his he-wolf howl and claiming the night as his, bending men's arms down on the bars, performing feats of strength, his bronzed face flushed with drink, his black eyes flashing, clad in overalls and blanket coat, his ear-flaps dangling and his gauntleted mittens swinging from the cord across the shoulders. But this time it was neither an ante nor a stake that he threw away, but a mere marker in the game that he who held so many markers would not miss.

As a night, it eclipsed anything that Dawson had ever seen. It was Daylight's desire to make it memorable, and his attempt was a success. A goodly portion of Dawson got drunk that night. The fall weather was on, and, though the freeze-up of the Yukon still delayed, the thermometer was down to twenty-five below zero and falling. Wherefore, it was necessary to organize gangs of life-savers, who patrolled the streets to pick up drunken men from where they fell in the snow and where an hour's sleep would be fatal. Daylight, whose whim it was to make them drunk by hundreds and by thousands, was the one who initiated this life saving. He wanted Dawson to have its night, but, in his deeper processes never careless nor wanton, he saw to it that it was a night without accident. And, like his olden nights, his ukase went forth that there should be no quarrelling nor fighting, offenders to be dealt with by him personally. Nor did he have to deal with any. Hundreds of devoted followers saw to it that the evilly disposed were rolled in the snow and hustled off to bed. In the great world, where great captains of industry die, all wheels under their erstwhile management are stopped for a minute. But in the Klondike, such was its hilarious sorrow at the departure of its captain, that for twenty-four hours no wheels revolved. Even great Ophir, with its thousand men on the pay-roll, closed down. On the day after the night there were no men present or fit to go to work.

Next morning, at break of day, Dawson said good-by. The thousands that lined the bank wore mittens and their ear-flaps pulled down and tied. It was thirty below zero, the rim-ice was thickening, and the Yukon carried a run of mush-ice. From the deck of the *Seattle*, Daylight waved and called his farewells. As the lines were cast off and the steamer swung out into the current, those near him saw the moisture well up in Daylight's eyes. In a way, it was to him departure from his native land, this grim Arctic region which was practically the only land he had known. He tore off his cap and waved it.

"Good-by, you-all!" he called. "Good-by, you-all!"

PART II

CHAPTER I

In no blaze of glory did Burning Daylight descend upon San Francisco. Not only had he been forgotten, but the Klondike along with him. The world was interested in other things, and the Alaskan adventure, like the Spanish War, was an old story. Many things had happened since then. Exciting things were happening every day, and the sensation-space of newspapers was limited. The effect of being ignored, however, was an exhilaration. Big man as he had been in the Arctic game, it merely showed how much bigger was this new game, when a man worth eleven millions, and with a history such as his, passed unnoticed.

He settled down in St. Francis Hotel, was interviewed by the cub-reporters on the hotel-run, and received brief paragraphs of notice for twenty-four hours. He grinned to himself, and began to look around and get acquainted with the new order of beings and things. He was very awkward and very self-possessed. In addition to the stiffening afforded his backbone by the conscious ownership of eleven millions, he possessed an enormous certitude. Nothing abashed him, nor was he appalled by the display and culture and power around him. It was another kind of wilderness, that was all; and it was for him to learn the ways of it, the signs and trails and water-holes where good hunting lay, and the bad stretches of field and flood to be avoided. As usual, he fought shy of the women. He was still too badly scared to come to close quarters with the dazzling and resplendent creatures his own millions made accessible. They looked and longed, but he so concealed his timidity that he had all the seeming of moving boldly among them. Nor was it his wealth alone that attracted them. He was too much a man, and too much an unusual type of man. Young yet, barely thirty-six, eminently handsome, magnificently strong, almost bursting with a splendid virility, his free trail-stride, never learned on pavements, and his black eyes, hinting of great spaces and unwearied with the close perspective of the city dwellers, drew many a curious and wayward feminine glance. He saw, grinned knowingly to himself, and faced them as so many dangers, with a cool demeanor that was a far greater personal achievement than had they been famine, frost, or flood.

He had come down to the States to play the man's game, not the woman's game; and the men he had not yet learned. They struck him as soft--soft physically; yet he divined them hard in their dealings, but hard under an exterior of supple softness. It struck him that there was something cat-like about them. He met them in the clubs, and wondered how real was the good-fellowship they displayed and how quickly they would unsheathe their claws and gouge and rend. "That's the proposition," he repeated to himself; "what will they-all do when the play is close and down to brass tacks?" He felt unwarrantably suspicious of them. "They're sure slick," was his secret judgment; and from bits of gossip dropped now and again he felt his judgment well buttressed. On the other hand, they radiated an atmosphere of manliness and the fair play that goes with manliness. They might gouge and rend in a fight--which was no more than natural; but he felt, somehow, that they would gouge and rend according to rule. This was the impression he got of them--a generalization tempered by knowledge that there was bound to be a certain percentage of scoundrels among them.

Several months passed in San Francisco during which time he studied the game and its rules, and prepared himself to take a hand. He even took private instruction in English, and succeeded in eliminating his worst faults, though in moments of excitement he was prone to lapse into "you-all," "knowed," "sure," and similar solecisms. He learned to eat and dress and generally comport himself after the manner of civilized man; but through it all he remained himself, not unduly reverential nor considerative, and never hesitating to stride rough-shod over any soft-faced convention if it got in his way and the provocation were great enough. Also, and unlike the average run of weaker men coming from back countries and far places, he failed to reverence the particular tin gods worshipped variously by the civilized tribes of men. He had seen totems before, and knew them for what they were.

Tiring of being merely an onlooker, he ran up to Nevada, where the new gold-mining boom was fairly started--"just to try a flutter," as he phrased it to himself. The flutter on the Tonopah Stock Exchange lasted just ten days, during which time his smashing, wild-bull game played ducks and drakes with the more stereotyped gamblers, and at the end of which time, having gambled Floridel into his fist, he let go for a net profit of half a million. Whereupon, smacking his lips, he departed for San Francisco and the St. Francis Hotel. It tasted good, and his hunger for the game became more acute.

And once more the papers sensationalized him. BURNING DAYLIGHT was a big-letter headline again. Interviewers flocked about him. Old files of magazines and newspapers were searched through, and the romantic and historic Elam Harnish, Adventurer of the Frost, King of the Klondike, and father of the Sourdoughs, strode upon the breakfast table of a million homes along with the toast and breakfast foods. Even before his elected time, he was forcibly launched into the game. Financiers and promoters, and all the flotsam and jetsam of the sea of speculation surged upon the shores of his eleven millions. In self-defence he was compelled to open offices. He had made them sit up and take notice, and now, willy-nilly, they were dealing him hands and clamoring for him to play. Well, play he would; he'd show 'em; even despite the elated prophesies made of how swiftly he would be trimmed--prophesies coupled with descriptions of the bucolic game he would play and of his wild and woolly appearance.

He dabbled in little things at first--"stalling for time," as he explained it to Holdsworthy, a friend he had made at the Alta-Pacific Club. Daylight himself was a member of the club, and Holdsworthy had proposed him. And it was well that Daylight played closely at first, for he was astounded by the multitudes of sharks--"ground-sharks," he called them--that flocked about him. He saw through their schemes readily enough, and even marveled that such numbers of them could find sufficient prey to keep them going. Their rascality and general dubiousness was so transparent that he could not understand how any one could be taken in by them.

And then he found that there were sharks and sharks. Holdsworthy treated him more like a brother than a mere fellow-clubman, watching over him, advising him, and introducing him to the magnates of the local financial world. Holdsworthy's family lived in a delightful bungalow near Menlo Park, and here Daylight spent a number of weekends, seeing a fineness and kindness of home life of which he had never dreamed. Holdsworthy was an enthusiast over flowers, and a half lunatic over raising prize poultry; and these engrossing madnesses were a source of perpetual joy to Daylight, who looked on in tolerant good humor. Such amiable weaknesses tokened the healthfulness of the man, and drew Daylight closer to him. A prosperous, successful business man without great ambition, was Daylight's estimate of him--a man too easily satisfied with the small stakes of the game ever to launch out in big play.

On one such week-end visit, Holdsworthy let him in on a good thing, a good little thing, a brickyard at Glen Ellen. Daylight listened closely to the other's description of the situation. It was a most reasonable venture, and Daylight's one objection was that it was so small a matter and so far out of his line; and he went into it only as a matter of friendship, Holdsworthy explaining that he was himself already in a bit, and that while it was a good thing, he would be compelled to make sacrifices in other directions in order to develop it. Daylight advanced the capital, fifty thousand dollars, and, as he laughingly explained afterward, "I was stung, all right, but it wasn't Holdsworthy that did it half as much as those blamed chickens and fruit-trees of his."

It was a good lesson, however, for he learned that there were few faiths in the business world, and that even the simple, homely faith of breaking bread and eating salt counted for little in the face of a worthless brickyard and fifty thousand dollars in cash. But the sharks and sharks of various orders and degrees, he concluded, were on the surface. Deep down, he divined, were the integrities and the stabilities. These big captains of industry and masters of finance, he decided, were the men to work with. By the very nature of their huge deals and enterprises they had to play fair. No room there for little sharpers' tricks and bunco games. It was to be expected that little men should salt gold-mines with a shotgun and work off worthless brick-yards on their friends, but in high finance such methods were not worth while. There the men were engaged in developing the country, organizing its railroads, opening up its mines, making accessible its vast natural resources. Their play was bound to be big and stable. "They sure can't afford tin-horn tactics," was his summing up.

So it was that he resolved to leave the little men, the Holdsworthys, alone; and, while he met them in good-fellowship, he chummed with none, and formed no deep friendships. He did not dislike the little men, the men of the Alta-Pacific, for instance. He merely did not elect to choose them for partners in the big game in which he intended to play. What that big game was, even he did not know. He was waiting to find it. And in the meantime he played small hands, investing in several arid-lands reclamation projects and keeping his eyes open for the big chance when it should come along.

And then he met John Dowsett, the great John Dowsett. The whole thing was fortuitous. This cannot be doubted, as Daylight himself knew, it was by the merest chance, when in Los Angeles, that he heard the tuna were running strong at Santa Catalina, and went over to the island instead of returning directly to San Francisco as he had planned. There he met John Dowsett, resting off for several days in the middle of a flying western trip. Dowsett had of course heard of the spectacular Klondike King and his rumored thirty millions, and he certainly found himself interested by the man in the acquaintance that was formed. Somewhere along in this acquaintanceship the idea must have popped into his brain. But he did not broach it, preferring to mature it carefully. So he talked in large general ways, and did his best to be agreeable and win Daylight's friendship.

It was the first big magnate Daylight had met face to face, and he was pleased and charmed. There was such a kindly humanness about the man, such a genial democraticness, that Daylight found it hard to realize that this was THE John Dowsett, president of a string of banks, insurance manipulator, reputed ally of the lieutenants of Standard Oil, and known ally of the Guggenhammers. Nor did his looks belie his reputation and his manner.

Physically, he guaranteed all that Daylight knew of him. Despite his sixty years and snow-white hair, his hand-shake was firmly hearty, and he showed no signs of decrepitude, walking with a quick, snappy step, making all movements definitely and decisively. His skin was a healthy pink, and his thin, clean lips knew the way to writhe heartily over a joke. He had honest blue eyes of palest blue; they looked out at one keenly and frankly from under shaggy gray brows. His mind showed itself disciplined and orderly, and its workings struck Daylight as having all the certitude of a steel trap. He was a man who KNEW and who never decorated his knowledge with foolish frills of sentiment or emotion. That he was accustomed to command was patent, and every word and gesture tingled with power. Combined with this was his sympathy and tact, and Daylight could note easily enough all the earmarks that distinguished him from a little man of the Holdsworthy caliber. Daylight knew also his history, the prime old American stock from which he had descended, his own war record, the John Dowsett before him who had been one of the banking buttresses of the Cause of the Union, the Commodore Dowsett of the War of 1812 the General Dowsett of Revolutionary fame, and that first far Dowsett, owner of lands and slaves in early New England.

"He's sure the real thing," he told one of his fellow-clubmen afterwards, in the smoking-room of the Alta-Pacific. "I tell you, Gallon, he was a genuine surprise to me. I knew the big ones had to be like that, but I had to see him to really know it. He's one of the fellows that does things. You can see it sticking out all over him. He's one in a thousand, that's straight, a man to tie to. There's no limit to any game he plays, and you can stack on it that he plays right up to the handle. I bet he can lose or win half a dozen million without batting an eye."

Gallon puffed at his cigar, and at the conclusion of the panegyric regarded the other curiously; but Daylight, ordering cocktails, failed to note this curious stare.

"Going in with him on some deal, I suppose," Gallon remarked.

"Nope, not the slightest idea. Here's kindness. I was just explaining that I'd come to understand how these big fellows do big things. Why, dye know, he gave me such a feeling that he knew everything, that I was plumb ashamed of myself."

"I guess I could give him cards and spades when it comes to driving a dog-team, though," Daylight observed, after a meditative pause. "And I really believe I could put him on to a few wrinkles in poker and placer mining, and maybe in paddling a birch canoe. And maybe I stand a better chance to learn the game he's been playing all his life than he would stand of learning the game I played up North."

CHAPTER 2

It was not long afterward that Daylight came on to New York. A letter from John Dowsett had been the cause--a simple little typewritten letter of several lines. But Daylight had thrilled as he read it. He remembered the thrill that was his, a callow youth of fifteen, when, in Tempas Butte, through lack of a fourth man, Tom Galsworthy, the gambler, had said, "Get in, Kid; take a hand." That thrill was his now. The bald, typewritten sentences seemed gorged with mystery. *"Our Mr. Howison will call upon you at your hotel. He is to be trusted. We must not be seen together. You will understand after we have had our talk."* Daylight conned the words over and over. That was it. The big game had arrived, and it looked as if he were being invited to sit in and take a hand. Surely, for no other reason would one man so peremptorily invite another man to make a journey across the continent.

They met--thanks to "our" Mr. Howison,--up the Hudson, in a magnificent country home. Daylight, according to instructions, arrived in a private motor-car which had been furnished him. Whose car it was he did not know any more than did he know the owner of the house, with its generous, rolling, tree-studded lawns. Dowsett was already there, and another man whom Daylight recognized before the introduction was begun. It was Nathaniel Letton, and none other. Daylight had seen his face a score of times in the magazines and newspapers, and read about his standing in the financial world and about his endowed University of Daratona. He, likewise, struck Daylight as a man of power, though he was puzzled in that he could find no likeness to Dowsett. Except in the matter of cleanness,--a cleanness that seemed to go down to the deepest fibers of him,--Nathaniel Letton was unlike the other in every particular. Thin to emaciation, he seemed a cold flame of a man, a man of a mysterious, chemic sort of flame, who, under a glacier-like exterior, conveyed, somehow, the impression of the ardent heat of a thousand suns. His large gray eyes were mainly responsible for this feeling, and they blazed out feverishly from what was almost a death's-head, so thin was the face, the skin of which was a ghastly, dull, dead white. Not more than fifty, thatched with a sparse growth of iron-gray hair, he looked several times the age of Dowsett. Yet Nathaniel Letton possessed control--Daylight could see that plainly. He was a thin-faced ascetic, living in a state of high, attenuated calm--a molten planet under a transcontinental ice sheet. And yet, above all most of all, Daylight was impressed by the terrific and almost awful cleanness of the man. There was no dross in him. He had all the seeming of having been purged by fire. Daylight had the feeling that a healthy man-oath would be a deadly offence to his ears, a sacrilege and a blasphemy.

They drank--that is, Nathaniel Letton took mineral water served by the smoothly operating machine of a lackey who inhabited the place, while Dowsett took Scotch and soda and Daylight a cocktail. Nobody seemed to notice the unusualness of a Martini at midnight, though Daylight looked sharply for that very thing; for he had long since learned that Martinis had their strictly appointed times and places. But he liked Martinis, and, being a natural man, he chose deliberately to drink when and how he pleased. Others had noticed this peculiar habit of his, but not so Dowsett and Letton; and Daylight's secret thought was: "They sure wouldn't bat an eye if I called for a glass of corrosive sublimate."

Leon Guggenhammer arrived in the midst of the drink, and ordered Scotch. Daylight studied him curiously. This was one of the great Guggenhammer family; a younger one, but nevertheless one of the crowd with which he had locked grapples in the North. Nor did Leon Guggenhammer fail to mention cognizance of that old affair. He complimented Daylight on his prowess-"The echoes of Ophir came down to us, you know. And I must say, Mr. Daylight--er, Mr. Harnish, that you whipped us roundly in that affair."

Echoes! Daylight could not escape the shock of the phrase--*echoes* had come down to them of the fight into which he had flung all his strength and the strength of his Klondike millions. The Guggenhammers sure must go some when a fight of that dimension was no more than a skirmish of which they deigned to hear echoes. "They sure play an almighty big game down here," was his conclusion, accompanied by a corresponding elation that it was just precisely that almighty big game in which he was about to be invited to play a hand. For the moment he poignantly regretted that rumor was not true, and that his eleven millions were not in reality thirty millions. Well, that much he would be frank about; he would let them know exactly how many stacks of chips he could buy.

Leon Guggenhammer was young and fat. Not a day more than thirty, his face, save for the adumbrated puff sacks under the eyes, was as smooth and lineless as a boy's. He, too, gave the impression of cleanness. He showed in the pink of health; his unblemished, smooth-shaven skin shouted advertisement of his splendid physical condition. In the face of that perfect skin, his very fatness and mature, rotund paunch could be nothing other than normal. He was constituted to be prone to fatness, that was all.

The talk soon centred down to business, though Guggenhammer had first to say his say about the forthcoming international yacht race and about his own palatial steam yacht, the *Electra*, whose recent engines were already antiquated. Dowsett broached the plan, aided by an occasional remark from the other two, while Daylight asked questions. Whatever the proposition was, he was going into it with his eyes open. And they filled his eyes with the practical vision of what they had in mind.

"They will never dream you are with us," Guggenhammer interjected, as the outlining of the matter drew to a close, his handsome Jewish eyes flashing enthusiastically. "They'll think you are raiding on your own in proper buccaneer style."

"Of course, you understand, Mr. Harnish, the absolute need for keeping our alliance in the dark," Nathaniel Letton warned gravely.

Daylight nodded his head.

"And you also understand," Letton went on, "that the result can only be productive of good. The thing is legitimate and right, and the only ones who may be hurt are the stock gamblers themselves. It is not an attempt to smash the market. As you see yourself, you are to bull the market. The honest investor will be the gainer."

"Yes, that's the very thing," Dowsett said. "The commercial need for copper is continually increasing. Ward Valley Copper, and all that it stands for,--practically one-quarter of the world's supply, as I have shown you,--is a big thing, how big, even we can scarcely estimate. Our arrangements are made. We have plenty of capital ourselves, and yet we want more. Also, there is too much Ward Valley out to suit our present plans. Thus we kill both birds with one stone-"

"And I am the stone," Daylight broke in with a smile.

"Yes, just that. Not only will you bull Ward Valley, but you will at the same time gather Ward Valley in. This will be of inestimable advantage to us, while you and all of us will profit by it as well. And as Mr. Letton has pointed out, the thing is legitimate and square. On the eighteenth the directors meet, and, instead of the customary dividend, a double dividend will be declared."

"And where will the shorts be then?" Leon Guggenhammer cried excitedly.

"The shorts will be the speculators," Nathaniel Letton explained, "the gamblers, the froth of Wall Street--you understand. The genuine investors will not be hurt. Furthermore, they will have learned for the thousandth time to have confidence in Ward Valley. And with their confidence we can carry through the large developments we have outlined to you."

"There will be all sorts of rumors on the street," Dowsett warned Daylight, "but do not let them frighten you. These rumors may even originate with us. You can see how and why clearly. But rumors are to be no concern of yours. You are on the inside. All you have to do is buy, buy, buy, and keep on buying to the last stroke, when the directors declare the double dividend. Ward Valley will jump so that it won't be feasible to buy after that."

"What we want," Letton took up the strain, pausing significantly to sip his mineral water, "what we want is to take large blocks of Ward Valley off the hands of the public. We could do this easily enough by depressing the market and frightening the holders. And we could do it more cheaply in such fashion. But we are absolute masters of the situation, and we are fair enough to buy Ward Valley on a rising market. Not that we are philanthropists, but that we need the investors in our big development scheme. Nor do we lose directly by the transaction. The instant the action of the directors becomes known, Ward Valley will rush heavenward. In addition, and outside the legitimate field of the transaction, we will pinch the shorts for a very large sum. But that is only incidental, you understand, and in a way, unavoidable. On the other hand, we shall not turn up our noses at that phase of it. The shorts shall be the veriest gamblers, of course, and they will get no more than they deserve."

"And one other thing, Mr. Harnish," Guggenhammer said, "if you exceed your available cash, or the amount you care to invest in the venture, don't fail immediately to call on us. Remember, we are behind you."

"Yes, we are behind you," Dowsett repeated.

Nathaniel Letton nodded his head in affirmation.

"Now about that double dividend on the eighteenth-" John Dowsett drew a slip of paper from his note-book and adjusted his glasses. "Let me show you the figures. Here, you see..."

And thereupon he entered into a long technical and historical explanation of the earnings and dividends of Ward Valley from the day of its organization.

The whole conference lasted not more than an hour, during which time Daylight lived at the topmost of the highest peak of life that he had ever scaled. These men were big players. They were powers. True, as he knew himself, they were not the real inner circle. They did not rank with the Morgans and Harrimans. And yet they were in touch with those giants and were themselves lesser giants. He was pleased, too, with their attitude toward him. They met him deferentially, but not patronizingly. It was the deference of equality, and Daylight could not escape the subtle flattery of it; for he was fully aware that in experience as well as wealth they were far and away beyond him.

"We'll shake up the speculating crowd," Leon Guggenhammer proclaimed jubilantly, as they rose to go. "And you are the man to do it, Mr. Harnish. They are bound to think you are on your own, and their shears are all sharpened for the trimming of newcomers like you."

"They will certainly be misled," Letton agreed, his eerie gray eyes blazing out from the voluminous folds of the huge Mueller with which he was swathing his neck to the ears. "Their minds run in ruts. It is the unexpected that upsets their stereotyped calculations--any new combination, any strange factor, any fresh variant. And you will be all that to them, Mr. Harnish. And I repeat, they are gamblers, and they will deserve all that befalls them. They clog and cumber all legitimate enterprise. You have no idea of the trouble they cause men like us--sometimes, by their gambling tactics, upsetting the soundest plans, even overturning the stablest institutions."

Dowsett and young Guggenhammer went away in one motor-car, and Letton by himself in another. Daylight, with still in the forefront of his consciousness all that had occurred in the preceding hour, was deeply impressed by the scene at the moment of departure. The three machines stood like weird night monsters at the gravelled foot of the wide stairway under the unlighted porte-cochere. It was a dark night, and the lights of the motor-cars cut as sharply through the blackness as knives would cut through solid substance. The obsequious lackey--the automatic genie of the house which belonged to none of the three men,--stood like a graven statue after having helped them in. The fur-coated chauffeurs bulked dimly in their seats. One after the other, like spurred steeds, the cars leaped into the blackness, took the curve of the driveway, and were gone.

Daylight's car was the last, and, peering out, he caught a glimpse of the unlighted house that loomed hugely through the darkness like a mountain. Whose was it? he wondered. How came they to use it for their secret conference? Would the lackey talk? How about the chauffeurs? Were they trusted men like "our" Mr. Howison? Mystery? The affair was alive with it. And hand in hand with mystery walked Power. He leaned back and inhaled his cigarette. Big things were afoot. The cards were shuffled even the for a mighty deal, and he was in on it. He remembered back to his poker games with Jack Kearns, and laughed aloud. He had played for thousands in those days on the turn of a card; but now he was playing for millions. And on the eighteenth, when that dividend was declared, he chuckled at the confusion that would inevitably descend upon the men with the sharpened shears waiting to trim him--him, Burning Daylight.

CHAPTER 3

Back at his hotel, though nearly two in the morning, he found the reporters waiting to interview him. Next morning there were more. And thus, with blare of paper trumpet, was he received by New York. Once more, with beating of toms-toms and wild hullaballoo, his picturesque figure strode across the printed sheet. The King of the Klondike, the hero of the Arctic, the thirty-million-dollar millionaire of the North, had come to New York. What had he come for? To trim the New Yorkers as he had trimmed the Tonopah crowd in Nevada? Wall Street had best watch out, for the wild man of Klondike had just come to town. Or, perchance, would Wall Street trim him? Wall Street had trimmed many wild men; would this be Burning Daylight's fate? Daylight grinned to himself, and gave out ambiguous interviews. It helped the game, and he grinned again, as he meditated that Wall Street would sure have to go some before it trimmed him.

They were prepared for him to play, and, when heavy buying of Ward Valley began, it was quickly decided that he was the operator. Financial gossip buzzed and hummed. He was after the Guggenhammers once more. The story of Ophir was told over again and sensationalized until even Daylight scarcely recognized it. Still, it was all grist to his mill. The stock gamblers were clearly befooled. Each day he increased his buying, and so eager were the sellers that Ward Valley rose but slowly. "It sure beats poker," Daylight whispered gleefully to himself, as he noted the perturbation he was causing. The newspapers hazarded countless guesses and surmises, and Daylight was constantly dogged by a small battalion of reporters. His own interviews were gems. Discovering the delight the newspapers took in his vernacular, in his "you-alls," and "sures," and "surge-ups," he even exaggerated these particularities of speech, exploiting the phrases he had heard other frontiersmen use, and inventing occasionally a new one of his own.

A wildly exciting time was his during the week preceding Thursday the eighteenth. Not only was he gambling as he had never gambled before, but he was gambling at the biggest table in the world and for stakes so large that even the case-hardened habitues of that table were compelled to sit up. In spite of the unlimited selling, his persistent buying compelled Ward Valley steadily to rise, and as Thursday approached, the situation became acute. Something had to smash. How much Ward Valley was this Klondike gambler going to buy? How much *could* he buy? What was the Ward Valley crowd doing all this time? Daylight appreciated the interviews with them that appeared--interviews delightfully placid and non-committal. Leon Guggenhammer even hazarded the opinion that this Northland Croesus might possibly be making a mistake. But not that they cared, John Dowsett explained. Nor did they object. While in the dark regarding his intentions, of one thing they were certain; namely, that he was bulling Ward Valley. And they did not mind that. No matter what happened to him and his spectacular operations, Ward Valley was all right, and would remain all right, as firm as the Rock of Gibraltar. No; they had no Ward Valley to sell, thank you. This purely fictitious state of the market was bound shortly to pass, and Ward Valley was not to be induced to change the even tenor of its way by any insane stock exchange flurry. "It is purely gambling from beginning to end," were Nathaniel Letton's words; "and we refuse to have anything to do with it or to take notice of it in any way."

During this time Daylight had several secret meetings with his partners--one with Leon Guggenhammer, one with John Dowsett, and two with Mr. Howison. Beyond congratulations, they really amounted to nothing; for, as he was informed, everything was going satisfactorily.

But on Tuesday morning a rumor that was disconcerting came to Daylight's ears. It was also published in the *Wall Street Journal,* and it was to the effect, on apparently straight inside information, that on Thursday, when the directors of Ward Valley met, instead of the customary dividend being declared, an assessment would be levied. It was the first check Daylight had received. It came to him with a shock that if the thing were so he was a broken man. And it also came to him that all this colossal operating of his was being done on his own money. Dowsett, Guggenhammer, and Letton were risking nothing. It was a panic, short-lived, it was true, but sharp enough while it lasted to make him remember Holdsworthy and the brick-yard, and to impel him to cancel all buying orders while he rushed to a telephone.

"Nothing in it--only a rumor," came Leon Guggenhammer's throaty voice in the receiver. "As you know," said Nathaniel Letton, "I am one of the directors, and I should certainly be aware of it were such action contemplated. And John Dowsett: "I warned you against just such rumors. There is not an iota of truth in it--certainly not. I tell you on my honor as a gentleman."

Heartily ashamed of himself for his temporary loss of nerve, Daylight returned to his task. The cessation of buying had turned the Stock Exchange into a bedlam, and down all the line of stocks the bears were smashing. Ward Valley, as the ape, received the brunt of the shock, and was already beginning to tumble. Daylight calmly doubled his buying orders. And all through Tuesday and Wednesday, and Thursday morning, he went on buying, while Ward Valley rose triumphantly higher. Still they sold, and still he bought, exceeding his power to buy many times over, when delivery was taken into account. What of that? On this day the double dividend would be declared, he assured himself. The pinch of delivery would be on the shorts. They would be making terms with him.

And then the thunderbolt struck. True to the rumor, Ward Valley levied the assessment. Daylight threw up his arms. He verified the report and quit. Not alone Ward Valley, but all securities were being hammered down by the triumphant bears. As for Ward Valley, Daylight did not even trouble to learn if it had fetched bottom or was still tumbling. Not stunned, not even bewildered, while Wall Street went mad, Daylight withdrew from the field to think it over. After a short conference with his brokers, he proceeded to his hotel, on the way picking up the evening papers and glancing at the head-lines. BURNING DAYLIGHT CLEANED OUT, he read; DAYLIGHT GETS HIS; ANOTHER WESTERNER FAILS TO FIND EASY MONEY. As he entered his hotel, a later edition announced the suicide of a young man, a lamb, who had followed Daylight's play. *What in hell did he want to kill himself for?* was Daylight's muttered comment.

He passed up to his rooms, ordered a Martini cocktail, took off his shoes, and sat down to think. After half an hour he roused himself to take the drink, and as he felt the liquor pass warmingly through his body, his features relaxed into a slow, deliberate, yet genuine grin. He was laughing at himself.

"Buncoed, by gosh!" he muttered.

Then the grin died away, and his face grew bleak and serious. Leaving out his interests in the several Western reclamation projects (which were still assessing heavily), he was a ruined man. But harder hit than this was his pride. He had been so easy. They had gold-bricked him, and he had nothing to show for it. The simplest farmer would have had documents, while he had nothing but a gentleman's agreement, and a verbal one at that. *Gentleman's agreement.* He snorted over it. John Dowsett's voice, just as he had heard it in the telephone receiver, sounded in his ears the words, *"On my honor as a gentleman."* They were sneak-thieves and swindlers, that was what they were, and they had given him the double-cross. The newspapers were right. He had come to New York to be trimmed, and Messrs. Dowsett, Letton, and Guggenhammer had done it. He was a little fish, and they had played with him ten days--ample time in which to swallow him, along with his eleven millions. Of course, they had been unloading on him all the time, and now they were buying Ward Valley back for a song ere the market righted itself. Most probably, out of his share of the swag, Nathaniel Letton would erect a couple of new buildings for that university of his. Leon Guggenhammer would buy new engines for that yacht, or a whole fleet of yachts. But what the devil Dowsett would do with his whack, was beyond him--most likely start another string of banks.

And Daylight sat and consumed cocktails and saw back in his life to Alaska, and lived over the grim years in which he had battled for his eleven millions. For a while murder ate at his heart, and wild ideas and sketchy plans of killing his betrayers flashed through his mind. That was what that young man should have done instead of killing himself. He should have gone gunning. Daylight unlocked his grip and took out his automatic pistol--a big Colt's .44. He released the safety catch with his thumb, and operating the sliding outer barrel, ran the contents of the clip through the mechanism. The eight cartridges slid out in a stream. He refilled the clip, threw a cartridge into the chamber, and, with the trigger at full cock, thrust up the safety ratchet. He shoved the weapon into the side pocket of his coat, ordered another Martini, and resumed his seat.

He thought steadily for an hour, but he grinned no more. Lines formed in his face, and in those lines were the travail of the North, the bite of the frost, all that he had achieved and suffered--the long, unending weeks of trail, the bleak tundra shore of Point Barrow, the smashing ice-jam of the Yukon, the battles with animals and men, the lean-dragged days of famine, the long months of stinging hell among the mosquitoes of the Koyokuk, the toil of pick and shovel, the scars and mars of pack-strap and tump-line, the straight meat diet with the dogs, and all the long procession of twenty full years of toil and sweat and endeavor.

At ten o'clock he arose and pored over the city directory. Then he put on his shoes, took a cab, and departed into the night. Twice he changed cabs, and finally fetched up at the night office of a detective agency. He superintended the thing himself, laid down money in advance in profuse quantities, selected the six men he needed, and gave them their instructions. Never, for so simple a task, had they been so well paid; for, to each, in addition to office charges, he gave a five-hundred-dollar bill, with the promise of another if he succeeded. Some time next day, he was convinced, if not sooner, his three silent partners would come together. To each one two of his detectives were to be attached. Time and place was all he wanted to learn.

"Stop at nothing, boys," were his final instructions. "I must have this information. Whatever you do, whatever happens, I'll sure see you through."

Returning to his hotel, he changed cabs as before, went up to his room, and with one more cocktail for a nightcap, went to bed and to sleep. In the morning he dressed and shaved, ordered breakfast and the newspapers sent up, and waited. But he did not drink. By nine o'clock his telephone began to ring and the reports to come in. Nathaniel Letton was taking the train at Tarrytown. John Dowsett was coming down by the subway. Leon Guggenhammer had not stirred out yet, though he was assuredly within. And in this fashion, with a map of the city spread out before him, Daylight followed the movements of his three men as they drew together. Nathaniel Letton was at his offices in the Mutual-Solander Building. Next arrived Guggenhammer. Dowsett was still in his own offices. But at eleven came the word that he also had arrived, and several minutes later Daylight was in a hired motor-car and speeding for the Mutual-Solander Building.

CHAPTER 4

Nathaniel Letton was talking when the door opened; he ceased, and with his two companions gazed with controlled perturbation at Burning Daylight striding into the room. The free, swinging movements of the trail-traveler were unconsciously exaggerated in that stride of his. In truth, it seemed to him that he felt the trail beneath his feet.

"Howdy, gentlemen, howdy," he remarked, ignoring the unnatural calm with which they greeted his entrance. He shook hands with them in turn, striding from one to another and gripping their hands so heartily that Nathaniel Letton could not forbear to wince. Daylight flung himself into a massive chair and sprawled lazily, with an appearance of fatigue. The leather grip he had brought into the room he dropped carelessly beside him on the floor

"Goddle mighty, but I've sure been going some," he sighed. "We sure trimmed them beautiful. It was real slick. And the beauty of the play never dawned on me till the very end. It was pure and simple knock down and drag out. And the way they fell for it was amazin'."

The geniality in his lazy Western drawl reassured them. He was not so formidable, after all. Despite the act that he had effected an entrance in the face of Letton's instructions to the outer office, he showed no indication of making a scene or playing rough.

"Well," Daylight demanded good-humoredly, "ain't you-all got a good word for your pardner? Or has his sure enough brilliance plumb dazzled you-all?"

Letton made a dry sound in his throat. Dowsett sat quietly and waited, while Leon Guggenhammer struggled into articulation.

"You have certainly raised Cain," he said.

Daylight's black eyes flashed in a pleased way.

"Didn't I, though!" he proclaimed jubilantly. "And didn't we fool 'em! I was totally surprised. I never dreamed they would be that easy.

"And now," he went on, not permitting the pause to grow awkward, "we-all might as well have an accounting. I'm pullin' West this afternoon on that blamed Twentieth Century." He tugged at his grip, got it open, and dipped into it with both his hands. "But don't forget, boys, when you-all want me to hornswoggle Wall Street another flutter, all you-all have to do is whisper the word. I'll sure be right there with the goods."

His hands emerged, clutching a great mass of stubs, check-books, and broker's receipts. These he deposited in a heap on the big table, and dipping again, he fished out the stragglers and added them to the pile. He consulted a slip of paper, drawn from his coat pocket, and read aloud: --

"Ten million twenty-seven thousand and forty-two dollars and sixty-eight cents is my figurin' on my expenses. Of course that-all's taken from the winnings before we-all get to figurin' on the whack-up. Where's your figures? It must a' been a Goddle mighty big clean-up."

The three men looked their bepuzzlement at one another. The man was a bigger fool than they had imagined, or else he was playing a game which they could not divine.

Nathaniel Letton moistened his lips and spoke up.

"It will take some hours yet, Mr. Harnish, before the full accounting can be made. Mr. Howison is at work upon it now. We--ah--as you say, it has been a gratifying clean-up. Suppose we have lunch together and talk it over. I'll have the clerks work through the noon hour, so that you will have ample time to catch your train."

81

Dowsett and Guggenhammer manifested a relief that was almost obvious. The situation was clearing. It was disconcerting, under the circumstances, to be pent in the same room with this heavy-muscled, Indian-like man whom they had robbed. They remembered unpleasantly the many stories of his strength and recklessness. If Letton could only put him off long enough for them to escape into the policed world outside the office door, all would be well; and Daylight showed all the signs of being put off.

"I'm real glad to hear that," he said. "I don't want to miss that train, and you-all have done me proud, gentlemen, letting me in on this deal. I just do appreciate it without being able to express my feelings. But I am sure almighty curious, and I'd like terrible to know, Mr. Letton, what your figures of our winning is. Can you-all give me a rough estimate?"

Nathaniel Letton did not look appealingly at his two friends, but in the brief pause they felt that appeal pass out from him. Dowsett, of sterner mould than the others, began to divine that the Klondiker was playing. But the other two were still older the blandishment of his child-like innocence.

"It is extremely--er--difficult," Leon Guggenhammer began. "You see, Ward Valley has fluctuated so, er--"

"That no estimate can possibly be made in advance," Letton supplemented.

"Approximate it, approximate it," Daylight counselled cheerfully. "It don't hurt if you-all are a million or so out one side or the other. The figures'll straighten that up. But I'm that curious I'm just itching all over. What d'ye say?"

"Why continue to play at cross purposes?" Dowsett demanded abruptly and coldly. "Let us have the explanation here and now. Mr. Harnish is laboring under a false impression, and he should be set straight. In this deal--"

But Daylight interrupted. He had played too much poker to be unaware or unappreciative of the psychological factor, and he headed Dowsett off in order to play the denouncement of the present game in his own way.

"Speaking of deals," he said, "reminds me of a poker game I once seen in Reno, Nevada. It wa'n't what you-all would call a square game. They-all was tin-horns that sat in. But they was a tenderfoot--short-horns they-all are called out there. He stands behind the dealer and sees that same dealer give hisself four aces offen the bottom of the deck. The tenderfoot is sure shocked. He slides around to the player facin' the dealer across the table.

"'Say,' he whispers, 'I seen the dealer deal hisself four aces.'

"'Well, an' what of it?' says the player.

"'I'm tryin' to tell you-all because I thought you-all ought to know,' says the tenderfoot. 'I tell you-all I seen him deal hisself four aces.'

"'Say, mister,' says the player, 'you-all'd better get outa here. You-all don't understand the game. It's *his* deal, ain't it?'"

The laughter that greeted his story was hollow and perfunctory, but Daylight appeared not to notice it.

"Your story has some meaning, I suppose," Dowsett said pointedly.

Daylight looked at him innocently and did not reply. He turned jovially to Nathaniel Letton.

"Fire away," he said. "Give us an approximation of our winning. As I said before, a million out one way or the other won't matter, it's bound to be such an almighty big winning."

By this time Letton was stiffened by the attitude Dowsett had taken, and his answer was prompt and definite.

"I fear you are under a misapprehension, Mr. Harnish. There are no winnings to be divided with you. Now don't get excited, I beg of you. I have but to press this button..."

Far from excited, Daylight had all the seeming of being stunned. He felt absently in his vest pocket for a match, lighted it, and discovered that he had no cigarette. The three men watched him with the tense closeness of cats. Now that it had come, they knew that they had a nasty few minutes before them.

"Do you-all mind saying that over again?" Daylight said. "Seems to me I ain't got it just exactly right. You-all said...?"

He hung with painful expectancy on Nathaniel Letton's utterance.

"I said you were under a misapprehension, Mr. Harnish, that was all. You have been stock gambling, and you have been hard hit. But neither Ward Valley, nor I, nor my associates, feel that we owe you anything."

Daylight pointed at the heap of receipts and stubs on the table.

"That-all represents ten million twenty-seven thousand and forty-two dollars and sixty-eight cents, hard cash. Ain't it good for anything here?"

Letton smiled and shrugged his shoulders.

Daylight looked at Dowsett and murmured: --

"I guess that story of mine had some meaning, after all." He laughed in a sickly fashion. "It was your deal all right, and you-all dole them right, too. Well, I ain't kicking. I'm like the player in that poker game. It was your deal, and you-all had a right to do your best. And you d-one it-cleaned me out slicker'n a whistle."

He gazed at the heap on the table with an air of stupefaction.

"And that-all ain't worth the paper it's written on. Gol dast it, you-all can sure deal 'em 'round when you get a chance. Oh, no, I ain't a-kicking. It was your deal, and you-all certainly done me, and a man ain't half a man that squeals on another man's deal. And now the hand is played out, and the cards are on the table, and the deal's over, but..."

His hand, dipping swiftly into his inside breast pocket, appeared with the big Colt's automatic.

"As I was saying, the old deal's finished. Now it's MY deal, and I'm a-going to see if I can hold them four aces-

"Take your hand away, you whited sepulchre!" he cried sharply.

Nathaniel Letton's hand, creeping toward the push-button on the desk, was abruptly arrested.

"Change cars," Daylight commanded. "Take that chair over there, you gangrene-livered skunk. Jump! By God! or I'll make you leak till folks'll think your father was a water hydrant and your mother a sprinkling-cart. You-all move your chair alongside, Guggenhammer; and you-all Dowsett, sit right there, while I just irrelevantly explain the virtues of this here automatic. She's loaded for big game and she goes off eight times. She's a sure hummer when she gets started.

"Preliminary remarks being over, I now proceed to deal. Remember, I ain't making no remarks about your deal. You done your darndest, and it was all right. But this is my deal, and it's up to me to do my darndest. In the first place, you-all know me. I'm Burning Daylight--savvee? Ain't afraid of God, devil, death, nor destruction. Them's my four aces, and they sure copper your bets. Look at that there living skeleton. Letton, you're sure afraid to die. Your bones is all rattling together you're that scared. And look at that fat Jew there. This little weapon's sure put the fear of God in his heart. He's yellow as a sick persimmon. Dowsett, you're a cool one. You-all ain't batted an eye nor turned a hair. That's because you're great on arithmetic. And that makes you-all dead easy in this deal of mine. You're sitting there and adding two and two together, and you-all know I sure got you skinned. You know me, and that I ain't afraid of nothing. And you-all adds up all your money and knows you ain't a-going to die if you can help it."

"I'll see you hanged," was Dowsett's retort.

"Not by a damned sight. When the fun starts, you're the first I plug. I'll hang all right, but you-all won't live to see it. You-all die here and now while I'll die subject to the law's delay--savvee? Being dead, with grass growing out of your carcasses, you won't know when I hang, but I'll sure have the pleasure a long time of knowing you-all beat me to it."

Daylight paused.

"You surely wouldn't kill us?" Letton asked in a queer, thin voice.

Daylight shook his head.

"It's sure too expensive. You-all ain't worth it. I'd sooner have my chips back. And I guess you-all'd sooner give my chips back than go to the dead-house."

A long silence followed.

"Well, I've done dealt. It's up to you-all to play. But while you're deliberating, I want to give you-all a warning: if that door opens and any one of you cusses lets on there's anything unusual, right here and then I sure start plugging. They ain't a soul'll get out the room except feet first."

A long session of three hours followed. The deciding factor was not the big automatic pistol, but the certitude that Daylight would use it. Not alone were the three men convinced of this, but Daylight himself was convinced. He was firmly resolved to kill the men if his money was not forthcoming. It was not an easy matter, on the spur of the moment, to raise ten millions in paper currency, and there were vexatious delays. A dozen times Mr. Howison and the head clerk were summoned into the room. On these occasions the pistol lay on Daylight's lap, covered carelessly by a newspaper, while he was usually engaged in rolling or lighting his brown-paper cigarettes. But in the end, the thing was accomplished. A suit-case was brought up by one of the clerks from the waiting motor-car, and Daylight snapped it shut on the last package of bills. He paused at the door to make his final remarks.

"There's three several things I sure want to tell you-all. When I get outside this door, you-all'll be set free to act, and I just want to warn you-all about what to do. In the first place, no warrants for my arrest--savvee? This money's mine, and I ain't robbed you of it. If it gets out how you gave me the double-cross and how I done you back again, the laugh'll be on you, and it'll sure be an almighty big laugh. You-all can't afford that laugh. Besides, having got back my stake that you-all robbed me of, if you arrest me and try to rob me a second time, I'll go gunning for you-all, and I'll sure get you. No little fraid-cat shrimps like you-all can skin Burning Daylight. If you win you lose, and there'll sure be some several unexpected funerals around this burg. Just look me in the eye, and you-all 'll savvee I mean business. Them stubs and receipts on the table is all yourn. Good day."

As the door shut behind him, Nathaniel Letton sprang for the telephone, and Dowsett intercepted him.

"What are you going to do?" Dowsett demanded.

"The police. It's downright robbery. I won't stand it. I tell you I won't stand it."

Dowsett smiled grimly, but at the same time bore the slender financier back and down into his chair.

"We'll talk it over," he said; and in Leon Guggenhammer he found an anxious ally.

And nothing ever came of it. The thing remained a secret with the three men. Nor did Daylight ever give the secret away, though that afternoon, leaning back in his stateroom on the Twentieth Century, his shoes off, and feet on a chair, he chuckled long and heartily. New York remained forever puzzled over the affair; nor could it hit upon a rational explanation. By all rights, Burning Daylight should have gone broke, yet it was known that he immediately reappeared in San Francisco possessing an apparently unimpaired capital. This was evidenced by the magnitude of the enterprises he engaged in, such as, for instance, Panama Mail, by sheer weight of money and fighting power wresting the control away from Shiftily and selling out in two months to the Harriman interests at a rumored enormous advance.

CHAPTER 5

Back in San Francisco, Daylight quickly added to his reputation In ways it was not an enviable reputation. Men were afraid of him. He became known as a fighter, a fiend, a tiger. His play was a ripping and smashing one, and no one knew where or how his next blow would fall. The element of surprise was large. He balked on the unexpected, and, fresh from the wild North, his mind not operating in stereotyped channels, he was able in unusual degree to devise new tricks and stratagems. And once he won the advantage, he pressed it remorselessly. "As relentless as a Red Indian," was said of him, and it was said truly.

On the other hand, he was known as "square." His word was as good as his bond, and this despite the fact that he accepted nobody's word. He always shied at propositions based on *gentlemen's agreements,* and a man who ventured his honor as a gentleman, in dealing with Daylight, inevitably was treated to an unpleasant time. Daylight never gave his own word unless he held the whip-hand. It was a case with the other fellow taking it or nothing.

Legitimate investment had no place in Daylight's play. It tied up his money, and reduced the element of risk. It was the gambling side of business that fascinated him, and to play in his slashing manner required that his money must be ready to hand. It was never tied up save for short intervals, for he was principally engaged in turning it over and over, raiding here, there, and everywhere, a veritable pirate of the financial main. A five-per cent safe investment had no attraction for him; but to risk millions in sharp, harsh skirmish, standing to lose everything or to win fifty or a hundred per cent, was the savor of life to him. He played according to the rules of the game, but he played mercilessly. When he got a man or a corporation down and they squealed, he gouged no less hard. Appeals for financial mercy fell on deaf ears. He was a free lance, and had no friendly business associations. Such alliances as were formed from time to time were purely affairs of expediency, and he regarded his allies as men who would give him the double-cross or ruin him if a profitable chance presented. In spite of this point of view, he was faithful to his allies. But he was faithful just as long as they were and no longer. The treason had to come from them, and then it was 'Ware Daylight.

The business men and financiers of the Pacific coast never forgot the lesson of Charles Klinkner and the California & Altamont Trust Company. Klinkner was the president. In partnership with Daylight, the pair raided the San Jose Interurban. The powerful Lake Power & Electric Lighting corporation came to the rescue, and Klinkner, seeing what he thought was the opportunity, went over to the enemy in the thick of the pitched battle. Daylight lost three millions before he was done with it, and before he was done with it he saw the California & Altamont Trust Company hopelessly wrecked, and Charles Klinkner a suicide in a felon's cell. Not only did Daylight lose his grip on San Jose Interurban, but in the crash of his battle front he lost heavily all along the line. It was conceded by those competent to judge that he could have compromised and saved much. But, instead, he deliberately threw up the battle with San Jose Interurban and Lake Power, and, apparently defeated, with Napoleonic suddenness struck at Klinkner. It was the last unexpected thing Klinkner would have dreamed of, and Daylight knew it. He knew, further, that the California & Altamont Trust Company has an intrinsically sound institution, but that just then it was in a precarious condition due to Klinkner's speculations with its money. He knew, also, that in a few months the Trust Company would be more firmly on its feet than ever, thanks to those same speculations, and that if he were to strike he must strike immediately. "It's just that much money in pocket and a whole lot more," he was reported to have said in connection with his heavy losses. "It's just so much insurance against the future. Henceforth, men who go in with me on deals will think twice before they try to double-cross me, and then some."

The reason for his savageness was that he despised the men with whom he played. He had a conviction that not one in a hundred of them was intrinsically square; and as for the square ones, he prophesied that, playing in a crooked game, they were sure to lose and in the long run go broke. His New York experience had opened his eyes. He tore the veils of illusion from the business game, and saw its nakedness. He generalized upon industry and society somewhat as follows: --

Society, as organized, was a vast bunco game. There were many hereditary inefficients--men and women who were not weak enough to be confined in feeble-minded homes, but who were not strong enough to be ought else than hewers of wood and drawers of water. Then there were the fools who took the organized bunco game seriously, honoring and respecting it. They were easy game for the others, who saw clearly and knew the bunco game for what it was.

Work, legitimate work, was the source of all wealth. That was to say, whether it was a sack of potatoes, a grand piano, or a seven-passenger touring car, it came into being only by the performance of work. Where the bunco came in was in the distribution of these things after labor had created them. He failed to see the horny-handed sons of toil enjoying grand pianos or riding in automobiles. How this came about was explained by the bunco. By tens of thousands and hundreds of thousands men sat up nights and schemed how they could get between the workers and the things the workers produced. These schemers were the business men. When they got between the worker and his product, they took a whack out of it for themselves The size of the whack was determined by no rule of equity; but by their own strength and swinishness. It was always a case of "all the traffic can bear." He saw all men in the business game doing this.

One day, in a mellow mood (induced by a string of cocktails and a hearty lunch), he started a conversation with Jones, the elevator boy. Jones was a slender, mop-headed, man-grown, truculent flame of an individual who seemed to go out of his way to insult his passengers. It was this that attracted Daylight's interest, and he was not long in finding out what was the matter with Jones. He was a proletarian, according to his own aggressive classification, and he had wanted to write for a living. Failing to win with the magazines, and compelled to find himself in food and shelter, he had gone to the little valley of Petacha, not a hundred miles from Los Angeles. Here, toiling in the day-time, he planned to write and study at night. But the railroad charged all the traffic would bear. Petacha was a desert valley, and produced only three things: cattle, fire-wood, and charcoal. For freight to Los Angeles on a carload of cattle the railroad charged eight dollars. This, Jones explained, was due to the fact that the cattle had legs and could be driven to Los Angeles at a cost equivalent to the charge per car load. But firewood had no legs, and the railroad charged just precisely twenty-four dollars a carload.

This was a fine adjustment, for by working hammer-and- tongs through a twelve-hour day, after freight had been deducted from the selling price of the wood in Los Angeles, the wood-chopper received one dollar and sixty cents. Jones had thought to get ahead of the game by turning his wood into charcoa. His estimates were satisfactory. But the railroad also made estimates. It issued a rate of forty-two dollars a car on charcoal. At the end of three months, Jones went over his figures, and found that he was still making one dollar and sixty cents a day.

"So I quit," Jones concluded. "I went hobbling for a year, and I got back at the railroads. Leaving out the little things, I came across the Sierras in the summer and touched a match to the snow-sheds. They only had a little thirty- thousand-dollar fire. I guess that squared up all balances due on Petacha."

"Son, ain't you afraid to be turning loose such information?" Daylight gravely demanded.

"Not on your life," quoth Jones. "They can't prove it. You could say I said so, and I could say I didn't say so, and a hell of a lot that evidence would amount to with a jury."

Daylight went into his office and meditated awhile. That was it: *All the traffic would bear.* From top to bottom, that was the rule of the game; and what kept the game going was the fact that a sucker was born every minute. If a Jones were born every minute, the game wouldn't last very long. Lucky for the players that the workers weren't Joneses.

But there were other and larger phases of the game. Little business men, shopkeepers, and such ilk took what whack they could out of the product of the worker; but, after all, it was the large business men who formed the workers through the little business men. When all was said and done, the latter, like Jones in Petacha Valley, got no more than wages out of their whack. In truth, they were hired men for the large business men. Still again, higher up, were the big fellows. They used vast and complicated paraphernalia for the purpose, on a large scale of getting between hundreds of thousands of workers and their products. These men were not so much mere robbers as gamblers. And, not content with their direct winnings, being essentially gamblers, they raided one another. They called this feature of the game *high finance.* They were all engaged primarily in robbing the worker, but every little while they formed combinations and robbed one another of the accumulated loot. This explained the fifty-thousand-dollar raid on him by Holdsworthy and the ten-million-dollar raid on him by Dowsett, Letton, and Guggenhammer. And when he raided Panama Mail he had done exactly the same thing. Well, he concluded, it was finer sport robbing the robbers than robbing the poor stupid workers.

Thus, all unread in philosophy, Daylight preempted for himself the position and vocation of a twentieth-century superman. He found, with rare and mythical exceptions, that there was *no noblesse oblige* among the business and financial supermen. As a clever traveler had announced in an after-dinner speech at the Alta-Pacific, "There was honor amongst thieves, and this was what distinguished thieves from honest men." That was it. It hit the nail on the head. These modern supermen were a lot of sordid banditti who had the successful effrontery to preach a code of right and wrong to their victims which they themselves did not practise. With them, a man's word was good just as long as he was compelled to keep it. *Thou shalt not steal* was only applicable to the honest worker. They, the supermen, were above such commandments. They certainly stole and were honored by their fellows according to the magnitude of their stealings.

The more Daylight played the game, the clearer the situation grew. Despite the fact that every robber was keen to rob every other robber, the band was well organized. It practically controlled the political machinery of society, from the ward politician up to the Senate of the United States. It passed laws that gave it privilege to rob. It enforced these laws by means of

88

the police, the marshals, the militia and regular army, and the courts. And it was a snap. A superman's chiefest danger was his fellow-superman. The great stupid mass of the people did not count. They were constituted of such inferior clay that the veriest chicanery fooled them. The superman manipulated the strings, and when robbery of the workers became too slow or monotonous, they turned loose and robbed one another.

Daylight was philosophical, but not a philosopher. He had never read the books. He was a hard-headed, practical man, and farthest from him was any intention of ever reading the books. He had lived life in the simple, where books were not necessary for an understanding of life, and now life in the complex appeared just as simple. He saw through its frauds and fictions, and found it as elemental as on the Yukon. Men were made of the same stuff. They had the same passions and desires. Finance was poker on a larger scale. The men who played were the men who had stakes. The workers were the fellows toiling for grubstakes. He saw the game played out according to the everlasting rules, and he played a hand himself. The gigantic futility of humanity organized and befuddled by the bandits did not shock him. It was the natural order. Practically all human endeavors were futile. He had seen so much of it. His partners had starved and died on the Stewart. Hundreds of old-timers had failed to locate on Bonanza and Eldorado, while Swedes and chechaquos had come in on the moose-pasture and blindly staked millions. It was life, and life was a savage proposition at best. Men in civilization robbed because they were so made. They robbed just as cats scratched, famine pinched, and frost bit.

So it was that Daylight became a successful financier. He did not go in for swindling the workers. Not only did he not have the heart for it, but it did not strike him as a sporting proposition. The workers were so easy, so stupid. It was more like slaughtering fat hand-reared pheasants on the English preserves he had heard about. The sport to him, was in waylaying the successful robbers and taking their spoils from them. There was fun and excitement in that, and sometimes they put up the very devil of a fight. Like Robin Hood of old, Daylight proceeded to rob the rich; and, in a small way, to distribute to the needy. But he was charitable after his own fashion. The great mass of human misery meant nothing to him. That was part of the everlasting order. He had no patience with the organized charities and the professional charity mongers. Nor, on the other hand, was what he gave a conscience dole. He owed no man, and restitution was unthinkable. What he gave was a largess, a free, spontaneous gift; and it was for those about him. He never contributed to an earthquake fund in Japan nor to an open-air fund in New York City. Instead, he financed Jones, the elevator boy, for a year that he might write a book. When he learned that the wife of his waiter at the St. Francis was suffering from tuberculosis, he sent her to Arizona, and later, when her case was declared hopeless, he sent the husband, too, to be with her to the end. Likewise, he bought a string of horse-hair bridles from a convict in a Western penitentiary, who spread the good news until it seemed to Daylight that half the convicts in that institution were making bridles for him. He bought them all, paying from twenty to fifty dollars each for them. They were beautiful and honest things, and he decorated all the available wall-space of his bedroom with them.

The grim Yukon life had failed to make Daylight hard. It required civilization to produce this result. In the fierce, savage game he now played, his habitual geniality imperceptibly slipped away from him, as did his lazy Western drawl. As his speech became sharp and nervous, so did his mental processes. In the swift rush of the game he found less and less time to spend on being merely good-natured. The change marked his face itself.

The lines grew sterner. Less often appeared the playful curl of his lips, the smile in the wrinkling corners of his eyes. The eyes themselves, black and flashing, like an Indian's, betrayed glints of cruelty and brutal consciousness of power. His tremendous vitality remained, and radiated from all his being, but it was vitality under the new aspect of the man-trampling man-conqueror. His battles with elemental nature had been, in a way, impersonal; his present battles were wholly with the males of his species, and the hardships of the trail, the river, and the frost marred him far less than the bitter keenness of the struggle with his fellows.

He still had recrudescence of geniality, but they were largely periodical and forced, and they were usually due to the cocktails he took prior to meal-time. In the North, he had drunk deeply and at irregular intervals; but now his drinking became systematic and disciplined. It was an unconscious development, but it was based upon physical and mental condition. The cocktails served as an inhibition. Without reasoning or thinking about it, the strain of the office, which was essentially due to the daring and audacity of his ventures, required check or cessation; and he found, through the weeks and months, that the cocktails supplied this very thing. They constituted a stone wall. He never drank during the morning, nor in office hours; but the instant he left the office he proceeded to rear this wall of alcoholic inhibition athwart his consciousness. The office became immediately a closed affair. It ceased to exist. In the afternoon, after lunch, it lived again for one or two hours, when, leaving it, he rebuilt the wall of inhibition. Of course, there were exceptions to this; and, such was the rigor of his discipline, that if he had a dinner or a conference before him in which, in a business way, he encountered enemies or allies and planned or prosecuted campaigns, he abstained from drinking. But the instant the business was settled, his everlasting call went out for a Martini, and for a double-Martini at that, served in a long glass so as not to excite comment.

CHAPTER 6

Into Daylight's life came Dede Mason. She came rather imperceptibly. He had accepted her impersonally along with the office furnishing, the office boy, Morrison, the chief, confidential, and only clerk, and all the rest of the accessories of a superman's gambling place of business. Had he been asked any time during the first months she was in his employ, he would have been unable to tell the color of her eyes. From the fact that she was a demiblonde, there resided dimly in his subconsciousness a conception that she was a brunette. Likewise he had an idea that she was not thin, while there was an absence in his mind of any idea that she was fat. As to how she dressed, he had no ideas at all. He had no trained eye in such matters, nor was he interested. He took it for granted, in the lack of any impression to the contrary, that she was dressed some how. He knew her as "Miss Mason," and that was all, though he was aware that as a stenographer she seemed quick and accurate. This impression, however, was quite vague, for he had had no experience with other stenographers, and naturally believed that they were all quick and accurate.

One morning, signing up letters, he came upon an *I shall*. Glancing quickly over the page for similar constructions, he found a number of I *wills*. The I *shall* was alone. It stood out conspicuously. He pressed the call-bell twice, and a moment later Dede Mason entered.

"Did I say that, Miss Mason?" he asked, extending the letter to her and pointing out the criminal phrase.

A shade of annoyance crossed her face. She stood convicted.

"My mistake," she said. "I am sorry. But it's not a mistake, you know," she added quickly.

"How do you make that out?" challenged Daylight. "It sure don't sound right, in my way of thinking."

She had reached the door by this time, and now turned the offending letter in her hand.

"It's right just the same."

"But that would make all those I wills wrong, then," he argued.

"It does," was her audacious answer. "Shall I change them?"

"I shall be over to look that affair up on Monday." Daylight repeated the sentence from the letter aloud. He did it with a grave, serious air, listening intently to the sound of his own voice. He shook his head. "It don't sound right, Miss Mason. It just don't sound right. Why, nobody writes to me that way. They all say I *will*--educated men, too, some of them. Ain't that so?"

"Yes," she acknowledged, and passed out to her machine to make the correction.

It chanced that day that among the several men with whom he sat at luncheon was a young Englishman, a mining engineer. Had it happened any other time it would have passed unnoticed, but, fresh from the tilt with his stenographer, Daylight was struck immediately by the Englishman's *I shall*. Several times, in the course of the meal, the phrase was repeated, and Daylight was certain there was no mistake about it.

After luncheon he cornered Macintosh, one of the members whom he knew to have been a college man, because of his football reputation.

"Look here, Bunny," Daylight demanded, "which is right, *I shall be over to look that affair up on Monday*, or *I will be over to look that affair up on Monday?*"

The ex-football captain debated painfully for a minute.

"Blessed if I know," he confessed. "Which way do I say it?

"Oh, I *will*, of course."

"Then the other is right, depend upon it. I always was rotten on grammar."

On the way back to the office, Daylight dropped into a bookstore and bought a grammar; and for a solid hour, his feet up on the desk, he toiled through its pages.

"Knock off my head with little apples if the girl ain't right," he communed aloud at the end of the session. For the first time it struck him that there was something about his stenographer. He had accepted her up to then, as a female creature and a bit of office furnishing. But now, having demonstrated that she knew more grammar than did business men and college graduates, she became an individual. She seemed to stand out in his consciousness as conspicuously as the *I shall* had stood out on the typed page, and he began to take notice.

He managed to watch her leaving that afternoon, and he was aware for the first time that she was well-formed, and that her manner of dress was satisfying. He knew none of the details of women's dress, and he saw none of the details of her neat shirt-waist and well-cut tailor suit. He saw only the effect in a general, sketchy way. She looked *right*. This was in the absence of anything wrong or out of the way.

"She's a trim little good-looker," was his verdict, when the outer office door closed on her.

The next morning, dictating, he concluded that he liked the way she did her hair, though for the life of him he could have given no description of it. The impression was pleasing, that was all. She sat between him and the window, and he noted that her hair was light brown, with hints of golden bronze. A pale sun, shining in, touched the golden bronze into smouldering fires that were very pleasing to behold. Funny, he thought, that he had never observed this phenomenon before.

In the midst of the letter he came to the construction which had caused the trouble the day before. He remembered his wrestle with the grammar, and dictated: --

"I shall meet you halfway this proposition--"

Miss Mason gave a quick look up at him. The action was purely involuntary, and, in fact, had been half a startle of surprise. The next instant her eyes had dropped again, and she sat waiting to go on with the dictation. But in that moment of her glance Daylight had noted that her eyes were gray. He was later to learn that at times there were golden lights in those same gray eyes; but he had seen enough, as it was, to surprise him, for he became suddenly aware that he had always taken her for a brunette with brown eyes, as a matter of course.

"You were right, after all," he confessed, with a sheepish grin that sat incongruously on his stern, Indian-like features.

Again he was rewarded by an upward glance and an acknowledging smile, and this time he verified the fact that her eyes were gray.

"But it don't sound right, just the same," he complained.

At this she laughed outright.

"I beg your pardon," she hastened to make amends, and then spoiled it by adding, "but you are so funny."

Daylight began to feel a slight awkwardness, and the sun would persist in setting her hair a-smouldering.

"I didn't mean to be funny," he said.

"That was why I laughed. But it *is* right, and perfectly good grammar."

"All right," he sighed--"*I shall meet you halfway in this proposition*--got that?"

And the dictation went on.

92

He discovered that in the intervals, when she had nothing to do, she read books and magazines, or worked on some sort of feminine fancy work.

Passing her desk, once, he picked up a volume of Kipling's poems and glanced bepuzzled through the pages.

"You like reading, Miss Mason?" he said, laying the book down.

"Oh, yes," was her answer; "very much."

Another time it was a book of Wells', *The Wheels of Change.*

"What's it all about?" Daylight asked.

"Oh, it's just a novel, a love-story.

" She stopped, but he still stood waiting, and she felt it incumbent to go on.

"It's about a little Cockney draper's assistant, who takes a vacation on his bicycle, and falls in with a young girl very much above him. Her mother is a popular writer and all that. And the situation is very curious, and sad, too, and tragic. Would you care to read it?"

"Does he get her?" Daylight demanded.

"No; that's the point of it. He wasn't--"

"And he doesn't get her, and you've read all them pages, hundreds of them, to find that out?" Daylight muttered in amazement.

Miss Mason was nettled as well as amused.

"But you read the mining and financial news by the hour," she retorted.

"But I sure get something out of that. It's business, and it's different. I get money out of it. What do you get out of books?"

"Points of view, new ideas, life."

"Not worth a cent cash."

"But life's worth more than cash," she argued.

"Oh, well," he said, with easy masculine tolerance, "so long as you enjoy it. That's what counts, I suppose; and there's no accounting for taste."

Despite his own superior point of view, he had an idea that she knew a lot, and he experienced a fleeting feeling like that of a barbarian face to face with the evidence of some tremendous culture. To Daylight culture was a worthless thing, and yet, somehow, he was vaguely troubled by a sense that there was more in culture than he imagined.

Again, on her desk, in passing, he noticed a book with which he was familiar. This time he did not stop, for he had recognized the cover. It was a magazine correspondent's book on the Klondike, and he knew that he and his photograph figured in it and he knew, also, of a certain sensational chapter concerned with a woman's suicide, and with one "Too much Daylight."

After that he did not talk with her again about books. He imagined what erroneous conclusions she had drawn from that particular chapter, and it stung him the more in that they were undeserved. Of all unlikely things, to have the reputation of being a lady-killer,--he, Burning Daylight,--and to have a woman kill herself out of love for him. He felt that he was a most unfortunate man and wondered by what luck that one book of all the thousands of books should have fallen into his stenographer's hands. For some days afterward he had an uncomfortable sensation of guiltiness whenever he was in Miss Mason's presence; and once he was positive that he caught her looking at him with a curious, intent gaze, as if studying what manner of man he was.

He pumped Morrison, the clerk, who had first to vent his personal grievance against Miss Mason before he could tell what little he knew of her.

"She comes from Siskiyou County. She's very nice to work with in the office, of course, but she's rather stuck on herself-- exclusive, you know."

"How do you make that out?" Daylight queried.

"Well, she thinks too much of herself to associate with those she works with, in the office here, for instance. She won't have anything to do with a fellow, you see. I've asked her out repeatedly, to the theatre and the chutes and such things. But nothing doing. Says she likes plenty of sleep, and can't stay up late, and has to go all the way to Berkeley--that's where she lives."

This phase of the report gave Daylight a distinct satisfaction. She was a bit above the ordinary, and no doubt about it. But Morrison's next words carried a hurt.

"But that's all hot air. She's running with the University boys, that's what she's doing. She needs lots of sleep and can't go to the theatre with me, but she can dance all hours with them. I've heard it pretty straight that she goes to all their hops and such things. Rather stylish and high-toned for a stenographer, I'd say. And she keeps a horse, too. She rides astride all over those hills out there. I saw her one Sunday myself. Oh, she's a high-flyer, and I wonder how she does it. Sixty-five a month don't go far. Then she has a sick brother, too."

"Live with her people?" Daylight asked.

"No; hasn't got any. They were well to do, I've heard. They must have been, or that brother of hers couldn't have gone to the University of California. Her father had a big cattle-ranch, but he got to fooling with mines or something, and went broke before he died. Her mother died long before that. Her brother must cost a lot of money. He was a husky once, played football, was great on hunting and being out in the mountains and such things. He got his accident breaking horses, and then rheumatism or something got into him. One leg is shorter than the other and withered up some. He has to walk on crutches. I saw her out with him once--crossing the ferry. The doctors have been experimenting on him for years, and he's in the French Hospital now, I think."

All of which side-lights on Miss Mason went to increase Daylight's interest in her. Yet, much as he desired, he failed to get acquainted with her. He had thoughts of asking her to luncheon, but his was the innate chivalry of the frontiersman, and the thoughts never came to anything. He knew a self-respecting, square-dealing man was not supposed to take his stenographer to luncheon. Such things did happen, he knew, for he heard the chaffing gossip of the club; but he did not think much of such men and felt sorry for the girls. He had a strange notion that a man had less rights over those he employed than over mere acquaintances or strangers. Thus, had Miss Mason not been his employee, he was confident that he would have had her to luncheon or the theatre in no time. But he felt that it was an imposition for an employer, because he bought the time of an employee in working hours, to presume in any way upon any of the rest of that employee's time. To do so was to act like a bully. The situation was unfair. It was taking advantage of the fact that the employee was dependent on one for a livelihood. The employee might permit the imposition through fear of angering the employer and not through any personal inclination at all.

In his own case he felt that such an imposition would be peculiarly obnoxious, for had she not read that cursed Klondike correspondent's book? A pretty idea she must have of him, a girl that was too high-toned to have anything to do with a good-looking, gentlemanly fellow like Morrison. Also, and down under all his other reasons, Daylight was timid. The only thing he had ever been afraid of in his life was woman, and he had been afraid all his life. Nor was that timidity to be put easily to flight now that he felt the first glimmering need and desire for woman. The specter of the apron-string

94

still haunted him, and helped him to find excuses for getting on no forwarder with Dede Mason.

CHAPTER 7

Not being favored by chance in getting acquainted with Dede Mason, Daylight's interest in her slowly waned. This was but natural, for he was plunged deep in hazardous operations, and the fascinations of the game and the magnitude of it accounted for all the energy that even his magnificent organism could generate. Such was his absorption that the pretty stenographer slowly and imperceptibly faded from the forefront of his consciousness. Thus, the first faint spur, in the best sense, of his need for woman ceased to prod. So far as Dede Mason was concerned, he possessed no more than a complacent feeling of satisfaction in that he had a very nice stenographer.

And, completely to put the quietus on any last lingering hopes he might have had of her, he was in the thick of his spectacular and intensely bitter fight with the Coastwise Steam Navigation Company, and the Hawaiian, Nicaraguan, and Pacific-Mexican Steamship-Company. He stirred up a bigger muss than he had anticipated, and even he was astounded at the wide ramifications of the struggle and at the unexpected and incongruous interests that were drawn into it. Every newspaper in San Francisco turned upon him. It was true, one or two of them had first intimated that they were open to subsidization, but Daylight's judgment was that the situation did not warrant such expenditure. Up to this time the press had been amusingly tolerant and good-naturedly sensational about him, but now he was to learn what virulent scrupulousness an antagonized press was capable of. Every episode of his life was resurrected to serve as foundations for malicious fabrications. Daylight was frankly amazed at the new interpretation put upon all he had accomplished and the deeds he had done. From an Alaskan hero he was metamorphosed into an Alaskan bully, liar, desperado, and all around "bad Man." Not content with this, lies upon lies, out of whole cloth, were manufactured about him. He never replied, though once he went to the extent of disburdening his mind to half a dozen reporters.

"Do your damnedest," he told them. "Burning Daylight's bucked bigger things than your dirty, lying sheets. And I don't blame you, boys... that is, not much. You can't help it. You've got to live. There's a mighty lot of women in this world that make their living in similar fashion to yours, because they're not able to do anything better. Somebody's got to do the dirty work, and it might as well be you. You're paid for it, and you ain't got the backbone to rustle cleaner jobs."

The socialist press of the city jubilantly exploited this utterance, scattering it broadcast over San Francisco in tens of thousands of paper dodgers. And the journalists, stung to the quick, retaliated with the only means in their power-printer's ink abuse. The attack became bitterer than ever. The whole affair sank to the deeper deeps of rancor and savageness. The poor woman who had killed herself was dragged out of her grave and paraded on thousands of reams of paper as a martyr and a victim to Daylight's ferocious brutality. Staid, statistical articles were published, proving that he had made his start by robbing poor miners of their claims, and that the capstone to his fortune had been put in place by his treacherous violation of faith with the Guggenhammers in the deal on Ophir. And there were editorials written in which he was called an enemy of society, possessed of the manners and culture of a caveman, a fomenter of wasteful business troubles, the destroyer of the city's prosperity in commerce and trade, an anarchist of dire menace; and one editorial gravely recommended that hanging would be a lesson to him and his ilk, and concluded with the fervent hope that some day his big motor-car would smash up and smash him with it.

He was like a big bear raiding a bee-hive and, regardless of the stings, he obstinately persisted in pawing for the honey. He gritted his teeth and struck back. Beginning with a raid on two steamship companies, it developed into a pitched battle with a city, a state, and a continental coastline. Very well; they wanted fight, and they would get it. It was what he wanted, and he felt justified in having come down from the Klondike, for here he was gambling at a bigger table than ever the Yukon had supplied. Allied with him, on a splendid salary, with princely pickings thrown in, was a lawyer, Larry Hegan, a young Irishman with a reputation to make, and whose peculiar genius had been unrecognized until Daylight picked up with him. Hegan had Celtic imagination and daring, and to such degree that Daylight's cooler head was necessary as a check on his wilder visions. Hegan's was a Napoleonic legal mind, without balance, and it was just this balance that Daylight supplied. Alone, the Irishman was doomed to failure, but directed by Daylight, he was on the highroad to fortune and recognition. Also, he was possessed of no more personal or civic conscience than Napoleon.

It was Hegan who guided Daylight through the intricacies of modern politics, labor organization, and commercial and corporation law. It was Hegan, prolific of resource and suggestion, who opened Daylight's eyes to undreamed possibilities in twentieth-century warfare; and it was Daylight, rejecting, accepting, and elaborating, who planned the campaigns and prosecuted them. With the Pacific coast from Peugeot Sound to Panama, buzzing and humming, and with San Francisco furiously about his ears, the two big steamship companies had all the appearance of winning. It looked as if Burning Daylight was being beaten slowly to his knees. And then he struck--at the steamship companies, at San Francisco, at the whole Pacific coast.

It was not much of a blow at first. A Christian Endeavor convention being held in San Francisco, a row was started by Express Drivers' Union No. 927 over the handling of a small heap of baggage at the Ferry Building. A few heads were broken, a score of arrests made, and the baggage was delivered. No one would have guessed that behind this petty wrangle was the fine Irish hand of Hegan, made potent by the Klondike gold of Burning Daylight. It was an insignificant affair at best--or so it seemed. But the Teamsters' Union took up the quarrel, backed by the whole Water Front Federation. Step by step, the strike became involved. A refusal of cooks and waiters to serve scab teamsters or teamsters' employers brought out the cooks and waiters. The butchers and meat-cutters refused to handle meat destined for unfair restaurants. The combined Employers' Associations put up a solid front, and found facing them the 40,000 organized laborers of San Francisco. The restaurant bakers and the bakery wagon drivers struck, followed by the milkers, milk drivers, and chicken pickers. The building trades asserted its position in unambiguous terms, and all San Francisco was in turmoil.

But still, it was only San Francisco. Hegan's intrigues were masterly, and Daylight's campaign steadily developed. The powerful fighting organization known as the Pacific Slope Seaman's Union refused to work vessels the cargoes of which were to be handled by scab longshoremen and freight-handlers. The union presented its ultimatum, and then called a strike. This had been Daylight's objective all the time. Every incoming coastwise vessel was boarded by the union officials and its crew sent ashore. And with the Seamen went the firemen, the engineers, and the sea

97

cooks and waiters. Daily the number of idle steamers increased. It was impossible to get scab crews, for the men of the Seaman's Union were fighters trained in the hard school of the sea, and when they went out it meant blood and death to scabs. This phase of the strike spread up and down the entire Pacific coast, until all the ports were filled with idle ships, and sea transportation was at a standstill. The days and weeks dragged out, and the strike held. The Coastwise Steam Navigation Company, and the Hawaiian, Nicaraguan, and Pacific-Mexican Steamship Company were tied up completely. The expenses of combating the strike were tremendous, and they were earning nothing, while daily the situation went from bad to worse, until "peace at any price" became the cry. And still there was no peace, until Daylight and his allies played out their hand, raked in the winnings, and allowed a goodly portion of a continent to resume business.

It was noted, in following years, that several leaders of workmen built themselves houses and blocks of renting flats and took trips to the old countries, while, more immediately, other leaders and "dark horses" came to political preferment and the control of the municipal government and the municipal moneys. In fact, San Francisco's boss-ridden condition was due in greater degree to Daylight's widespreading battle than even San Francisco ever dreamed. For the part he had played, the details of which were practically all rumor and guesswork, quickly leaked out, and in consequence he became a much-execrated and well-hated man. Nor had Daylight himself dreamed that his raid on the steamship companies would have grown to such colossal proportions.

But he had got what he was after. He had played an exciting hand and won, beating the steamship companies down into the dust and mercilessly robbing the stockholders by perfectly legal methods before he let go. Of course, in addition to the large sums of money he had paid over, his allies had rewarded themselves by gobbling the advantages which later enabled them to loot the city. His alliance with a gang of cutthroats had brought about a lot of cutthroating. But his conscience suffered no twinges. He remembered what he had once heard an old preacher utter, namely, that they who rose by the sword perished by the sword. One took his chances when he played with cutting throats, and his, Daylight's, throat was still intact. That was it! And he had won. It was all gamble and war between the strong men. The fools did not count. They were always getting hurt; and that they always had been getting hurt was the conclusion he drew from what little he knew of history. San Francisco had wanted war, and he had given it war. It was the game. All the big fellows did the same, and they did much worse, too.

"Don't talk to me about morality and civic duty," he replied to a persistent interviewer. "If you quit your job tomorrow and went to work on another paper, you would write just what you were told to write. It's morality and civic duty now with you; on the new job it would be backing up a thieving railroad with... morality and civic duty, I suppose. Your price, my son, is just about thirty per week. That's what you sell for. But your paper would sell for a bit more. Pay its price to-day, and it would shift its present rotten policy to some other rotten policy; but it would never let up on morality and civic duty.

"And all because a sucker is born every minute. So long as the people stand for it, they'll get it good and plenty, my son. And the shareholders and business interests might as well shut up squawking about how much they've been hurt. You never hear ary squeal out of them when they've got the other fellow down and are gouging him. This is the time *they* got gouged, and that's all there is to it. Talk about mollycoddles! Son, those same fellows would steal crusts from starving men and pull gold fillings from the mouths of corpses, yep, and squawk like Sam Scratch if some blamed corpse hit back. They're all tarred with the same brush, little and big. Look at your Sugar Trust--with all its millions stealing water like a common thief from New York City, and short-weighing the government on its foney scales. Morality and civic duty! Son, forget it."

CHAPTER 8

Daylight's coming to civilization had not improved him. True, he wore better clothes, had learned slightly better manners, and spoke better English. As a gambler and a man-trampler he had developed remarkable efficiency. Also, he had become used to a higher standard of living, and he had whetted his wits to razor sharpness in the fierce, complicated struggle of fighting males. But he had hardened, and at the expense of his old-time, whole-souled geniality. Of the essential refinements of civilization he knew nothing. He did not know they existed. He had become cynical, bitter, and brutal. Power had its effect on him that it had on all men. Suspicious of the big exploiters, despising the fools of the exploited herd, he had faith only in himself. This led to an undue and erroneous exaltation of his ego, while kindly consideration of others--nay, even simple respect--was destroyed, until naught was left for him but to worship at the shrine of self.

Physically, he was not the man of iron muscles who had come down out of the Arctic. He did not exercise sufficiently, ate more than was good for him, and drank altogether too much. His muscles were getting flabby, and his tailor called attention to his increasing waistband. In fact, Daylight was developing a definite paunch. This physical deterioration was manifest likewise in his face. The lean Indian visage was suffering a city change. The slight hollows in the cheeks under the high cheek-bones had filled out. The beginning of puff-sacks under the eyes was faintly visible. The girth of the neck had increased, and the first crease and fold of a double chin were becoming plainly discernible. The old effect of asceticism, bred of terrific hardships and toil, had vanished; the features had become broader and heavier, betraying all the stigmata of the life he lived, advertising the man's self-indulgence, harshness, and brutality.

Even his human affiliations were descending. Playing a lone hand, contemptuous of most of the men with whom he played, lacking in sympathy or understanding of them, and certainly independent of them, he found little in common with those to be encountered, say at the Alta-Pacific. In point of fact, when the battle with the steamship companies was at its height and his raid was inflicting incalculable damage on all business interests, he had been asked to resign from the Alta-Pacific. The idea had been rather to his liking, and he had found new quarters in clubs like the Riverside, organized and practically maintained by the city bosses. He found that he really liked such men better. They were more primitive and simple, and they did not put on airs. They were honest buccaneers, frankly in the game for what they could get out of it, on the surface more raw and savage, but at least not glossed over with oily or graceful hypocrisy. The Alta-Pacific had suggested that his resignation be kept a private matter, and then had privily informed the newspapers. The latter had made great capital out of the forced resignation, but Daylight had grinned and silently gone his way, though registering a black mark against more than one club member who was destined to feel, in the days to come, the crushing weight of the Klondiker's financial paw.

The storm-centre of a combined newspaper attack lasting for months, Daylight's character had been torn to shreds. There was no fact in his history that had not been distorted into a criminality or a vice. This public making of him over into an iniquitous monster had pretty well crushed any lingering hope he had of getting acquainted with Dede Mason. He felt that there was no chance for her ever to look kindly on a man of his caliber, and, beyond increasing her salary to seventy-five dollars a month, he proceeded

100

gradually to forget about her. The increase was made known to her through Morrison, and later she thanked Daylight, and that was the end of it.

One week-end, feeling heavy and depressed and tired of the city and its ways, he obeyed the impulse of a whim that was later to play an important part in his life. The desire to get out of the city for a whiff of country air and for a change of scene was the cause. Yet, to himself, he made the excuse of going to Glen Ellen for the purpose of inspecting the brickyard with which Holdsworthy had goldbricked him.

He spent the night in the little country hotel, and on Sunday morning, astride a saddle-horse rented from the Glen Ellen butcher, rode out of the village. The brickyard was close at hand on the flat beside the Sonoma Creek. The kilns were visible among the trees, when he glanced to the left and caught sight of a cluster of wooded knolls half a mile away, perched on the rolling slopes of Sonoma Mountain. The mountain, itself wooded, towered behind. The trees on the knolls seemed to beckon to him. The dry, early-summer air, shot through with sunshine, was wine to him. Unconsciously he drank it in deep breaths. The prospect of the brickyard was uninviting. He was jaded with all things business, and the wooded knolls were calling to him. A horse was between his legs--a good horse, he decided; one that sent him back to the cayuses he had ridden during his eastern Oregon boyhood. He had been somewhat of a rider in those early days, and the champ of bit and creak of saddle-leather sounded good to him now.

Resolving to have his fun first, and to look over the brickyard afterward, he rode on up the hill, prospecting for a way across country to get to the knolls. He left the country road at the first gate he came to and cantered through a hayfield. The grain was waist-high on either side the wagon road, and he sniffed the warm aroma of it with delighted nostrils. Larks flew up before him, and from everywhere came mellow notes. From the appearance of the road it was patent that it had been used for hauling clay to the now idle brickyard. Salving his conscience with the idea that this was part of the inspection, he rode on to the clay-pit--a huge scar in a hillside. But he did not linger long, swinging off again to the left and leaving the road. Not a farm-house was in sight, and the change from the city crowding was essentially satisfying. He rode now through open woods, across little flower-scattered glades, till he came upon a spring. Flat on the ground, he drank deeply of the clear water, and, looking about him, felt with a shock the beauty of the world. It came to him like a discovery; he had never realized it before, he concluded, and also, he had forgotten much. One could not sit in at high finance and keep track of such things. As he drank in the air, the scene, and the distant song of larks, he felt like a poker-player rising from a night-long table and coming forth from the pent atmosphere to taste the freshness of the morn.

At the base of the knolls he encountered a tumble-down stake-and-rider fence. From the look of it he judged it must be forty years old at least--the work of some first pioneer who had taken up the land when the days of gold had ended. The woods were very thick here, yet fairly clear of underbrush, so that, while the blue sky was screened by the arched branches, he was able to ride beneath. He now found himself in a nook of several acres, where the oak and manzanita and madrono gave way to clusters of stately redwoods. Against the foot of a steep-sloped knoll he came upon a magnificent group of redwoods that seemed to have gathered about a tiny gurgling spring.

He halted his horse, for beside the spring uprose a wild California lily. It was a wonderful flower, growing there in the cathedral nave of lofty trees. At least eight feet in height, its stem rose straight and slender, green and bare for two-thirds its length, and then burst into a shower of snow-white waxen bells. There were hundreds of these blossoms, all from the one stem, delicately poised and ethereally frail. Daylight had never seen anything like it. Slowly his gaze wandered from it to all that was about him. He took off his hat, with almost a vague religious feeling. This was different. No room for contempt and evil here. This was clean and fresh and beautiful --something he could respect. It was like a church. The atmosphere was one of holy calm. Here man felt the prompting of nobler things. Much of this and more was in Daylight's heart as he looked about him. But it was not a concept of his mind. He merely felt it without thinking about it at all.

On the steep incline above the spring grew tiny maidenhair ferns, while higher up were larger ferns and brakes. Great, moss-covered trunks of fallen trees lay here and there, slowly sinking back and merging into the level of the forest mould. Beyond, in a slightly clearer space, wild grape and honeysuckle swung in green riot from gnarled old oak trees. A gray Douglas squirrel crept out on a branch and watched him. From somewhere came the distant knocking of a woodpecker. This sound did not disturb the hush and awe of the place. Quiet woods, noises belonged there and made the solitude complete. The tiny bubbling ripple of the spring and the gray flash of tree-squirrel were as yardsticks with which to measure the silence and motionless repose.

"Might be a million miles from anywhere," Daylight whispered to himself.

But ever his gaze returned to the wonderful lily beside the bubbling spring.

He tethered the horse and wandered on foot among the knolls. Their tops were crowned with century-old spruce trees, and their sides clothed with oaks and madronos and native holly. But to the perfect redwoods belonged the small but deep canon that threaded its way among the knolls. Here he found no passage out for his horse, and he returned to the lily beside the spring. On foot, tripping, stumbling, leading the animal, he forced his way up the hillside. And ever the ferns carpeted the way of his feet, ever the forest climbed with him and arched overhead, and ever the clean joy and sweetness stole in upon his senses.

On the crest he came through an amazing thicket of velvet-trunked young madronos, and emerged on an open hillside that led down into a tiny valley. The sunshine was at first dazzling in its brightness, and he paused and rested, for he was panting from the exertion. Not of old had he known shortness of breath such as this, and muscles that so easily tired at a stiff climb. A tiny stream ran down the tiny valley through a tiny meadow that was carpeted knee-high with grass and blue and white nemophila. The hillside was covered with Mariposa lilies and wild hyacinth, down through which his horse dropped slowly, with circumspect feet and reluctant gait.

Crossing the stream, Daylight followed a faint cattle trail over a low, rocky hill and through a wine-wooded forest of manzanita, and emerged upon another tiny valley, down which filtered another spring-fed, meadow-bordered streamlet. A jack-rabbit bounded from a bush under his horse's nose, leaped the stream, and vanished up the opposite hillside of scrub-oak. Daylight watched it admiringly as he rode on to the head of the meadow. Here he startled up a many-pronged buck, that seemed to soar across the meadow, and to soar over the stake-and-rider fence, and, still soaring, disappeared in a friendly copse beyond.

Daylight's delight was unbounded. It seemed to him that he had never been so happy. His old woods' training was aroused, and he was keenly interested in everything in the moss on the trees and branches; in the bunches of mistletoe hanging in the oaks; in the nest of a wood-rat; in the water-cress growing in the sheltered eddies of the little stream; in the butterflies drifting through the rifted sunshine and shadow; in the blue jays that flashed in splashes of gorgeous color across the forest aisles; in the tiny birds, like wrens, that hopped among the bushes and imitated certain minor quail-calls; and in the crimson-crested woodpecker that ceased its knocking and cocked its head on one side to survey him. Crossing the stream, he struck faint vestiges of a wood-road, used, evidently, a generation back, when the meadow had been cleared of its oaks. He found a hawk's nest on the lightning-shattered tipmost top of a six-foot redwood. And to complete it all his horse stumbled upon several large broods of half-grown quail, and the air was filled with the thrum of their flight. He halted and watched the young ones "petrifying" and disappearing on the ground before his eyes, and listening to the anxious calls of the old ones hidden in the thickets.

"It sure beats country places and bungalows at Menlo Park," he communed aloud; "and if ever I get the hankering for country life, it's me for this every time."

The old wood-road led him to a clearing, where a dozen acres of grapes grew on wine-red soil. A cow-path, more trees and thickets, and he dropped down a hillside to the southeast exposure. Here, poised above a big forested canon, and looking out upon Sonoma Valley, was a small farm-house. With its barn and outhouses it snuggled into a nook in the hillside, which protected it from west and north. It was the erosion from this hillside, he judged, that had formed the little level stretch of vegetable garden. The soil was fat and black, and there was water in plenty, for he saw several faucets running wide open.

Forgotten was the brickyard. Nobody was at home, but Daylight dismounted and ranged the vegetable garden, eating strawberries and green peas, inspecting the old adobe barn and the rusty plough and harrow, and rolling and smoking cigarettes while he watched the antics of several broods of young chickens and the mother hens. A foottrail that led down the wall of the big canyon invited him, and he proceeded to follow it. A water-pipe, usually above ground, paralleled the trail, which he concluded led upstream to the bed of the creek. The wall of the canon was several hundred feet from top to bottom, and magnificent were the untouched trees that the place was plunged in perpetual shade. He measured with his eye spruces five and six feet in diameter and redwoods even larger. One such he passed, a twister that was at least ten or eleven feet through. The trail led straight to a small dam where was the intake for the pipe that watered the vegetable garden. Here, beside the stream, were alders and laurel trees, and he walked through fern-brakes higher than his head. Velvety moss was everywhere, out of which grew maiden-hair and gold-back ferns.

Save for the dam, it was a virgin wild. No ax had invaded, and the trees died only of old age and stress of winter storm. The huge trunks of those that had fallen lay moss-covered, slowly resolving back into the soil from which they sprang. Some had lain so long that they were quite gone, though their faint outlines, level with the mould, could still be seen. Others bridged the stream, and from beneath the bulk of one monster half a dozen younger trees, overthrown and crushed by the fall, growing out along the ground, still lived and prospered, their roots bathed by the stream, their upshooting branches catching the sunlight through the gap that had been made in the forest roof.

Back at the farm-house, Daylight mounted and rode on away from the ranch and into the wilder canons and steeper steeps beyond. Nothing could satisfy his holiday spirit now but the ascent of Sonoma Mountain. And here on the crest, three hours afterward, he emerged, tired and sweaty, garments torn and face and hands scratched, but with sparkling eyes and an unwonted zestfulness of expression. He felt the illicit pleasure of a schoolboy playing truant. The big gambling table of San Francisco seemed very far away. But there was more than illicit pleasure in his mood. It was as though he were going through a sort of cleansing bath. No room here for all the sordidness, meanness, and viciousness that filled the dirty pool of city existence. Without pondering in detail upon the matter at all, his sensations were of purification and uplift. Had he been asked to state how he felt, he would merely have said that he was having a good time; for he was unaware in his self-consciousness of the potent charm of nature that was percolating through his city-rotted body and brain--potent, in that he came of an abysmal past of wilderness dwellers, while he was himself coated with but the thinnest rind of crowded civilization.

There were no houses in the summit of Sonoma Mountain, and, all alone under the azure California sky, he reined in on the southern edge of the peak. He saw open pasture country, intersected with wooded canons, descending to the south and west from his feet, crease on crease and roll on roll, from lower level to lower level, to the floor of Petaluma Valley, flat as a billiard-table, a cardboard affair, all patches and squares of geometrical regularity where the fat freeholds were farmed. Beyond, to the west, rose range on range of mountains cuddling purple mists of atmosphere in their valleys; and still beyond, over the last range of all, he saw the silver sheen of the Pacific. Swinging his horse, he surveyed the west and north, from Santa Rosa to St. Helena, and on to the east, across Sonoma to the chaparral-covered range that shut off the view of Napa Valley. Here, part way up the eastern wall of Sonoma Valley, in range of a line intersecting the little village of Glen Ellen, he made out a scar upon a hillside. His first thought was that it was the dump of a mine tunnel, but remembering that he was not in gold-bearing country, he dismissed the scar from his mind and continued the circle of his survey to the southeast, where, across the waters of San Pablo Bay, he could see, sharp and distant, the twin peaks of Mount Diablo. To the south was Mount Tamalpais, and, yes, he was right, fifty miles away, where the draughty winds of the Pacific blew in the Golden Gate, the smoke of San Francisco made a low-lying haze against the sky.

"I ain't seen so much country all at once in many a day," he thought aloud.

He was loath to depart, and it was not for an hour that he was able to tear himself away and take the descent of the mountain. Working out a new route just for the fun of it, late afternoon was upon him when he arrived back at the wooded knolls. Here, on the top of one of them, his keen eyes caught a glimpse of a shade of green sharply differentiated from any he had seen all day. Studying it for a minute, he concluded that it was composed of three cypress trees, and he knew that nothing else than the hand of man could have planted them there. Impelled by curiosity purely boyish, he made up his mind to investigate. So densely wooded was the knoll, and so steep, that he had to dismount and go up on foot, at times even on hands and knees struggling hard to force a way through the thicker underbrush. He came out abruptly upon the cypresses. They were enclosed in a small square of ancient fence; the pickets he could plainly see had been hewn and sharpened by hand. Inside were the mounds of two children's graves.

104

Two wooden headboards, likewise hand-hewn, told the story: *Little David, born 1855, died 1859; and Little Lily, born 1853, died 1860.*

"The poor little kids," Daylight muttered.

The graves showed signs of recent care. Withered bouquets of wild flowers were on the mounds, and the lettering on the headboards was freshly painted. Guided by these clews, Daylight cast about for a trail, and found one leading down the side opposite to his ascent. Circling the base of the knoll, he picked up with his horse and rode on to the farm-house. Smoke was rising from the chimney and he was quickly in conversation with a nervous, slender young man, who, he learned, was only a tenant on the ranch. How large was it? A matter of one hundred and eighty acres, though it seemed much larger. This was because it was so irregularly shaped. Yes, it included the clay-pit and all the knolls, and its boundary that ran along the big canon was over a mile long.

"You see," the young man said, "it was so rough and broken that when they began to farm this country the farmers bought in the good land to the edge of it. That's why its boundaries are all gouged and jagged."

"Oh, yes, he and his wife managed to scratch a living without working too hard. They didn't have to pay much rent. Hillard, the owner, depended on the income from the clay-pit. Hillard was well off, and had big ranches and vineyards down on the flat of the valley. The brickyard paid ten cents a cubic yard for the clay. As for the rest of the ranch, the land was good in patches, where it was cleared, like the vegetable garden and the vineyard, but the rest of it was too much up-and-down.

"You're not a farmer," Daylight said.

The young man laughed and shook his head.

"No; I'm a telegraph operator. But the wife and I decided to take a two years' vacation, and... here we are But the time's about up. I'm going back into the office this fall after I get the grapes off."

Yes, there were about eleven acres in the vineyard--wine grapes. The price was usually good. He grew most of what they ate. If he owned the place, he'd clear a patch of land on the side-hill above the vineyard and plant a small home orchard. The soil was good. There was plenty of pasturage all over the ranch, and there were several cleared patches, amounting to about fifteen acres in all, where he grew as much mountain hay as could be found. It sold for three to five dollars more a ton than the rank-stalked valley hay.

As Daylight listened, there came to him a sudden envy of this young fellow living right in the midst of all this which Daylight had travelled through the last few hours.

"What in thunder are you going back to the telegraph office for?" he demanded.

The young man smiled with a certain wistfulness.

"Because we can't get ahead here..." (he hesitated an instant), "and because there are added expenses coming. The rent, small as it is, counts; and besides, I'm not strong enough to effectually farm the place. If I owned it, or if I were a real husky like you, I'd ask nothing better. Nor would the wife." Again the wistful smile hovered on his face. "You see, we're country born, and after bucking with cities for a few years, we kind of feel we like the country best. We've planned to get ahead, though, and then some day we'll buy a patch of land and stay with it."

The graves of the children? Yes, he had relettered them and hoed the weeds out. It had become the custom. Whoever lived on the ranch did that. For years, the story ran, the father and mother had returned each summer to the graves. But there had come a time when they came no more, and

105

then old Hillard started the custom. The scar across the valley? An old mine. It had never paid. The men had worked on it, off and on, for years, for the indications had been good. But that was years and years ago. No paying mine had ever been struck in the valley, though there had been no end of prospect-holes put down and there had been a sort of rush there thirty years back.

A frail-looking young woman came to the door to call the young man to supper. Daylight's first thought was that city living had not agreed with her. And then he noted the slight tan and healthy glow that seemed added to her face, and he decided that the country was the place for her. Declining an invitation to supper, he rode on for Glen Ellen sitting slack-kneed in the saddle and softly humming forgotten songs. He dropped down the rough, winding road through covered pasture, with here and there thickets of manzanita and vistas of open glades. He listened greedily to the quail calling, and laughed outright, once, in sheer joy, at a tiny chipmunk that fled scolding up a bank, slipping on the crumbly surface and falling down, then dashing across the road under his horse's nose and, still scolding, scrabbling up a protecting oak.

Daylight could not persuade himself to keep to the travelled roads that day, and another cut across country to Glen Ellen brought him upon a canon that so blocked his way that he was glad to follow a friendly cow-path. This led him to a small frame cabin. The doors and windows were open, and a cat was nursing a litter of kittens in the doorway, but no one seemed at home. He descended the trail that evidently crossed the canon. Part way down, he met an old man coming up through the sunset. In his hand he carried a pail of foamy milk. He wore no hat, and in his face, framed with snow-white hair and beard, was the ruddy glow and content of the passing summer day. Daylight thought that he had never seen so contented-looking a being.

"How old are you, daddy?" he queried.

"Eighty-four," was the reply. "Yes, sirree, eighty-four, and spryer than most."

"You must a' taken good care of yourself," Daylight suggested.

"I don't know about that. I ain't loafed none. I walked across the Plains with an ox-team and fit Injuns in '51, and I was a family man then with seven youngsters. I reckon I was as old then as you are now, or pretty nigh on to it."

"Don't you find it lonely here?"

The old man shifted the pail of milk and reflected.

"That all depends," he said oracularly. "I ain't never been lonely except when the old wife died. Some fellers are lonely in a crowd, and I'm one of them. That's the only time I'm lonely, is when I go to 'Frisco. But I don't go no more, thank you 'most to death. This is good enough for me. I've ben right here in this valley since '54--one of the first settlers after the Spaniards."

Daylight started his horse, saying: --

"Well, good night, daddy. Stick with it. You got all the young bloods skinned, and I guess you've sure buried a mighty sight of them."

The old man chuckled, and Daylight rode on, singularly at peace with himself and all the world. It seemed that the old contentment of trail and camp he had known on the Yukon had come back to him. He could not shake from his eyes the picture of the old pioneer coming up the trail through the sunset light. He was certainly going some for eighty-four. The thought of following his example entered Daylight's mind, but the big game of San Francisco vetoed the idea.

"Well, anyway," he decided, "when I get old and quit the game, I'll settle down in a place something like this, and the city can go to hell."

CHAPTER 9

Instead of returning to the city on Monday, Daylight rented the butcher's horse for another day and crossed the bed of the valley to its eastern hills to look at the mine. It was dryer and rockier here than where he had been the day before, and the ascending slopes supported mainly chaparral, scrubby and dense and impossible to penetrate on horseback. But in the canyons water was plentiful and also a luxuriant forest growth. The mine was an abandoned affair, but he enjoyed the half-hour's scramble around. He had had experience in quartz-mining before he went to Alaska, and he enjoyed the recrudescence of his old wisdom in such matters. The story was simple to him: good prospects that warranted the starting of the tunnel into the side-hill; the three months' work and the getting short of money; the lay-off while the men went away and got jobs; then the return and a new stretch of work, with the "pay" ever luring and ever receding into the mountain, until, after years of hope, the men had given up and vanished. Most likely they were dead by now, Daylight thought, as he turned in the saddle and looked back across the canyon at the ancient dump and dark mouth of the tunnel.

As on the previous day, just for the joy of it, he followed cattle-trails at haphazard and worked his way up toward the summits. Coming out on a wagon road that led upward, he followed it for several miles, emerging in a small, mountain-encircled valley, where half a dozen poor ranchers farmed the wine-grapes on the steep slopes. Beyond, the road pitched upward. Dense chaparral covered the exposed hillsides but in the creases of the canons huge spruce trees grew, and wild oats and flowers.

Half an hour later, sheltering under the summits themselves, he came out on a clearing. Here and there, in irregular patches where the steep and the soil favored, wine grapes were growing. Daylight could see that it had been a stiff struggle, and that wild nature showed fresh signs of winning--chaparral that had invaded the clearings; patches and parts of patches of vineyard, unpruned, grassgrown, and abandoned; and everywhere old stake-and-rider fences vainly striving to remain intact. Here, at a small farm-house surrounded by large outbuildings, the road ended. Beyond, the chaparral blocked the way.

He came upon an old woman forking manure in the barnyard, and reined in by the fence.

"Hello, mother," was his greeting; "ain't you got any men-folk around to do that for you?"

She leaned on her pitchfork, hitched her skirt in at the waist, and regarded him cheerfully. He saw that her toil-worn, weather-exposed hands were like a man's, callused, large-knuckled, and gnarled, and that her stockingless feet were thrust into heavy man's brogans.

"Nary a man," she answered. "And where be you from, and all the way up here? Won't you stop and hitch and have a glass of wine?"

Striding clumsily but efficiently, like a laboring-man, she led him into the largest building, where Daylight saw a hand-press and all the paraphernalia on a small scale for the making of wine. It was too far and too bad a road to haul the grapes to the valley wineries, she explained, and so they were compelled to do it themselves. "They," he learned, were she and her daughter, the latter a widow of forty-odd. It had been easier before the grandson died and before he went away to fight savages in the Philippines. He had died out there in battle.

Daylight drank a full tumbler of excellent Riesling, talked a few minutes, and accounted for a second tumbler. Yes, they just managed not to starve.

Her husband and she had taken up this government land in '57 and cleared it and farmed it ever since, until he died, when she had carried it on. It actually didn't pay for the toil, but what were they to do? There was the wine trust, and wine was down. That Riesling? She delivered it to the railroad down in the valley for twenty-two cents a gallon. And it was a long haul. It took a day for the round trip. Her daughter was gone now with a load.

Daylight knew that in the hotels, Riesling, not quite so good even, was charged for at from a dollar and a half to two dollars a quart. And she got twenty-two cents a gallon. That was the game. She was one of the stupid lowly, she and her people before her--the ones that did the work, drove their oxen across the Plains, cleared and broke the virgin land, toiled all days and all hours, paid their taxes, and sent their sons and grandsons out to fight and die for the flag that gave them such ample protection that they were able to sell their wine for twenty-two cents. The same wine was served to him at the St. Francis for two dollars a quart, or eight dollars a short gallon. That was it.

Between her and her hand-press on the mountain clearing and him ordering his wine in the hotel was a difference of seven dollars and seventy-eight cents. A clique of sleek men in the city got between her and him to just about that amount. And, besides them, there was a horde of others that took their whack. They called it railroading, high finance, banking, wholesaling, real estate, and such things, but the point was that they got it, while she got what was left,--twenty-two cents. Oh, well, a sucker was born every minute, he sighed to himself, and nobody was to blame; it was all a game, and only a few could win, but it was damned hard on the suckers.

"How old are you, mother?" he asked.

"Seventy-nine come next January."

"Worked pretty hard, I suppose?"

"Sense I was seven. I was bound out in Michigan state until I was woman-grown. Then I married, and I reckon the work got harder and harder."

"When are you going to take a rest?"

She looked at him, as though she chose to think his question facetious, and did not reply.

"Do you believe in God?"

She nodded her head.

"Then you get it all back," he assured her; but in his heart he was wondering about God, that allowed so many suckers to be born and that did not break up the gambling game by which they were robbed from the cradle to the grave.

"How much of that Riesling you got?"

She ran her eyes over the casks and calculated. "Just short of eight hundred gallons."

He wondered what he could do with all of it, and speculated as to whom he could give it away.

"What would you do if you got a dollar a gallon for it?" he asked.

"Drop dead, I suppose."

"No; speaking seriously."

"Get me some false teeth, shingle the house, and buy a new wagon. The road's mighty hard on wagons."

"And after that?"

"Buy me a coffin."

"Well, they're yours, mother, coffin and all."

109

She looked her incredulity.

"No; I mean it. And there's fifty to bind the bargain. Never mind the receipt. It's the rich ones that need watching, their memories being so infernal short, you know. Here's my address. You've got to deliver it to the railroad. And now, show me the way out of here. I want to get up to the top."

On through the chaparral he went, following faint cattle. trails and working slowly upward till he came out on the divide and gazed down into Napa Valley and back across to Sonoma Mountain.

"A sweet land," he muttered, "an almighty sweet land."

Circling around to the right and dropping down along the cattle-trails, he quested for another way back to Sonoma Valley; but the cattle-trails seemed to fade out, and the chaparral to grow thicker with a deliberate viciousness and even when he won through in places, the canon and small feeders were too precipitous for his horse, and turned him back. But there was no irritation about it. He enjoyed it all, for he was back at his old game of bucking nature. Late in the afternoon he broke through, and followed a well-defined trail down a dry canon. Here he got a fresh thrill. He had heard the baying of the hound some minutes before, and suddenly, across the bare face of the hill above him, he saw a large buck in flight. And not far behind came the deer-hound, a magnificent animal. Daylight sat tense in his saddle and watched until they disappeared, his breath just a trifle shorter, as if he, too, were in the chase, his nostrils distended, and in his bones the old hunting ache and memories of the days before he came to live in cities.

The dry canon gave place to one with a slender ribbon of running water. The trail ran into a wood-road, and the wood-road emerged across a small flat upon a slightly travelled county road. There were no farms in this immediate section, and no houses. The soil was meagre, the bed-rock either close to the surface or constituting the surface itself. Manzanita and scrub-oak, however, flourished and walled the road on either side with a jungle growth. And out a runway through this growth a man suddenly scuttled in a way that reminded Daylight of a rabbit.

He was a little man, in patched overalls; bareheaded, with a cotton shirt open at the throat and down the chest. The sun was ruddy-brown in his face, and by it his sandy hair was bleached on the ends to peroxide blond. He signed to Daylight to halt, and held up a letter.

"If you're going to town, I'd be obliged if you mail this."

"I sure will." Daylight put it into his coat pocket. "Do you live hereabouts, stranger?"

But the little man did not answer. He was gazing at Daylight in a surprised and steadfast fashion.

"I know you," the little man announced. "You're Elam Harnish--Burning Daylight, the papers call you. Am I right?"

Daylight nodded.

"But what under the sun are you doing here in the chaparral?"

Daylight grinned as he answered, "Drumming up trade for a free rural delivery route."

"Well, I'm glad I wrote that letter this afternoon," the little man went on, "or else I'd have missed seeing you. I've seen your photo in the papers many a time, and I've a good memory for faces. I recognized you at once. My name's Ferguson."

"Do you live hereabouts?" Daylight repeated his query.

"Oh, yes. I've got a little shack back here in the bush a hundred yards, and a pretty spring, and a few fruit trees and berry bushes. Come in and take a look. And that spring is a dandy. You never tasted water like it. Come in and try it."

Walking and leading his horse, Daylight followed the quick-stepping eager little man through the green tunnel and emerged abruptly upon the clearing, if clearing it might be called, where wild nature and man's earth-scratching were inextricably blended. It was a tiny nook in the hills, protected by the steep walls of a canon mouth. Here were several large oaks, evidencing a richer soil. The erosion of ages from the hillside had slowly formed this deposit of fat earth. Under the oaks, almost buried in them, stood a rough, unpainted cabin, the wide verandah of which, with chairs and hammocks, advertised an out-of doors bedchamber. Daylight's keen eyes took in every thing. The clearing was irregular, following the patches of the best soil, and every fruit tree and berry bush, and even each vegetable plant, had the water personally conducted to it. The tiny irrigation channels were every where, and along some of them the water was running.

Ferguson looked eagerly into his visitor's face for signs of approbation. "What do you think of it, eh?"

"Hand-reared and manicured, every blessed tree," Daylight laughed, but the joy and satisfaction that shone in his eyes contented the little man.

"Why, d'ye know, I know every one of those trees as if they were sons of mine. I planted them, nursed them, fed them, and brought them up. Come on and peep at the spring."

"It's sure a hummer," was Daylight's verdict, after due inspection and sampling, as they turned back for the house.

The interior was a surprise. The cooking being done in the small, lean-to kitchen, the whole cabin formed a large living room. A great table in the middle was comfortably littered with books and magazines. All the available wall space, from floor to ceiling, was occupied by filled bookshelves. It seemed to Daylight that he had never seen so many books assembled in one place. Skins of wildcat, 'coon, and deer lay about on the pine-board floor.

"Shot them myself, and tanned them, too," Ferguson proudly asserted.

The crowning feature of the room was a huge fireplace of rough stones and boulders.

"Built it myself," Ferguson proclaimed, "and, by God, she drew! Never a wisp of smoke anywhere save in the pointed channel, and that during the big southeasters."

Daylight found himself charmed and made curious by the little man. Why was he hiding away here in the chaparral, he and his books? He was nobody's fool, anybody could see that. Then why? The whole affair had a tinge of adventure, and Daylight accepted an invitation to supper, half prepared to find his host a raw-fruit-and-nut-eater or some similar sort of health faddest. At table, while eating rice and jack-rabbit curry (the latter shot by Ferguson), they talked it over, and Daylight found the little man had no food "views." He ate whatever he liked, and all he wanted, avoiding only such combinations that experience had taught him disagreed with his digestion.

Next, Daylight surmised that he might be touched with religion; but, quest about as he would, in a conversation covering the most divergent topics, he could find no hint of queerness or unusualness. So it was, when between them they had washed and wiped the dishes and put them away, and had settled down to a comfortable smoke, that Daylight put his question.

"Look here, Ferguson. Ever since we got together, I've been casting about to find out what's wrong with you, to locate a screw loose somewhere, but I'll be danged if I've succeeded. What are you doing here, anyway? What made you come here? What were you doing for a living before you came here? Go ahead and elucidate yourself."

Ferguson frankly showed his pleasure at the questions.

"First of all," he began, "the doctors wound up by losing all hope for me. Gave me a few months at best, and that, after a course in sanatoriums and a trip to Europe and another to Hawaii. They tried electricity, and forced feeding, and fasting. I was a graduate of about everything in the curriculum. They kept me poor with their bills while I went from bad to worse. The trouble with me was two fold: first, I was a born weakling; and next, I was living unnaturally--too much work, and responsibility, and strain. I was managing editor of the *Times-Tribune*--"

Daylight gasped mentally, for the *Times-Tribune* was the biggest and most influential paper in San Francisco, and always had been so.

"--and I wasn't strong enough for the strain. Of course my body went back on me, and my mind, too, for that matter. It had to be bolstered up with whiskey, which wasn't good for it any more than was the living in clubs and hotels good for my stomach and the rest of me. That was what ailed me; I was living all wrong."

He shrugged his shoulders and drew at his pipe.

"When the doctors gave me up, I wound up my affairs and gave the doctors up. That was fifteen years ago. I'd been hunting through here when I was a boy, on vacations from college, and when I was all down and out it seemed a yearning came to me to go back to the country. So I quit, quit everything, absolutely, and came to live in the Valley of the Moon--that's the Indian name, you know, for Sonoma Valley. I lived in the lean-to the first year; then I built the cabin and sent for my books. I never knew what happiness was before, nor health. Look at me now and dare to tell me that I look forty-seven."

"I wouldn't give a day over forty," Daylight confessed.

"Yet the day I came here I looked nearer sixty, and that was fifteen years ago."

They talked along, and Daylight looked at the world from new angles. Here was a man, neither bitter nor cynical, who laughed at the city-dwellers and called them lunatics; a man who did not care for money, and in whom the lust for power had long since died. As for the friendship of the city-dwellers, his host spoke in no uncertain terms.

"What did they do, all the chaps I knew, the chaps in the clubs with whom I'd been cheek by jowl for heaven knows how long? I was not beholden to them for anything, and when I slipped out there was not one of them to drop me a line and say, 'How are you, old man? Anything I can do for you?' For several weeks it was: 'What's become of Ferguson?' After that I became a reminiscence and a memory. Yet every last one of them knew I had nothing but my salary and that I'd always lived a lap ahead of it."

"But what do you do now?" was Daylight's query. "You must need cash to buy clothes and magazines?"

"A week's work or a month's work, now and again, ploughing in the winter, or picking grapes in the fall, and there's always odd jobs with the farmers through the summer. I don't need much, so I don't have to work much. Most of my time I spend fooling around the place. I could do hack work for the magazines and newspapers; but I prefer the ploughing and the grape picking. Just look at me and you can see why. I'm hard as rocks. And I like the work. But I tell you a chap's got to break in to it. It's a great thing when he's learned to pick grapes a whole long day and come home at the end of it with that tired happy feeling, instead of being in a state of physical collapse. That fireplace--those big stones--I was soft, then, a little, anemic, alcoholic degenerate, with the spunk of a rabbit and about one per cent as much stamina, and some of those big stones nearly broke my back and my heart. But I persevered, and used my body in the way Nature intended it should be used--not bending over a desk and swilling whiskey... and, well, here I am, a better man for it, and there's the fireplace, fine and dandy, eh?

"And now tell me about the Klondike, and how you turned San Francisco upside down with that last raid of yours. You're a bonny fighter, you know, and you touch my imagination, though my cooler reason tells me that you are a lunatic like the rest. The lust for power! It's a dreadful affliction. Why didn't you stay in your Klondike? Or why don't you clear out and live a natural life, for instance, like mine? You see, I can ask questions, too. Now you talk and let me listen for a while."

It was not until ten o'clock that Daylight parted from Ferguson. As he rode along through the starlight, the idea came to him of buying the ranch on the other side of the valley. There was no thought in his mind of ever intending to live on it. His game was in San Francisco. But he liked the ranch, and as soon as he got back to the office he would open up negotiations with Hillard. Besides, the ranch included the clay-pit, and it would give him the whip-hand over Holdsworthy if he ever tried to cut up any didoes.

113

CHAPTER 10

The time passed, and Daylight played on at the game. But the game had entered upon a new phase. The lust for power in the mere gambling and winning was metamorphosing into the lust for power in order to revenge. There were many men in San Francisco against whom he had registered black marks, and now and again, with one of his lightning strokes, he erased such a mark. He asked no quarter; he gave no quarter. Men feared and hated him, and no one loved him, except Larry Hegan, his lawyer, who would have laid down his life for him. But he was the only man with whom Daylight was really intimate, though he was on terms of friendliest camaraderie with the rough and unprincipled following of the bosses who ruled the Riverside Club.

On the other hand, San Francisco's attitude toward Daylight had undergone a change. While he, with his slashing buccaneer methods, was a distinct menace to the more orthodox financial gamblers, he was nevertheless so grave a menace that they were glad enough to leave him alone. He had already taught them the excellence of letting a sleeping dog lie. Many of the men, who knew that they were in danger of his big bear-paw when it reached out for the honey vats, even made efforts to placate him, to get on the friendly side of him. The Alta-Pacific approached him confidentially with an offer of reinstatement, which he promptly declined. He was after a number of men in that club, and, whenever opportunity offered, he reached out for them and mangled them. Even the newspapers, with one or two blackmailing exceptions, ceased abusing him and became respectful. In short, he was looked upon as a bald-faced grizzly from the Arctic wilds to whom it was considered expedient to give the trail. At the time he raided the steamship companies, they had yapped at him and worried him, the whole pack of them, only to have him whirl around and whip them in the fiercest pitched battle San Francisco had ever known. Not easily forgotten was the Pacific Slope Seaman's strike and the giving over of the municipal government to the labor bosses and grafters. The destruction of Charles Klinkner and the California and Altamont Trust Company had been a warning. But it was an isolated case; they had been confident in strength in numbers--until he taught them better.

Daylight still engaged in daring speculations, as, for instance, at the impending outbreak of the Japanese-Russian War, when, in the face of the experience and power of the shipping gamblers, he reached out and clutched practically a monopoly of available steamer-charters. There was scarcely a battered tramp on the Seven Seas that was not his on time charter. As usual, his position was, "You've got to come and see me"; which they did, and, to use another of his phrases, they "paid through the nose" for the privilege. And all his venturing and fighting had now but one motive. Some day, as he confided to Hegan, when he'd made a sufficient stake, he was going back to New York and knock the spots out of Messrs. Dowsett, Letton, and Guggenhammer. He'd show them what an all-around general buzz-saw he was and what a mistake they'd made ever to monkey with him. But he never lost his head, and he knew that he was not yet strong enough to go into death-grapples with those three early enemies. In the meantime the black marks against them remained for a future easement day.

Dede Mason was still in the office. He had made no more overtures, discussed no more books and no more grammar. He had no active interest in her, and she was to him a pleasant memory of what had never happened, a joy, which, by his essential nature, he was barred from ever knowing. Yet, while his interest had gone to sleep and his energy was consumed in the endless battles he waged, he knew every trick of the light on her hair, every quick denote mannerism of movement, every line of her figure as expounded by her tailor-made gowns. Several times, six months or so apart, he had increased her salary, until now she was receiving ninety dollars a month. Beyond this he dared not go, though he had got around it by making the work easier. This he had accomplished after her return from a vacation, by retaining her substitute as an assistant. Also, he had changed his office suite, so that now the two girls had a room by themselves.

His eye had become quite critical wherever Dede Mason was concerned. He had long since noted her pride of carriage. It was unobtrusive, yet it was there. He decided, from the way she carried it, that she deemed her body a thing to be proud of, to be cared for as a beautiful and valued possession. In this, and in the way she carried her clothes, he compared her with her assistant, with the stenographers he encountered in other offices, with the women he saw on the sidewalks. "She's sure well put up," he communed with himself; "and she sure knows how to dress and carry it off without being stuck on herself and without laying it on thick."

The more he saw of her, and the more he thought he knew of her, the more unapproachable did she seem to him. But since he had no intention of approaching her, this was anything but an unsatisfactory fact. He was glad he had her in his office, and hoped she'd stay, and that was about all.

Daylight did not improve with the passing years. The life was not good for him. He was growing stout and soft, and there was unwonted flabbiness in his muscles. The more he drank cocktails, the more he was compelled to drink in order to get the desired result, the inhibitions that eased him down from the concert pitch of his operations. And with this went wine, too, at meals, and the long drinks after dinner of Scotch and soda at the Riverside. Then, too, his body suffered from lack of exercise; and, from lack of decent human associations, his moral fibres were weakening. Never a man to hide anything, some of his escapades became public, such as speeding, and of joy-rides in his big red motor-car down to San Jose with companions distinctly sporty--incidents that were narrated as good fun and comically in the newspapers.

Nor was there anything to save him. Religion had passed him by. "A long time dead" was his epitome of that phase of speculation. He was not interested in humanity. According to his rough-hewn sociology, it was all a gamble. God was a whimsical, abstract, mad thing called Luck. As to how one happened to be born--whether a sucker or a robber--was a gamble to begin with; Luck dealt out the cards, and the little babies picked up the hands allotted them. Protest was vain. Those were their cards and they had to play them, willy-nilly, hunchbacked or straight backed, crippled or clean-limbed, addle-pated or clear- headed. There was no fairness in it. The cards most picked up put them into the sucker class; the cards of a few enabled them to become robbers. The playing of the cards was life--the crowd of players, society. The table was the earth, and the earth, in lumps and chunks, from loaves of bread to big red motor-cars, was the stake. And in the end, lucky and unlucky, they were all a long time dead.

It was hard on the stupid lowly, for they were coppered to lose from the start; but the more he saw of the others, the apparent winners, the less it seemed to him that they had anything to brag about. They, too, were a long time dead, and their living did not amount to much. It was a wild animal fight; the strong trampled the weak, and the strong, he had already discovered,--men like Dowsett, and Letton, and Guggenhammer,--were not necessarily the best. He remembered his miner comrades of the Arctic. They were the stupid lowly, they did the hard work and were robbed of the fruit of their toil just as was the old woman making wine in the Sonoma hills; and yet they had finer qualities of truth, and loyalty, and square-dealing than did the men who robbed them. The winners seemed to be the crooked ones, the unfaithful ones, the wicked ones. And even they had no say in the matter. They played the cards that were given them; and Luck, the monstrous, mad-god thing, the owner of the whole shebang, looked on and grinned. It was he who stacked the universal card-deck of existence.

There was no justice in the deal. The little men that came, the little pulpy babies, were not even asked if they wanted to try a flutter at the game. They had no choice. Luck jerked them into life, slammed them up against the jostling table, and told them: "Now play, damn you, play!" And they did their best, poor little devils. The play of some led to steam yachts and mansions; of others, to the asylum or the pauper's ward. Some played the one same card, over and over, and made wine all their days in the chaparral, hoping, at the end, to pull down a set of false teeth and a coffin. Others quit the game early, having drawn cards that called for violent death, or famine in the Barrens, or loathsome and lingering disease. The hands of some called for kingship and irresponsible and numerated power; other hands called for ambition, for wealth in untold sums, for disgrace and shame, or for women and wine.

As for himself, he had drawn a lucky hand, though he could not see all the cards. Somebody or something might get him yet. The mad god, Luck, might be tricking him along to some such end. An unfortunate set of circumstances, and in a month's time the robber gang might be war-dancing around his financial carcass. This very day a street-car might run him down, or a sign fall from a building and smash in his skull. Or there was disease, ever rampant, one of Luck's grimmest whims. Who could say? To-morrow, or some other day, a ptomaine bug, or some other of a thousand bugs, might jump out upon him and drag him down. There was Doctor Bascom, Lee Bascom who had stood beside him a week ago and talked and argued, a picture of magnificent youth, and strength, and health. And in three days he was dead--pneumonia, rheumatism of the heart, and heaven knew what else--at the end screaming in agony that could be heard a block away. That had been terrible. It was a fresh, raw stroke in Daylight's consciousness. And when would his own turn come? Who could say?

In the meantime there was nothing to do but play the cards he could see in his hand, and they were *battle, revenge, and cocktails*. And Luck sat over all and grinned.

CHAPTER 11

One Sunday, late in the afternoon, found Daylight across the bay in the Piedmont hills back of Oakland. As usual, he was in a big motor-car, though not his own, the guest of Swiftwater Bill, Luck's own darling, who had come down to spend the clean-up of the seventh fortune wrung from the frozen Arctic gravel. A notorious spender, his latest pile was already on the fair road to follow the previous six. He it was, in the first year of Dawson, who had cracked an ocean of champagne at fifty dollars a quart; who, with the bottom of his gold-sack in sight, had cornered the egg-market, at twenty-four dollars per dozen, to the tune of one hundred and ten dozen, in order to pique the lady-love who had jilted him; and he it was, paying like a prince for speed, who had chartered special trains and broken all records between San Francisco and New York. And here he was once more, the "luck-pup of hell," as Daylight called him, throwing his latest fortune away with the same old-time facility.

It was a merry party, and they had made a merry day of it, circling the bay from San Francisco around by San Jose and up to Oakland, having been thrice arrested for speeding, the third time, however, on the Haywards stretch, running away with their captor. Fearing that a telephone message to arrest them had been flashed ahead, they had turned into the back-road through the hills, and now, rushing in upon Oakland by a new route, were boisterously discussing what disposition they should make of the constable.

"We'll come out at Blair Park in ten minutes," one of the men announced. "Look here, Swiftwater, there's a crossroads right ahead, with lots of gates, but it'll take us backcountry clear into Berkeley. Then we can come back into Oakland from the other side, sneak across on the ferry, and send the machine back around to-night with the chauffeur."

But Swiftwater Bill failed to see why he should not go into Oakland by way of Blair Park, and so decided.

The next moment, flying around a bend, the back-road they were not going to take appeared. Inside the gate leaning out from her saddle and just closing it, was a young woman on a chestnut sorrel. With his first glimpse, Daylight felt there was something strangely familiar about her. The next moment, straightening up in the saddle with a movement he could not fail to identify, she put the horse into a gallop, riding away with her back toward them. It was Dede Mason--he remembered what Morrison had told him about her keeping a riding horse, and he was glad she had not seen him in this riotous company. Swiftwater Bill stood up, clinging with one hand to the back of the front seat and waving the other to attract her attention. His lips were pursed for the piercing whistle for which he was famous and which Daylight knew of old, when Daylight, with a hook of his leg and a yank on the shoulder, slammed the startled Bill down into his seat.

"You m-m-must know the lady," Swiftwater Bill spluttered.

"I sure do," Daylight answered, "so shut up."

"Well, I congratulate your good taste, Daylight. She's a peach, and she rides like one, too."

Intervening trees at that moment shut her from view, and Swiftwater Bill plunged into the problem of disposing of their constable, while Daylight, leaning back with closed eyes, was still seeing Dede Mason gallop off down the country road. Swiftwater Bill was right. She certainly could ride. And, sitting astride, her seat was perfect. Good for Dede! That was an added point, her having the courage to ride in the only natural and logical manner. Her head as screwed on right, that was one thing sure.

On Monday morning, coming in for dictation, he looked at her with new interest, though he gave no sign of it; and the stereotyped business passed off in the stereotyped way. But the following Sunday found him on a horse himself, across the bay and riding through the Piedmont hills. He made a long day of it, but no glimpse did he catch of Dede Mason, though he even took the back-road of many gates and rode on into Berkeley. Here, along the lines of multitudinous houses, up one street and down another, he wondered which of them might be occupied by her. Morrison had said long ago that she lived in Berkeley, and she had been headed that way in the late afternoon of the previous Sunday--evidently returning home.

It had been a fruitless day, so far as she was concerned; and yet not entirely fruitless, for he had enjoyed the open air and the horse under him to such purpose that, on Monday, his instructions were out to the dealers to look for the best chestnut sorrel that money could buy. At odd times during the week he examined numbers of chestnut sorrels, tried several, and was unsatisfied. It was not till Saturday that he came upon Bob. Daylight knew him for what he wanted the moment he laid eyes on him. A large horse for a riding animal, he was none too large for a big man like Daylight. In splendid condition, Bob's coat in the sunlight was a flame of fire, his arched neck a jeweled conflagration.

"He's a sure winner," was Daylight's comment; but the dealer was not so sanguine. He was selling the horse on commission, and its owner had insisted on Bob's true charactor being given. The dealer gave it.

"Not what you'd call a real vicious horse, but a dangerous one. Full of vinegar and all-round cussedness, but without malice. Just as soon kill you as not, but in a playful sort of way, you understand, without meaning to at all. Personally, I wouldn't think of riding him. But he's a stayer. Look at them lungs. And look at them legs. Not a blemish. He's never been hurt or worked. Nobody ever succeeded in taking it out of him. Mountain horse, too, trail-broke and all that, being raised in rough country. Sure-footed as a goat, so long as he don't get it into his head to cut up. Don't shy. Ain't really afraid, but makes believe. Don't buck, but rears. Got to ride him with a martingale. Has a bad trick of whirling around without cause It's his idea of a joke on his rider. It's all just how he feels One day he'll ride along peaceable and pleasant for twenty miles. Next day, before you get started, he's well-nigh unmanageable. Knows automobiles so he can lay down alongside of one and sleep or eat hay out of it. He'll let nineteen go by without batting an eye, and mebbe the twentieth, just because he's feeling frisky, he'll cut up over like a range cayuse. Generally speaking, too lively for a gentleman, and too unexpected. Present owner nicknamed him Judas Iscariot, and refuses to sell without the buyer knowing all about him first. There, that's about all I know, except look at that mane and tail. Ever see anything like it? Hair as fine as a baby's."

The dealer was right. Daylight examined the mane and found it finer than any horse's hair he had ever seen. Also, its color was unusual in that it was almost auburn. While he ran his fingers through it, Bob turned his head and playfully nuzzled Daylight's shoulder

"Saddle him up, and I'll try him," he told the dealer. "I wonder if he's used to spurs. No English saddle, mind. Give me a good Mexican and a curb bit--not too severe, seeing as he likes to rear."

Daylight superintended the preparations, adjusting the curb strap and the stirrup length, and doing the cinching. He shook his head at the martingale, but yielded to the dealer's advice and allowed it to go on. And

118

Bob, beyond spirited restlessness and a few playful attempts, gave no trouble. Nor in the hour's ride that followed, save for some permissible curveting and prancing, did he misbehave. Daylight was delighted; the purchase was immediately made; and Bob, with riding gear and personal equipment, was despatched across the bay forthwith to take up his quarters in the stables of the Oakland Riding Academy.

The next day being Sunday, Daylight was away early, crossing on the ferry and taking with him Wolf, the leader of his sled team, the one dog which he had selected to bring with him when he left Alaska. Quest as he would through the Piedmont hills and along the many-gated back-road to Berkeley, Daylight saw nothing of Dede Mason and her chestnut sorrel. But he had little time for disappointment, for his own chestnut sorrel kept him busy. Bob proved a handful of impishness and contrariety, and he tried out his rider as much as his rider tried him out. All of Daylight's horse knowledge and horse sense was called into play, while Bob, in turn, worked every trick in his lexicon. Discovering that his martingale had more slack in it than usual, he proceeded to give an exhibition of rearing and hind-leg walking. After ten hopeless minutes of it, Daylight slipped off and tightened the martingale, whereupon Bob gave an exhibition of angelic goodness. He fooled Daylight completely. At the end of half an hour of goodness, Daylight, lured into confidence, was riding along at a walk and rolling a cigarette, with slack knees and relaxed seat, the reins lying on the animal's neck. Bob whirled abruptly and with lightning swiftness, pivoting on his hind legs, his fore legs just lifted clear of the ground. Daylight found himself with his right foot out of the stirrup and his arms around the animal's neck; and Bob took advantage of the situation to bolt down the road. With a hope that he should not encounter Dede Mason at that moment, Daylight regained his seat and checked in the horse.

Arrived back at the same spot, Bob whirled again. This time Daylight kept his seat, but, beyond a futile rein across the neck, did nothing to prevent the evolution. He noted that Bob whirled to the right, and resolved to keep him straightened out by a spur on the left. But so abrupt and swift was the whirl that warning and accomplishment were practically simultaneous.

"Well, Bob," he addressed the animal, at the same time wiping the sweat from his own eyes, "I'm free to confess that you're sure the blamedest all-fired quickest creature I ever saw. I guess the way to fix you is to keep the spur just a-touching--ah! you brute!"

For, the moment the spur touched him, his left hind leg had reached forward in a kick that struck the stirrup a smart blow. Several times, out of curiosity, Daylight attempted the spur, and each time Bob's hoof landed the stirrup. Then Daylight, following the horse's example of the unexpected, suddenly drove both spurs into him and reached him underneath with the quirt.

"You ain't never had a real licking before," he muttered as Bob, thus rudely jerked out of the circle of his own impish mental processes, shot ahead.

Half a dozen times spurs and quirt bit into him, and then Daylight settled down to enjoy the mad magnificent gallop. No longer punished, at the end of a half mile Bob eased down into a fast canter. Wolf, toiling in the rear, was catching up, and everything was going nicely.

"I'll give you a few pointers on this whirling game, my boy," Daylight was saying to him, when Bob whirled.

He did it on a gallop, breaking the gallop off short by fore legs stiffly planted. Daylight fetched up against his steed's neck with clasped arms, and at the same instant, with fore feet clear of the ground, Bob whirled around. Only an excellent rider could have escaped being unhorsed, and as it was, Daylight was nastily near to it. By the time he recovered his seat, Bob was in full career, bolting the way he had come, and making Wolf side-jump to the bushes.

"All right, darn you!" Daylight grunted, driving in spurs and quirt again and again. "Back-track you want to go, and back-track you sure will go till you're dead sick of it."

When, after a time, Bob attempted to ease down the mad pace, spurs and quirt went into him again with undiminished vim and put him to renewed effort. And when, at last, Daylight decided that the horse had had enough, he turned him around abruptly and put him into a gentle canter on the forward track. After a time he reined him in to a stop to see if he were breathing painfully. Standing for a minute, Bob turned his head and nuzzled his rider's stirrup in a roguish, impatient way, as much as to intimate that it was time they were going on.

"Well, I'll be plumb gosh darned!" was Daylight's comment. "No ill-will, no grudge, no nothing-and after that lambasting! You're sure a hummer, Bob."

Once again Daylight was lulled into fancied security. For an hour Bob was all that could be desired of a spirited mount, when, and as usual without warning, he took to whirling and bolting. Daylight put a stop to this with spurs and quirt, running him several punishing miles in the direction of his bolt. But when he turned him around and started forward, Bob proceeded to feign fright at trees, cows, bushes, Wolf, his own shadow--in short, at every ridiculously conceivable object. At such times, Wolf lay down in the shade and looked on, while Daylight wrestled it out.

So the day passed. Among other things, Bob developed a trick of making believe to whirl and not whirling. This was as exasperating as the real thing, for each time Daylight was fooled into tightening his leg grip and into a general muscular tensing of all his body. And then, after a few make-believe attempts, Bob actually did whirl and caught Daylight napping again and landed him in the old position with clasped arms around the neck. And to the end of the day, Bob continued to be up to one trick or another; after passing a dozen automobiles on the way into Oakland, suddenly electing to go mad with fright at a most ordinary little runabout. And just before he arrived back at the stable he capped the day with a combined whirling and rearing that broke the martingale and enabled him to gain a perpendicular position on his hind legs. At this juncture a rotten stirrup leather parted, and Daylight was all but unhorsed.

But he had taken a liking to the animal, and repented not of his bargain. He realized that Bob was not vicious nor mean, the trouble being that he was bursting with high spirits and was endowed with more than the average horse's intelligence. It was the spirits and the intelligence, combined with inordinate roguishness, that made him what he was. What was required to control him was a strong hand, with tempered sternness and yet with the requisite touch of brutal dominance.

"It's you or me, Bob," Daylight told him more than once that day.

And to the stableman, that night: --

"My, but ain't he a looker! Ever see anything like him? Best piece of horseflesh I ever straddled, and I've seen a few in my time."

And to Bob, who had turned his head and was up to his playful nuzzling:--

"Good-by, you little bit of all right. See you again next Sunday A.M., and just you bring along your whole basket of tricks, you old son-of-a-gun."

CHAPTER 12

Throughout the week Daylight found himself almost as much interested in Bob as in Dede; and, not being in the thick of any big deals, he was probably more interested in both of them than in the business game. Bob's trick of whirling was of especial moment to him. How to overcome it,--that was the thing. Suppose he did meet with Dede out in the hills; and suppose, by some lucky stroke of fate, he should manage to be riding alongside of her; then that whirl of Bob's would be most disconcerting and embarrassing. He was not particularly anxious for her to see him thrown forward on Bob's neck. On the other hand, suddenly to leave her and go dashing down the back-track, plying quirt and spurs, wouldn't do, either.

What was wanted was a method wherewith to prevent that lightning whirl. He must stop the animal before it got around. The reins would not do this. Neither would the spurs. Remained the quirt. But how to accomplish it? Absent-minded moments were many that week, when, sitting in his office chair, in fancy he was astride the wonderful chestnut sorrel and trying to prevent an anticipated whirl. One such moment, toward the end of the week, occurred in the middle of a conference with Hegan. Hegan, elaborating a new and dazzling legal vision, became aware that Daylight was not listening. His eyes had gone lack-lustre, and he, too, was seeing with inner vision.

"Got it" he cried suddenly. "Hegan, congratulate me. It's as simple as rolling off a log. All I've got to do is hit him on the nose, and hit him hard."

Then he explained to the startled Hegan, and became a good listener again, though he could not refrain now and again from making audible chuckles of satisfaction and delight. That was the scheme. Bob always whirled to the right. Very well. He would double the quirt in his hand and, the instant of the whirl, that doubled quirt would rap Bob on the nose. The horse didn't live, after it had once learned the lesson, that would whirl in the face of the doubled quirt.

More keenly than ever, during that week in the office did Daylight realize that he had no social, nor even human contacts with Dede. The situation was such that he could not ask her the simple question whether or not she was going riding next Sunday. It was a hardship of a new sort, this being the employer of a pretty girl. He looked at her often, when the routine work of the day was going on, the question he could not ask her tickling at the founts of speech--*Was she going riding next Sunday?* And as he looked, he wondered how old she was, and what love passages she had had, must have had, with those college whippersnappers with whom, according to Morrison, she herded and danced. His mind was very full of her, those six days between the Sundays, and one thing he came to know thoroughly well; he wanted her. And so much did he want her that his old timidity of the apron-string was put to rout. He, who had run away from women most of his life, had now grown so courageous as to pursue. Some Sunday, sooner or later, he would meet her outside the office, somewhere in the hills, and then, if they did not get acquainted, it would be because she did not care to get acquainted.

Thus he found another card in the hand the mad god had dealt him. How important that card was to become he did not dream, yet he decided that it was a pretty good card. In turn, he doubted. Maybe it was a trick of Luck to bring calamity and disaster upon him. Suppose Dede wouldn't have him, and suppose he went on loving her more and more, harder and harder? All his old generalized terrors of love revived. He remembered the disastrous love affairs of men and women he had known in the past. There was Bertha Doolittle, old Doolittle's daughter, who had been madly in love with Dartworthy, the rich Bonanza fraction owner; and Dartworthy, in turn, not loving Bertha at all, but madly loving Colonel Walthstone's wife and eloping down the Yukon with her; and Colonel Walthstone himself, madly loving his own wife and lighting out in pursuit of the fleeing couple. And what had been the outcome? Certainly Bertha's love had been unfortunate and tragic, and so had the love of the other three. Down below Minook, Colonel Walthstone and Dartworthy had fought it out. Dartworthy had been killed. A bullet through the Colonel's lungs had so weakened him that he died of pneumonia the following spring. And the Colonel's wife had no one left alive on earth to love.

And then there was Freda, drowning herself in the running mush-ice because of some man on the other side of the world, and hating him, Daylight, because he had happened along and pulled her out of the mush-ice and back to life. And the Virgin.... The old memories frightened him. If this love-germ gripped him good and hard, and if Dede wouldn't have him, it might be almost as bad as being gouged out of all he had by Dowsett, Letton, and Guggenhammer. Had his nascent desire for Dede been less, he might well have been frightened out of all thought of her. As it was, he found consolation in the thought that some love affairs did come out right. And for all he knew, maybe Luck had stacked the cards for him to win. Some men were born lucky, lived lucky all their days, and died lucky. Perhaps, too, he was such a man, a born luck-pup who could not lose.

Sunday came, and Bob, out in the Piedmont hills, behaved like an angel. His goodness, at times, was of the spirited prancing order, but otherwise he was a lamb. Daylight, with doubled quirt ready in his right hand, ached for a whirl, just one whirl, which Bob, with an excellence of conduct that was tantalizing, refused to perform. But no Dede did Daylight encounter. He vainly circled about among the hill roads and in the afternoon took the steep grade over the divide of the second range and dropped into Maraga Valley. Just after passing the foot of the descent, he heard the hoof beats of a cantering horse. It was from ahead and coming toward him. What if it were Dede? He turned Bob around and started to return at a walk. If it were Dede, he was born to luck, he decided; for the meeting couldn't have occurred under better circumstances. Here they were, both going in the same direction, and the canter would bring her up to him just where the stiff grade would compel a walk. There would be nothing else for her to do than ride with him to the top of the divide; and, once there, the equally stiff descent on the other side would compel more walking.

The canter came nearer, but he faced straight ahead until he heard the horse behind check to a walk. Then he glanced over his shoulder. It was Dede. The recognition was quick, and, with her, accompanied by surprise. What more natural thing than that, partly turning his horse, he should wait till she caught up with him; and that, when abreast they should continue abreast on up the grade? He could have sighed with relief. The thing was accomplished, and so easily. Greetings had been exchanged; here they were side by side and going in the same direction with miles and miles ahead of them.

He noted that her eye was first for the horse and next for him.

"Oh, what a beauty" she had cried at sight of Bob. From the shining light in her eyes, and the face filled with delight, he would scarcely have believed that it belonged to a young woman he had known in the office, the young woman with the controlled, subdued office face

"I didn't know you rode," was one of her first remarks. "I imagined you were wedded to get-there-quick machines."

"I've just taken it up lately," was his answer. "Beginning to get stout; you know, and had to take it off somehow."

She gave a quick sidewise glance that embraced him from head to heel, including seat and saddle, and said: --

"But you've ridden before."

She certainly had an eye for horses and things connected with horses was his thought, as he replied: --

"Not for many years. But I used to think I was a regular rip-snorter when I was a youngster up in Eastern Oregon, sneaking away from camp to ride with the cattle and break cayuses and that sort of thing."

Thus, and to his great relief, were they launched on a topic of mutual interest. He told her about Bob's tricks, and of the whirl and his scheme to overcome it; and she agreed that horses had to be handled with a certain rational severity, no matter how much one loved them. There was her Mab, which she had for eight years and which she had had break of stall-kicking. The process had been painful for Mab, but it had cured her.

"You've ridden a lot," Daylight said.

"I really can't remember the first time I was on a horse," she told him. "I was born on a ranch, you know, and they couldn't keep me away from the horses. I must have been born with the love for them. I had my first pony, all my own, when I was six. When I was eight I knew what it was to be all day in the saddle along with Daddy. By the time I was eleven he was taking me on my first deer hunts. I'd be lost without a horse. I hate indoors, and without Mab here I suppose I'd have been sick and dead long ago."

"You like the country?" he queried, at the same moment catching his first glimpse of a light in her eyes other than gray.

"As much as I detest the city," she answered. "But a woman can't earn a living in the country. So I make the best of it--along with Mab."

And thereat she told him more of her ranch life in the days before her father died. And Daylight was hugely pleased with himself. They were getting acquainted. The conversation had not lagged in the full half hour they had been together.

"We come pretty close from the same part of the country," he said. "I was raised in Eastern Oregon, and that's none so far from Siskiyou."

The next moment he could have bitten out his tongue for her quick question was: --

"How did you know I came from Siskiyou? I'm sure I never mentioned it."

"I don't know," he floundered temporarily. "I heard somewhere that you were from thereabouts."

Wolf, sliding up at that moment, sleek-footed and like a shadow, caused her horse to shy and passed the awkwardness off, for they talked Alaskan dogs until the conversation drifted back to horses. And horses it was, all up the grade and down the other side.

When she talked, he listened and followed her, and yet all the while he was following his own thoughts and impressions as well. It was a nervy thing for her to do, this riding astride, and he didn't know, after all, whether he liked it or not. His ideas of women were prone to be old-fashioned; they were the ones he had imbibed in the early-day, frontier life of his youth, when no woman was seen on anything but a side-saddle. He had grown up to the tacit fiction that women on horseback were not bipeds. It came to him with a shock, this sight of her so manlike in her saddle. But he had to confess that the sight looked good to him just

Two other immediate things about her struck him. First, there were the golden spots in her eyes. Queer that he had never noticed them before.

Perhaps the light in the office had not been right, and perhaps they came and went. No; they were glows of color--a sort of diffused, golden light. Nor was it golden, either, but it was nearer that than any color he knew. It certainly was not any shade of yellow. A lover's thoughts are ever colored, and it is to be doubted if any one else in the world would have called Dede's eyes golden. But Daylight's mood verged on the tender and melting, and he preferred to think of them as golden, and therefore they were golden.

And then she was so natural. He had been prepared to find her a most difficult young woman to get acquainted with. Yet here it was proving so simple. There was nothing highfalutin about her company manners--it was by this homely phrase that he differentiated this Dede on horseback from the Dede with the office manners whom he had always known. And yet, while he was delighted with the smoothness with which everything was going, and with the fact that they had found plenty to talk about, he was aware of an irk under it all. After all, this talk was empty and idle. He was a man of action, and he wanted her, Dede Mason, the woman; he wanted her to love him and to be loved by him; and he wanted all this glorious consummation then and there. Used to forcing issues used to gripping men and things and bending them to his will, he felt, now, the same compulsive prod of mastery. He wanted to tell her that he loved her and that there was nothing else for her to do but marry him. And yet he did not obey the prod. Women were fluttery creatures, and here mere mastery would prove a bungle. He remembered all his hunting guile, the long patience of shooting meat in famine when a hit or a miss meant life or death. Truly, though this girl did not yet mean quite that, nevertheless she meant much to him--more, now, than ever, as he rode beside her, glancing at her as often as he dared, she in her corduroy riding-habit, so bravely manlike, yet so essentially and revealingly woman, smiling, laughing, talking, her eyes sparkling, the flush of a day of sun and summer breeze warm in her cheeks.

CHAPTER 13

Another Sunday man and horse and dog roved the Piedmont hills. And again Daylight and Dede rode together. But this time her surprise at meeting him was tinctured with suspicion; or rather, her surprise was of another order. The previous Sunday had been quite accidental, but his appearing a second time among her favorite haunts hinted of more than the fortuitous. Daylight was made to feel that she suspected him, and he, remembering that he had seen a big rock quarry near Blair Park, stated offhand that he was thinking of buying it. His one-time investment in a brickyard had put the idea into his head--an idea that he decided was a good one, for it enabled him to suggest that she ride along with him to inspect the quarry.

So several hours he spent in her company, in which she was much the same girl as before, natural, unaffected, lighthearted, smiling and laughing, a good fellow, talking horses with unflagging enthusiasm, making friends with the crusty-tempered Wolf, and expressing the desire to ride Bob, whom she declared she was more in love with than ever. At this last Daylight demurred. Bob was full of dangerous tricks, and he wouldn't trust any one on him except his worst enemy.

"You think, because I'm a girl, that I don't know anything about horses," she flashed back. "But I've been thrown off and bucked off enough not to be over-confident. And I'm not a fool. I wouldn't get on a bucking horse. I've learned better. And I'm not afraid of any other kind. And you say yourself that Bob doesn't buck."

"But you've never seen him cutting up didoes," Daylight

"But you must remember I've seen a few others, and I've been on several of them myself. I brought Mab here to electric cars, locomotives, and automobiles. She was a raw range colt when she came to me. Broken to saddle that was all. Besides, I won't hurt your horse."

Against his better judgment, Daylight gave in, and, on an unfrequented stretch of road, changed saddles and bridles.

"Remember, he's greased lightning," he warned, as he helped her to mount.

She nodded, while Bob pricked up his ears to the knowledge that he had a strange rider on his back. The fun came quickly enough--too quickly for Dede, who found herself against Bob's neck as he pivoted around and bolted the other way. Daylight followed on her horse and watched. He saw her check the animal quickly to a standstill, and immediately, with rein across neck and a decisive prod of the left spur, whirl him back the way he had come and almost as swiftly.

"Get ready to give him the quirt on the nose," Daylight called.

But, too quickly for her, Bob whirled again, though this time, by a severe effort, she saved herself from the undignified position against his neck. His bolt was more determined, but she pulled him into a prancing walk, and turned him roughly back with her spurred heel. There was nothing feminine in the way she handled him; her method was imperative and masculine. Had this not been so, Daylight would have expected her to say she had had enough. But that little preliminary exhibition had taught him something of Dede's quality. And if it had not, a glance at her gray eyes, just perceptibly angry with herself, and at her firm-set mouth, would have told him the same thing. Daylight did not suggest anything, while he hung almost gleefully upon her actions in anticipation of what the fractious Bob was going to get. And Bob got it, on his next whirl, or attempt, rather, for he was no more than halfway around when the quirt met him smack on his tender nose. There and then, in his bewilderment, surprise, and pain, his fore feet, just skimming above the road, dropped down.

"Great!" Daylight applauded. "A couple more will fix him. He's too smart not to know when he's beaten."

Again Bob tried. But this time he was barely quarter around when the doubled quirt on his nose compelled him to drop his fore feet to the road. Then, with neither rein nor spur, but by the mere threat of the quirt, she straightened him out.

Dede looked triumphantly at Daylight.

"Let me give him a run?" she asked.

Daylight nodded, and she shot down the road. He watched her out of sight around the bend, and watched till she came into sight returning. She certainly could sit her horse, was his thought, and she was a sure enough hummer. God, she was the wife for a man! Made most of them look pretty slim. And to think of her hammering all week at a typewriter. That was no place for her. She should be a man's wife, taking it easy, with silks and satins and diamonds (his frontier notion of what befitted a wife beloved), and dogs, and horses, and such things--"And we'll see, Mr. Burning Daylight, what you and me can do about it," he murmured to himself! and aloud to her: --

"You'll do, Miss Mason; you'll do. There's nothing too good in horseflesh you don't deserve, a woman who can ride like that. No; stay with him, and we'll jog along to the quarry." He chuckled. "Say, he actually gave just the least mite of a groan that last time you fetched him. Did you hear it? And did you see the way he dropped his feet to the road--just like he'd struck a stone wall. And he's got savvee enough to know from now on that that same stone wall will be always there ready for him to lam into."

When he parted from her that afternoon, at the gate of the road that led to Berkeley, he drew off to the edge of the intervening clump of trees, where, unobserved, he watched her out of sight. Then, turning to ride back into Oakland, a thought came to him that made him grin ruefully as he muttered: "And now it's up to me to make good and buy that blamed quarry. Nothing less than that can give me an excuse for snooping around these hills."

But the quarry was doomed to pass out of his plans for a time, for on the following Sunday he rode alone. No Dede on a chestnut sorrel came across the back-road from Berkeley that day, nor the day a week later. Daylight was beside himself with impatience and apprehension, though in the office he contained himself. He noted no change in her, and strove to let none show in himself. The same old monotonous routine went on, though now it was irritating and maddening. Daylight found a big quarrel on his hands with a world that wouldn't let a man behave toward his stenographer after the way of all men and women. What was the good of owning millions anyway? he demanded one day of the desk-calendar, as she passed out after receiving his dictation.

As the third week drew to a close and another desolate Sunday confronted him, Daylight resolved to speak, office or no office. And as was his nature, he went simply and directly to the point She had finished her work with him, and was gathering her note pad and pencils together to depart, when he said: --

"Oh, one thing more, Miss Mason, and I hope you won't mind my being frank and straight out. You've struck me right along as a sensible-minded girl, and I don't think you'll take offence at what I'm going to say. You know how long you've been in the office--it's years, now, several of them, anyway; and you know I've always been straight and aboveboard with you. I've never what you call--presumed. Because you were in my office I've tried to be more careful than if--if you wasn't in my office--you understand. But just the same, it don't make me any the less human. I'm a lonely sort of a fellow--don't take that as a bid for kindness. What I mean by it is to try and tell you just how much those two rides with you have meant. And now I hope you won't mind my just asking why you haven't been out riding the last two Sundays?"

He came to a stop and waited, feeling very warm and awkward, the perspiration starting in tiny beads on his forehead. She did not speak immediately, and he stepped across the room and raised the window higher.

"I have been riding," she answered; "in other directions."

"But why...?" He failed somehow to complete the question. "Go ahead and be frank with me," he urged. "Just as frank as I am with you. Why didn't you ride in the Piedmont hills? I hunted for you everywhere.

"And that is just why." She smiled, and looked him straight in the eyes for a moment, then dropped her own. "Surely, you understand, Mr. Harnish."

He shook his head glumly.

"I do, and I don't. I ain't used to city ways by a long shot. There's things one mustn't do, which I don't mind as long as I don't want to do them."

"But when you do?" she asked quickly.

"Then I do them." His lips had drawn firmly with this affirmation of will, but the next instant he was amending the statement "That is, I mostly do. But what gets me is the things you mustn't do when they're not wrong and they won't hurt anybody--this riding, for instance."

She played nervously with a pencil for a time, as if debating her reply, while he waited patiently.

"This riding," she began; "it's not what they call the right thing. I leave it to you. You know the world. You are Mr. Harnish, the millionaire-"

"Gambler," he broke in harshly

She nodded acceptance of his term and went on.

"And I'm a stenographer in your office--"

"You're a thousand times better than me--" he attempted to interpolate, but was in turn interrupted.

"It isn't a question of such things. It's a simple and fairly common situation that must be considered. I work for you. And it isn't what you or I might think, but what other persons will think. And you don't need to be told any more about that. You know yourself."

Her cool, matter-of-fact speech belied her--or so Daylight thought, looking at her perturbed feminineness, at the rounded lines of her figure, the breast that deeply rose and fell, and at the color that was now excited in her cheeks.

"I'm sorry I frightened you out of your favorite stamping ground," he said rather aimlessly.

"You didn't frighten me," she retorted, with a touch of fire. "I'm not a silly seminary girl. I've taken care of myself for a long time now, and I've done it without being frightened. We were together two Sundays, and I'm sure I wasn't frightened of Bob, or you. It isn't that. I have no fears of taking care of myself, but the world insists on taking care of one as well. That's the trouble. It's what the world would have to say about me and my employer meeting regularly and riding in the hills on Sundays. It's funny, but it's so. I could ride with one of the clerks without remark, but with you--no."

"But the world don't know and don't need to know," he cried.

"Which makes it worse, in a way, feeling guilty of nothing and yet sneaking around back-roads with all the feeling of doing something wrong. It would be finer and braver for me publicly..."

"To go to lunch with me on a week-day," Daylight said, divining the drift of her uncompleted argument.

She nodded.

"I didn't have that quite in mind, but it will do. I'd prefer doing the brazen thing and having everybody know it, to doing the furtive thing and being found out. Not that I'm asking to be invited to lunch," she added, with a smile; "but I'm sure you understand my position."

"Then why not ride open and aboveboard with me in the hills?" he urged.

She shook her head with what he imagined was just the faintest hint of regret, and he went suddenly and almost maddeningly hungry for her.

"Look here, Miss Mason, I know you don't like this talking over of things in the office. Neither do I. It's part of the whole thing, I guess; a man ain't supposed to talk anything but business with his stenographer. Will you ride with me next Sunday, and we can talk it over thoroughly then and reach some sort of a conclusion. Out in the hills is the place where you can talk something besides business. I guess you've seen enough of me to know I'm pretty square. I--I do honor and respect you, and... and all that, and I .." He was beginning to flounder, and the hand that rested on the desk blotter was visibly trembling. He strove to pull himself together. "I just want to harder than anything ever in my life before. I--I--I can't explain myself, but I do, that's all. Will you?--Just next Sunday? To-morrow?"

Nor did he dream that her low acquiescence was due, as much as anything else, to the beads of sweat on his forehead, his trembling hand, and his all too-evident general distress.

CHAPTER 14

"Of course, there's no way of telling what anybody wants from what they say." Daylight rubbed Bob's rebellious ear with his quirt and pondered with dissatisfaction the words he had just uttered. They did not say what he had meant them to say. "What I'm driving at is that you say flatfooted that you won't meet me again, and you give your reasons, but how am I to know they are your real reasons? Mebbe you just don't want to get acquainted with me, and won't say so for fear of hurting my feelings. Don't you see? I'm the last man in the world to shove in where I'm not wanted. And if I thought you didn't care a whoop to see anything more of me, why, I'd clear out so blamed quick you couldn't see me for smoke."

Dede smiled at him in acknowledgment of his words, but rode on silently. And that smile, he thought, was the most sweetly wonderful smile he had ever seen. There was a difference in it, he assured himself, from any smile she had ever given him before. It was the smile of one who knew him just a little bit, of one who was just the least mite acquainted with him. Of course, he checked himself up the next moment, it was unconscious on her part. It was sure to come in the intercourse of any two persons. Any stranger, a business man, a clerk, anybody after a few casual meetings would show similar signs of friendliness. It was bound to happen, but in her case it made more impression on him; and, besides, it was such a sweet and wonderful smile. Other women he had known had never smiled like that; he was sure of it.

It had been a happy day. Daylight had met her on the back-road from Berkeley, and they had had hours together. It was only now, with the day drawing to a close and with them approaching the gate of the road to Berkeley, that he had broached the important subject.

She began her answer to his last contention, and he listened gratefully.

"But suppose, just suppose, that the reasons I have given are the only ones?--that there is no question of my not wanting to know you?"

"Then I'd go on urging like Sam Scratch," he said quickly. "Because, you see, I've always noticed that folks that incline to anything are much more open to hearing the case stated. But if you did have that other reason up your sleeve, if you didn't want to know me, if--if, well, if you thought my feelings oughtn't to be hurt just because you had a good job with me..." Here, his calm consideration of a possibility was swamped by the fear that it was an actuality, and he lost the thread of his reasoning. "Well, anyway, all you have to do is to say the word and I'll clear out. And with no hard feelings; it would be just a case of bad luck for me. So be honest, Miss Mason, please, and tell me if that's the reason--I almost got a hunch that it is."

She glanced up at him, her eyes abruptly and slightly moist, half with hurt, half with anger.

"Oh, but that isn't fair," she cried. "You give me the choice of lying to you and hurting you in order to protect myself by getting rid of you, or of throwing away my protection by telling you the truth, for then you, as you said yourself, would stay and urge."

Her cheeks were flushed, her lips tremulous, but she continued to look him frankly in the eyes.

Daylight smiled grimly with satisfaction.

"I'm real glad, Miss Mason, real glad for those words."

"But they won't serve you," she went on hastily. "They can't serve you. I refuse to let them. This is our last ride, and... here is the gate."

Ranging her mare alongside, she bent, slid the catch, and followed the opening gate.

"No; please, no," she said, as Daylight started to follow.

Humbly acquiescent, he pulled Bob back, and the gate swung shut between them. But there was more to say, and she did not ride on.

"Listen, Miss Mason," he said, in a low voice that shook with sincerity; "I want to assure you of one thing. I'm not just trying to fool around with you. I like you, I want you, and I was never more in earnest in my life. There's nothing wrong in my intentions or anything like that. What I mean is strictly honorable--"

But the expression of her face made him stop. She was angry, and she was laughing at the same time.

"The last thing you should have said," she cried. "It's like a--a matrimonial bureau: intentions strictly honorable; object, matrimony. But it's no more than I deserved. This is what I suppose you call urging like Sam Scratch."

The tan had bleached out of Daylight's skin since the time he came to live under city roofs, so that the flush of blood showed readily as it crept up his neck past the collar and overspread his face. Nor in his exceeding discomfort did he dream that she was looking upon him at that moment with more kindness than at any time that day. It was not in her experience to behold big grown-up men who blushed like boys, and already she repented the sharpness into which she had been surprised.

"Now, look here, Miss Mason," he began, slowly and stumblingly at first, but accelerating into a rapidity of utterance that was almost incoherent; "I'm a rough sort of a man, I know that, and I know I don't know much of anything. I've never had any training in nice things. I've never made love before, and I've never been in love before either--and I don't know how to go about it any more than a thundering idiot. What you want to do is get behind my tomfool words and get a feel of the man that's behind them. That's me, and I mean all right, if I don't know how to go about it."

Dede Mason had quick, birdlike ways, almost flitting from mood to mood; and she was all contrition on the instant.

"Forgive me for laughing," she said across the gate. "It wasn't really laughter. I was surprised off my guard, and hurt, too. You see, Mr. Harnish, I've not been..."

She paused, in sudden fear of completing the thought into which her birdlike precipitancy had betrayed her.

"What you mean is that you've not been used to such sort of proposing," Daylight said; "a sort of on-the-run, 'Howdy, glad-to-make-your-acquaintance, won't-you-be-mine' proposition."

She nodded and broke into laughter, in which he joined, and which served to pass the awkwardness away. He gathered heart at this, and went on in greater confidence, with cooler head and tongue.

"There, you see, you prove my case. You've had experience in such matters. I don't doubt you've had slathers of proposals. Well, I haven't, and I'm like a fish out of water. Besides, this ain't a proposal. It's a peculiar situation, that's all, and I'm in a corner. I've got enough plain horse-sense to know a man ain't supposed to argue marriage with a girl as a reason for getting acquainted with her. And right there was where I was in the hole. Number one, I can't get acquainted with you in the office. Number two, you say you won't see me out of the office to give me a chance. Number three, your reason is that folks will talk because you work for me. Number four, I just got to get acquainted with you, and I just got to get you to see that I mean fair and all right. Number five, there you are on one side the gate getting ready to go, and me here on the other side the gate pretty desperate and bound to say something to make you reconsider. Number six, I said it. And now and finally, I just do want you to reconsider."

And, listening to him, pleasuring in the sight of his earnest, perturbed face and in the simple, homely phrases that but emphasized his earnestness and marked the difference between him and the average run of men she had known, she forgot to listen and lost herself in her own thoughts. The love of a strong man is ever a lure to a normal woman, and never more strongly did Dede feel the lure than now, looking across the closed gate at Burning Daylight. Not that she would ever dream of marrying him--she had a score of reasons against it; but why not at least see more of him? He was certainly not repulsive to her. On the contrary, she liked him, had always liked him from the day she had first seen him and looked upon his lean Indian face and into his flashing Indian eyes. He was a figure of a man in more ways than his mere magnificent muscles. Besides, Romance had gilded him, this doughty, rough-hewn adventurer of the North, this man of many deeds and many millions, who had come down out of the Arctic to wrestle and fight so masterfully with the men of the South.

Savage as a Red Indian, gambler and profligate, a man without morals, whose vengeance was never glutted and who stamped on the faces of all who opposed him--oh, yes, she knew all the hard names he had been called. Yet she was not afraid of him. There was more than that in the connotation of his name. *Burning Daylight* called up other things as well. They were there in the newspapers, the magazines, and the books on the Klondike. When all was said, *Burning Daylight* had a mighty connotation--one to touch any woman's imagination, as it touched hers, the gate between them, listening to the wistful and impassioned simplicity of his speech. Dede was after all a woman, with a woman's sex-vanity, and it was this vanity that was pleased by the fact that such a man turned in his need to her.

And there was more that passed through her mind--sensations of tiredness and loneliness; trampling squadrons and shadowy armies of vague feelings and vaguer prompting; and deeper and dimmer whisperings and echoings, the flutterings of forgotten generations crystallized into being and fluttering anew and always, undreamed and unguessed, subtle and potent, the spirit and essence of life that under a thousand deceits and masks forever makes for life. It was a strong temptation, just to ride with this man in the hills. It would be that only and nothing more, for she was firmly convinced that his way of life could never be her way. On the other hand, she was vexed by none of the ordinary feminine fears and timidities. That she could take care of herself under any and all circumstances she never doubted. Then why not? It was such a little thing, after all.

She led an ordinary, humdrum life at best. She ate and slept and worked, and that was about all. As if in review, her anchorite existence passed before her: six days of the week spent in the office and in journeying back and forth on the ferry; the hours stolen before bedtime for snatches of song at the piano, for doing her own special laundering, for sewing and mending and casting up of meagre accounts; the two evenings a week of social diversion she permitted herself; the other stolen hours and Saturday afternoons spent with her brother at the hospital; and the seventh day, Sunday, her day of solace, on Mab's back, out among the blessed hills. But it was lonely, this solitary riding. Nobody of her acquaintance rode. Several girls at the University had been persuaded into trying it, but after a Sunday or two on hired livery hacks they had lost interest. There was Madeline, who bought her own horse and rode enthusiastically for several months, only to get married and go away to live in Southern California. After years of it, one did get tired of this eternal riding alone.

He was such a boy, this big giant of a millionaire who had half the rich men of San Francisco afraid of him. Such a boy! She had never imagined this side of his nature.

"How do folks get married?" he was saying. "Why, number one, they meet; number two, like each other's looks; number three, get acquainted; and number four, get married or not, according to how they like each other after getting acquainted. But how in thunder we're to have a chance to find out whether we like each other enough is beyond my savvee, unless we make that chance ourselves. I'd come to see you, call on you, only I know you're just rooming or boarding, and that won't do."

Suddenly, with a change of mood, the situation appeared to Dede ridiculously absurd. She felt a desire to laugh--not angrily, not hysterically, but just jolly. It was so funny. Herself, the stenographer, he, the notorious and powerful gambling millionaire, and the gate between them across which poured his argument of people getting acquainted and married. Also, it was an impossible situation. On the face of it, she could not go on with it. This program of furtive meetings in the hills would have to discontinue. There would never be another meeting. And if, denied this, he tried to woo her in the office, she would be compelled to lose a very good position, and that would be an end of the episode. It was not nice to contemplate; but the world of men, especially in the cities, she had not found particularly nice. She had not worked for her living for years without losing a great many of her illusions.

"We won't do any sneaking or hiding around about it," Daylight was explaining. "We'll ride around as bold if you please, and if anybody sees us, why, let them. If they talk--well, so long as our consciences are straight we needn't worry. Say the word, and Bob will have on his back the happiest man alive."

She shook her head, pulled in the mare, who was impatient to be off for home, and glanced significantly at the lengthening shadows.

"It's getting late now, anyway," Daylight hurried on, "and we've settled nothing after all. Just one more Sunday, anyway--that's not asking much--to settle it in."

"We've had all day," she said.

"But we started to talk it over too late. We'll tackle it earlier next time. This is a big serious proposition with me, I can tell you. Say next Sunday?"

"Are men ever fair?" she asked. "You know thoroughly well that by 'next Sunday' you mean many Sundays."

"Then let it be many Sundays," he cried recklessly, while she thought that she had never seen him looking handsomer. "Say the word. Only say the word. Next Sunday at the quarry..."

She gathered the reins into her hand preliminary to starting.

"Good night," she said, "and--"

"Yes," he whispered, with just the faintest touch of impressiveness.

"Yes," she said, her voice low but distinct.

At the same moment she put the mare into a canter and went down the road without a backward glance, intent on an analysis of her own feelings. With her mind made up to say no--and to the last instant she had been so resolved--her lips nevertheless had said yes. Or at least it seemed the lips. She had not intended to consent. Then why had she? Her first surprise and bewilderment at so wholly unpremeditated an act gave way to consternation as she considered its consequences. She knew that Burning Daylight was not a man to be trifled with, that under his simplicity and

132

boyishness he was essentially a dominant male creature, and that she had pledged herself to a future of inevitable stress and storm. And again she demanded of herself why she had said yes at the very moment when it had been farthest from her intention.

CHAPTER 15

Life at the office went on much the way it had always gone. Never, by word or look, did they acknowledge that the situation was in any wise different from what it had always been. Each Sunday saw the arrangement made for the following Sunday's ride; nor was this ever referred to in the office. Daylight was fastidiously chivalrous on this point. He did not want to lose her from the office. The sight of her at her work was to him an undiminishing joy. Nor did he abuse this by lingering over dictation or by devising extra work that would detain her longer before his eyes. But over and beyond such sheer selfishness of conduct was his love of fair play. He scorned to utilize the accidental advantages of the situation. Somewhere within him was a higher appeasement of love than mere possession. He wanted to be loved for himself, with a fair field for both sides.

On the other hand, had he been the most artful of schemers he could not have pursued a wiser policy. Bird-like in her love of individual freedom, the last woman in the world to be bullied in her affections, she keenly appreciated the niceness of his attitude. She did this consciously, but deeper than all consciousness, and intangible as gossamer, were the effects of this. All unrealizable, save for some supreme moment, did the web of Daylight's personality creep out and around her. Filament by filament, these secret and undreamable bonds were being established. They it was that could have given the cue to her saying yes when she had meant to say no. And in some such fashion, in some future crisis of greater moment, might she not, in violation of all dictates of sober judgment, give another unintentional consent?

Among other good things resulting from his growing intimacy with Dede, was Daylight's not caring to drink so much as formerly. There was a lessening in desire for alcohol of which even he at last became aware. In a way she herself was the needed inhibition. The thought of her was like a cocktail. Or, at any rate, she substituted for a certain percentage of cocktails. From the strain of his unnatural city existence and of his intense gambling operations, he had drifted on to the cocktail route. A wall must forever be built to give him easement from the high pitch, and Dede became a part of this wall. Her personality, her laughter, the intonations of her voice, the impossible golden glow of her eyes, the light on her hair, her form, her dress, her actions on horseback, her merest physical mannerisms--all, pictured over and over in his mind and dwelt upon, served to take the place of many a cocktail or long Scotch and soda.

In spite of their high resolve, there was a very measurable degree of the furtive in their meetings. In essence, these meetings were stolen. They did not ride out brazenly together in the face of the world. On the contrary, they met always unobserved, she riding across the many-gated backroad from Berkeley to meet him halfway. Nor did they ride on any save unfrequented roads, preferring to cross the second range of hills and travel among a church-going farmer folk who would scarcely have recognized even Daylight from his newspaper photographs.

He found Dede a good horsewoman--good not merely in riding but in endurance. There were days when they covered sixty, seventy, and even eighty miles; nor did Dede ever claim any day too long, nor--another strong recommendation to Daylight--did the hardest day ever the slightest chafe of the chestnut sorrel's back. "A sure enough hummer," was Daylight's stereotyped but ever enthusiastic verdict to himself.

They learned much of each other on these long, uninterrupted rides. They had nothing much to talk about but themselves, and, while she received a liberal education concerning Arctic travel and gold-mining, he, in turn, touch by touch, painted an ever clearer portrait of her. She amplified the ranch life of her girlhood, prattling on about horses and dogs and persons and things until it was as if he saw the whole process of her growth and her becoming. All this he was able to trace on through the period of her father's failure and death, when she had been compelled to leave the university and go into office work. The brother, too, she spoke of, and of her long struggle to have him cured and of her now fading hopes. Daylight decided that it was easier to come to an understanding of her than he had anticipated, though he was always aware that behind and under all he knew of her was the mysterious and baffling woman and sex. There, he was humble enough to confess to himself, was a chartless, shoreless sea, about which he knew nothing and which he must nevertheless somehow navigate.

His lifelong fear of woman had originated out of non-understanding and had also prevented him from reaching any understanding. Dede on horseback, Dede gathering poppies on a summer hillside, Dede taking down dictation in her swift shorthand strokes--all this was comprehensible to him. But he did not know the Dede who so quickly changed from mood to mood, the Dede who refused steadfastly to ride with him and then suddenly consented, the Dede in whose eyes the golden glow forever waxed and waned and whispered hints and messages that were not for his ears. In all such things he saw the glimmering profundities of sex, acknowledged their lure, and accepted them as incomprehensible.

There was another side of her, too, of which he was consciously ignorant. She knew the books, was possessed of that mysterious and awful thing called "culture." And yet, what continually surprised him was that this culture was never obtruded on their intercourse. She did not talk books, nor art, nor similar folderols. Homely minded as he was himself, he found her almost equally homely minded. She liked the simple and the out-of-doors, the horses and the hills, the sunlight and the flowers. He found himself in a partly new flora, to which she was the guide, pointing out to him all the varieties of the oaks, making him acquainted with the madrono and the manzanita, teaching him the names, habits, and habitats of unending series of wild flowers, shrubs, and ferns. Her keen woods eye was another delight to him. It had been trained in the open, and little escaped it. One day, as a test, they strove to see which could discover the greater number of birds' nests. And he, who had always prided himself on his own acutely trained observation, found himself hard put to keep his score ahead. At the end of the day he was but three nests in the lead, one of which she challenged stoutly and of which even he confessed serious doubt. He complimented her and told her that her success must be due to the fact that she was a bird herself, with all a bird's keen vision and quick-flashing ways.

The more he knew her the more he became convinced of this birdlike quality in her. That was why she liked to ride, he argued. It was the nearest approach to flying. A field of poppies, a glen of ferns, a row of poplars on a country lane, the tawny brown of a hillside, the shaft of sunlight on a distant peak--all such were provocative of quick joys which seemed to him like so many outbursts of song. Her joys were in little things, and she seemed always singing. Even in sterner things it was the same. When she rode Bob and fought with that magnificent brute for mastery, the qualities of an eagle were uppermost in her.

These quick little joys of hers were sources of joy to him. He joyed in her joy, his eyes as excitedly fixed on her as bears were fixed on the object of her attention. Also through her he came to a closer discernment and keener appreciation of nature. She showed him colors in the landscape that he would never have dreamed were there. He had known only the primary colors. All colors of red were red. Black was black, and brown was just plain brown until it became yellow, when it was no longer brown. Purple he had always imagined was red, something like blood, until she taught him better. Once they rode out on a high hill brow where wind-blown poppies blazed about their horses' knees, and she was in an ecstasy over the lines of the many distances. Seven, she counted, and he, who had gazed on landscapes all his life, for the first time learned what a "distance" was. After that, and always, he looked upon the face of nature with a more seeing eye, learning a delight of his own in surveying the serried ranks of the upstanding ranges, and in slow contemplation of the purple summer mists that haunted the languid creases of the distant hills.

But through it all ran the golden thread of love. At first he had been content just to ride with Dede and to be on comradely terms with her; but the desire and the need for her increased. The more he knew of her, the higher was his appraisal. Had she been reserved and haughty with him, or been merely a giggling, simpering creature of a woman, it would have been different. Instead, she amazed him with her simplicity and wholesomeness, with her great store of comradeliness. This latter was the unexpected. He had never looked upon woman in that way. Woman, the toy; woman, the harpy; woman, the necessary wife and mother of the race's offspring,--all this had been his expectation and understanding of woman. But woman, the comrade and playfellow and joyfellow--this was what Dede had surprised him in. And the more she became worth while, the more ardently his love burned, unconsciously shading his voice with caresses, and with equal unconsciousness flaring up signal fires in his eyes. Nor was she blind to it yet, like many women before her, she thought to play with the pretty fire and escape the consequent conflagration.

"Winter will soon be coming on," she said regretfully, and with provocation, one day, "and then there won't be any more riding."

"But I must see you in the winter just the same," he cried hastily.

She shook her head.

"We have been very happy and all that," she said, looking at him with steady frankness. "I remember your foolish argument for getting acquainted, too; but it won't lead to anything; it can't. I know myself too well to be mistaken."

Her face was serious, even solicitous with desire not to hurt, and her eyes were unwavering, but in them was the light, golden and glowing--the abyss of sex into which he was now unafraid to gaze.

"I've been pretty good," he declared. "I leave it to you if I haven't. It's been pretty hard, too, I can tell you. You just think it over. Not once have I said a word about love to you, and me loving you all the time. That's going some for a man that's used to having his own way. I'm somewhat of a rusher when it comes to travelling. I reckon I'd rush God Almighty if it came to a race over the ice. And yet I didn't rush you. I guess this fact is an indication of how much I do love you. Of course I want you to marry me. Have I said a word about it, though? Nary a chirp, nary a flutter. I've been quiet and good, though it's almost made me sick at times, this keeping quiet. I haven't asked you to marry me. I'm not asking you now. Oh, not but what you satisfy me. I sure know you're the wife for me. But how about myself? Do you know me well enough know your own mind?" He shrugged his shoulders. "I don't know, and I ain't going to take chances on it now. You've got to know for sure whether you think you could get along with me or not, and I'm playing a slow conservative game. I ain't a-going to lose for overlooking my hand."

This was love-making of a sort beyond Dede's experience. Nor had she ever heard of anything like it. Furthermore, its lack of ardor carried with it a shock which she could overcome only by remembering the way his hand had trembled in the past, and by remembering the passion she had seen that very day and every day in his eyes, or heard in his voice. Then, too, she recollected what he had said to her weeks before: "Maybe you don't know what patience is," he had said, and thereat told her of shooting squirrels with a big rifle the time he and Elijah Davis had starved on the Stewart River.

"So you see," he urged, "just for a square deal we've got to see some more of each other this winter. Most likely your mind ain't made up yet--"

"But it is," she interrupted. "I wouldn't dare permit myself to care for you. Happiness, for me, would not lie that way. I like you, Mr. Harnish, and all that, but it can never be more than that."

"It's because you don't like my way of living," he charged, thinking in his own mind of the sensational joyrides and general profligacy with which the newspapers had credited him--thinking this, and wondering whether or not, in maiden modesty, she would disclaim knowledge of it.

To his surprise, her answer was flat and uncompromising.

"No; I don't."

"I know I've been brash on some of those rides that got into the papers," he began his defense, "and that I've been travelling with a lively crowd--"

"I don't mean that," she said, "though I know about it too, and can't say that I like it. But it is your life in general, your business. There are women in the world who could marry a man like you and be happy, but I couldn't. And the more I cared for such a man, the more unhappy I should be. You see, my unhappiness, in turn, would tend to make him unhappy. I should make a mistake, and he would make an equal mistake, though his would not be so hard on him because he would still have his business."

"Business!" Daylight gasped. "What's wrong with my business? I play fair and square. There's nothing under hand about it, which can't be said of most businesses, whether of the big corporations or of the cheating, lying, little corner-grocerymen. I play the straight rules of the game, and I don't have to lie or cheat or break my word."

Dede hailed with relief the change in the conversation and at the same time the opportunity to speak her mind.

"In ancient Greece," she began pedantically, "a man was judged a good citizen who built houses, planted trees--" She did not complete the quotation, but drew the conclusion hurriedly. "How many houses have you built? How many trees have you planted?"

He shook his head noncommittally, for he had not grasped the drift of the argument.

"Well," she went on, "two winters ago you cornered coal--"

"Just locally," he grinned reminiscently, "just locally. And I took advantage of the car shortage and the strike in British Columbia."

"But you didn't dig any of that coal yourself. Yet you forced it up four dollars a ton and made a lot of money. That was your business. You made the poor people pay more for their coal. You played fair, as you said, but you put your hands down into all their pockets and took their money away from them. I know. I burn a grate fire in my sitting-room at Berkeley. And instead of eleven dollars a ton for Rock Wells, I paid fifteen dollars that winter. You robbed me of four dollars. I could stand it. But there were thousands of the very poor who could not stand it. You might call it legal gambling, but to me it was downright robbery."

Daylight was not abashed. This was no revelation to him. He remembered the old woman who made wine in the Sonoma hills and the millions like her who were made to be robbed.

"Now look here, Miss Mason, you've got me there slightly, I grant. But you've seen me in business a long time now, and you know I don't make a practice of raiding the poor people. I go after the big fellows. They're my meat. They rob the poor, and I rob them. That coal deal was an accident. I wasn't after the poor people in that, but after the big fellows, and I got them, too. The poor people happened to get in the way and got hurt, that was all.

"Don't you see," he went on, "the whole game is a gamble. Everybody gambles in one way or another. The farmer gambles against the weather and the market on his crops. So does the United States Steel Corporation. The business of lots of men is straight robbery of the poor people. But I've never made that my business. You know that. I've always gone after the robbers."

"I missed my point," she admitted. "Wait a minute."

And for a space they rode in silence.

"I see it more clearly than I can state it, but it's something like this. There is legitimate work, and there's work that--well, that isn't legitimate. The farmer works the soil and produces grain. He's making something that is good for humanity. He actually, in a way, creates something, the grain that will fill the mouths of the hungry."

"And then the railroads and market-riggers and the rest proceed to rob him of that same grain," Daylight broke in.

Dede smiled and held up her hand.

"Wait a minute. You'll make me lose my point. It doesn't hurt if they rob him of all of it so that he starves to death. The point is that the wheat he grew is still in the world. It exists. Don't you see? The farmer created something, say ten tons of wheat, and those ten tons exist. The railroads haul the wheat to market, to the mouths that will eat it. This also is legitimate. It's like some one bringing you a glass of water, or taking a cinder out of your eye. Something has been done, in a way been created, just like the wheat."

"But the railroads rob like Sam Scratch," Daylight objected.

"Then the work they do is partly legitimate and partly not. Now we come to you. You don't create anything. Nothing new exists when you're done with your business. Just like the coal. You didn't dig it. You didn't haul it to market. You didn't deliver it. Don't you see? that's what I meant by planting the trees and building the houses. You haven't planted one tree nor built a single house."

"I never guessed there was a woman in the world who could talk business like that," he murmured admiringly. "And you've got me on that point. But there's a lot to be said on my side just the same. Now you listen to me. I'm going to talk under three heads. Number one: We live a short time, the best of us, and we're a long time dead. Life is a big gambling game. Some are born lucky and some are born unlucky. Everybody sits in at the table, and everybody tries to rob everybody else. Most of them get robbed. They're born suckers. A fellow like me comes along and sizes up the proposition. I've got two choices. I can herd with the suckers, or I can herd with the robbers. As a sucker, I win nothing. Even the crusts of bread are snatched out of my mouth by the robbers. I work hard all my days, and die working. And I ain't never had a flutter. I've had nothing but work, work, work. They talk about the dignity of labor. I tell you there ain't no dignity in that sort of labor. My other choice is to herd with the robbers, and I herd with them. I play that choice wide open to win. I get the automobiles, and the porterhouse steaks, and the soft beds.

"Number two: There ain't much difference between playing halfway robber like the railroad hauling that farmer's wheat to market, and playing all robber and robbing the robbers like I do. And, besides, halfway robbery is too slow a game for me to sit in. You don't win quick enough for me."

"But what do you want to win for?" Dede demanded. "You have millions and millions, already. You can't ride in more than one automobile at a time, sleep in more than one bed at a time."

"Number three answers that," he said, "and here it is: Men and things are so made that they have different likes. A rabbit likes a vegetarian diet. A lynx likes meat. Ducks swim; chickens are scairt of water. One man collects postage stamps, another man collects butterflies. This man goes in for paintings, that man goes in for yachts, and some other fellow for hunting big game. One man thinks horse-racing is It, with a big I, and another man finds the biggest satisfaction in actresses. They can't help these likes. They have them, and what are they going to do about it? Now I like gambling. I like to play the game. I want to play it big and play it quick. I'm just made that way. And I play it."

"But why can't you do good with all your money?"

Daylight laughed.

"Doing good with your money! It's like slapping God in the face, as much as to tell him that he don't know how to run his world and that you'll be much obliged if he'll stand out of the way and give you a chance. Thinking about God doesn't keep me sitting up nights, so I've got another way of looking at it. Ain't it funny, to go around with brass knuckles and a big club breaking folks' heads and taking their money away from them until I've got a pile, and then, repenting of my ways, going around and bandaging up the heads the other robbers are breaking? I leave it to you. That's what doing good with money amounts to. Every once in a while some robber turns soft-hearted and takes to driving an ambulance. That's what Carnegie did. He smashed heads in pitched battles at Homestead, regular wholesale head-breaker he was, held up the suckers for a few hundred million, and now he goes around dribbling it back to them. funny? I leave it to you."

He rolled a cigarette and watched her half curiously, half amusedly. His replies and harsh generalizations of a harsh school were disconcerting, and she came back to her earlier position.

"I can't argue with you, and you know that. No matter how right a woman is, men have such a way about them well, what they say sounds most convincing, and yet the woman is still certain they are wrong. But there is one thing--the creative joy. Call it gambling if you will, but just the same it seems to me more satisfying to create something, make something, than just to roll dice out of a dice-box all day long. Why, sometimes, for exercise, or when I've got to pay fifteen dollars for coal, I curry Mab and give her a whole half hour's brushing. And when I see her coat clean and shining and satiny, I feel a satisfaction in what I've done. So it must be with the man who builds a house or plants a tree. He can look at it. He made it. It's his handiwork. Even if somebody like you comes along and takes his tree away from him, still it is there, and still did he make it. You can't rob him of that, Mr. Harnish, with all your millions. It's the creative joy, and it's a higher joy than mere gambling. Haven't you ever made things yourself--a log cabin up in the Yukon, or a canoe, or raft, or something? And don't you remember how satisfied you were, how good you felt, while you were doing it and after you had it done?"

While she spoke his memory was busy with the associations she recalled. He saw the deserted flat on the river bank by the Klondike, and he saw the log cabins and warehouses spring up, and all the log structures he had built, and his sawmills working night and day on three shifts.

"Why, dog-gone it, Miss Mason, you're right--in a way. I've built hundreds of houses up there, and I remember I was proud and glad to see them go up. I'm proud now, when I remember them. And there was Ophir--the most God-forsaken moose-pasture of a creek you ever laid eyes on. I made that into the big Ophir. Why, I ran the water in there from the Rinkabilly, eighty miles away. They all said I couldn't, but I did it, and I did it by myself. The dam and the flume cost me four million. But you should have seen that Ophir--power plants, electric lights, and hundreds of men on the pay-roll, working night and day. I guess I do get an inkling of what you mean by making a thing. I made Ophir, and by God, she was a sure hummer--I beg your pardon. I didn't mean to cuss. But that Ophir !--I sure am proud of her now, just as the last time I laid eyes on her."

"And you won something there that was more than mere money," Dede encouraged. "Now do you know what I would do if I had lots of money and simply had to go on playing at business? Take all the southerly and westerly slopes of these bare hills. I'd buy them in and plant eucalyptus on them. I'd do it for the joy of doing it anyway; but suppose I had that gambling twist in me which you talk about, why, I'd do it just the same and make money out of the trees. And there's my other point again. Instead of raising the price of coal without adding an ounce of coal to the market supply, I'd be making thousands and thousands of cords of firewood--making something where nothing was before. And everybody who ever crossed on the ferries would look up at these forested hills and be made glad. Who was made glad by your adding four dollars a ton to Rock Wells?"

It was Daylight's turn to be silent for a time while she waited an answer.

"Would you rather I did things like that?" he asked at last.

"It would be better for the world, and better for you," she answered non-committally.

CHAPTER 16

All week every one in the office knew that something new and big was afoot in Daylight's mind. Beyond some deals of no importance, he had not been interested in anything for several months. But now he went about in an almost unbroken brown study, made unexpected and lengthy trips across the bay to Oakland, or sat at his desk silent and motionless for hours. He seemed particularly happy with what occupied his mind. At times men came in and conferred with him--and with new faces and differing in type from those that usually came to see him.

On Sunday Dede learned all about it.

"I've been thinking a lot of our talk," he began, "and I've got an idea I'd like to give it a flutter. And I've got a proposition to make your hair stand up. It's what you call legitimate, and at the same time it's the gosh-dangdest gamble a man ever went into. How about planting minutes wholesale, and making two minutes grow where one minute grew before? Oh, yes, and planting a few trees, too--say several million of them. You remember the quarry I made believe I was looking at? Well, I'm going to buy it. I'm going to buy these hills, too, clear from here around to Berkeley and down the other way to San Leandro. I own a lot of them already, for that matter. But mum is the word. I'll be buying a long time to come before anything much is guessed about it, and I don't want the market to jump up out of sight. You see that hill over there. It's my hill running clear down its slopes through Piedmont and halfway along those rolling hills into Oakland. And it's nothing to all the things I'm going to buy."

He paused triumphantly.

"And all to make two minutes grow where one grew before?" Dede queried, at the same time laughing heartily at his affectation of mystery.

He stared at her fascinated. She had such a frank, boyish way of throwing her head back when she laughed. And her teeth were an unending delight to him. Not small, yet regular and firm, without a blemish, he considered then the healthiest, whitest, prettiest teeth he had ever seen. And for months he had been comparing them with the teeth of every woman he met.

It was not until her laughter was over that he was able to continue.

"The ferry system between Oakland and San Francisco is the worst one-horse concern in the United States. You cross on it every day, six days in the week. That's say, twenty-five days a month, or three hundred a year. Now long does it take you one way? Forty minutes, if you're lucky. I'm going to put you across in twenty minutes. If that ain't making two minutes grow where one grew before, knock off my head with little apples. I'll save you twenty minutes each way. That's forty minutes a day, times three hundred, equals twelve thousand minutes a year, just for you, just for one person. Let's see: that's two hundred whole hours. Suppose I save two hundred hours a year for thousands of other folks,--that's farming some, ain't it?"

Dede could only nod breathlessly. She had caught the contagion of his enthusiasm, though she had no clew as to how this great time-saving was to be accomplished.

"Come on," he said. "Let's ride up that hill, and when I get you out on top where you can see something, I'll talk sense."

A small footpath dropped down to the dry bed of the canon, which they crossed before they began the climb. The slope was steep and covered with matted brush and bushes, through which the horses slipped and lunged. Bob, growing disgusted, turned back suddenly and attempted to pass Mab. The mare was thrust sidewise into the denser bush, where she nearly fell.

Recovering, she flung her weight against Bob. Both riders' legs were caught in the consequent squeeze, and, as Bob plunged ahead down hill, Dede was nearly scraped off. Daylight threw his horse on to its haunches and at the same time dragged Dede back into the saddle. Showers of twigs and leaves fell upon them, and predicament followed predicament, until they emerged on the hilltop the worse for wear but happy and excited. Here no trees obstructed the view. The particular hill on which they were, out-jutted from the regular line of the range, so that the sweep of their vision extended over three-quarters of the circle. Below, on the flat land bordering the bay, lay Oakland, and across the bay was San Francisco. Between the two cities they could see the white ferry-boats on the water. Around to their right was Berkeley, and to their left the scattered villages between Oakland and San Leandro. Directly in the foreground was Piedmont, with its desultory dwellings and patches of farming land, and from Piedmont the land rolled down in successive waves upon Oakland.

"Look at it," said Daylight, extending his arm in a sweeping gesture. "A hundred thousand people there, and no reason there shouldn't be half a million. There's the chance to make five people grow where one grows now. Here's the scheme in a nutshell. Why don't more people live in Oakland? No good service with San Francisco, and, besides, Oakland is asleep. It's a whole lot better place to live in than San Francisco. Now, suppose I buy in all the street railways of Oakland, Berkeley, Alameda, San Leandro, and the rest,--bring them under one head with a competent management? Suppose I cut the time to San Francisco one-half by building a big pier out there almost to Goat Island and establishing a ferry system with modern up-to-date boats? Why, folks will want to live over on this side. Very good. They'll need land on which to build. So, first I buy up the land. But the land's cheap now. Why? Because it's in the country, no electric roads, no quick communication, nobody guessing that the electric roads are coming. I'll build the roads. That will make the land jump up. Then I'll sell the land as fast as the folks will want to buy because of the improved ferry system and transportation facilities.

"You see, I give the value to the land by building the roads. Then I sell the land and get that value back, and after that, there's the roads, all carrying folks back and forth and earning big money. Can't lose. And there's all sorts of millions in it. I'm going to get my hands on some of that water front and the tide-lands. Take between where I'm going to build my pier and the old pier. It's shallow water. I can fill and dredge and put in a system of docks that will handle hundreds of ships. San Francisco's water front is congested. No more room for ships. With hundreds of ships loading and unloading on this side right into the freight cars of three big railroads, factories will start up over here instead of crossing to San Francisco. That means factory sites. That means me buying in the factory sites before anybody guesses the cat is going to jump, much less, which way. Factories mean tens of thousands of workingmen and their families. That means more houses and more land, and that means me, for I'll be there to sell them the land. And tens of thousands of families means tens of thousands of nickels every day for my electric cars. The growing population will mean more stores, more banks, more everything. And that'll mean me, for I'll be right there with business property as well as home property. What do you think of it?"

Before she could answer, he was off again, his mind's eye filled with this new city of his dream which he builded on the Alameda hills by the gateway to the Orient.

142

"Do you know--I've been looking it up--the Firth Of Clyde, where all the steel ships are built, isn't half as wide as Oakland Creek down there, where all those old hulks lie? Why ain't it a Firth of Clyde? Because the Oakland City Council spends its time debating about prunes and raisins. What is needed is somebody to see things, and, after that, organization. That's me. I didn't make Ophir for nothing. And once things begin to hum, outside capital will pour in. All I do is start it going. 'Gentlemen,' I say, 'here's all the natural advantages for a great metropolis. God Almighty put them advantages here, and he put me here to see them. Do you want to land your tea and silk from Asia and ship it straight East? Here's the docks for your steamers, and here's the railroads. Do you want factories from which you can ship direct by land or water? Here's the site, and here's the modern, up-to-date city, with the latest improvements for yourselves and your workmen, to live in.'"

"Then there's the water. I'll come pretty close to owning the watershed. Why not the waterworks too? There's two water companies in Oakland now, fighting like cats and dogs and both about broke. What a metropolis needs is a good water system. They can't give it. They're stick-in-the-muds. I'll gobble them up and deliver the right article to the city. There's money there, too--money everywhere. Everything works in with everything else. Each improvement makes the value of everything else pump up. It's people that are behind the value. The bigger the crowd that herds in one place, the more valuable is the real estate. And this is the very place for a crowd to herd. Look at it. Just look at it! You could never find a finer site for a great city. All it needs is the herd, and I'll stampede a couple of hundred thousand people in here ins two years. And what's more it won't be one of these wild cat land booms. It will be legitimate. Twenty years for now there'll be a million people on this side the bay. Another thing is hotels. There isn't a decent one in the town. I'll build a couple of up-to-date ones that'll make them sit up and take notice. I won't care if they don't pay for years. Their effect will more than give me my money back out of the other holdings. And, oh, yes, I'm going to plant eucalyptus, millions of them, on these hills."

"But how are you going to do it?" Dede asked. "You haven't enough money for all that you've planned."

"I've thirty million, and if I need more I can borrow on the land and other things. Interest on mortgages won't anywhere near eat up the increase in land values, and I'll be selling land right along."

In the weeks that followed, Daylight was a busy man. He spent most of his time in Oakland, rarely coming to the office. He planned to move the office to Oakland, but, as he told Dede, the secret preliminary campaign of buying had to be put through first. Sunday by Sunday, now from this hilltop and now from that, they looked down upon the city and its farming suburbs, and he pointed out to her his latest acquisitions. At first it was patches and sections of land here and there; but as the weeks passed it was the unowned portions that became rare, until at last they stood as islands surrounded by Daylight's land.

It meant quick work on a colossal scale, for Oakland and the adjacent country was not slow to feel the tremendous buying. But Daylight had the ready cash, and it had always been his policy to strike quickly. Before the others could get the warning of the boom, he quietly accomplished many things. At the same time that his agents were purchasing corner lots and entire blocks in the heart of the business section and the waste lands for factory sites, Day was rushing franchises through the city council, capturing the two exhausted water companies and the eight or nine independent street railways, and getting his grip on the Oakland Creek and the bay tide-lands for his dock system. The tide-lands had been in litigation for years, and he took the bull by the horns--buying out the private owners and at the same time leasing from the city fathers.

By the time that Oakland was aroused by this unprecedented activity in every direction and was questioning excitedly the meaning of it, Daylight secretly bought the chief Republican newspaper and the chief Democratic organ, and moved boldly into his new offices. Of necessity, they were on a large scale, occupying four floors of the only modern office building in the town--the only building that wouldn't have to be torn down later on, as Daylight put it. There was department after department, a score of them, and hundreds of clerks and stenographers. As he told Dede: --

"I've got more companies than you can shake a stick at. There's the Alameda & Contra Costa Land Syndicate, the Consolidated Street Railways, the Yerba Buena Ferry Company, the United Water Company, the Piedmont Realty Company, the Fairview and Portola Hotel Company, and half a dozen more that I've got to refer to a notebook to remember. There's the Piedmont Laundry Farm, and Redwood Consolidated Quarries. Starting in with our quarry, I just kept a-going till I got them all. And there's the ship-building company I ain't got a name for yet. Seeing as I had to have ferry-boats, I decided to build them myself. They'll be done by the time the pier is ready for them. Phew! It all sure beats poker. And I've had the fun of gouging the robber gangs as well. The water company bunches are squealing yet. I sure got them where the hair was short. They were just about all in when I came along and finished them off."

"But why do you hate them so?" Dede asked.

"Because they're such cowardly skunks."

"But you play the same game they do."

"Yes; but not in the same way." Daylight regarded her thoughtfully. "When I say cowardly skunks, I mean just that,--cowardly skunks. They set up for a lot of gamblers, and there ain't one in a thousand of them that's got the nerve to be a gambler. They're four-flushers, if you know what that means. They're a lot of little cottontail rabbits making believe they're big rip-snorting timber wolves. They set out to everlastingly eat up some proposition but at the first sign of trouble they turn tail and stampede for the brush. Look how it works. When the big fellows wanted to unload Little Copper, they sent Jakey Fallow into the New York Stock Exchange to yell out: 'I'll buy all or any part of Little Copper at fifty five,' Little Copper being at fifty-four. And in thirty minutes them cottontails-- *financiers*, some folks call them--bid up Little Copper to sixty. And an hour after that, stampeding for the brush, they were throwing Little Copper overboard at forty-five and even forty.

"They're catspaws for the big fellows. Almost as fast as they rob the suckers, the big fellows come along and hold them up. Or else the big fellows use them in order to rob each other. That's the way the Chattanooga Coal and Iron Company was swallowed up by the trust in the last panic. The trust made that panic. It had to break a couple of big banking companies and squeeze half a dozen big fellows, too, and it did it by stampeding the cottontails. The cottontails did the rest all right, and the trust gathered in Chattanooga Coal and Iron. Why, any man, with nerve and savvee, can start them cottontails jumping for the brush. I don't exactly hate them myself, but I haven't any regard for chicken-hearted four-flushers."

144

CHAPTER 17

For months Daylight was buried in work. The outlay was terrific, and there was nothing coming in. Beyond a general rise in land values, Oakland had not acknowledged his irruption on the financial scene. The city was waiting for him to show what he was going to do, and he lost no time about it. The best skilled brains on the market were hired by him for the different branches of the work. Initial mistakes he had no patience with, and he was determined to start right, as when he engaged Wilkinson, almost doubling his big salary, and brought him out from Chicago to take charge of the street railway organization. Night and day the road gangs toiled on the streets. And night and day the pile-drivers hammered the big piles down into the mud of San Francisco Bay. The pier was to be three miles long, and the Berkeley hills were denuded of whole groves of mature eucalyptus for the piling.

At the same time that his electric roads were building out through the hills, the hay-fields were being surveyed and broken up into city squares, with here and there, according to best modern methods, winding boulevards and strips of park. Broad streets, well graded, were made, with sewers and water-pipes ready laid, and macadamized from his own quarries. Cement sidewalks were also laid, so that all the purchaser had to do was to select his lot and architect and start building. The quick service of Daylight's new electric roads into Oakland made this big district immediately accessible, and long before the ferry system was in operation hundreds of residences were going up. The profit on this land was enormous. In a day, his onslaught of wealth had turned open farming country into one of the best residential districts of the city.

But this money that flowed in upon him was immediately poured back into his other investments. The need for electric cars was so great that he installed his own shops for building them. And even on the rising land market, he continued to buy choice factory sites and building properties. On the advice of Wilkinson, practically every electric road already in operation was rebuilt. The light, old fashioned rails were torn out and replaced by the heaviest that were manufactured. Corner lots, on the sharp turns of narrow streets, were bought and ruthlessly presented to the city in order to make wide curves for his tracks and high speed for his cars. Then, too, there were the main-line feeders for his ferry system, tapping every portion of Oakland, Alameda, and Berkeley, and running fast expresses to the pier end. The same large-scale methods were employed in the water system. Service of the best was needed, if his huge land investment was to succeed. Oakland had to be made into a worth-while city, and that was what he intended to do. In addition to his big hotels, he built amusement parks for the common people, and art galleries and club-house country inns for the more finicky classes. Even before there was any increase in population, a marked increase in street-railway traffic took place. There was nothing fanciful about his schemes. They were sound investments.

"What Oakland wants is a first-class theatre," he said, and, after vainly trying to interest local capital, he started the building of the theatre himself; for he alone had vision for the two hundred thousand new people that were coming to the town.

But no matter what pressure was on Daylight, his Sundays he reserved for his riding in the hills. It was not the winter weather, however, that brought these rides with Dede to an end. One Saturday afternoon in the office she told him not to expect to meet her next day, and, when he pressed for an explanation: --

145

"I've sold Mab."

Daylight was speechless for the moment. Her act meant one of so many serious things that he couldn't classify it. It smacked almost of treachery. She might have met with financial disaster.

It might be her way of letting him know she had seen enough of him. Or...

"What's the matter?" he managed to ask.

"I couldn't afford to keep her with hay forty-five dollars a ton," Dede answered.

"Was that your only reason?" he demanded, looking at her steadily; for he remembered her once telling him how she had brought the mare through one winter, five years before, when hay had gone as high as sixty dollars a ton.

"No. My brother's expenses have been higher, as well, and I was driven to the conclusion that since I could not afford both, I'd better let the mare go and keep the brother."

Daylight felt inexpressibly saddened. He was suddenly aware of a great emptiness. What would a Sunday be without Dede? And Sundays without end without her? He drummed perplexedly on the desk with his fingers.

"Who bought her?" he asked.

Dede's eyes flashed in the way long since familiar to him when she was angry.

"Don't you dare buy her back for me," she cried. "And don't deny that that was what you had in mind."

"No, I won't deny it. It was my idea to a tee. But I wouldn't have done it without asking you first, and seeing how you feel about it, I won't even ask you. But you thought a heap of that mare, and it's pretty hard on you to lose her. I'm sure sorry. And I'm sorry, too, that you won't be riding with me tomorrow. I'll be plumb lost. I won't know what to do with myself."

"Neither shall I," Dede confessed mournfully, "except that I shall be able to catch up with my sewing."

"But I haven't any sewing."

Daylight's tone was whimsically plaintive, but secretly he was delighted with her confession of loneliness. It was almost worth the loss of the mare to get that out of her. At any rate, he meant something to her. He was not utterly unliked.

"I wish you would reconsider, Miss Mason," he said softly. "Not alone for the mare's sake, but for my sake. Money don't cut any ice in this. For me to buy that mare wouldn't mean as it does to most men to send a bouquet of flowers or a box of candy to a young lady. And I've never sent you flowers or candy." He observed the warning flash of her eyes, and hurried on to escape refusal. "I'll tell you what we'll do. Suppose I buy the mare and own her myself, and lend her to you when you want to ride. There's nothing wrong in that. Anybody borrows a horse from anybody, you know."

Again he saw refusal, and headed her off.

"Lots of men take women buggy-riding. There's nothing wrong in that. And the man always furnishes the horse and buggy. Well, now, what's the difference between my taking you buggy-riding and furnishing the horse and buggy, and taking you horse-back-riding and furnishing the horses?"

She shook her head, and declined to answer, at the same time looking at the door as if to intimate that it was time for this unbusinesslike conversation to end. He made one more effort.

"Do you know, Miss Mason, I haven't a friend in the world outside you? I mean a real friend, man or woman, the kind you chum with, you know, and that you're glad to be with and sorry to be away from. Hegan is the

146

nearest man I get to, and he's a million miles away from me. Outside business, we don't hitch. He's got a big library of books, and some crazy kind of culture, and he spends all his off times reading things in French and German and other outlandish lingoes--when he ain't writing plays and poetry. There's nobody I feel chummy with except you, and you know how little we've chummed--once a week, if it didn't rain, on Sunday. I've grown kind of to depend on you. You're a sort of--of--of--"

"A sort of habit," she said with a smile.

"That's about it. And that mare, and you astride of her, coming along the road under the trees or through the sunshine--why, with both you and the mare missing, there won't be anything worth waiting through the week for. If you'd just let me buy her back--"

"No, no; I tell you no." Dede rose impatiently, but her eyes were moist with the memory of her pet. "Please don't mention her to me again. If you think it was easy to part with her, you are mistaken. But I've seen the last of her, and I want to forget her."

Daylight made no answer, and the door closed behind him.

Half an hour later he was conferring with Jones, the erstwhile elevator boy and rabid proletarian whom Daylight long before had grubstaked to literature for a year. The resulting novel had been a failure. Editors and publishers would not look at it, and now Daylight was using the disgruntled author in a little private secret service system he had been compelled to establish for himself. Jones, who affected to be surprised at nothing after his crushing experience with railroad freight rates on firweood and charcoal, betrayed no surprise now when the task was given to him to locate the purchaser of a certain sorrel mare.

"How high shall I pay for her?" he asked.

"Any price. You've got to get her, that's the point. Drive a sharp bargain so as not to excite suspicion, but her. Then you deliver her to that address up in Sonoma County. The man's the caretaker on a little ranch I have there. Tell him he's to take whacking good care of her. And after that forget all about it. Don't tell me the name of the man you buy her from. Don't tell me anything about it except that you've got her and delivered her. Savvee?"

But the week had not passed, when Daylight noted the flash in Dede's eyes that boded trouble.

"Something's gone wrong--what is it?" he asked boldly.

"Mab," she said. "The man who bought her has sold her already. If I thought you had anything to do with it--"

"I don't even know who you sold her to," was Daylight's answer. "And what's more, I'm not bothering my head about her. She was your mare, and it's none of my business what you did with her. You haven't got her, that's sure and worse luck. And now, while we're on touchy subjects, I'm going to open another one with you. And you needn't get touchy about it, for it's not really your business at all."

She waited in the pause that followed, eyeing him almost suspiciously.

"It's about that brother of yours. He needs more than you can do for him. Selling that mare of yours won't send him to Germany. And that's what his own doctors say he needs--that crack German specialist who rips a man's bones and muscles into pulp and then molds them all over again. Well, I want to send him to Germany and give that crack a flutter, that's all."

"If it were only possible" she said, half breathlessly, and wholly without anger. "Only it isn't, and you know it isn't. I can't accept money from you--"

"Hold on, now," he interrupted. "Wouldn't you accept a drink of water from one of the Twelve Apostles if you was dying of thirst? Or would you be afraid of his evil intentions"--she made a gesture of dissent "--or of folks might say about it?"

"But that's different," she began.

"Now look here, Miss Mason. You've got to get some foolish notions out of your head. This money notion is one of the funniest things I've seen. Suppose you was falling over a cliff, wouldn't it be all right for me to reach out and hold you by the arm? Sure it would. But suppose you ended another sort of help--instead of the strength of arm, the strength of my pocket? That would be all and that's what they all say. But why do they say it. Because the robber gangs want all the suckers to be honest and respect money. If the suckers weren't honest and didn't respect money, where would the robbers be? Don't you see? The robbers don't deal in arm-holds; they deal in dollars. Therefore arm-holds are just common and ordinary, while dollars are sacred--so sacred that you didn't let me lend you a hand with a few.

"Or here's another way," he continued, spurred on by her mute protest. "It's all right for me to give the strength of my arm when you're falling over a cliff. But if I take that same strength of arm and use it at pick-and-shovel work for a day and earn two dollars, you won't have anything to do with the two dollars. Yet it's the same old strength of arm in a new form, that's all. Besides, in this proposition it won't be a claim on you. It ain't even a loan to you. It's an arm-hold I'm giving your brother--just the same sort of arm-hold as if he was falling over a cliff. And a nice one you are, to come running out and yell 'Stop!' at me, and let your brother go on over the cliff. What he needs to save his legs is that crack in Germany, and that's the arm-hold I'm offering.

"Wish you could see my rooms. Walls all decorated with horsehair bridles--scores of them--hundreds of them. They're no use to me, and they cost like Sam Scratch. But there's a lot of convicts making them, and I go on buying. Why, I've spent more money in a single night on whiskey than would get the best specialists and pay all the expenses of a dozen cases like your brother's. And remember, you've got nothing to do with this. If your brother wants to look on it as a loan, all right. It's up to him, and you've got to stand out of the way while I pull him back from that cliff."

Still Dede refused, and Daylight's argument took a more painful turn.

"I can only guess that you're standing in your brother's way on account of some mistaken idea in your head that this is my idea of courting. Well, it ain't. You might as well think I'm courting all those convicts I buy bridles from. I haven't asked you to marry me, and if I do I won't come trying to buy you into consenting. And there won't be anything underhand when I come a-asking."

Dede's face was flushed and angry.

"If you knew how ridiculous you are, you'd stop," she blurted out. "You can make me more uncomfortable than any man I ever knew. Every little while you give me to understand that you haven't asked me to marry you yet. I'm not waiting to be asked, and I warned you from the first that you had no chance. And yet you hold it over my head that some time, some day, you're going to ask me to marry you. Go ahead and ask me now, and get your answer and get it over and done with."

He looked at her in honest and pondering admiration. "I want you so bad, Miss Mason, that I don't dast to ask you now," he said, with such whimsicality and earnestness as to make her throw her head back in a frank boyish laugh. "Besides, as I told you, I'm green at it. I never went a-courting before, and I don't want to make any mistakes."

"But you're making them all the time," she cried impulsively. "No man ever courted a woman by holding a threatened proposal over her head like a club."

"I won't do it any more," he said humbly. "And anyway, we're off the argument. My straight talk a minute ago still holds. You're standing in your brother's way. No matter what notions you've got in your head, you've got to get out of the way and give him a chance. Will you let me go and see him and talk it over with him? I'll make it a hard and fast business proposition. I'll stake him to get well, that's all, and charge him interest."

She visibly hesitated.

"And just remember one thing, Miss Mason: it's HIS leg, not yours."

Still she refrained from giving her answer, and Daylight went on strengthening his position.

"And remember, I go over to see him alone. He's a man, and I can deal with him better without womenfolks around. I'll go over to-morrow afternoon."

CHAPTER 18

Daylight had been wholly truthful when he told Dede that he had no real friends. On speaking terms with thousands, on fellowship and drinking terms with hundreds, he was a lonely man. He failed to find the one man, or group of several men, with whom he could be really intimate. Cities did not make for comradeship as did the Alaskan trail. Besides, the types of men were different. Scornful and contemptuous of business men on the one hand, on the other his relations with the San Francisco bosses had been more an alliance of expediency than anything else. He had felt more of kinship for the franker brutality of the bosses and their captains, but they had failed to claim any deep respect. They were too prone to crookedness. Bonds were better than men's word in this modern world, and one had to look carefully to the bonds. In the old Yukon days it had been different. Bonds didn't go. A man said he had so much, and even in a poker game his appeasement was accepted.

Larry Hegan, who rose ably to the largest demands of Daylight's operations and who had few illusions and less hypocrisy, might have proved a chum had it not been for his temperamental twist. Strange genius that he was, a Napoleon of the law, with a power of visioning that far exceeded Daylight's, he had nothing in common with Daylight outside the office. He spent his time with books, a thing Daylight could not abide. Also, he devoted himself to the endless writing of plays which never got beyond manuscript form, and, though Daylight only sensed the secret taint of it, was a confirmed but temperate eater of hasheesh. Hegan lived all his life cloistered with books in a world of agitation. With the out-of-door world he had no understanding nor tolerance. In food and drink he was abstemious as a monk, while exercise was a thing abhorrent.

Daylight's friendships, in lieu of anything closer, were drinking friendships and roistering friendships. And with the passing of the Sunday rides with Dede, he fell back more and more upon these for diversion. The cocktail wall of inhibition he reared more assiduously than ever. The big red motor-car was out more frequently now, while a stable hand was hired to give Bob exercise. In his early San Francisco days, there had been intervals of easement between his deals, but in this present biggest deal of all the strain was unremitting. Not in a month, or two, or three, could his huge land investment be carried to a successful consummation. And so complete and wide-reaching was it that complications and knotty situations constantly arose. Every day brought its problems, and when he had solved them in his masterful way, he left the office in his big car, almost sighing with relief at anticipation of the approaching double Martini. Rarely was he made tipsy. His constitution was too strong for that. Instead, he was that direst of all drinkers, the steady drinker, deliberate and controlled, who averaged a far higher quantity of alcohol than the irregular and violent drinker.

For six weeks hard-running he had seen nothing of Dede except in the office, and there he resolutely refrained from making approaches. But by the seventh Sunday his hunger for her overmastered him. It was a stormy day. A heavy southeast gale was blowing, and squall after squall of rain and wind swept over the city. He could not take his mind off of her, and a persistent picture came to him of her sitting by a window and sewing feminine fripperies of some sort. When the time came for his first pre-luncheon cocktail to be served to him in his rooms, he did not take it. Filled with a daring determination, he glanced at his note book for Dede's telephone number, and called for the switch.

At first it was her landlady's daughter who was raised, but in a minute he heard the voice he had been hungry to hear.

"I just wanted to tell you that I'm coming out to see you," he said. "I didn't want to break in on you without warning, that was all."

"Has something happened?" came her voice.

"I'll tell you when I get there," he evaded.

He left the red car two blocks away and arrived on foot at the pretty, three-storied, shingled Berkeley house. For an instant only, he was aware of an inward hesitancy, but the next moment he rang the bell. He knew that what he was doing was in direct violation of her wishes, and that he was setting her a difficult task to receive as a Sunday caller the multimillionaire and notorious Elam Harnish of newspaper fame. On the other hand, the one thing he did not expect of her was what he would have termed "silly female capers."

And in this he was not disappointed.

She came herself to the door to receive him and shake hands with him. He hung his mackintosh and hat on the rack in the comfortable square hall and turned to her for direction.

"They are busy in there," she said, indicating the parlor from which came the boisterous voices of young people, and through the open door of which he could see several college youths. "So you will have to come into my rooms."

She led the way through the door opening out of the hall to the right, and, once inside, he stood awkwardly rooted to the floor, gazing about him and at her and all the time trying not to gaze. In his perturbation he failed to hear and see her invitation to a seat. So these were her quarters. the intimacy of it and her making no fuss about it was startling, but it was no more than he would have expected of her. It was almost two rooms in one, the one he was in evidently the sitting-room, and the one he could see into, the bedroom. Beyond an oaken dressing-table, with an orderly litter of combs and brushes and dainty feminine knickknacks, there was no sign of its being used as a bedroom. The broad couch, with a cover of old rose and banked high with cushions, he decided must be the bed, but it was farthest from any experience of a civilized bed he had ever had.

Not that he saw much of detail in that awkward moment of standing. His general impression was one of warmth and comfort and beauty. There were no carpets, and on the hardwood floor he caught a glimpse of several wolf and coyote skins. What captured and perceptibly held his eye for a moment was a Crouched Venus that stood on a Steinway upright against a background of mountain-lion skin on the wall.

But it was Dede herself that smote most sharply upon sense and perception. He had always cherished the idea that she was very much a woman--the lines of her figure, her hair, her eyes, her voice, and birdlike laughing ways had all contributed to this; but here, in her own rooms, clad in some flowing, clinging gown, the emphasis of sex was startling. He had been accustomed to her only in trim tailor suits and shirtwaists, or in riding costume of velvet corduroy, and he was not prepared for this new revelation. She seemed so much softer, so much more pliant, and tender, and lissome. She was a part of this atmosphere of quietude and beauty. She fitted into it just as she had fitted in with the sober office furnishings.

"Won't you sit down?" she repeated.

He felt like an animal long denied food. His hunger for her welled up in him, and he proceeded to "wolf" the dainty morsel before him. Here was no patience, no diplomacy. The straightest, direct way was none too quick for him and, had he known it, the least unsuccessful way he could have chosen.

"Look here," he said, in a voice that shook with passion, "there's one thing I won't do, and that's propose to you in the office. That's why I'm here. Dede Mason, I want you. I just want you."

While he spoke he advanced upon her, his black eyes burning with bright fire, his aroused blood swarthy in his cheek.

So precipitate was he, that she had barely time to cry out her involuntary alarm and to step back, at the same time catching one of his hands as he attempted to gather her into his arms.

In contrast to him, the blood had suddenly left her cheeks. The hand that had warded his off and that still held it, was trembling. She relaxed her fingers, and his arm dropped to his side. She wanted to say something, do something, to pass on from the awkwardness of the situation, but no intelligent thought nor action came into her mind. She was aware only of a desire to laugh. This impulse was party hysterical and partly spontaneous humor--the latter growing from instant to instant. Amazing as the affair was, the ridiculous side of it was not veiled to her. She felt like one who had suffered the terror of the onslaught of a murderous footpad only to find out that it was an innocent pedestrian asking the time.

Daylight was the quicker to achieve action.

"Oh, I know I'm a sure enough fool," he said. "I--I guess I'll sit down. Don't be scairt, Miss Mason. I'm not real dangerous."

"I'm not afraid," she answered, with a smile, slipping down herself into a chair, beside which, on the floor, stood a sewing-basket from which, Daylight noted, some white fluffy thing of lace and muslin overflowed. Again she smiled. "Though I confess you did startle me for the moment."

"It's funny," Daylight sighed, almost with regret; "here I am, strong enough to bend you around and tie knots in you. Here I am, used to having my will with man and beast and anything. And here I am sitting in this chair, as weak and helpless as a little lamb. You sure take the starch out of me."

Dede vainly cudgeled her brains in quest of a reply to these remarks. Instead, her thought dwelt insistently upon the significance of his stepping aside, in the middle of a violent proposal, in order to make irrelevant remarks. What struck her was the man's certitude. So little did he doubt that he would have her, that he could afford to pause and generalize upon love and the effects of love.

She noted his hand unconsciously slipping in the familiar way into the side coat pocket where she knew he carried his tobacco and brown papers.

"You may smoke, if you want to," she said.

He withdrew his hand with a jerk, as if something in the pocket had stung him.

"No, I wasn't thinking of smoking. I was thinking of you. What's a man to do when he wants a woman but ask her to marry him? That's all that I'm doing. I can't do it in style. I know that. But I can use straight English, and that's good enough for me. I sure want you mighty bad, Miss Mason. You're in my mind 'most all the time, now. And what I want to know is--well, do you want me? That's all."

"I--I wish you hadn't asked," she said softly.

"Mebbe it's best you should know a few things before you give me an answer," he went on, ignoring the fact that the answer had already been given. "I never went after a woman before in my life, all reports to the contrary not withstanding. The stuff you read about me in the papers and books, about me being a lady-killer, is all wrong. There's not an iota of truth in it. I guess I've done more than my share of card-playing and whiskey-drinking, but women I've let alone. There was a woman that killed herself, but I didn't know she wanted me that bad or else I'd have married her--not for love, but to keep her from killing herself. She was the best of the boiling, but I never gave her any encouragement. I'm telling you all this because you've read about it, and I want you to get it straight from me.

"Lady-killer! " he snorted. "Why, Miss Mason, I don't mind telling you that I've sure been scairt of women all my life. You're the first one I've not been afraid of. That's the strange thing about it. I just plumb worship you, and yet I'm not afraid of you. Mebbe it's because you're different from the women I know. You've never chased me. Lady-killer! Why, I've been running away from ladies ever since I can remember, and I guess all that saved me was that I was strong in the wind and that I never fell down and broke a leg or anything.

"I didn't ever want to get married until after I met you, and until a long time after I met you. I cottoned to you from the start; but I never thought it would get as bad as marriage. Why, I can't get to sleep nights, thinking of you and wanting you."

He came to a stop and waited. She had taken the lace and muslin from the basket, possibly to settle her nerves and wits, and was sewing upon it. As she was not looking at him, he devoured her with his eyes. He noted the firm, efficient hands--hands that could control a horse like Bob, that could run a typewriter almost as fast as a man could talk, that could sew on dainty garments, and that, doubtlessly, could play on the piano over there in the corner. Another ultra-feminine detail he noticed--her slippers. They were small and bronze. He had never imagined she had such a small foot. Street shoes and riding boots were all that he had ever seen on her feet, and they had given no advertisement of this. The bronze slippers fascinated him, and to them his eyes repeatedly turned.

A knock came at the door, which she answered. Daylight could not help hearing the conversation. She was wanted at the telephone.

"Tell him to call up again in ten minutes," he heard her say, and the masculine pronoun caused in him a flashing twinge of jealousy. Well, he decided, whoever it was, Burning Daylight would give him a run for his money. The marvel to him was that a girl like Dede hadn't been married long since.

She came back, smiling to him, and resumed her sewing. His eyes wandered from the efficient hands to the bronze slippers and back again, and he swore to himself that there were mighty few stenographers like her in existence. That was because she must have come of pretty good stock, and had a pretty good raising. Nothing else could explain these rooms of hers and the clothes she wore and the way she wore them.

"Those ten minutes are flying," he suggested.

"I can't marry you," she said.

"You don't love me?"

She shook her head.

"Do you like me--the littlest bit?"

This time she nodded, at the same time allowing the smile of amusement to play on her lips. But it was amusement without contempt. The humorous side of a situation rarely appealed in vain to her.

"Well, that's something to go on," he announced. "You've got to make a start to get started. I just liked you at first, and look what it's grown into. You recollect, you said you didn't like my way of life. Well, I've changed it a heap. I ain't gambling like I used to. I've gone into what you called the legitimate, making two minutes grow where one grew before, three hundred

153

thousand folks where only a hundred thousand grew before. And this time next year there'll be two million eucalyptus growing on the hills. Say do you like me more than the littlest bit?"

She raised her eyes from her work and looked at him as she answered:--

"I like you a great deal, but--"

He waited a moment for her to complete the sentence, failing which, he went on himself.

"I haven't an exaggerated opinion of myself, so I know I ain't bragging when I say I'll make a pretty good husband. You'd find I was no hand at nagging and fault-finding. I can guess what it must be for a woman like you to be independent. Well, you'd be independent as my wife. No strings on you. You could follow your own sweet will, and nothing would be too good for you. I'd give you everything your heart desired--"

"Except yourself," she interrupted suddenly, almost sharply.

Daylight's astonishment was momentary.

"I don't know about that. I'd be straight and square, and live true. I don't hanker after divided affections."

"I don't mean that," she said. "Instead of giving yourself to your wife, you would give yourself to the three hundred thousand people of Oakland, to your street railways and ferry-routes, to the two million trees on the hills --to everything business--and--and to all that that means."

"I'd see that I didn't," he declared stoutly. "I'd be yours to command--"

"You think so, but it would turn out differently." She suddenly became nervous. "We must stop this talk. It is too much like attempting to drive a bargain. 'How much will you give?' 'I'll give so much.' 'I want more,' and all that. I like you, but not enough to marry you, and I'll never like you enough to marry you."

"How do you know that?" he demanded.

"Because I like you less and less."

Daylight sat dumbfounded. The hurt showed itself plainly in his face.

"Oh, you don't understand," she cried wildly, beginning to lose self-control--"It's not that way I mean. I do like you; the more I've known you the more I've liked you. And at the same time the more I've known you the less would I care to marry you."

This enigmatic utterance completed Daylight's perplexity.

"Don't you see?" she hurried on. "I could have far easier married the Elam Harnish fresh from Klondike, when I first laid eyes on him long ago, than marry you sitting before me now."

He shook his head slowly.

"That's one too many for me. The more you know and like a man the less you want to marry him. Familiarity breeds contempt--I guess that's what you mean."

"No, no," she cried, but before she could continue, a knock came on the door.

"The ten minutes is up," Daylight said.

His eyes, quick with observation like an Indian's, darted about the room while she was out. The impression of warmth and comfort and beauty predominated, though he was unable to analyze it; while the simplicity delighted him--expensive simplicity, he decided, and most of it leftovers from the time her father went broke and died. He had never before appreciated a plain hardwood floor with a couple of wolfskins; it sure beat all the carpets in creation. He stared solemnly at a bookcase containing acCouple of hundred books. There was mystery. He could not understand what people found so much to write about. Writing things and reading

154

things were not the same as doing things, and himself primarily a man of action, doing things was alone comprehensible.

His gaze passed on from the Crouched Venus to a little tea-table with all its fragile and exquisite accessories, and to a shining copper kettle and copper chafing-dish. Chafing dishes were not unknown to him, and he wondered if she concocted suppers on this one for some of those University young men he had heard whispers about. One or two water-colors on the wall made him conjecture that she had painted them herself. There were photographs of horses and of old masters, and the trailing purple of a Burial of Christ held him for a time. But ever his gaze returned to that Crouched Venus on the piano. To his homely, frontier-trained mind, it seemed curious that a nice young woman should have such a bold, if not sinful, object on display in her own room. But he reconciled himself to it by an act of faith. Since it was Dede, it must be eminently all right. Evidently such things went along with culture. Larry Hegan had similar casts and photographs in his book-cluttered quarters. But then, Larry Hegan was different. There was that hint of unhealth about him that Daylight invariably sensed in his presence, while Dede, on the contrary, seemed always so robustly wholesome, radiating an atmosphere compounded of the sun and wind and dust of the open road. And yet, if such a clean, healthy woman as she went in for naked women crouching on her piano, it must be all right. Dede made it all right. She could come pretty close to making anything all right. Besides, he didn't understand culture anyway.

She reentered the room, and as she crossed it to her chair, he admired the way she walked, while the bronze slippers were maddening.

"I'd like to ask you several questions," he began immediately "Are you thinking of marrying somebody?"

She laughed merrily and shook her head.

"Do you like anybody else more than you like me?--that man at the 'phone just now, for instance?"

"There isn't anybody else. I don't know anybody I like well enough to marry. For that matter, I don't think I am a marrying woman. Office work seems to spoil one for that."

Daylight ran his eyes over her, from her face to the tip of a bronze slipper, in a way that made the color mantle in her cheeks. At the same time he shook his head sceptically.

"It strikes me that you're the most marryingest woman that ever made a man sit up and take notice. And now another question. You see, I've just got to locate the lay of the land. Is there anybody you like as much as you like me?"

But Dede had herself well in hand.

"That's unfair," she said. "And if you stop and consider, you will find that you are doing the very thing you disclaimed--namely, nagging. I refuse to answer any more of your questions. Let us talk about other things. How is Bob?"

Half an hour later, whirling along through the rain on Telegraph Avenue toward Oakland, Daylight smoked one of his brown-paper cigarettes and reviewed what had taken place. It was not at all bad, was his summing up, though there was much about it that was baffling. There was that liking him the more she knew him and at the same time wanting to marry him less. That was a puzzler.

But the fact that she had refused him carried with it a certain elation. In refusing him she had refused his thirty million dollars. That was going some for a ninety dollar-a-month stenographer who had known better ties. She wasn't after money, that was patent. Every woman he had encountered had seemed willing to swallow him down for the sake of his money. Why, he had doubled his fortune, made fifteen millions, since the day she first came to work for him, and behold, any willingness to marry him she might have possessed had diminished as his money had increased.

"Gosh!" he muttered. "If I clean up a hundred million on this land deal she won't even be on speaking terms with me."

But he could not smile the thing away. It remained to baffle him, that enigmatic statement of hers that she could more easily have married the Elam Harnish fresh from the Klondike than the present Elam Harnish. Well, he concluded, the thing to do was for him to become more like that old-time Daylight who had come down out of the North to try his luck at the bigger game. But that was impossible. He could not set back the flight of time. Wishing wouldn't do it, and there was no other way. He might as well wish himself a boy again.

Another satisfaction he cuddled to himself from their interview. He had heard of stenographers before, who refused their employers, and who invariably quit their positions immediately afterward. But Dede had not even hinted at such a thing. No matter how baffling she was, there was no nonsensical silliness about her. She was level headed. But, also, he had been level-headed and was partly responsible for this. He hadn't taken advantage of her in the office. True, he had twice overstepped the bounds, but he had not followed it up and made a practice of it. She knew she could trust him. But in spite of all this he was confident that most young women would have been silly enough to resign a position with a man they had turned down. And besides, after he had put it to her in the right light, she had not been silly over his sending her brother to Germany.

"Gee!" he concluded, as the car drew up before his hotel. "If I'd only known it as I do now, I'd have popped the question the first day she came to work. According to her say-so, that would have been the proper moment. She likes me more and more, and the more she likes me the less she'd care to marry me! Now what do you think of that? She sure must be fooling."

CHAPTER 19

Once again, on a rainy Sunday, weeks afterward, Daylight proposed to Dede. As on the first time, he restrained himself until his hunger for her overwhelmed him and swept him away in his red automobile to Berkeley. He left the machine several blocks away and proceeded to the house on foot. But Dede was out, the landlady's daughter told him, and added, on second thought, that she was out walking in the hills. Furthermore, the young lady directed him where Dede's walk was most likely to extend.

Daylight obeyed the girl's instructions, and soon the street he followed passed the last house and itself ceased where began the first steep slopes of the open hills. The air was damp with the on-coming of rain, for the storm had not yet burst, though the rising wind proclaimed its imminence. As far as he could see, there was no sign of Dede on the smooth, grassy hills. To the right, dipping down into a hollow and rising again, was a large, full-grown eucalyptus grove. Here all was noise and movement, the lofty, slender trunked trees swaying back and forth in the wind and clashing their branches together. In the squalls, above all the minor noises of creaking and groaning, arose a deep thrumming note as of a mighty harp. Knowing Dede as he did, Daylight was confident that he would find her somewhere in this grove where the storm effects were so pronounced. And find her he did, across the hollow and on the exposed crest of the opposing slope where the gale smote its fiercest blows.

There was something monotonous, though not tiresome, about the way Daylight proposed. Guiltless of diplomacy subterfuge, he was as direct and gusty as the gale itself. had time neither for greeting nor apology.

"It's the same old thing," he said. "I want you and I've come for you. You've just got to have me, Dede, for the more I think about it the more certain I am that you've got a Sneaking liking for me that's something more than just Ordinary liking. And you don't dast say that it isn't; now dast you?"

He had shaken hands with her at the moment he began speaking, and he had continued to hold her hand. Now, when she did not answer, she felt a light but firmly insistent pressure as of his drawing her to him. Involuntarily, she half-yielded to him, her desire for the moment stronger than her will. Then suddenly she drew herself away, though permitting her hand still to remain in his.

"You sure ain't afraid of me?" he asked, with quick compunction.

"No." She smiled woefully. "Not of you, but of myself."

"You haven't taken my dare," he urged under this encouragement.

"Please, please," she begged. "We can never marry, so don't let us discuss it."

"Then I copper your bet to lose." He was almost gay, now, for success was coming faster than his fondest imagining. She liked him, without a doubt; and without a doubt she liked him well enough to let him hold her hand, well enough to be not repelled by the nearness of him.

She shook her head.

"No, it is impossible. You would lose your bet."

For the first time a dark suspicion crossed Daylight's mind--a clew that explained everything.

"Say, you ain't been let in for some one of these secret marriages have you?"

The consternation in his voice and on his face was too much for her, and her laugh rang out, merry and spontaneous as a burst of joy from the throat of a bird.

Daylight knew his answer, and, vexed with himself decided that action was more efficient than speech. So he stepped between her and the wind and drew her so that she stood close in the shelter of him. An unusually stiff squall blew about them and thrummed overhead in the tree-tops and both paused to listen. A shower of flying leaves enveloped them, and hard on the heel of the wind came driving drops of rain. He looked down on her and on her hair wind-blown about her face; and because of her closeness to him and of a fresher and more poignant realization of what she meant to him, he trembled so that she was aware of it in the hand that held hers.

She suddenly leaned against him, bowing her head until it rested lightly upon his breast. And so they stood while another squall, with flying leaves and scattered drops of rain, rattled past. With equal suddenness she lifted her head and looked at him.

"Do you know," she said, "I prayed last night about you. I prayed that you would fail, that you would lose everything -- everything."

Daylight stared his amazement at this cryptic utterance. "That sure beats me. I always said I got out of my depth with women, and you've got me out of my depth now. Why you want me to lose everything, seeing as you like me--"

"I never said so."

"You didn't dast say you didn't. So, as I was saying: liking me, why you'd want me to go broke is clean beyond my simple understanding. It's right in line with that other puzzler of yours, the more-you-like-me-the-less-you-want-to-marry-me one. Well, you've just got to explain, that's all."

His arms went around her and held her closely, and this time she did not resist. Her head was bowed, and he had not see her face, yet he had a premonition that she was crying. He had learned the virtue of silence, and he waited her will in the matter. Things had come to such a pass that she was bound to tell him something now. Of that he was confident.

"I am not romantic," she began, again looking at him as he spoke. "It might be better for me if I were. Then I could make a fool of myself and be unhappy for the rest of my life. But my abominable common sense prevents. And that doesn't make me a bit happier, either."

"I'm still out of my depth and swimming feeble," Daylight said, after waiting vainly for her to go on. "You've got to show me, and you ain't shown me yet. Your common sense and praying that I'd go broke is all up in the air to me. Little woman, I just love you mighty hard, and I want you to marry me. That's straight and simple and right off the bat. Will you marry me?"

She shook her head slowly, and then, as she talked, seemed to grow angry, sadly angry; and Daylight knew that this anger was against him.

"Then let me explain, and just as straight and simply as you have asked." She paused, as if casting about for a beginning. "You are honest and straightforward. Do you want me to be honest and straightforward as a woman is not supposed to be?--to tell you things that will hurt you?--to make confessions that ought to shame me? to behave in what many men would think was an unwomanly manner?"

The arm around her shoulder pressed encouragement, but he did not speak.

"I would dearly like to marry you, but I am afraid. I am proud and humble at the same time that a man like you should care for me. But you have too much money. There's where my abominable common sense steps in. Even if we did marry, you could never be my man--my lover and my husband. You would be your money's man. I know I am a foolish woman, but I want my man for myself. You would not be free for me. Your money possesses you, taking your time, your thoughts, your energy, ever thing, bidding you go here and go there, do this and do that. Don't you see? Perhaps it's pure silliness, but I feel that I can love much, give much--give all, and in return, though I don't want all, I want much--and I want much more than your money would permit you to give me.

"And your money destroys you; it makes you less and less nice. I am not ashamed to say that I love you, because I shall never marry you. And I loved you much when I did not know you at all, when you first came down from Alaska and I first went into the office. You were my hero. You were the Burning Daylight of the gold-diggings, the daring traveler and miner. And you looked it. I don't see how any woman could have looked at you without loving you--then. But you don't look it now.

"Please, please, forgive me for hurting you. You wanted straight talk, and I am giving it to you. All these last years you have been living unnaturally. You, a man of the open, have been cooping yourself up in the cities with all that that means. You are not the same man at all, and your money is destroying you. You are becoming something different, something not so healthy, not so clean, not so nice. Your money and your way of life are doing it. You know it. You haven't the same body now that you had then. You are putting on flesh, and it is not healthy flesh. You are kind and genial with me, I know, but you are not kind and genial to all the world as you were then. You have become harsh and cruel. And I know. Remember, I have studied you six days a week, month after month, year after year; and I know more about the most insignificant parts of you than you know of all of me. The cruelty is not only in your heart and thoughts, but it is there in face. It has put its lines there. I have watched them come and grow. Your money, and the life it compels you to lead have done all this. You are being brutalized and degraded. And this process can only go on and on until you are hopelessly destroyed--"

He attempted to interrupt, but she stopped him, herself breathless and her voice trembling.

"No, no; let me finish utterly. I have done nothing but think, think, think, all these months, ever since you came riding with me, and now that I have begun to speak I am going to speak all that I have in me. I do love you, but I cannot marry you and destroy love. You are growing into a thing that I must in the end despise. You can't help it. More than you can possibly love me, do you love this business game. This business--and it's all perfectly useless, so far as you are concerned--claims all of you. I sometimes think it would be easier to share you equitably with another woman than to share you with this business. I might have half of you, at any rate. But this business would claim, not half of you, but nine-tenths of you, or ninety-nine hundredths.

"Remember, the meaning of marriage to me is not to get a man's money to spend. I want the man. You say you want ME. And suppose I consented, but gave you only one-hundredth part of me. Suppose there was something else in my life that took the other ninety-nine parts, and, furthermore, that ruined my figure, that put pouches under my eyes and crows-feet in the corners, that made me unbeautiful to look upon and that made my spirit unbeautiful. Would you be satisfied with that one-hundredth part of me? Yet that is all you are offering me of yourself. Do you wonder that I won't marry you?--that I can't?"

Daylight waited to see if she were quite done, and she went on again.

"It isn't that I am selfish. After all, love is giving, not receiving. But I see so clearly that all my giving could not do you any good. You are like a sick man. You don't play business like other men. You play it heart and and all of you. No matter what you believed and intended a wife would be only a brief diversion. There is that magnificent Bob, eating his head off in the stable. You would buy me a beautiful mansion and leave me in it to yawn my head off, or cry my eyes out because of my helplessness and inability to save you. This disease of business would be corroding you and marring you all the time. You play it as you have played everything else, as in Alaska you played the life of the trail. Nobody could be permitted to travel as fast and as far as you, to work as hard or endure as much. You hold back nothing; you put all you've got into whatever you are doing."

"Limit is the sky," he grunted grim affirmation.

"But if you would only play the lover-husband that way--"

Her voice faltered and stopped, and a blush showed in her wet cheeks as her eyes fell before his.

"And now I won't say another word," she added. "I've delivered a whole sermon."

She rested now, frankly and fairly, in the shelter of his arms, and both were oblivious to the gale that rushed past them in quicker and stronger blasts. The big downpour of rain had not yet come, but the mist-like squalls were more frequent. Daylight was openly perplexed, and he was still perplexed when he began to speak.

"I'm stumped. I'm up a tree. I'm clean flabbergasted, Miss Mason--or Dede, because I love to call you that name. I'm free to confess there's a mighty big heap in what you say. As I understand it, your conclusion is that you'd marry me if I hadn't a cent and if I wasn't getting fat. No, no; I'm not joking. I acknowledge the corn, and that's just my way of boiling the matter down and summing it up. If I hadn't a cent, and if I was living a healthy life with all the time in the world to love you and be your husband instead of being awash to my back teeth in business and all the rest--why, you'd marry me.

"That's all as clear as print, and you're correcter than I ever guessed before. You've sure opened my eyes a few. But I'm stuck. What can I do? My business has sure roped, thrown, and branded me. I'm tied hand and foot, and I can't get up and meander over green pastures. I'm like the man that got the bear by the tail. I can't let go; and I want you, and I've got to let go to get you.

"I don't know what to do, but something's sure got to happen--I can't lose you. I just can't. And I'm not going to. Why, you're running business a close second right now. Business never kept me awake nights.

"You've left me no argument. I know I'm not the same man that came from Alaska. I couldn't hit the trail with the dogs as I did in them days. I'm soft in my muscles, and my mind's gone hard. I used to respect men. I despise them now. You see, I spent all my life in the open, and I reckon I'm an open-air man. Why, I've got the prettiest little ranch you ever laid eyes on, up in Glen Ellen. That's where I got stuck for that brick-yard. You recollect handling the correspondence. I only laid eyes on the ranch that one time, and I so fell in love with it that I bought it there and then. I just rode around the hills, and was happy as a kid out of school. I'd be a better man living in the country. The city doesn't make me better. You're plumb right there. I know it. But suppose your prayer should be answered and I'd go clean broke and have to work for day's wages?"

She did not answer, though all the body of her seemed to urge consent.

"Suppose I had nothing left but that little ranch, and was satisfied to grow a few chickens and scratch a living somehow--would you marry me then, Dede?"

"Why, we'd be together all the time!" she cried.

"But I'd have to be out ploughing once in a while, he warned, "or driving to town to get the grub."

"But there wouldn't be the office, at any rate, and no man to see, and men to see without end. But it is all foolish and impossible, and we'll have to be starting back now if we're to escape the rain."

Then was the moment, among the trees, where they began the descent of the hill, that Daylight might have drawn her closely to him and kissed her once. But he was too perplexed with the new thoughts she had put into his head to take advantage of the situation. He merely caught her by the arm and helped her over the rougher footing.

"It's darn pretty country up there at Glen Ellen," he said meditatively. "I wish you could see it."

At the edge of the grove he suggested that it might be better for them to part there.

"It's your neighborhood, and folks is liable to talk."

But she insisted that he accompany her as far as the house.

"I can't ask you in," she said, extending her hand at the foot of the steps.

The wind was humming wildly in sharply recurrent gusts, but still the rain held off.

"Do you know," he said, "taking it by and large, it's the happiest day of my life." He took off his hat, and the wind rippled and twisted his black hair as he went on solemnly, "And I'm sure grateful to God, or whoever or whatever is responsible for your being on this earth. For you do like me heaps. It's been my joy to hear you say so to-day. It's--" He left the thought arrested, and his face assumed the familiar whimsical expression as he murmured: "Dede, Dede, we've just got to get married. It's the only way, and trust to luck for it's coming out all right--".

But the tears were threatening to rise in her eyes again, as she shook her head and turned and went up the steps.

161

CHAPTER 20

When the ferry system began to run, and the time between Oakland and San Francisco was demonstrated to be cut in half, the tide of Daylight's terrific expenditure started to turn. Not that it really did turn, for he promptly went into further investments. Thousands of lots in his residence tracts were sold, and thousands of homes were being built. Factory sites also were selling, and business properties in the heart of Oakland. All this tended to a steady appreciation in value of Daylight's huge holdings. But, as of old, he had his hunch and was riding it. Already he had begun borrowing from the banks. The magnificent profits he made on the land he sold were turned into more land, into more development; and instead of paying off old loans, he contracted new ones. As he had pyramided in Dawson City, he now pyramided in Oakland; but he did it with the knowledge that it was a stable enterprise rather than a risky placer-mining boom.

In a small way, other men were following his lead, buying and selling land and profiting by the improvement work he was doing. But this was to be expected, and the small fortunes they were making at his expense did not irritate him. There was an exception, however. One Simon Dolliver, with money to go in with, and with cunning and courage to back it up, bade fair to become a several times millionaire at Daylight's expense. Dolliver, too, pyramided, playing quickly and accurately, and keeping his money turning over and over. More than once Daylight found him in the way, as he himself had got in the way of the Guggenhammers when they first set their eyes on Ophir Creek.

Work on Daylight's dock system went on apace, yet was one of those enterprises that consumed money dreadfully and that could not be accomplished as quickly as a ferry system. The engineering difficulties were great, the dredging and filling a cyclopean task. The mere item of piling was anything but small. A good average pile, by the time it was delivered on the ground, cost a twenty-dollar gold piece, and these piles were used in unending thousands. All accessible groves of mature eucalyptus were used, and as well, great rafts of pine piles were towed down the coast from Peugeot Sound.

Not content with manufacturing the electricity for his street railways in the old-fashioned way, in power-houses, Daylight organized the Sierra and Salvador Power Company. This immediately assumed large proportions. Crossing the San Joaquin Valley on the way from the mountains, and plunging through the Contra Costa hills, there were many towns, and even a robust city, that could be supplied with power, also with light; and it became a street- and house-lighting project as well. As soon as the purchase of power sites in the Sierras was rushed through, the survey parties were out and building operations begun.

And so it went. There were a thousand maws into which he poured unceasing streams of money. But it was all so sound and legitimate, that Daylight, born gambler that he was, and with his clear, wide vision, could not play softly and safely. It was a big opportunity, and to him there was only one way to play it, and that was the big way. Nor did his one confidential adviser, Larry Hegan, aid him to caution. On the contrary, it was Daylight who was compelled to veto the wilder visions of that able hasheesh dreamer. Not only did Daylight borrow heavily from the banks and trust companies, but on several of his corporations he was compelled to issue stock. He did this grudgingly however, and retained most of his big enterprises of his own. Among the companies in which he reluctantly allowed the investing public to join were the Golden Gate Dock Company, and Recreation Parks Company, the United Water Company, the Uncial Shipbuilding Company, and the Sierra and Salvador Power Company. Nevertheless, between himself and Hegan, he retained the controlling share in each of these enterprises.

His affair with Dede Mason only seemed to languish. While delaying to grapple with the strange problem it presented, his desire for her continued to grow. In his gambling simile, his conclusion was that Luck had dealt him the most remarkable card in the deck, and that for years he had overlooked it. Love was the card, and it beat them all. Love was the king card of trumps, the fifth ace, the joker in a game of tenderfoot poker. It was the card of cards, and play it he would, to the limit, when the opening came. He could not see that opening yet. The present game would have to play to some sort of a conclusion first.

Yet he could not shake from his brain and vision the warm recollection of those bronze slippers, that clinging gown, and all the feminine softness and pliancy of Dede in her pretty Berkeley rooms. Once again, on a rainy Sunday, he telephoned that he was coming. And, as has happened ever since man first looked upon woman and called her good, again he played the blind force of male compulsion against the woman's secret weakness to yield. Not that it was Daylight's way abjectly to beg and entreat. On the contrary, he was masterful in whatever he did, but he had a trick of whimsical wheedling that Dede found harder to resist than the pleas of a suppliant lover. It was not a happy scene in its outcome, for Dede, in the throes of her own desire, desperate with weakness and at the same time with her better judgment hating her weakness cried out: --

"You urge me to try a chance, to marry you now and trust to luck for it to come out right. And life is a gamble say. Very well, let us gamble. Take a coin and toss it in the air. If it comes heads, I'll marry you. If it doesn't, you are forever to leave me alone and never mention marriage again."

A fire of mingled love and the passion of gambling came into Daylight's eyes. Involuntarily his hand started for his pocket for the coin. Then it stopped, and the light in his eyes was troubled.

"Go on," she ordered sharply. "Don't delay, or I may change my mind, and you will lose the chance."

"Little woman." His similes were humorous, but there was no humor in their meaning. His thought was as solemn as his voice. "Little woman, I'd gamble all the way from Creation to the Day of Judgment; I'd gamble a golden harp against another man's halo; I'd toss for pennies on the front steps of the New Jerusalem or set up a faro layout just outside the Pearly Gates; but I'll be everlastingly damned if I'll gamble on love. Love's too big to me to take a chance on. Love's got to be a sure thing, and between you and me it is a sure thing. If the odds was a hundred to one on my winning this flip, just the same, nary a flip."

In the spring of the year the Great Panic came on. The first warning was when the banks began calling in their unprotected loans. Daylight promptly paid the first several of his personal notes that were presented; then he divined that these demands but indicated the way the wind was going to blow, and that one of those terrific financial storms he had heard about was soon to sweep over the United States. How terrific this particular storm was to be he did not anticipate. Nevertheless, he took every precaution in his power, and had no anxiety about his weathering it out.

Money grew tighter. Beginning with the crash of several of the greatest Eastern banking houses, the tightness spread, until every bank in the country was calling in its credits. Daylight was caught, and caught because of the fact that for the first time he had been playing the legitimate business game. In the old days, such a panic, with the accompanying extreme shrinkage of values, would have been a golden harvest time for him. As it was, he watched the gamblers, who had ridden the wave of prosperity and made preparation for the slump, getting out from under and safely scurrying to cover or proceeding to reap a double harvest. Nothing remained for him but to stand fast and hold up.

He saw the situation clearly. When the banks demanded that he pay his loans, he knew that the banks were in sore need of the money. But he was in sorer need. And he knew that the banks did not want his collateral which they held. It would do them no good. In such a tumbling of values was no time to sell. His collateral was good, all of it, eminently sound and worth while; yet it was worthless at such a moment, when the one unceasing cry was money, money, money. Finding him obdurate, the banks demanded more collateral, and as the money pinch tightened they asked for two and even three times as much as had been originally accepted. Sometimes Daylight yielded to these demands, but more often not, and always battling fiercely.

He fought as with clay behind a crumbling wall. All portions of the wall were menaced, and he went around constantly strengthening the weakest parts with clay. This clay was money, and was applied, a sop here and a sop there, as fast as it was needed, but only when it was directly needed. The strength of his position lay in the Yerba Buena Ferry Company, the Consolidated Street Railways, and the United Water Company. Though people were no longer buying residence lots and factory and business sites, they were compelled to ride on his cars and ferry-boats and to consume his water. When all the financial world was clamoring for money and perishing through lack of it, the first of each month many thousands of dollars poured into his coffers from the water-rates, and each day ten thousand dollars, in dime and nickels, came in from his street railways and ferries.

Cash was what was wanted, and had he had the use of all this steady river of cash, all would have been well with him. As it was, he had to fight continually for a portion of it. Improvement work ceased, and only absolutely essential repairs were made. His fiercest fight was with the operating expenses, and this was a fight that never ended. There was never any let-up in his turning the thumb-screws of extended credit and economy. From the big wholesale suppliers down through the salary list to office stationery and postage stamps, he kept the thumb-screws turning. When his superintendents and heads of departments performed prodigies of cutting down, he patted them on the back and demanded more. When they threw down their hands in despair, he showed them how more could be accomplished.

"You are getting eight thousand dollars a year," he told Matthewson. "It's better pay than you ever got in your life before. Your fortune is in the same sack with mine. You've got to stand for some of the strain and risk. You've got personal credit in this town. Use it. Stand off butcher and baker and all the rest. Savvee? You're drawing down something like six hundred and sixty dollars a month. I want that cash. From now on, stand everybody off and draw down a hundred. I'll pay you interest on the rest till this blows over."

Two weeks later, with the pay-roll before them, it was:--

"Matthewson, who's this bookkeeper, Rogers? Your nephew? I thought so. He's pulling down eighty-five a month. After--this let him draw thirty-five. The forty can ride with me at interest."

164

"Impossible! " Matthewson cried. "He can't make ends meet on his salary as it is, and he has a wife and two kids--"

Daylight was upon him with a mighty oath.

"Can't! Impossible! What in hell do you think I'm running? A home for feeble-minded? Feeding and dressing and wiping the little noses of a lot of idiots that can't take care of themselves? Not on your life. I'm hustling, and now's the time that everybody that works for me has got to hustle. I want no fair-weather birds holding down my office chairs or anything else. This is nasty weather, damn nasty weather, and they've got to buck into it just like me. There are ten thousand men out of work in Oakland right now, and sixty thousand more in San Francisco. Your nephew, and everybody else on your pay-roll, can do as I say right now or quit. Savvee? If any of them get stuck, you go around yourself and guarantee their credit with the butchers and grocers. And you trim down that pay-roll accordingly. I've been carrying a few thousand folks that'll have to carry themselves for a while now, that's all."

"You say this filter's got to be replaced," he told his chief of the water-works. "We'll see about it. Let the people of Oakland drink mud for a change. It'll teach them to appreciate good water. Stop work at once. Get those men off the pay-roll. Cancel all orders for material. The contractors will sue? Let 'em sue and be damned. We'll be busted higher'n a kite or on easy street before they can get judgment."

And to Wilkinson: --

"Take off that owl boat. Let the public roar and come home early to its wife. And there's that last car that connects with the 12:45 boat at Twenty-second and Hastings. Cut it out. I can't run it for two or three passengers. Let them take an earlier boat home or walk. This is no time for philanthropy. And you might as well take off a few more cars in the rush hours. Let the strap-hangers pay. It's the strap-hangers that'll keep us from going under."

And to another chief, who broke down under the excessive strain of retrenchment: --

"You say I can't do that and can't do this. I'll just show you a few of the latest patterns in the can-and-can't line. You'll be compelled to resign? All right, if you think so I never saw the man yet that I was hard up for. And when any man thinks I can't get along without him, I just show him the latest pattern in that line of goods and give him his walking-papers."

And so he fought and drove and bullied and even wheedled his way along. It was fight, fight, fight, and no let-up, from the first thing in the morning till nightfall. His private office saw throngs every day. All men came to see him, or were ordered to come. Now it was an optimistic opinion on the panic, a funny story, a serious business talk, or a straight take-it-or-leave-it blow from the shoulder. And there was nobody to relieve him. It was a case of drive, drive, drive, and he alone could do the driving. And this went on day after day, while the whole business world rocked around him and house after house crashed to the ground.

"It's all right, old man," he told Hegan every morning; and it was the same cheerful word that he passed out all day long, except at such times when he was in the thick of fighting to have his will with persons and things.

Eight o'clock saw him at his desk each morning. By ten o'clock, it was into the machine and away for a round of the banks. And usually in the machine with him was the ten thousand and more dollars that had been earned by his ferries and railways the day before. This was for the weakest spot in the financial dike. And with one bank president after another similar scenes were enacted. They were paralyzed with fear, and first of all he played his role of the big vital optimist. Times were improving. Of course they were. The signs were already in the air. All that anybody had to do was to sit tight a little longer and hold on. That was all. Money was already more active in the East. Look at the trading on Wall Street of the last twenty-four hours. That was the straw that showed the wind. Hadn't Ryan said so and so? and wasn't it reported that Morgan was preparing to do this and that?

As for himself, weren't the street-railway earnings increasing steadily? In spite of the panic, more and more people were coming to Oakland right along. Movements were already beginning in real estate. He was dickering even then to sell over a thousand of his suburban acres. Of course it was at a sacrifice, but it would ease the strain on all of them and bolster up the faint-hearted. That was the trouble--the faint-hearts. Had there been no faint-hearts there would have been no panic. There was that Eastern syndicate, negotiating with him now to take the majority of the stock in the Sierra and Salvador Power Company off his hands. That showed confidence that better times were at hand.

And if it was not cheery discourse, but prayer and entreaty or show down and fight on the part of the banks, Daylight had to counter in kind. If they could bully, he could bully. If the favor he asked were refused, it became the thing he demanded. And when it came down to raw and naked fighting, with the last veil of sentiment or illusion torn off, he could take their breaths away.

But he knew, also, how and when to give in. When he saw the wall shaking and crumbling irretrievably at a particular place, he patched it up with sops of cash from his three cash-earning companies. If the banks went, he went too. It was a case of their having to hold out. If they smashed and all the collateral they held of his was thrown on the chaotic market, it would be the end. And so it was, as the time passed, that on occasion his red motor-car carried, in addition to the daily cash, the most gilt-edged securities he possessed; namely, the Ferry Company, United Water and Consolidated Railways. But he did this reluctantly, fighting inch by inch.

As he told the president of the Merchants San Antonio who made the plea of carrying so many others: --

"They're small fry. Let them smash. I'm the king pin here. You've got more money to make out of me than them. Of course, you're carrying too much, and you've got to choose, that's all. It's root hog or die for you or them. I'm too strong to smash. You could only embarrass me and get yourself tangled up. Your way out is to let the small fry go, and I'll lend you a hand to do it."

And it was Daylight, also, in this time of financial anarchy, who sized up Simon Dolliver's affairs and lent the hand that sent that rival down in utter failure. The Golden Gate National was the keystone of Dolliver's strength, and to the president of that institution Daylight said: --

"Here I've been lending you a hand, and you now in the last ditch, with Dolliver riding on you and me all the time. It don't go. You hear me, it don't go. Dolliver couldn't cough up eleven dollars to save you. Let him get off and walk, and I'll tell you what I'll do. I'll give you the railway nickels for four days--that's forty thousand cash. And on the sixth of the month you can count on twenty thousand more from the Water Company." He shrugged his shoulders. "Take it or leave it. Them's my terms."

"It's dog eat dog, and I ain't overlooking any meat that's floating around," Daylight proclaimed that afternoon to Hegan; and Simon Dolliver went the way of the unfortunate in the Great Panic who were caught with plenty of paper and no money.

Daylight's shifts and devices were amazing. Nothing however large or small, passed his keen sight unobserved. The strain he was under was terrific. He no longer ate lunch. The days were too short, and his noon hours and his office were as crowded as at any other time. By the end of the day he was exhausted, and, as never before, he sought relief behind his wall of alcoholic inhibition. Straight to his hotel he was driven, and straight to his rooms he went, where immediately was mixed for him the first of a series of double Martinis. By dinner, his brain was well clouded and the panic forgotten. By bedtime, with the assistance of Scotch whiskey, he was full--not violently nor uproariously full, nor stupefied, but merely well under the influence of a pleasant and mild anesthetic.

Next morning he awoke with parched lips and mouth, and with sensations of heaviness in his head which quickly passed away. By eight o'clock he was at his desk, buckled down to the fight, by ten o'clock on his personal round of the banks, and after that, without a moment's cessation, till nightfall, he was handling the knotty tangles of industry, finance, and human nature that crowded upon him. And with nightfall it was back to the hotel, the double Martinis and the Scotch; and this was his program day after day until the days ran into weeks.

CHAPTER 21

Though Daylight appeared among his fellows hearty voiced, inexhaustible, spilling over with energy and vitality, deep down he was a very weary man. And sometime under the liquor drug, snatches of wisdom came to him far more lucidity than in his sober moments, as, for instance, one night, when he sat on the edge of the bed with one shoe in his hand and meditated on Dede's aphorism to the effect that he could not sleep in more than one bed at a time. Still holding the shoe, he looked at the array of horsehair bridles on the walls. Then, carrying the shoe, he got up and solemnly counted them, journeying into the two adjoining rooms to complete the tale. Then he came back to the bed and gravely addressed his shoe: --

"The little woman's right. Only one bed at a time. One hundred and forty hair bridles, and nothing doing with ary one of them. One bridle at a time! I can't ride one horse at a time. Poor old Bob. I'd better be sending you out to pasture. Thirty million dollars, and a hundred million or nothing in sight, and what have I got to show for it? There's lots of things money can't buy. It can't buy the little woman. It can't buy capacity. What's the good of thirty millions when I ain't got room for more than a quart of cocktails a day? If I had a hundred-quart-cocktail thirst, it'd be different. But one quart--one measly little quart! Here I am, a thirty times over millionaire, slaving harder every day than any dozen men that work for me, and all I get is two meals that don't taste good, one bed, a quart of Martini, and a hundred and forty hair bridles to look at on the wall." He stared around at the array disconsolately. "Mr. Shoe, I'm sizzled. Good night."

Far worse than the controlled, steady drinker is the solitary drinker, and it was this that Daylight was developing into. He rarely drank sociably any more, but in his own room, by himself. Returning weary from each day's unremitting effort, he drugged himself to sleep, knowing that on the morrow he would rise up with a dry and burning mouth and repeat the program.

But the country did not recover with its wonted elasticity. Money did not become freer, though the casual reader of Daylight's newspapers, as well as of all the other owned and subsidised newspapers in the country, could only have concluded that the money tightness was over and that the panic was past history. All public utterances were cheery and optimistic, but privately many of the utters were in desperate straits. The scenes enacted in the privacy of Daylight's office, and of the meetings of his boards of directors, would have given the lie to the editorials in his newspapers; as, for instance, when he addressed the big stockholders in the Sierra and Salvador Power Company, the United Water Company, and the several other stock companies: --

"You've got to dig. You've got a good thing, but you'll have to sacrifice in order to hold on. There ain't no use spouting hard times explanations. Don't I know the hard times is on? Ain't that what you're here for? As I said before, you've got to dig. I run the majority stock, and it's come to a case of assess. It's that or smash. If ever I start going you won't know what struck you, I'll smash that hard. The small fry can let go, but you big ones can't. This ship won't sink as long as you stay with her. But if you start to leave her, down you'll sure go before you can get to shore. This assessment has got to be met that's all."

The big wholesale supply houses, the caterers for his hotels, and all the crowd that incessantly demanded to be paid, had their hot half-hours with him. He summoned them to his office and displayed his latest patterns of can and can't and will and won't.

"By God, you've got to carry me!" he told them. "If you think this is a pleasant little game of parlor whist and that you can quit and go home whenever you want, you're plumb wrong. Look here, Watkins, you remarked five minutes ago that you wouldn't stand for it. Now let me tell you a few. You're going to stand for it and keep on standin's for it. You're going to continue supplying me and taking my paper until the pinch is over. How you're going to do it is your trouble, not mine. You remember what I did to Klinkner and the Altamont Trust Company? I know the inside of your business better than you do yourself, and if you try to drop me I'll smash you. Even if I'd be going to smash myself, I'd find a minute to turn on you and bring you down with me. It's sink or swim for all of us, and I reckon you'll find it to your interest to keep me on top the puddle."

Perhaps his bitterest fight was with the stockholders of the United Water Company, for it was practically the whole of the gross earnings of this company that he voted to lend to himself and used to bolster up his wide battle front. Yet he never pushed his arbitrary rule too far. Compelling sacrifice from the men whose fortunes were tied up with his, nevertheless when any one of them was driven to the wall and was in dire need, Daylight was there to help him back into the line. Only a strong man could have saved so complicated a situation in such time of stress, and Daylight was that man. He turned and twisted, schemed and devised, bludgeoned and bullied the weaker ones, kept the faint-hearted in the fight, and had no mercy on the deserter.

And in the end, when early summer was on, everything began to mend. Came a day when Daylight did the unprecedented. He left the office an hour earlier than usual, and for the reason that for the first time since the panic there was not an item of work waiting to be done. He dropped into Hegan's private office, before leaving, for a chat, and as he stood up to go, he said:--

"Hegan, we're all hunkadory. We're pulling out of the financial pawnshop in fine shape, and we'll get out without leaving one unredeemed pledge behind. The worst is over, and the end is in sight. Just a tight rein for a couple more weeks, just a bit of a pinch or a flurry or so now and then, and we can let go and spit on our hands."

For once he varied his program. Instead of going directly to his hotel, he started on a round of the bars and cafes, drinking a cocktail here and a cocktail there, and two or three when he encountered men he knew. It was after an hour or so of this that he dropped into the bar of the Parthenon for one last drink before going to dinner. By this time all his being was pleasantly warmed by the alcohol, and he was in the most genial and best of spirits. At the corner of the bar several young men were up to the old trick of resting their elbows and attempting to force each other's hands down. One broad-shouldered young giant never removed his elbow, but put down every hand that came against him. Daylight was interested.

"It's Slosson," the barkeeper told him, in answer to his query. "He's the heavy-hammer thrower at the U.C. Broke all records this year, and the world's record on top of it. He's a husky all right all right."

Daylight nodded and went over to him, placing his own arm in opposition.

"I'd like to go you a flutter, son, on that proposition," he said.

The young man laughed and locked hands with him; and to Daylight's astonishment it was his own hand that was forced down on the bar

"Hold on," he muttered. "Just one more flutter. I reckon I wasn't just ready that time."

Again the hands locked. It happened quickly. The offensive attack of Daylight's muscles slipped instantly into defense, and, resisting vainly, his hand was forced over and down. Daylight was dazed. It had been no trick. The skill was equal, or, if anything, the superior skill had been his. Strength, sheer strength, had done it. He called for the drinks, and, still dazed and pondering, held up his own arm, and looked at it as at some new strange thing. He did not know this arm. It certainly was not the arm he had carried around with him all the years. The old arm? Why, it would have been play to turn down that young husky's. But this arm--he continued to look at it with such dubious perplexity as to bring a roar of laughter from the young men.

This laughter aroused him. He joined in it at first, and then his face slowly grew grave. He leaned toward the hammer-thrower.

"Son," he said, "let me whisper a secret. Get out of here and quit drinking before you begin."

The young fellow flushed angrily, but Daylight held steadily on.

"You listen to your dad, and let him say a few. I'm a young man myself, only I ain't. Let me tell you, several years ago for me to turn your hand down would have been like committing assault and battery on a kindergarten."

Slosson looked his incredulity, while the others grinned and clustered around Daylight encouragingly.

"Son, I ain't given to preaching. This is the first time I ever come to the penitent form, and you put me there yourself--hard. I've seen a few in my time, and I ain't fastidious so as you can notice it. But let me tell you right not that I'm worth the devil alone knows how many millions, and that I'd sure give it all, right here on the bar, to turn down your hand. Which means I'd give the whole shooting match just to be back where I was before I quit sleeping under the stars and come into the hen-coops of cities to drink cocktails and lift up my feet and ride. Son, that's that's the matter with me, and that's the way I feel about it. The game ain't worth the candle. You just take care of yourself, and roll my advice over once in a while. Good night."

He turned and lurched out of the place, the moral effect of his utterance largely spoiled by the fact that he was so patently full while he uttered it.

Still in a daze, Daylight made to his hotel, accomplished his dinner, and prepared for bed.

"The damned young whippersnapper!" he muttered. "Put my hand down easy as you please. My hand!"

He held up the offending member and regarded it with stupid wonder. The hand that had never been beaten! The hand that had made the Circle City giants wince! And a kid from college, with a laugh on his face, had put it down--twice! Dede was right. He was not the same man. The situation would bear more serious looking into than he had ever given it. But this was not the time. In the morning, after a good sleep, he would give it consideration.

CHAPTER 22

Daylight awoke with the familiar parched mouth and lips and throat, took a long drink of water from the pitcher beside his bed, and gathered up the train of thought where he had left it the night before. He reviewed the easement of the financial strain. Things were mending at last. While the going was still rough, the greatest dangers were already past. As he had told Hegan, a tight rein and careful playing were all that was needed now. Flurries and dangers were bound to come, but not so grave as the ones they had already weathered. He had been hit hard, but he was coming through without broken bones, which was more than Simon Dolliver and many another could say. And not one of his business friends had been ruined. He had compelled them to stay in line to save himself, and they had been saved as well.

His mind moved on to the incident at the corner of the bar of the Parthenon, when the young athlete had turned his hand down. He was no longer stunned by the event, but he was shocked and grieved, as only a strong man can be, at this passing of his strength. And the issue was too clear for him to dodge, even with himself. He knew why his hand had gone down. Not because he was an old man. He was just in the first flush of his prime, and, by rights, it was the hand of the hammer-thrower which should have gone down. Daylight knew that he had taken liberties with himself. He had always looked upon this strength of his as permanent, and here, for years, it had been steadily oozing from him. As he had diagnosed it, he had come in from under the stars to roost in the coops of cities. He had almost forgotten how to walk. He had lifted up his feet and been ridden around in automobiles, cabs and carriages, and electric cars. He had not exercised, and he had dry-rotted his muscles with alcohol.

And was it worth it? What did all his money mean after all? Dede was right. It could buy him no more than one bed at a time, and at the same time it made him the abjectest of slaves. It tied him fast. He was tied by it right now. Even if he so desired, he could not lie abed this very day. His money called him. The office whistle would soon blow, and he must answer it. The early sunshine was streaming through his window--a fine day for a ride in the hills on Bob, with Dede beside him on her Mab. Yet all his millions could not buy him this one day. One of those flurries might come along, and he had to be on the spot to meet it. Thirty millions! And they were powerless to persuade Dede to ride on Mab--Mab, whom he had bought, and who was unused and growing fat on pasture. What were thirty millions when they could not buy a man a ride with the girl he loved? Thirty millions!--that made him come here and go there, that rode upon him like so many millstones, that destroyed him while they grew, that put their foot down and prevented him from winning this girl who worked for ninety dollars a month.

Which was better? he asked himself. All this was Dede's own thought. It was what she had meant when she prayed he would go broke. He held up his offending right arm. It wasn't the same old arm. Of course she could not love that arm and that body as she had loved the strong, clean arm and body of years before. He didn't like that arm and body himself. A young whippersnapper had been able to take liberties with it. It had gone back on him. He sat up suddenly. No, by God, he had gone back on it! He had gone back on himself. He had gone back on Dede. She was right, a thousand times right, and she had sense enough to know it, sense enough to refuse to marry a money slave with a whiskey-rotted carcass.

171

He got out of bed and looked at himself in the long mirror on the wardrobe door. He wasn't pretty. The old-time lean cheeks were gone. These were heavy, seeming to hang down by their own weight. He looked for the lines of cruelty Dede had spoken of, and he found them, and he found the harshness in the eyes as well, the eyes that were muddy now after all the cocktails of the night before, and of the months and years before. He looked at the clearly defined pouches that showed under his eyes, and they've shocked him. He rolled up the sleeve of his pajamas. No wonder the hammer-thrower had put his hand down. Those weren't muscles. A rising tide of fat had submerged them. He stripped off the pajama coat. Again he was shocked, this time but the bulk of his body. It wasn't pretty. The lean stomach had become a paunch. The ridged muscles of chest and shoulders and abdomen had broken down into rolls of flesh.

He sat down on the bed, and through his mind drifted pictures of his youthful excellence, of the hardships he had endured over other men, of the Indians and dogs he had run off their legs in the heart-breaking days and nights on the Alaskan trail, of the feats of strength that had made him king over a husky race of frontiersmen.

And this was age. Then there drifted across the field of vision of his mind's eye the old man he had encountered at Glen Ellen, corning up the hillside through the fires of sunset, white-headed and white-bearded, eighty-four, in his hand the pail of foaming milk and in his face all the warm glow and content of the passing summer day. That had been age. "Yes siree, eighty-four, and spryer than most," he could hear the old man say. "And I ain't loafed none. I walked across the Plains with an ox-team and fit Injuns in '51, and I was a family man then with seven youngsters."

Next he remembered the old woman of the chaparral, pressing grapes in her mountain clearing; and Ferguson, the little man who had scuttled into the road like a rabbit, the one-time managing editor of a great newspaper, who was content to live in the chaparral along with his spring of mountain water and his hand-reared and manicured fruit trees. Ferguson had solved a problem. A weakling and an alcoholic, he had run away from the doctors and the chicken-coop of a city, and soaked up health like a thirsty sponge. Well, Daylight pondered, if a sick man whom the doctors had given up could develop into a healthy farm laborer, what couldn't a merely stout man like himself do under similar circumstances? He caught a vision of his body with all its youthful excellence returned, and thought of Dede, and sat down suddenly on the bed, startled by the greatness of the idea that had come to him.

He did not sit long. His mind, working in its customary way, like a steel trap, canvassed the idea in all its bearings. It was big--bigger than anything he had faced before. And he faced it squarely, picked it up in his two hands and turned it over and around and looked at it. The simplicity of it delighted him. He chuckled over it, reached his decision, and began to dress. Midway in the dressing he stopped in order to use the telephone.

Dede was the first he called up.

"Don't come to the office this morning," he said. "I'm coming out to see you for a moment."

He called up others. He ordered his motor-car. To Jones he gave instructions for the forwarding of Bob and Wolf to Glen Ellen. Hegan he surprised by asking him to look up the deed of the Glen Ellen ranch and make out a new one in Dede Mason's name. "Who?" Hegan demanded. "Dede Mason," Daylight replied imperturbably the 'phone must be indistinct this morning. "D-e-d-e M-a-s-o-n. Got it?"

Half an hour later he was flying out to Berkeley. And for the first time the big red car halted directly before the house. Dede offered to receive him in the parlor, but he shook his head and nodded toward her rooms.

"In there," he said. "No other place would suit."

As the door closed, his arms went out and around her. Then he stood with his hands on her shoulders and looking down into her face.

"Dede, if I tell you, flat and straight, that I'm going up to live on that ranch at Glen Ellen, that I ain't taking a cent with me, that I'm going to scratch for every bite I eat, and that I ain't going to play ary a card at the business game again, will you come along with me?"

She gave a glad little cry, and he nestled her in closely. But the next moment she had thrust herself out from him to the old position at arm's length.

"I--I don't understand," she said breathlessly.

"And you ain't answered my proposition, though I guess no answer is necessary. We're just going to get married right away and start. I've sent Bob and Wolf along already. When will you be ready?"

Dede could not forbear to smile. "My, what a hurricane of a man it is. I'm quite blown away. And you haven't explained a word to me."

Daylight smiled responsively.

"Look here, Dede, this is what card-sharps call a show-down. No more philandering and frills and long-distance sparring between you and me. We're just going to talk straight out in meeting--the truth, the whole truth, and nothing but the truth. Now you answer some questions for me, and then I'll answer yours." He paused. "Well, I've got only one question after all: Do you love me enough to marry me?"

"But--" she began.

"No buts," he broke in sharply. "This is a show-down. When I say marry, I mean what I told you at first, that we'd go up and live on the ranch. Do you love me enough for that?"

She looked at him for a moment, then her lids dropped, and all of her seemed to advertise consent.

"Come on, then, let's start." The muscles of his legs tensed involuntarily as if he were about to lead her to the door. "My auto's waiting outside. There's nothing to delay excepting getting on your hat."

He bent over her. "I reckon it's allowable," he said, as he kissed her.

It was a long embrace, and she was the first to speak.

"You haven't answered my questions. How is this possible? How can you leave your business? Has anything happened?"

"No, nothing's happened yet, but it's going to, blame quick. I've taken your preaching to heart, and I've come to the penitent form. You are my Lord God, and I'm sure going to serve you. The rest can go to thunder. You were sure right. I've been the slave to my money, and since I can't serve two masters I'm letting the money slide. I'd sooner have you than all the money in the world, that's all." Again he held her closely in his arms. "And I've sure got you, Dede. I've sure got you.

"And I want to tell you a few more. I've taken my last drink. You're marrying a whiskey-soak, but your husband won't be that. He's going to grow into another man so quick you won't know him. A couple of months from now, up there in Glen Ellen, you'll wake up some morning and find you've got a perfect stranger in the house with you, and you'll have to get introduced to him all over again. You'll say, 'I'm Mrs. Harnish, who are you?' And I'll say, 'I'm Elam Harnish's younger brother. I've just arrived from Alaska to attend the funeral.' 'What funeral?' you'll say. And I'll say, 'Why, the funeral of that good-for-nothing, gambling, whiskey-drinking

173

Burning Daylight--the man that died of fatty degeneration of the heart from sitting in night and day at the business game 'Yes ma'am,' I'll say, 'he's sure a gone 'coon, but I've come to take his place and make you happy. And now, ma'am, if you'll allow me, I'll just meander down to the pasture and milk the cow while you're getting breakfast.'"

Again he caught her hand and made as if to start with her for the door. When she resisted, he bent and kissed her again and again.

"I'm sure hungry for you, little woman," he murmured "You make thirty millions look like thirty cents."

"Do sit down and be sensible," she urged, her cheeks flushed, the golden light in her eyes burning more golden than he had ever seen it before.

But Daylight was bent on having his way, and when he sat down it was with her beside him and his arm around her.

"'Yes, ma'am,' I'll say, 'Burning Daylight was a pretty good cuss, but it's better that he's gone. He quit rolling up in his rabbit-skins and sleeping in the snow, and went to living in a chicken-coop. He lifted up his legs and quit walking and working, and took to existing on Martini cocktails and Scotch whiskey. He thought he loved you, ma'am, and he did his best, but he loved his cocktails more, and he loved his money more, and himself more, and 'most everything else more than he did you.' And then I'll say, 'Ma'am, you just run your eyes over me and see how different I am. I ain't got a cocktail thirst, and all the money I got is a dollar and forty cents and I've got to buy a new ax, the last one being plumb wore out, and I can love you just about eleven times as much as your first husband did. You see, ma'am, he went all to fat. And there ain't ary ounce of fat on me.' And I'll roll up my sleeve and show you, and say, 'Mrs. Harnish, after having experience with being married to that old fat money-bags, do you-all mind marrying a slim young fellow like me?' And you'll just wipe a tear away for poor old Daylight, and kind of lean toward me with a willing expression in your eye, and then I'll blush maybe some, being a young fellow, and put my arm around you, like that, and then--why, then I'll up and marry my brother's widow, and go out and do the chores while she's cooking a bite to eat."

"But you haven't answered my questions," she reproached him, as she emerged, rosy and radiant, from the embrace that had accompanied the culmination of his narrative.

"Now just what do you want to know?" he asked.

"I want to know how all this is possible? How you are able to leave your business at a time like this? What you meant by saying that something was going to happen quickly? I--" She hesitated and blushed. "I answered your question, you know."

"Let's go and get married," he urged, all the whimsicality of his utterance duplicated in his eyes. "You know I've got to make way for that husky young brother of mine, and I ain't got long to live." She made an impatient moue, and he continued seriously. "You see, it's like this, Dede. I've been working like forty horses ever since this blamed panic set in, and all the time some of those ideas you'd given me were getting ready to sprout. Well, they sprouted this morning, that's all. I started to get up, expecting to go to the office as usual. But I didn't go to the office. All that sprouting took place there and then. The sun was shining in the window, and I knew it was a fine day in the hills. And I knew I wanted to ride in the hills with you just about thirty million times more than I wanted to go to the office. And I knew all the time it was impossible. And why? Because of the office. The office wouldn't let me. All my money reared right up on its hind legs and got in the way and wouldn't let me. It's a way that blamed money has of getting in the way. You know that yourself.

"And then I made up my mind that I was to the dividing of the ways. One way led to the office. The other way led to Berkeley.

And I took the Berkeley road. I'm never going to set foot in the office again. That's all gone, finished, over and done with, and I'm letting it slide clean to smash and then some. My mind's set on this. You see, I've got religion, and it's sure the old-time religion; it's love and you, and it's older than the oldest religion in the world. It's IT, that's what it is--IT, with a capital I-T."

She looked at him with a sudden, startled expression.

"You mean--?" she began.

"I mean just that. I'm wiping the slate clean. I'm letting it all go to smash. When them thirty million dollars stood up to my face and said I couldn't go out with you in the hills to-day, I knew the time had come for me to put my foot down. And I'm putting it down. I've got you, and my strength to work for you, and that little ranch in Sonoma. That's all I want, and that's all I'm going to save out, along with Bob and Wolf, a suit case and a hundred and forty hair bridles. All the rest goes, and good riddance. It's that much junk."

But Dede was insistent.

"Then this--this tremendous loss is all unnecessary?" she asked.

"Just what I haven't been telling you. It IS necessary. If that money thinks it can stand up right to my face and say I can't go riding with you--"

"No, no; be serious," Dede broke in. "I don't mean that, and you know it. What I want to know is, from a standpoint of business, is this failure necessary?"

He shook his head.

"You bet it isn't necessary. That's the point of it. I'm not letting go of it because I'm licked to a standstill by the panic and have got to let go. I'm firing it out when I've licked the panic and am winning, hands down. That just shows how little I think of it. It's you that counts, little woman, and I make my play accordingly."

But she drew away from his sheltering arms.

"You are mad, Elam."

"Call me that again," he murmured ecstatically. "It's sure sweeter than the chink of millions."

All this she ignored.

"It's madness. You don't know what you are doing--"

"Oh, yes, I do," he assured her. "I'm winning the dearest wish of my heart. Why, your little finger is worth more--"

"Do be sensible for a moment."

"I was never more sensible in my lie. I know what I want, and I'm going to get it. I want you and the open air. I want to get my foot off the paving-stones and my ear away from the telephone.

I want a little ranch-house in one of the prettiest bits of country God ever made, and I want to do the chores around that ranch-house--milk cows, and chop wood, and curry horses, and plough the ground, and all the rest of it; and I want you there in the ranch-house with me. I'm plumb tired of everything else, and clean wore out. And I'm sure the luckiest man alive, for I've got what money can't buy. I've got you, and thirty millions couldn't buy you, nor three thousand millions, nor thirty cents--"

A knock at the door interrupted him, and he was left to stare delightedly at the Crouched Venus and on around the room at Dede's dainty possessions, while she answered the telephone.

"It is Mr. Hegan," she said, on returning. "He is holding the line. He says it is important."

Daylight shook his head and smiled.

"Please tell Mr. Hegan to hang up. I'm done with the office and I don't want to hear anything about anything."

A minute later she was back again.

"He refuses to hang up. He told me to tell you that Unwin is in the office now, waiting to see you, and Harrison, too. Mr. Hegan said that Grimshaw and Hodgkins are in trouble. That it looks as if they are going to break. And he said something about protection."

It was startling information. Both Unwin and Harrison represented big banking corporations, and Daylight knew that if the house of Grimshaw and Hodgkins went it would precipitate a number of failures and start a flurry of serious dimensions. But Daylight smiled, and shook his head, and mimicked the stereotyped office tone of voice as he said: --

"Miss Mason, you will kindly tell Mr. Hegan that there is nothing doing and to hang up."

"But you can't do this," she pleaded.

"Watch me," he grimly answered.

"Elam!"

"Say it again" he cried. "Say it again, and a dozen Grimshaws and Hodgkins can smash!"

He caught her by the hand and drew her to him.

"You let Hegan hang on to that line till he's tired. We can't be wasting a second on him on a day like this. He's only in love with books and things, but I've got a real live woman in my arms that's loving me all the time she's kicking over the traces."

CHAPTER 23

"But I know something of the fight you have been making," Dede contended. "If you stop now, all the work you have done, everything, will be destroyed. You have no right to do it. You can't do it."

Daylight was obdurate. He shook his head and smiled tantalizingly.

"Nothing will be destroyed, Dede, nothing. You don't understand this business game. It's done on paper. Don't you see? Where's the gold I dug out of Klondike? Why, it's in twenty-dollar gold pieces, in gold watches, in wedding rings. No matter what happens to me, the twenty-dollar pieces, the watches, and the wedding rings remain. Suppose I died right now. It wouldn't affect the gold one iota. It's sure the same with this present situation. All I stand for is paper. I've got the paper for thousands of acres of land. All right. Burn up the paper, and burn me along with it. The land remains, don't it? The rain falls on it, the seeds sprout in it, the trees grow out of it, the houses stand on it, the electric cars run over it. It's paper that business is run on. I lose my paper, or I lose my life, it's all the same; it won't alter one grain of sand in all that land, or twist one blade of grass around sideways.

"Nothing is going to be lost--not one pile out of the docks, not one railroad spike, not one ounce of steam out of the gauge of a ferry-boat. The cars will go on running, whether I hold the paper or somebody else holds it. The tide has set toward Oakland. People are beginning to pour in. We're selling building lots again. There is no stopping that tide. No matter what happens to me or the paper, them three hundred thousand folks are coming in the same. And there'll be cars to carry them around, and houses to hold them, and good water for them to drink and electricity to give them light, and all the rest."

By this time Hegan had arrived in an automobile. The honk of it came in through the open window, and they saw, it stop alongside the big red machine. In the car were Unwin and Harrison, while Jones sat with the chauffeur

"I'll see Hegan," Daylight told Dede. "There's no need for the rest. They can wait in the machine."

"Is he drunk?" Hegan whispered to Dede at the door.

She shook her head and showed him in.

"Good morning, Larry," was Daylight's greeting. "Sit down and rest your feet. You sure seem to be in a flutter."

"I am," the little Irishman snapped back. "Grimshaw and Hodgkins are going to smash if something isn't done quick. Why didn't you come to the office? What are you going to do about it?"

"Nothing," Daylight drawled lazily. "Except let them smash, I guess--"

"But--"

"I've had no dealings with Grimshaw and Hodgkins. I don't owe them anything. Besides, I'm going to smash myself. Look here, Larry, you know me. You know when I make up my mind I mean it. Well, I've sure made up my mind. I'm tired of the whole game. I'm letting go of it as fast as I can, and a smash is the quickest way to let go."

Hegan stared at his chief, then passed his horror-stricken gaze on to Dede, who nodded in sympathy.

"So let her smash, Larry," Daylight went on. "All you've got to do is to protect yourself and all our friends. Now you listen to me while I tell you what to do. Everything is in good shape to do it. Nobody must get hurt. Everybody that stood by me must come through without damage. All the back wages and salaries must be paid pronto. All the money I've switched away from the water company, the street cars, and the ferries must be switched back. And you won't get hurt yourself none. Every company you got stock in will come through--"

"You are crazy, Daylight!" the little lawyer cried out. "This is all babbling lunacy. What is the matter with you? You haven't been eating a drug or something?"

"I sure have!" Daylight smiled reply. "And I'm now coughing it up. I'm sick of living in a city and playing business--I'm going off to the sunshine, and the country, and the green grass. And Dede, here, is going with me. So you've got the chance to be the first to congratulate me."

"Congratulate the--the devil!" Hegan spluttered. "I'm not going to stand for this sort of foolishness."

"Oh, yes, you are; because if you don't there'll be a bigger smash and some folks will most likely get hurt. You're worth a million or more yourself, now, and if you listen to me you come through with a whole skin. I want to get hurt, and get hurt to the limit. That's what I'm looking for, and there's no man or bunch of men can get between me and what I'm looking for. Savvee, Hegan? Savvee?"

"What have you done to him?" Hegan snarled at Dede.

"Hold on there, Larry." For the first time Daylight's voice was sharp, while all the old lines of cruelty in his face stood forth. "Miss Mason is going to be my wife, and while I don't mind your talking to her all you want, you've got to use a different tone of voice or you'll be heading for a hospital, which will sure be an unexpected sort of smash. And let me tell you one other thing. This-all is my doing. She says I'm crazy, too."

Hegan shook his head in speechless sadness and continued to stare.

"There'll be temporary receiverships, of course," Daylight advised; "but they won't bother none or last long. What you must do immediately is to save everybody--the men that have been letting their wages ride with me, all the creditors, and all the concerns that have stood by. There's the wad of land that New Jersey crowd has been dickering for. They'll take all of a couple of thousand acres and will close now if you give them half a chance. That Fairmount section is the cream of it, and they'll dig up as high as a thousand dollars an acre for a part of it. That'll help out some. That five-hundred acre tract beyond, you'll be lucky if they pay two hundred an acre."

Dede, who had been scarcely listening, seemed abruptly to make up her mind, and stepped forward where she confronted the two men. Her face was pale, but set with determination, so that Daylight, looking at it, was reminded of the day when she first rode Bob.

"Wait," she said. "I want to say something. Elam, if you do this insane thing, I won't marry you. I refuse to marry you."

Hegan, in spite of his misery, gave her a quick, grateful look.

"I'll take my chance on that," Daylight began.

"Wait!" she again interrupted. "And if you don't do this thing, I will marry you."

"Let me get this proposition clear." Daylight spoke with exasperating slowness and deliberation. "As I understand it, if I keep right on at the business game, you'll sure marry me? You'll marry me if I keep on working my head off and drinking Martinis?"

After each question he paused, while she nodded an affirmation.

"And you'll marry me right away?"

"Yes."

"To-day? Now?"

"Yes."

He pondered for a moment.

"No, little woman, I won't do it. It won't work, and you know it yourself. I want you--all of you; and to get it I'll have to give you all of myself, and there'll be darn little of myself left over to give if I stay with the business game. Why, Dede, with you on the ranch with me, I'm sure of you--and of myself. I'm sure of you, anyway. You can talk will or won't all you want, but you're sure going to marry me just the same. And now, Larry, you'd better be going. I'll be at the hotel in a little while, and since I'm not going a step into the office again, bring all papers to sign and the rest over to my rooms. And you can get me on the 'phone there any time. This smash is going through. Savvee? I'm quit and done."

He stood up as a sign for Hegan to go. The latter was plainly stunned. He also rose to his feet, but stood looking helplessly around.

"Sheer, downright, absolute insanity," he muttered.

Daylight put his hand on the other's shoulder.

"Buck up, Larry. You're always talking about the wonders of human nature, and here I am giving you another sample of it and you ain't appreciating it. I'm a bigger dreamer than you are, that's all, and I'm sure dreaming what's coming true. It's the biggest, best dream I ever had, and I'm going after it to get it--"

"By losing all you've got," Hegan exploded at him.

"Sure--by losing all I've got that I don't want. But I'm hanging on to them hundred and forty hair bridles just the same. Now you'd better hustle out to Unwin and Harrison and get on down town. I'll be at the hotel, and you can call me up any time."

He turned to Dede as soon as Hegan was gone, and took her by the hand.

"And now, little woman, you needn't come to the office any more. Consider yourself discharged. And remember I was your employer, so you've got to come to me for recommendation, and if you're not real good, I won't give you one. In the meantime, you just rest up and think about what things you want to pack, because we'll just about have to set up housekeeping on your stuff--leastways, the front part of the house."

"But, Elam, I won't, I won't! If you do this mad thing I never will marry you."

She attempted to take her hand away, but he closed on it with a protecting, fatherly clasp.

"Will you be straight and honest? All right, here goes. Which would you sooner have--me and the money, or me and the ranch?"

"But--" she began.

"No buts. Me and the money?"

She did not answer.

"Me and the ranch?"

Still she did not answer, and still he was undisturbed.

"You see, I know your answer, Dede, and there's nothing more to say. Here's where you and I quit and hit the high places for Sonoma. You make up your mind what you want to pack, and I'll have some men out here in a couple of days to do it for you. It will be about the last work anybody else ever does for us. You and I will do the unpacking and the arranging ourselves."

She made a last attempt.

"Elam, won't you be reasonable? There is time to reconsider. I can telephone down and catch Mr. Hegan as soon as he reaches the office--"

"Why, I'm the only reasonable man in the bunch right now," he rejoined. "Look at me--as calm as you please, and as happy as a king, while they're

179

fluttering around like a lot of cranky hens whose heads are liable to be cut off."

"I'd cry, if I thought it would do any good," she threatened.

"In which case I reckon I'd have to hold you in my arms some more and sort of soothe you down," he threatened back. "And now I'm going to go. It's too bad you got rid of Mab. You could have sent her up to the ranch. But see you've got a mare to ride of some sort or other."

As he stood at the top of the steps, leaving, she said: --

"You needn't send those men. There will be no packing, because I am not going to marry you."

"I'm not a bit scared," he answered, and went down the steps.

CHAPTER 24

Three days later, Daylight rode to Berkeley in his red car. It was for the last time, for on the morrow the big machine passed into another's possession. It had been a strenuous three days, for his smash had been the biggest the panic had precipitated in California. The papers had been filled with it, and a great cry of indignation had gone up from the very men who later found that Daylight had fully protected their interests. It was these facts, coming slowly to light, that gave rise to the widely repeated charge that Daylight had gone insane. It was the unanimous conviction among business men that no sane man could possibly behave in such fashion. On the other hand, neither his prolonged steady drinking nor his affair with Dede became public, so the only conclusion attainable was that the wild financier from Alaska had gone lunatic. And Daylight had grinned and confirmed the suspicion by refusing to see the reporters.

He halted the automobile before Dede's door, and met her with his same rushing tactics, enclosing her in his arms before a word could be uttered. Not until afterward, when she had recovered herself from him and got him seated, did he begin to speak.

"I've done it," he announced. "You've seen the newspapers, of course. I'm plumb cleaned out, and I've just called around to find out what day you feel like starting for Glen Ellen. It'll have to be soon, for it's real expensive living in Oakland these days. My board at the hotel is only paid to the end of the week, and I can't afford to stay after that. And beginning with to-morrow I've got to use the street cars, and they sure eat up the nickels."

He paused, and waited, and looked at her. Indecision and trouble showed on her face. Then the smile he knew so well began to grow on her lips and in her eyes, until she threw back her head and laughed in the old forthright boyish way.

"When are those men coming to pack for me?" she asked.

And again she laughed and simulated a vain attempt to escape his bearlike arms.

"Dear Elam," she whispered; "dear Elam." And of herself, for the first time, she kissed him.

She ran her hand caressingly through his hair.

"Your eyes are all gold right now," he said. "I can look in them and tell just how much you love me."

"They have been all gold for you, Elam, for a long time. I think, on our little ranch, they will always be all gold."

"Your hair has gold in it, too, a sort of fiery gold." He turned her face suddenly and held it between his hands and looked long into her eyes. "And your eyes were full of gold only the other day, when you said you wouldn't marry me."

She nodded and laughed.

"You would have your will," she confessed. "But I couldn't be a party to such madness. All that money was yours, not mine. But I was loving you all the time, Elam, for the great big boy you are, breaking the thirty-million toy with which you had grown tired of playing. And when I said no, I knew all the time it was yes. And I am sure that my eyes were golden all the time. I had only one fear, and that was that you would fail to lose everything. Because, dear, I knew I should marry you anyway, and I did so want just you and the ranch and Bob and Wolf and those horse-hair bridles. Shall I tell you a secret? As soon as you left, I telephoned the man to whom I sold Mab."

181

She hid her face against his breast for an instant, and then looked at him again, gladly radiant.

"You see, Elam, in spite of what my lips said, my mind was made up then. I--I simply had to marry you. But I was praying you would succeed in losing everything. And so I tried to find what had become of Mab. But the man had sold her and did not know what had become of her. You see, I wanted to ride with you over the Glen Ellen hills, on Mab and you on Bob, just as I had ridden with you through the Piedmont hills."

The disclosure of Mab's whereabouts trembled on Daylight's lips, but he forbore.

"I'll promise you a mare that you'll like just as much as Mab," he said.

But Dede shook her head, and on that one point refused to be comforted.

"Now, I've got an idea," Daylight said, hastening to get the conversation on less perilous ground. "We're running away from cities, and you have no kith nor kin, so it don't seem exactly right that we should start off by getting married in a city. So here's the idea: I'll run up to the ranch and get things in shape around the house and give the caretaker his walking-papers. You follow me in a couple of days, coming on the morning train. I'll have the preacher fixed and waiting. And here's another idea. You bring your riding togs in a suit case. And as soon as the ceremony's over, you can go to the hotel and change. Then out you come, and you find me waiting with a couple of horses, and we'll ride over the landscape so as you can see the prettiest parts of the ranch the first thing. And she's sure pretty, that ranch. And now that it's settled, I'll be waiting for you at the morning train day after to-morrow."

Dede blushed as she spoke.

"You are such a hurricane."

"Well, ma'am," he drawled, "I sure hate to burn daylight. And you and I have burned a heap of daylight. We've been scandalously extravagant. We might have been married years ago."

Two days later, Daylight stood waiting outside the little Glen Ellen hotel. The ceremony was over, and he had left Dede to go inside and change into her riding-habit while he brought the horses. He held them now, Bob and Mab, and in the shadow of the watering-trough Wolf lay and looked on. Already two days of ardent California sun had touched with new fires the ancient bronze in Daylight's face. But warmer still was the glow that came into his cheeks and burned in his eyes as he saw Dede coming out the door, riding-whip in hand, clad in the familiar corduroy skirt and leggings of the old Piedmont days. There was warmth and glow in her own face as she answered his gaze and glanced on past him to the horses. Then she saw Mab. But her gaze leaped back to the man.

"Oh, Elam!" she breathed.

It was almost a prayer, but a prayer that included a thousand meanings Daylight strove to feign sheepishness, but his heart was singing too wild a song for mere playfulness. All things had been in the naming of his name--reproach, refined away by gratitude, and all compounded of joy and love.

She stepped forward and caressed the mare, and again turned and looked at the man, and breathed: --

"Oh, Elam! "

And all that was in her voice was in her eyes, and in them Daylight glimpsed a profundity deeper and wider than any speech or thought--the whole vast inarticulate mystery and wonder of sex and love.

Again he strove for playfulness of speech, but it was too great a moment for even love fractiousness to enter in. Neither spoke. She gathered the reins, and, bending, Daylight received her foot in his hand. She sprang, as he lifted and gained the saddle. The next moment he was mounted and beside her, and, with Wolf sliding along ahead in his typical wolf-trot, they went up the hill that led out of town--two lovers on two chestnut sorrel steeds, riding out and away to honeymoon through the warm summer day. Daylight felt himself drunken as with wine. He was at the topmost pinnacle of life. Higher than this no man could climb nor had ever climbed. It was his day of days, his love-time and his mating-time, and all crowned by this virginal possession of a mate who had said "Oh, Elam," as she had said it, and looked at him out of her soul as she had looked.

They cleared the crest of the hill, and he watched the joy mount in her face as she gazed on the sweet, fresh land. He pointed out the group of heavily wooded knolls across the rolling stretches of ripe grain.

"They're ours," he said. "And they're only a sample of the ranch. Wait till you see the big canon. There are 'coons down there, and back here on the Sonoma there are mink. And deer!-- why, that mountain's sure thick with them, and I reckon we can scare up a mountain-lion if we want to real hard. And, say, there's a little meadow=-well, I ain't going to tell you another word. You wait and see for yourself."

They turned in at the gate, where the road to the clay-pit crossed the fields, and both sniffed with delight as the warm aroma of the ripe hay rose in their nostrils. As on his first visit, the larks were uttering their rich notes and fluttering up before the horses until the woods and the flower-scattered glades were reached, when the larks gave way to blue jays and woodpeckers.

"We're on our land now," he said, as they left the hayfield behind. "It runs right across country over the roughest parts. Just you wait and see."

As on the first day, he turned aside from the clay-pit and worked through the woods to the left, passing the first spring and jumping the horses over the ruined remnants of the stake-and-rider fence. From here on, Dede was in an unending ecstasy. By the spring that gurgled among the redwoods grew another great wild lily, bearing on its slender stalk the prodigious outburst of white waxen bells. This time he did not dismount, but led the way to the deep canon where the stream had cut a passage among the knolls. He had been at work here, and a steep and slippery horse trail now crossed the creek, so they rode up beyond, through the somber redwood twilight, and, farther on, through a tangled wood of oak and madrono. They came to a small clearing of several acres, where the grain stood waist high.

"Ours," Daylight said.

She bent in her saddle, plucked a stalk of the ripe grain, and nibbled it between her teeth.

"Sweet mountain hay," she cried. "The kind Mab likes."

And throughout the ride she continued to utter cries and ejaculations of surprise and delight.

"And you never told me all this!" she reproached him, as they looked across the little clearing and over the descending slopes of woods to the great curving sweep of Sonoma Valley.

"Come," he said; and they turned and went back through the forest shade, crossed the stream and came to the lily by the spring.

Here, also, where the way led up the tangle of the steep hill, he had cut a rough horse trail. As they forced their way up the zigzags, they caught glimpses out and down through the sea of foliage. Yet always were their farthest glimpses stopped by the closing vistas of green, and, yet always, as they climbed, did the forest roof arch overhead, with only here and there rifts that permitted shattered shafts of sunlight to penetrate. And all about them were ferns, a score of varieties, from the tiny gold-backs and maidenhair to huge brakes six and eight feet tall. Below them, as they mounted, they glimpsed great gnarled trunks and branches of ancient trees, and above them were similar great gnarled branches.

Dede stopped her horse and sighed with the beauty of it all.

"It is as if we are swimmers," she said, "rising out of a deep pool of green tranquillity. Up above is the sky and the sun, but this is a pool, and we are fathoms deep."

They started their horses, but a dog-tooth violet, shouldering amongst the maidenhair, caught her eye and made her rein in again.

They cleared the crest and emerged from the pool as if into another world, for now they were in the thicket of velvet-trunked young madronos and looking down the open, sun-washed hillside, across the nodding grasses, to the drifts of blue and white nemophilae that carpeted the tiny meadow on either side the tiny stream. Dede clapped her hands.

"It's sure prettier than office furniture," Daylight remarked.

"It sure is," she answered.

And Daylight, who knew his weakness in the use of the particular word sure, knew that she had repeated it deliberately and with love.

They crossed the stream and took the cattle track over the low rocky hill and through the scrub forest of manzanita, till they emerged on the next tiny valley with its meadow-bordered streamlet.

"If we don't run into some quail pretty soon, I'll be surprised some," Daylight said.

And as the words left his lips there was a wild series of explosive thrumming as the old quail arose from all about Wolf, while the young ones scuttled for safety and disappeared miraculously before the spectators' very eyes.

He showed her the hawk's nest he had found in the lightning-shattered top of the redwood, and she discovered a wood-rat's nest which he had not seen before. Next they took the old wood-road and came out on the dozen acres of clearing where the wine grapes grew in the wine-colored volcanic soil. Then they followed the cow-path through more woods and thickets and scattered glades, and dropped down the hillside to where the farm-house, poised on the lip of the big canon, came into view only when they were right upon it.

Dede stood on the wide porch that ran the length of the house while Daylight tied the horses. To Dede it was very quiet. It was the dry, warm, breathless calm of California midday. All the world seemed dozing. From somewhere pigeons were cooing lazily. With a deep sigh of satisfaction, Wolf, who had drunk his fill at all the streams along the way, dropped down in the cool shadow of the porch. She heard the footsteps of Daylight returning, and caught her breath with a quick intake. He took her hand in his, and, as he turned the door-knob, felt her hesitate. Then he put his arm around her; the door swung open, and together they passed in.

184

CHAPTER 25

Many persons, themselves city-bred and city-reared, have fled to the soil and succeeded in winning great happiness. In such cases they have succeeded only by going through a process of savage disillusionment. But with Dede and Daylight it was different. They had both been born on the soil, and they knew its naked simplicities and rawer ways. They were like two persons, after far wandering, who had merely come home again. There was less of the unexpected in their dealings with nature, while theirs was all the delight of reminiscence. What might appear sordid and squalid to the fastidiously reared, was to them eminently wholesome and natural. The commerce of nature was to them no unknown and untried trade. They made fewer mistakes. They already knew, and it was a joy to remember what they had forgotten.

And another thing they learned was that it was easier for one who has gorged at the flesh-pots to content himself with the meagerness of a crust, than for one who has known only the crust. Not that their life was meagre. It was that they found keener delights and deeper satisfactions in little things. Daylight, who had played the game in its biggest and most fantastic aspects, found that here, on the slopes of Sonoma Mountain, it was still the same old game. Man had still work to perform, forces to combat, obstacles to overcome. When he experimented in a small way at raising a few pigeons for market, he found no less zest in calculating in squabs than formerly when he had calculated in millions. Achievement was no less achievement, while the process of it seemed more rational and received the sanction of his reason.

The domestic cat that had gone wild and that preyed on his pigeons, he found, by the comparative standard, to be of no less paramount menace than a Charles Klinkner in the field of finance, trying to raid him for several millions. The hawks and weasels and 'coons were so many Dowsetts, Lettons, and Guggenhammers that struck at him secretly. The sea of wild vegetation that tossed its surf against the boundaries of all his clearings and that sometimes crept in and flooded in a single week was no mean enemy to contend with and subdue. His fat-soiled vegetable-garden in the nook of hills that failed of its best was a problem of engrossing importance, and when he had solved it by putting in drain-tile, the joy of the achievement was ever with him. He never worked in it and found the soil unpacked and tractable without experiencing the thrill of accomplishment.

There was the matter of the plumbing. He was enabled to purchase the materials through a lucky sale of a number of his hair bridles. The work he did himself, though more than once he was forced to call in Dede to hold tight with a pipe-wrench. And in the end, when the bath-tub and the stationary tubs were installed and in working order, he could scarcely tear himself away from the contemplation of what his hands had wrought. The first evening, missing him, Dede sought and found him, lamp in hand, staring with silent glee at the tubs. He rubbed his hand over their smooth wooden lips and laughed aloud, and was as shamefaced as any boy when she caught him thus secretly exulting in his own prowess.

It was this adventure in wood-working and plumbing that brought about the building of the little workshop, where he slowly gathered a collection of loved tools. And he, who in the old days, out of his millions, could purchase immediately whatever he might desire, learned the new joy of the possession that follows upon rigid economy and desire long delayed. He waited three months before daring the extravagance of a Yankee screw-driver, and his glee in the marvelous little mechanism was so keen that Dede conceived forthright a great idea. For six months she saved her egg-money, which was hers by right of allotment, and on his birthday presented him with a turning-lathe of wonderful simplicity and multifarious efficiencies. And their mutual delight in the tool, which was his, was only equalled by their delight in Mab's first foal, which was Dede's special private property.

It was not until the second summer that Daylight built the huge fireplace that outrivalled Ferguson's across the valley. For all these things took time, and Dede and Daylight were not in a hurry. Theirs was not the mistake of the average city-dweller who flees in ultra-modern innocence to the soil. They did not essay too much. Neither did they have a mortgage to clear, nor did they desire wealth. They wanted little in the way of food, and they had no rent to pay. So they planned unambiguously, reserving their lives for each other and for the compensations of country-dwelling from which the average country-dweller is barred. From Ferguson's example, too, they profited much. Here was a man who asked for but the plainest fare; who ministered to his own simple needs with his own hands; who worked out as a laborer only when he needed money to buy books and magazines; and who saw to it that the major portion of his waking time was for enjoyment. He loved to loaf long afternoons in the shade with his books or to be up with the dawn and away over the hills.

On occasion he accompanied Dede and Daylight on deer hunts through the wild canons and over the rugged steeps of Hood Mountain, though more often Dede and Daylight were out alone. This riding was one of their chief joys. Every wrinkle and crease in the hills they explored, and they came to know every secret spring and hidden dell in the whole surrounding wall of the valley. They learned all the trails and cow-paths; but nothing delighted them more than to essay the roughest and most impossible rides, where they were glad to crouch and crawl along the narrowest deer-runs, Bob and Mab struggling and forcing their way along behind.

Back from their rides they brought the seeds and bulbs of wild flowers to plant in favoring nooks on the ranch. Along the foot trail which led down the side of the big canon to the intake of the water-pipe, they established their fernery. It was not a formal affair, and the ferns were left to themselves. Dede and Daylight merely introduced new ones from time to time, changing them from one wild habitat to another. It was the same with the wild lilac, which Daylight had sent to him from Mendocino County. It became part of the wildness of the ranch, and, after being helped for a season, was left to its own devices. they used to gather the seeds of the California poppy and scatter them over their own acres, so that the orange-colored blossoms spangled the fields of mountain hay and prospered in flaming drifts in the fence corners and along the edges of the clearings.

Dede, who had a fondness for cattails, established a fringe of them along the meadow stream, where they were left to fight it out with the water-cress. And when the latter was threatened with extinction, Daylight developed one of the shaded springs into his water-cress garden and declared war upon any invading cattail. On her wedding day Dede had discovered a long dog-tooth violet by the zigzag trail above the redwood spring, and here she continued to plant more and more. The open hillside above the tiny meadow became a colony of Mariposa lilies. This was due mainly to her efforts, while Daylight, who rode with a short-handled ax on his saddle-bow, cleared the little manzanita wood on the rocky hill of all its dead and dying and overcrowded weaklings.

They did not labor at these tasks. Nor were they tasks. Merely in passing, they paused, from time to time, and lent a hand to nature. These flowers and shrubs grew of themselves, and their presence was no violation of the natural environment. The man and the woman made no effort to introduce a flower or shrub that did not of its own right belong. Nor did they protect them from their enemies. The horses and the colts and the cows and the calves ran at pasture among them or over them, and flower or shrub had to take its chance. But the beasts were not noticeably destructive, for they were few in number and the ranch was large. On the other hand, Daylight could have taken in fully a dozen horses to pasture, which would have earned him a dollar and a half per head per month. But this he refused to do, because of the devastation such close pasturing would produce.

Ferguson came over to celebrate the housewarming that followed the achievement of the great stone fireplace. Daylight had ridden across the valley more than once to confer with him about the undertaking, and he was the only other present at the sacred function of lighting the first fire. By removing a partition, Daylight had thrown two rooms into one, and this was the big living-room where Dede's treasures were placed--her books, and paintings and photographs, her piano, the Crouched Venus, the chafing-dish and all its glittering accessories. Already, in addition to her own wild-animal skins, were those of deer and coyote and one mountain-lion which Daylight had killed. The tanning he had done himself, slowly and laboriously, in frontier fashion.

He handed the match to Dede, who struck it and lighted the fire. The crisp manzanita wood crackled as the flames leaped up and assailed the dry bark of the larger logs. Then she leaned in the shelter of her husband's arm, and the three stood and looked in breathless suspense. When Ferguson gave judgment, it was with beaming face and extended hand.

"She draws! By crickey, she draws" he cried.

He shook Daylight's hand ecstatically, and Daylight shook his with equal fervor, and, bending, kissed Dede on the lips. They were as exultant over the success of their simple handiwork as any great captain at astonishing victory. In Ferguson's eyes was actually a suspicious moisture while the woman pressed even more closely against the man whose achievement it was. He caught her up suddenly in his arms and whirled her away to the piano, crying out: "Come on, Dede! The *Gloria!* The *Gloria!*"

And while the flames in the fireplace that worked, the triumphant strains of the Twelfth Mass rolled forth.

CHAPTER 26

Daylight had made no assertion of total abstinence though he had not taken a drink for months after the day he resolved to let his business go to smash. Soon he proved himself strong enough to dare to take a drink without taking a second. On the other hand, with his coming to live in the country, had passed all desire and need for drink. He felt no yearning for it, and even forgot that it existed. Yet he refused to be afraid of it, and in town, on occasion, when invited by the storekeeper, would reply: "All right, son. If my taking a drink will make you happy here goes. Whiskey for mine."

But such a drink began no desire for a second. It made no impression. He was too profoundly strong to be affected by a thimbleful. As he had prophesied to Dede, Burning Daylight, the city financier, had died a quick death on the ranch, and his younger brother, the Daylight from Alaska, had taken his place. The threatened inundation of fat had subsided, and all his old-time Indian leanness and of muscle had returned. So, likewise, did the old slight hollows in his cheeks come back. For him they indicated the pink of physical condition. He became the acknowledged strong man of Sonoma Valley, the heaviest lifter and hardest winded among a husky race of farmer folk. And once a year he celebrated his birthday in the old-fashioned frontier way, challenging all the valley to come up the hill to the ranch and be put on its back. And a fair portion of the valley responded, brought the women-folk and children along, and picnicked for the day.

At first, when in need of ready cash, he had followed Ferguson's example of working at day's labor; but he was not long in gravitating to a form of work that was more stimulating and more satisfying, and that allowed him even more time for Dede and the ranch and the perpetual riding through the hills. Having been challenged by the blacksmith, in a spirit of banter, to attempt the breaking of a certain incorrigible colt, he succeeded so signally as to earn quite a reputation as a horse-breaker. And soon he was able to earn whatever money he desired at this, to him, agreeable work.

A sugar king, whose breeding farm and training stables were at Caliente, three miles away, sent for him in time of need, and, before the year was out, offered him the management of the stables. But Daylight smiled and shook his head. Furthermore, he refused to undertake the breaking of as many animals as were offered. "I'm sure not going to die from overwork," he assured Dede; and he accepted such work only when he had to have money. Later, he fenced off a small run in the pasture, where, from time to time, he took in a limited number of incorrigibles.

"We've got the ranch and each other," he told his wife, "and I'd sooner ride with you to Hood Mountain any day than earn forty dollars. You can't buy sunsets, and loving wives, and cool spring water, and such folderols, with forty dollars; and forty million dollars can't buy back for me one day that I didn't ride with you to Hood Mountain."

His life was eminently wholesome and natural. Early to bed, he slept like an infant and was up with the dawn. Always with something to do, and with a thousand little things that enticed but did not clamor, he was himself never overdone. Nevertheless, there were times when both he and Dede were not above confessing tiredness at bedtime after seventy or eighty miles in the saddle. Sometimes, when he had accumulated a little money, and when the season favored, they would mount their horses, with saddle-bags behind, and ride away over the wall of the valley and down into the other valleys. When night fell, they put up at the first convenient farm or village, and on the morrow they would ride on, without definite plan, merely continuing to ride on, day after day, until their money gave out and they were compelled to return. On such trips they would be gone anywhere from a week to ten days or two weeks, and once they managed a three weeks' trip. They even planned ambitiously some day when they were disgracefully prosperous, to ride all the way up to Daylight's boyhood home in Eastern Oregon, stopping on the way at Dede's girlhood home in Siskiyou. And all the joys of anticipation were theirs a thousand times as they contemplated the detailed delights of this grand adventure.

One day, stopping to mail a letter at the Glen Ellen post office, they were hailed by the blacksmith.

"Say, Daylight," he said, "a young fellow named Slosson sends you his regards. He came through in an auto, on the way to Santa Rosa. He wanted to know if you didn't live hereabouts, but the crowd with him was in a hurry. So he sent you his regards and said to tell you he'd taken your advice and was still going on breaking his own record."

Daylight had long since told Dede of the incident.

"Slosson?" he meditated, "Slosson? That must be the hammer-thrower. He put my hand down twice, the young scamp." He turned suddenly to Dede. "Say, it's only twelve miles to Santa Rosa, and the horses are fresh."

She divined what was in his mind, of which his twinkling eyes and sheepish, boyish grin gave sufficient advertisement, and she smiled and nodded acquiescence.

"We'll cut across by Bennett Valley," he said. "It's nearer that way."

There was little difficulty, once in Santa Rosa, of finding Slosson. He and his party had registered at the Oberlin Hotel, and Daylight encountered the young hammer-thrower himself in the office.

"Look here, son," Daylight announced, as soon as he had introduced Dede, "I've come to go you another flutter at that hand game. Here's a likely place."

Slosson smiled and accepted. The two men faced each other, the elbows of their right arms on the counter, the hands clasped. Slosson's hand quickly forced backward and down.

"You're the first man that ever succeeded in doing it," he said. "Let's try it again."

"Sure," Daylight answered. "And don't forget, son, that you're the first man that put mine down. That's why I lit out after you to-day."

Again they clasped hands, and again Slosson's hand went down. He was a broad-shouldered, heavy-muscled young giant, at least half a head taller than Daylight, and he frankly expressed his chagrin and asked for a third trial. This time he steeled himself to the effort, and for a moment the issue was in doubt. With flushed face and set teeth he met the other's strength till his crackling muscles failed him. The air exploded sharply from his tensed lungs, as he relaxed in surrender, and the hand dropped limply down.

"You're too many for me," he confessed. "I only hope you'll keep out of the hammer-throwing game."

Daylight laughed and shook his head.

"We might compromise, and each stay in his own class. You stick to hammer-throwing, and I'll go on turning down hands."

But Slosson refused to accept defeat.

"Say," he called out, as Daylight and Dede, astride their horses, were preparing to depart. "Say--do you mind if I look you up next year? I'd like to tackle you again."

189

"Sure, son. You're welcome to a flutter any time. Though I give you fair warning that you'll have to go some. You'll have to train up, for I'm ploughing and chopping wood and breaking colts these days."

Now and again, on the way home, Dede could hear her big boy-husband chuckling gleefully. As they halted their horses on the top of the divide out of Bennett Valley, in order to watch the sunset, he ranged alongside and slipped his arm around her waist.

"Little woman," he said, "you're sure responsible for it all. And I leave it to you, if all the money in creation is worth as much as one arm like that when it's got a sweet little woman like this to go around."

For of all his delights in the new life, Dede was his greatest. As he explained to her more than once, he had been afraid of love all his life only in the end to come to find it the greatest thing in the world. Not alone were the two well mated, but in coming to live on the ranch they had selected the best soil in which their love would prosper. In spite of her books and music, there was in her a wholesome simplicity and love of the open and natural, while Daylight, in every fiber of him, was essentially an open-air man.

Of one thing in Dede, Daylight never got over marveling about, and that was her efficient hands--the hands that he had first seen taking down flying shorthand notes and ticking away at the typewriter; the hands that were firm to hold a magnificent brute like Bob, that wonderfully flashed over the keys of the piano, that were unhesitant in household tasks, and that were twin miracles to caress and to run rippling fingers through his hair. But Daylight was not unduly uxorious. He lived his man's life just as she lived her woman's life. There was proper division of labor in the work they individually performed. But the whole was entwined and woven into a fabric of mutual interest and consideration. He was as deeply interested in her cooking and her music as she was in his agricultural adventures in the vegetable garden. And he, who resolutely declined to die of overwork, saw to it that she should likewise escape so dire a risk.

In this connection, using his man's judgment and putting his man's foot down, he refused to allow her to be burdened with the entertaining of guests. For guests they had, especially in the warm, long summers, and usually they were her friends from the city, who were put to camp in tents which they cared for themselves, and where, like true campers, they had also to cook for themselves. Perhaps only in California, where everybody knows camp life, would such a program have been possible. But Daylight's steadfast contention was that his wife should not become cook, waitress, and chambermaid because she did not happen to possess a household of servants. On the other hand, chafing-dish suppers in the big living-room for their camping guests were a common happening, at which times Daylight allotted them their chores and saw that they were performed. For one who stopped only for the night it was different. Likewise it was different with her brother, back from Germany, and again able to sit a horse. On his vacations he became the third in the family, and to him was given the building of the fires, the sweeping, and the washing of the dishes.

Daylight devoted himself to the lightening of Dede's labors, and it was her brother who incited him to utilize the splendid water-power of the ranch that was running to waste. It required Daylight's breaking of extra horses to pay for the materials, and the brother devoted a three weeks' vacation to assisting, and together they installed a Pelting wheel. Besides sawing wood and turning his lathe and grindstone, Daylight connected the power with the churn; but his great triumph was when he put his arm around Dede's waist and led her out to inspect a washing-machine, run by the Pelton wheel, which really worked and really washed clothes.

190

Dede and Ferguson, between them, after a patient struggle, taught Daylight poetry, so that in the end he might have been often seen, sitting slack in the saddle and dropping down the mountain trails through the sun-flecked woods, chanting aloud Kipling's "Tomlinson," or, when sharpening his ax, singing into the whirling grindstone Henley's "Song of the Sword." Not that he ever became consummately literary in the way his two teachers were. Beyond "Fra Lippo Lippi" and "Caliban and Setebos," he found nothing in Browning, while George Meredith was ever his despair. It was of his own initiative, however, that he invested in a violin, and practised so assiduously that in time he and Dede beguiled many a happy hour playing together after night had fallen.

So all went well with this well-mated pair. Time never dragged. There were always new wonderful mornings and still cool twilights at the end of day; and ever a thousand interests claimed him, and his interests were shared by her. More thoroughly than he knew, had he come to a comprehension of the relativity of things. In this new game he played he found in little things all the intensities of gratification and desire that he had found in the frenzied big things when he was a power and rocked half a continent with the fury of the blows he struck. With head and hand, at risk of life and limb, to bit and break a wild colt and win it to the service of man, was to him no less great an achievement. And this new table on which he played the game was clean. Neither lying, nor cheating, nor hypocrisy was here. The other game had made for decay and death, while this new one made for clean strength and life. And so he was content, with Dede at his side, to watch the procession of the days and seasons from the farm-house perched on the canon-lip; to ride through crisp frosty mornings or under burning summer suns; and to shelter in the big room where blazed the logs in the fireplace he had built, while outside the world shuddered and struggled in the storm-clasp of a southeaster.

Once only Dede asked him if he ever regretted, and his answer was to crush her in his arms and smother her lips with his. His answer, a minute later, took speech.

"Little woman, even if you did cost thirty millions, you are sure the cheapest necessity of life I ever indulged in." And then he added, "Yes, I do have one regret, and a monstrous big one, too. I'd sure like to have the winning of you all over again. I'd like to go sneaking around the Piedmont hills looking for you. I'd like to meander into those rooms of yours at Berkeley for the first time. And there's no use talking, I'm plumb soaking with regret that I can't put my arms around you again that time you leaned your head on my breast and cried in the wind and rain."

CHAPTER 27

But there came the day, one year, in early April, when Dede sat in an easy chair on the porch, sewing on certain small garments, while Daylight read aloud to her. It was in the afternoon, and a bright sun was shining down on a world of new green. Along the irrigation channels of the vegetable garden streams of water were flowing, and now and again Daylight broke off from his reading to run out and change the flow of water. Also, he was teasingly interested in the certain small garments on which Dede worked, while she was radiantly happy over them, though at times, when his tender fun was too insistent, she was rosily confused or affectionately resentful.

From where they sat they could look out over the world. Like the curve of a skirting blade, the Valley of the Moon stretched before them, dotted with farm-houses and varied by pasture-lands, hay-fields, and vineyards. Beyond rose the wall of the valley, every crease and wrinkle of which Dede and Daylight knew, and at one place, where the sun struck squarely, the white dump of the abandoned mine burned like a jewel. In the foreground, in the paddock by the barn, was Mab, full of pretty anxieties for the early spring foal that staggered about her on tottery legs. The air shimmered with heat, and altogether it was a lazy, basking day. Quail whistled to their young from the thicketed hillside behind the house. there was a gentle cooing of pigeons, and from the green depths of the big canon arose the sobbing wood note of a mourning dove. Once, there was a warning chorus from the foraging hens and a wild rush for cover, as a hawk, high in the blue, cast its drifting shadow along the ground.

It was this, perhaps, that aroused old hunting memories in Wolf. At any rate, Dede and Daylight became aware of excitement in the paddock, and saw harmlessly reenacted a grim old tragedy of the Younger World. Curiously eager, velvet-footed and silent as a ghost, sliding and gliding and crouching, the dog that was mere domesticated wolf stalked the enticing bit of young life that Mab had brought so recently into the world. And the mare, her own ancient instincts aroused and quivering, circled ever between the foal and this menace of the wild young days when all her ancestry had known fear of him and his hunting brethren. Once, she whirled and tried to kick him, but usually she strove to strike him with her fore-hoofs, or rushed upon him with open mouth and ears laid back in an effort to crunch his backbone between her teeth. And the wolf-dog, with ears flattened down and crouching, would slide silkily away, only to circle up to the foal from the other side and give cause to the mare for new alarm. Then Daylight, urged on by Dede's solicitude, uttered a low threatening cry; and Wolf, drooping and sagging in all the body of him in token of his instant return to man's allegiance, slunk off behind the barn.

It was a few minutes later that Daylight, breaking off from his reading to change the streams of irrigation, found that the water had ceased flowing. He shouldered a pick and shovel, took a hammer and a pipe-wrench from the tool-house, and returned to Dede on the porch.

"I reckon I'll have to go down and dig the pipe out," he told her. "It's that slide that's threatened all winter. I guess she's come down at last."

"Don't you read ahead, now," he warned, as he passed around the house and took the trail that led down the wall of the canon.

Halfway down the trail, he came upon the slide. It was a small affair, only a few tons of earth and crumbling rock; but, starting from fifty feet above, it had struck the water pipe with force sufficient to break it at a connection. Before proceeding to work, he glanced up the path of the slide,

192

and he glanced with the eye of the earth-trained miner. And he saw what made his eyes startle and cease for the moment from questing farther.

"Hello," he communed aloud, "look who's here."

His glance moved on up the steep broken surface, and across it from side to side. Here and there, in places, small twisted manzanitas were rooted precariously, but in the main, save for weeds and grass, that portion of the canon was bare. There were signs of a surface that had shifted often as the rains poured a flow of rich eroded soil from above over the lip of the canon.

"A true fissure vein, or I never saw one," he proclaimed softly.

And as the old hunting instincts had aroused that day in the wolf-dog, so in him recrudesced all the old hot desire of gold-hunting. Dropping the hammer and pipe-wrench, but retaining pick and shovel, he climbed up the slide to where a vague line of outputting but mostly soil-covered rock could be seen. It was all but indiscernible, but his practised eye had sketched the hidden formation which it signified. Here and there, along this wall of the vein, he attacked the crumbling rock with the pick and shoveled the encumbering soil away. Several times he examined this rock. So soft was some of it that he could break it in his fingers. Shifting a dozen feet higher up, he again attacked with pick and shovel. And this time, when he rubbed the soil from a chunk of rock and looked, he straightened up suddenly, gasping with delight. And then, like a deer at a drinking pool in fear of its enemies, he flung a quick glance around to see if any eye were gazing upon him. He grinned at his own foolishness and returned to his examination of the chunk. A slant of sunlight fell on it, and it was all aglitter with tiny specks of unmistakable free gold.

"From the grass roots down," he muttered in an awestricken voice, as he swung his pick into the yielding surface.

He seemed to undergo a transformation. No quart of cocktails had ever put such a flame in his cheeks nor such a fire in his eyes. As he worked, he was caught up in the old passion that had ruled most of his life. A frenzy seized him that markedly increased from moment to moment. He worked like a madman, till he panted from his exertions and the sweat dripped from his face to the ground. He quested across the face of the slide to the opposite wall of the vein and back again. And, midway, he dug down through the red volcanic earth that had washed from the disintegrating hill above, until he uncovered quartz, rotten quartz, that broke and crumbled in his hands and showed to be alive with free gold.

Sometimes he started small slides of earth that covered up his work and compelled him to dig again. Once, he was swept fifty feet down the canon-side; but he floundered and scrambled up again without pausing for breath. He hit upon quartz that was so rotten that it was almost like clay, and here the gold was richer than ever. It was a veritable treasure chamber. For a hundred feet up and down he traced the walls of the vein. He even climbed over the canon-lip to look along the brow of the hill for signs of the outcrop. But that could wait, and he hurried back to his find.

He toiled on in the same mad haste, until exhaustion and an intolerable ache in his back compelled him to pause. He straightened up with even a richer piece of gold-laden quartz. Stooping, the sweat from his forehead had fallen to the ground. It now ran into his eyes, blinding him. He wiped it from him with the back of his hand and returned to a scrutiny of the gold.

It would run thirty thousand to the ton, fifty thousand, anything - -he knew that. And as he gazed upon the yellow lure, and panted for air, and wiped the sweat away, his quick vision leaped and set to work. He saw the spur-track that must run up from the valley and across the upland pastures, and he ran the grades and built the bridge that would span the canon, until it was real before his eyes. Across the canon was the place for the mill, and there he erected it; and he erected, also, the endless chain of buckets, suspended from a cable and operated by gravity, that would carry the ore across the canon to the quartz-crusher. Likewise, the whole mine grew before him and beneath him-tunnels, shafts, and galleries, and hoisting plants. The blasts of the miners were in his ears, and from across the canon he could hear the roar of the stamps. The hand that held the lump of quartz was trembling, and there was a tired, nervous palpitation apparently in the pit of his stomach. It came to him abruptly that what he wanted was a drink--whiskey, cocktails, anything, a drink. And even then, with this new hot yearning for the alcohol upon him, he heard, faint and far, drifting down the green abyss of the canon, Dede's voice, crying:--

"Here, chick, chick, chick, chick, chick! Here, chick, chick, chick!"

He was astounded at the lapse of time. She had left her sewing on the porch and was feeding the chickens preparatory to getting supper. The afternoon was gone. He could not conceive that he had been away that long.

Again came the call: *"Here, chick, chick, chick, chick, chick! Here, chick, chick, chick!"*

It was the way she always called--first five, and then three. He had long since noticed it. And from these thoughts of her arose other thoughts that caused a great fear slowly to grow in his face. For it seemed to him that he had almost lost her. Not once had he thought of her in those frenzied hours, and for that much, at least, had she truly been lost to him.

He dropped the piece of quartz, slid down the slide, and started up the trail, running heavily. At the edge of the clearing he eased down and almost crept to a point of vantage whence he could peer out, himself unseen. She was feeding the chickens, tossing to them handfuls of grain and laughing at their antics.

The sight of her seemed to relieve the panic fear into which he had been flung, and he turned and ran back down the trail. Again he climbed the slide, but this time he climbed higher, carrying the pick and shovel with him. And again he toiled frenziedly, but this time with a different purpose. He worked artfully, loosing slide after slide of the red soil and sending it streaming down and covering up all he had uncovered, hiding from the light of day the treasure he had discovered. He even went into the woods and scooped armfuls of last year's fallen leaves which he scattered over the slide. But this he gave up as a vain task; and he sent more slides of soil down upon the scene of his labor, until no sign remained of the out-jutting walls of the vein.

Next he repaired the broken pipe, gathered his tools together, and started up the trail. He walked slowly, feeling a great weariness, as of a man who had passed through a frightful crisis. He put the tools away, took a great drink of the water that again flowed through the pipes, and sat down on the bench by the open kitchen door. Dede was inside, preparing supper, and the sound of her footsteps gave him a vast content.

He breathed the balmy mountain air in great gulps, like a diver fresh-risen from the sea. And, as he drank in the air, he gazed with all his eyes at the clouds and sky and valley, as if he were drinking in that, too, along with the air.

Dede did not know he had come back, and at times he turned his head and stole glances in at her--at her efficient hands, at the bronze of her brown hair that smouldered with fire when she crossed the path of sunshine that streamed through the window, at the promise of her figure

194

that shot through him a pang most strangely sweet and sweetly dear. He heard her approaching the door, and kept his head turned resolutely toward the valley. And next, he thrilled, as he had always thrilled, when he felt the caressing gentleness of her fingers through his hair.

"I didn't know you were back," she said. "Was it serious?"

"Pretty bad, that slide," he answered, still gazing away and thrilling to her touch. "More serious than I reckoned. But I've got the plan. Do you know what I'm going to do?--I'm going to plant eucalyptus all over it. They'll hold it. I'll plant them thick as grass, so that even a hungry rabbit can't squeeze between them; and when they get their roots agoing, nothing in creation will ever move that dirt again."

"Why, is it as bad as that?"

He shook his head.

"Nothing exciting. But I'd sure like to see any blamed old slide get the best of me, that's all. I'm going to seal that slide down so that it'll stay there for a million years. And when the last trump sounds, and Sonoma Mountain and all the other mountains pass into nothingness, that old slide will be still a-standing there, held up by the roots."

He passed his arm around her and pulled her down on his knees.

"Say, little woman, you sure miss a lot by living here on the ranch--music, and theatres, and such things. Don't you ever have a hankering to drop it all and go back?"

So great was his anxiety that he dared not look at her, and when she laughed and shook her head he was aware of a great relief. Also, he noted the undiminished youth that rang through that same old-time boyish laugh of hers.

"Say," he said, with sudden fierceness, "don't you go fooling around that slide until after I get the trees in and rooted. It's mighty dangerous, and I sure can't afford to lose you now."

He drew her lips to his and kissed her hungrily and passionately.

"What a lover!" she said; and pride in him and in her own womanhood was in her voice.

"Look at that, Dede." He removed one encircling arm and swept it in a wide gesture over the valley and the mountains beyond. "The Valley of the Moon--a good name, a good name. Do you know, when I look out over it all, and think of you and of all it means, it kind of makes me ache in the throat, and I have things in my heart I can't find the words to say, and I have a feeling that I can almost understand Browning and those other high-flying poet-fellows. Look at Hood Mountain there, just where the sun's striking. It was down in that crease that we found the spring."

"And that was the night you didn't milk the cows till ten o'clock," she laughed. "And if you keep me here much longer, supper won't be any earlier than it was that night."

Both arose from the bench, and Daylight caught up the milk-pail from the nail by the door. He paused a moment longer to look out over the valley.

"It's sure grand," he said.

"It's sure grand," she echoed, laughing joyously at him and with him and herself and all the world, as she passed in through the door.

And Daylight, like the old man he once had met, himself went down the hill through the fires of sunset with a milk pail on his arm.

Milton Keynes UK
Ingram Content Group UK Ltd.
UKHW051350170624
444327UK00020B/209